CHAOS
ASCENDANT
& OTHER TALES

Book Eleven of
the Thulian Chronicles

Art Wiederhold

Order this book online at www.trafford.com
or email orders@trafford.com

Most Trafford titles are also available at major online book retailers.

Printed in the United States of America.

ISBN: 978-1-4907-4785-9 (sc)
ISBN: 978-1-4907-4784-2 (e)

Trafford rev.   09/29/2014

 www.trafford.com

North America & international
toll-free: 1 888 232 4444 (USA & Canada)
fax: 812 355 4082

Contents

Chaos Ascendant

In the 56ᵗʰ year of the reign of Arka-Dal

Arka-Dal had just turned 78.

For 56 of those years, he had served his people as the Emperor of Thule. Despite this, there was no gray in his hair, or deep lines on his face and he still had the same speed and strength as he had at the age of 20.

The average man of the Second Age lived to be around 130 years. By now, even Arka-Dal should have shown some signs of aging.

Yet he didn't.

Neither did any of his wives or close friends. Even Leo, his long-term mentor and advisor, who was also ten years his senior, looked the same as he always had, albeit he'd packed on a few extra pounds.

All of them looked to be around 35 or 40 years. It was as if something—or someone—had caused them to cease aging.

Arka-Dal smiled.

This was all Merlin's doing. The wizard had magically extended their lives because he did not want Thule to go the way of Camelot. Thule was the shining light of the Second Age. Both Merlin and Gorinna feared that light might be extinguished after Arka-Dal's death and take the rest of mankind with it.

Yes, Arka-Dal understood why Merlin had extended his life.

He accepted it, but still didn't approve of it.

He was mulling this over as he dressed for an official meeting with a group of foreign dignitaries. He checked his reflection in the mirror and shrugged.

"Just how much longer will I live?" he asked aloud.

"At least three to four normal lifetimes—barring accidents," came a voice from behind him.

He turned and smiled at Merlin.

"Another 300 years?" he asked.

"Something like that. Perhaps longer," Merlin replied smugly. "By then, Thule should be so well established that your passing wouldn't bring it crashing down."

"What of my children? Did you extend their lives as well?" Arka-Dal asked as they walked down the hall.

"I extended the lives of everyone in the Dal line," Merlin said.

"Is that wise?" Arka-Dal asked.

Merlin shrugged.

"Only time will tell," he said. "Many paths lie before each of them. It is up to them to choose which paths they will follow and endure the consequences of those choices."

"Would you have done the same for Arthur?" Arka-Dal asked.

"No. I realized he was neither wise nor worthy enough. He was eaten up by jealousy and lust and the desire for vengeance. He was far too weak to rule. Extending his time on Earth would not have saved Camelot or the lofty ideals it pretended to aspire to," Merlin replied. "Arthur started out with the best of intentions, as did I. But we all know what road good intentions pave."

"But another came after him," Arka-Dal pointed out.

"Yes indeed. And he helped to establish one of the greatest, most just, yet contradictory nations in human history. Those who came after him eventually brought it—and the entire First Age—to a most terrible end," Merlin said. "There's much about you that reminds me of him. You have his strength of character, his wisdom and his incorruptible nobility."

Arka-Dal laughed.

"Is there anything in me that reminds you of Arthur?" he asked.

"Thankfully no!" Merlin said with a grin.

"I second that," said a female voice from behind them.

Arka-Dal smiled as Galya, his fourth wife, linked arms with him. Merlin smiled at her warmly.

Galya was the Devil's daughter. She'd been sent by her father to try and tempt Arka-Dal into crossing over into the dark side. Instead, she fell in love with him. They soon married and she bore him two children, Hawk and Melody. Like his other wives, Galya was fiercely loyal to Arka-Dal and she loved him above all else in the universe. Even her famous father had become quite fond of him. And they respected each other.

"Arthur had a nasty disposition and was prone to uncontrollable fits of rage. When his jealousy was roused, which was often, he was quite easy to corrupt. He was also weak-willed and black hearted. You are nothing at like him, my love," Galya said as they kissed. "He *feigned* nobility. You actually *possess* it."

"All this high praise might turn my head. Before long, you'll have *me* believing it," Arka-Dal joked. "I am no better than the next man down the street and I see things that remind me of that each and every day. It keeps me humble and appreciative."

"And *that, my boy, is your greatest strength*," Merlin said as he patted him on the back.

"That's one of the things that made me fall so madly in love with you," Galya smiled as she touched his cheek adoringly. "No other but you could have captured my heart or earned the respect of Father. He thinks you're quite exceptional."

"That's enough of that. Let's go and greet our guests," Arka-Dal said as they walked out into the hall.

As usual, the palace was alive with the sounds of children at play. The eldest children, Alexander and Ivar, were now in training with Masaichi Koto, the palace weaponmaster. But they, too, liked to join the fun with their younger siblings.

Mayumi, Arka-Dal's first wife and Empress, was proud of Alexander, who was the mirror image of his father and also had his quick mind and endless curiosity. His half brother, Ivar, looked more like his mother, Medusa but also had Arka-Dal's deep brown eyes. He and Alexander were nearly inseparable and loved to compete against each other.

Lorco and his sister Mara, resembled their mother Chatha, the pretty warrior queen of Atlantis. Mara was more into sports and horseback riding than "girl stuff" while Lorco enjoyed reading anything he could lay his hands on. He was also rough and tough when he had to be. A real chip off the old block as Chatha called him.

Both Melody and Hawk had inherited Galya's telekinetic abilities and spent much of their time testing their limits—with often hilarious results. Melody had attached herself to Lorco and used her powers to play practical jokes on him whenever she could—especially if he tried to ignore her.

Hawk palled around with young Hercemes, Arka-Dal's adopted son—unless of course, Mut, Arka-Dal's granddaughter was visiting. When Mut was there, Hawk followed her around like a lovesick puppy.

Mut had long dark hair, pale blue eyes and almost white skin like her mother Idut, but otherwise showed no other wraithlike traits, such as having perpetually cold skin. She was also rather bossy and opinionated and made it clear that when she was there, *she* was in charge. Anyone who disagreed was threatened with a knuckle sandwich. The only one she didn't try to boss around was Alexander. In fact, she seemed rather awed by him.

And there was more.

Chatha, Arka-Dal's youngest wife, had recently given birth to a son she named Theron after a long-ago king of Atlantis. The newborn was received with a grand celebration by the people of Thule, which included feasting, entertainment, fireworks and all sorts of sporting events—just like the births of all of the other Dal children.

And Arka-Dal had recently acquired yet another wife in the lovely Dihhuri queen, Zhijima. She had divorced Pandaar-Vli, one of Arka-Dal's best friends in order to marry him.[1]

The entire episode occurred when she caught Pandaar-Vli, her husband, rolling around on their bed with one of the palace maids. The angry and scorned Zhijima threw herself at Arka-Dal. This ignited several highly comical arguments with Pandaar and the rest of Arka-Dal's wives who pleaded with him to marry Zhijima.

At the bottom of the stairs was a large open space furnished with large comfortable sofas, wing backed chairs, gaming tables, a bar, several hand woven rugs from Sundar and Parthia and a grand, open fireplace with a marble mantle. Above the fireplace hung the famed Excalibur which Merlin had bestowed on Arka-Dal. Next to the fireplace sat Arka-Dal's teardrop shaped shield with the double headed eagle symbol emblazoned on it.

This was the living room.

It was informal.

Relaxing and fun to be in.

And it was the center of household activity.

This is where the children played on rainy days and where Arka-Dal gathered before and after meals with his friends and visitors to talk, play

---

[1]   Read From the depths of Evil & Other Tales

chess and throw darts. Usually, at least a half dozen cats lounged on the sofas and chairs or lay curled up on the rug in front of the fireplace.

This day was no different.

Arka-Dal and Leo met with the delegation from far away Sheba. Their enigmatic queen had sent them to Thule on what was best described as a fact finding tour. They were sent by her to learn as much as possible about Thule, its customs, inhabitants and way of life and to initiate diplomatic and possible trade relations.

Arka-Dal bade them to travel the Empire and get to know its land and people.

"After you've learned more about us, come back to the palace. I'll answer any and all questions you may have. Then you can decide what to do afterward," he said.

The delegates joined them for the usual lengthy family dinner and met everyone in Arka-Dal's family and inner circle. Around midnight, a maid showed the delegates to the guest rooms and wished them good night.

Arka-Dal stayed up another hour to play chess with Leo while sipping brandy, then retired to his chambers. Leo went up after a short chat with Merlin and the palace became almost eerily quite.

Two hours passed.

Merlin was seated on the sofa in front of the fireplace sipping brandy when the rustling of fine silk caught his attention. He glanced up and watched as Galya descended the stairs clad in her robe.

Her movements were graceful and fluid as always.

She smiled when she saw him. Merlin slid over to make room on the sofa for her. She sat next to him and crossed her legs.

"You're up late," she observed.

"So are you," he said.

"I'm still a creature of the night. I need far less sleep than the others," she said. "You seem troubled. Is there anything I can help with?"

"I'm not certain—yet," he responded. "There's something amiss in the grand scheme of the universe. Ned and I have been unable to put our fingers on it. Yet, I feel this is something that will prove to be highly disturbing."

"This even has the Knower stumped? Now there's a first!" Galya said.

"Indeed," Merlin said. "I do know that it has something to do with those who dwell beyond the Abyss."

"You mean the Others?" Galya asked.

Merlin nodded.

He drained his glass and went to the bar to pour himself another. At the same time, he brought a glass of brandy to Galya. She accepted it with a smile as he sat back down.

"What do you know about the Others?" he asked.

"Almost nothing," she replied. "Our kind never venture into the Abyss, much less beyond it. Father says the Others are twisted, unspeakable nightmares who feast upon the souls of the dead. I do know that for the last 2,000 years they have been trying to fight their way into the Abyss."

"And with good reason. Something has driven them from their world. Something dark and terrible. Something they are unable to stand against. When the Others invaded the Abyss, they drove Mephistos' people toward our world. They invaded Earth en masse, much like the hordes of Barbarians who were driven toward Rome by stronger waves of invaders during the First Age. As nasty as the Others are reputed to be, the obvious question is who or what drives them?" Merlin said.

"If something is driving the Others from their plane, it must be very powerful and terrifying. The Others supposedly fear nothing. That also suggests that another world lies beyond their realm," Galya said.

"And there are many more beyond that. The universe *is* infinite after all. There are more worlds and parallel worlds and planes than we can possible ever count. No one can know all of them. Not even Ned," Merlin said.

"Does Father know of this?" Galya asked.

"Yes. It is he who brought this our attention several months ago," Merlin replied. "Very little gets past *your* father."

Galya laughed.

"He says the same about *you*," she said.

Ned the Knower, was the oldest and most enigmatic being in the universe. He was tall and thin with blond hair, pointed ears and deep green eyes with uplifted brows. He looked for all the world like an Elf.

But Ned was older than the Elves.

Far older.

According to the legends, he was even older than the gods themselves and he occupied a space that was not exactly a space on a world that was not exactly a world. He could cross space and time at will, which he often did in his endless quest for knowledge.

Hence the sobriquet "Knower".

It was said that he knew all that was worth knowing—and quite a bit more. Arka-Dal and Merlin considered him a good friend, albeit a sometimes frustrating one. The ever Mercurial Knower came and went as he desired and had an uncanny knack for arriving on the scene at just the right moment.

Or wrong moment, depending on one's point of view.

Usually, when Ned made an appearance, there was trouble afoot.

This time, was no exception.

The Devil and Ned were not exactly friends.

Nor were they enemies.

Both had a grudging respect for the other and neither interfered with the other's workings. The Devil didn't venture into Ned's space and Ned didn't bother him unless he had to. So when the Knower suddenly popped into being right next to him, the Devil just about jumped out of his skin.

"I come in peace!" Ned announced as he raised his hand.

The Devil smiled.

"I wish you'd knock or something before you just appear from nowhere," he said. "To what do I owe your visit?"

"Something wicked this way comes," Ned replied.

"Then you saw what I saw?" the Devil asked.

"Indeed I did. Never in all my years of existence have I beheld anything like that. Now, I understand why you brought this to my attention. It is just as you feared. Perhaps worse!" Ned replied.

"Then those that dwell beyond the realm of the Others have awakened the Beast?" the Devil asked.

"Not yet—but the signs are there. The Minions are multiplying. Even now, they drive the Others before them and the Others seek to drive the dwellers of the Abyss before them. If the Beast fully wakes, its Minions will overrun the Abyss and eventually find their way into *your* domain," Ned explained.

The Devil nodded and paced the floor.

"The Beast wakes to feed every 10,000 years. When it does, it devours entire worlds. It has been so long since it last stirred, I had almost forgotten about it. Even so, I never imagined it would follow this particular path," he said.

"If the Beast enters the Abyss, it will devour Mephistos' people and those who seek to drive them. If the Abyss falls, Hell and all of its vast and numerous planes, will be its next target," Ned warned.

"And after that, Earth," the Devil said.

"You saw what it did to the *last* world it entered. That must not be allowed to happen again," Ned said. "We must stop the Beast before it wakes. Before it can do the same to this Earth as it did to the countless others it left in its wake."

"I don't know that the Beast *can* be stopped—but we must try," the Devil agreed. "It's time to put the plan we discussed into action. Let's alert Merlin."

"I already *have!*" Ned assured him.

The next day was much like any other day in Thule. The city was alive with people conducting their daily business and visitors from every nation and race imaginable were everywhere to be seen. Thulians were accustomed to seeing foreign travelers. After all, their city was the commercial hub of the Second Age and a major draw for tourists.

But one such visitor was particularly striking.

Seated astride a cloud-white stallion, the warrior cut quite an impressive figure as he slowly rode through the crowded streets of Thule. Just about everyone stopped what they were doing to watch as he rode past and many of the women commented on his rugged good looks.

A few winked and whistled at him. A couple playfully offered to marry him.

He paid them no mind.

Michael, the last survivor of the race known as Archangels, had come to Thule for a purpose. Like many others before him, he had come to seek refuge in the Empire and to offer his sword to its famous ruler.

Michael stood seven feet tall and had a lean, muscular body. His eyes were emerald and his golden hair hung loosely about his neck and shoulders. He wore a loose-fitting blue tunic and trousers, topped by a shimmering metal breastplate and bracers. A large metal shield, bow and a quiver filled with arrows hung across his back. A heavy broadsword with a wide hand guard and a golden hilt, hung at his left hip. Everything about him screamed "warrior".

In his glory days, Michael had served in the army of God with courage and honor. The War of Forever, as it was known, had lasted for thousands of years. It ended with one great, decisive battle at the edge of the universe and Michael found himself on the losing side.

He thought back to that final battle. He and a handful of loyal soldiers found themselves surrounded by a sea of demons and devils. On that fateful day, they swore an oath to each other. They would fight to the death. There could be no surrender. The forces of the Devil never took prisoners anyway. They were fighting to exterminate every last member of God's host.

That final battle lasted for weeks.

Maybe months.

Time has no meaning in the Outer Realms. There's no way to mark it.

In the end, only he remained.

He was badly wounded and bleeding from more than a dozen places. His wings were broken and useless. His armor and shield were battered and cracked and his arms ached from wielding his weapons. He dropped his arms and waited for the final blow. Instead, the demons bound him with strong chains and dragged him across the field to their commander, Galya.

In those days, she was the leader of the Devil's finest legions. It was the first time he'd ever seen her up close and she looked resplendently sinister in her jet-black, gold trimmed armor and flared helmet. He expected her to order her soldiers to execute him on the spot. Instead, she ordered them to take him to her father.

"And make certain he gets there unharmed if you know what's good for you!" she warned. Then she smiled at him and said, "Father's orders."

Her tone of voice was soft and calm. He detected no anger or malice in it.

His trip through the many planes of Hell were an epiphany. He realized that the Devil's forces numbered in the *billions*. It was then he realized that no matter how hard or how long his side would have fought, the outcome would have been the same. Hell's army could not be defeated. All the misery, death and destruction had been for nothing.

When they reached the last plane, the victorious demons brought Michael into the Devil's lair and forced him to kneel before their master.

He watched as the Devil slowly approached him then stopped not two feet away.

"I've been expecting you," the Devil said.

He was at the Devil's mercy then. He thought he'd be cast into the fires of Hell or suffer a fate much worse.

Instead—and to Michaels' astonishment—the Devil waved his hand and freed him from the chains. He then returned his sword, shield and bow to him and helped him to stand. Then he smiled.

"The war is ended now. You may go. Live in peace," he said.

Struck dumb by this turn of events, Michael bowed his head respectfully and walked out the same way he had entered. The sea of demons parted to let him pass. No one touched him. No one said anything. They simply saluted him out of respect. Not knowing what else to do, he returned their salute and went on his way.

The Devil had spared his life and by doing so, he'd thrown the Archangel into a state of mental turmoil that left him with far more questions than answers. While all of his brethren had been slaughtered, he was the only one to be spared.

Why?

It took him centuries to find his way out of Hell. During his travels, he met and got to know many demons of all types and humor. None molested him. None insulted him. They simply allowed him safe passage out of the Lower Planes. At one point, a demonic smith repaired his damaged shield, armor and sword, but warned him that the weapon could never again be used against anyone from Hell. The smith's craftsmanship was above reproach, too.

Everywhere he went, demons and devils greeted or saluted him. They answered any and all of his questions about Hell and the many types of people that dwelled on its many planes. He was amazed at what he learned.

And humbled.

But none could tell why the Devil had spared his life.

And Michael never understood why.

When he finally found his way out of Hell, Michael roamed the bleak landscape of Earth during the Great Darkness and realized there was still much use for his sword as he defended the tattered remnants of the human race from unspeakable horrors. He fought terrifying monsters. Destroyed countless killer machines. He slew vampires and other nasty creatures that preyed upon the helpless remnants of the human race and he watched as another civilization took root and flowered in the Valley after a century of war between several city-states.

His glory days were gone.

As were his wings.

Broken and useless, he'd had a demonic surgeon remove them centuries before. That's when he took to riding horses. As he traveled, he rid regions of bandits, slew all sorts of hideous monsters, and rescued damsels in distress from those who would enslave them, and performed many other great and heroic deeds. His fame and fortune grew.

Some people even made up songs and poems about his exploits.

He was St. Michael, the Archangel. Protector of the weak. Slayer of the wicked.

But something was missing.

Something very important.

God had created his Archangels to serve him as elite warriors. Without someone to serve, Michael's life had no real meaning.

No purpose.

God's death had actually benefited the Archangel. It freed him from servitude. Freed him to go where he wished and to serve whomever he chose. For the first time in his long existence, Michael had free will.

It was the very thing the Devil had given to mankind and the very thing God tried to take away. The irony did not escape him.

But he was created to be a warrior.

A soldier.

He knew nothing else. A soldier must have someone to serve or a cause to fight for. He must have a reason to exist.

That's when he heard about Thule and its almost legendary emperor, Arka-Dal. And the more he heard about them, the more he realized it was there he truly belonged.

Who better to serve than the famed Arka-Dal?

What better cause to protect than the most enlightened empire mankind had ever produced?

Surely Arka-Dal would accept him into the Army of Thule. Surely he would find a home there. A new purpose. A banner to stand and fight under.

And what a banner.

The double-headed eagle symbolized freedom and justice to millions of people throughout the world. Thule was what previous empires had aspired to be—and had failed so miserably to achieve. And he'd seen many of them rise and fall, from Republican Rome to enlightened Athens to Camelot and the United States. All had begun with lofty ideals and intentions. All had fallen due to corruption from within. After the fall of the United States at the start of Great Disaster, humankind had reverted to its tribal beginnings. It had taken nearly 2,000 years for men to claw their way out of the darkness and recreate the ancient city states of the First Age. And even they teetered on extinction thanks to centuries of warfare as each city-state strove for dominion over others. The Second Age might have ended before it had a chance to begin if not for Arka-Dal.

This minor prince from a warring city-state had risen from near obscurity to forge the most amazing empire the world had ever seen.

Michael had spent decades studying Arka-Dal and decided he was the only person on Earth worthy enough to serve. But first he traveled to Thule to learn all he could about the Empire and its people. The more he traveled, the more he learned and the more he liked what he saw.

Thule was like no other empire or nation that came before it and its people had made it what it was. Michael had never met anyone like them.

Thulians were prosperous and happy. Proud of their Empire. And they loved their Emperor passionately. They were confident in him, his inner circle, the stability of the Empire and themselves. They were well-educated and informed thanks to a system of public schools and universities and a host of newspapers.

As he explored the nation, he never heard anyone speak badly of Arka-Dal nor blame him for their lot in life. In fact, most of the people idolized him and they adored his family as much as they did their own.

"He's one of us," was the phrase he heard most often. "So's everyone else in his family."

Thulians themselves came in all shapes, sizes, colors and races. Michael was amazed to see Alfar, Dwarfs, Mongoblins and even minor Devils and Demons wandering through the market places and along Thule's streets. He even saw Trolls and Gnomes, which never frequented other human cities. He also encountered people from every known nation on Earth. Many were citizens. Others were merchants and tourists.

He was also surprised to see temples and churches of all denominations scattered throughout the land. Thulians were guaranteed religious freedom by their Constitution and all were welcome—as long as they obeyed the laws of the land and didn't practice human or animal sacrifices.

There was no state or official religion. No official gods or goddesses.

And no one cared a bit about anyone's race or religion.

In fact, Thule was a magnet for people seeking freedom from religious persecution.

Michael also decided to visit some of the military outposts and asked questions about their lives and training. He discovered that Thulian soldiers were well-paid and provided for and highly skilled and professional.

These soldiers were uncommonly loyal to Arka-Dal and the Empire. They told Michael that Arka-Dal was more than their commander-in-chief. He was one of *them*. He led them in the field. He ate what they ate. Lived as they lived and fought shoulder-to-shoulder with them. He would never ask his men to do anything he himself wouldn't do and they assured Michael they would follow Arka-Dal intro Hell or anywhere else he wanted to lead them without giving it a single thought.

Arka-Dal also knew many of them by name and always stopped to speak with and encourage them when encamped. He also joked with them, sang with them, drank with them and wept for them and their families if they fell in battle.

"He's one of us—a soldier. He'll always be one of us," one man-at-arms told him. "That's what makes him special."

Thulian engineering also amazed him.

The Empire had good, even roads that connected major cities and smaller towns to each other and to the capital. Dams, bridges and clever irrigation projects, aqueducts, and water purification plants were everywhere to be seen.

Most of the bigger cities had electric lights that were either solar powered or produced by massive hydroelectric plants. A railway system was also being constructed to make travel faster and easier. Radio and telegraph systems covered every corner of the Empire and even connected Arka-Dal to his ships at sea and close allies. And everywhere he went, he saw that businesses thrived in the open markets, seaports, shops and factories. Thulians not only imported goods from all over the world, they manufactured much of what they used themselves.

The cities and towns were neat, clean and safe. The highways were well-patrolled by cavalry units and the borders were protected by a series of small, interconnected forts and outposts.

Thule, the capital city of the Empire, was a marvel in civil and military engineering. It spanned both sides of the river and covered more than 60 square miles. The two halves were connected by a series of drawbridges that were raised to allow tall ships to sail up and down the river. During times of war, the bridges remained in the up position. On each side of the river stood rows of docks and piers. Some were private marinas containing yachts and pleasure boats. Some held warships. Most were crowded with fishing boats and trading vessels from all over the world. The docks were lined with warehouses, shops, inns and restaurants, all of which seemed incredibly busy.

Michael knew that the royal palace stood on a hill in the western half of the city. As he rode through the tall, heavy wood and iron gates, he was amazed at the height and breadth of the city's defensive walls and towers. All were made of reinforced stone and brick and painted white with gold, blue, red and green trim. The gates were open and unguarded and led to the main avenue.

The city itself was clean and beautiful. Stately trees of many varieties lined the streets. There were fine sculptures and fountains. Bright benches and small city parks. The first major structure he came to was the Great Arena and Sports Field, where the annual games—and baseball, the Emperor's favorite sport--were played. There were fine eateries, souvenir shops, taverns and hotels along the boulevard. He passed open air markets crowded with vendors and customers, universities, museums and even a zoo.

He stopped a passerby and asked where the palace was located. The man pointed to the top of a large hill.

"It's up there, on the other side of the rose garden," he said. "Just stay on this street."

The rose garden delighted him. To his surprise, it was a large public park. Everywhere he looked, he saw couples and families strolling along the winding paths or picnicking on the grassy lawns. There were playgrounds and athletic fields crowded with children and venders hawking cooked food, cold drinks and souvenirs.

The garden itself was a treat for the senses. It had roses of every imaginable variety as well as trees, shrubs and flowers from all over the world. There were man-made ponds covered with lily pads, ornate fountains, marble benches, mazes and even electric light poles.

He saw pairs of soldiers lazily patrolling and gardeners tending to the plants and shrubs and cleaning in general. He followed the main path to a large domed structure with many columns and windows. A sign outside proclaimed it to be the Hall of Heroes. He tied his horse to a tree and decided to check it out. He wondered what sort of heroes Thulians had.

The building was a rotunda modeled after a similar building of the First Age. The dome was more than 100 feet high and painted with scenes depicting long-ago battles and events. The dome was open at the top to allow sunlight to enter. It cast a warm, almost peaceful glow over the circular atrium which contained a circle of marble benches surrounding a tall, bubbling fountain.

The walls were of polished marble with 100 arched niches. Forty contained life-sized statues. Unlike most monuments which featured plain white statues, these sculptures were painted in vivid, life-like colors. The works were so well done, Michael thought he could see some of them breathing.

As he walked around, he was surprised at the array of heroes. Many were great men from the First Age, like Alexander of Macedon, Julius Caesar, Cincinnatus and Hannibal. All were famous military commanders and conquerors. He also saw statues of Washington, Jefferson, Franklin and Madison as well as Thulian heroes who had fallen in battle.

Michael asked one of the attendants why there was no statue of Arka-Dal on display. The man told him that the Emperor refuses to allow it.

"He says that the Hall is for those who are no longer with us so that they should never be forgotten—and *he's* still alive. He also says that he's not worthy to be included among such great people," the man explained.

"He sounds very modest. Especially so for a man in his lofty position," Michael commented.

The attendant laughed.

"That's why everybody likes him. He doesn't put himself above us. You'll like him, too—once you meet him," he said.

"And just how do you know where I'm going?" Michael inquired.

The man smiled.

"Where *else* would an unusual warrior like *you* go?" he said. "You've obviously come here to offer your services to Arka-Dal. And, if you're as formidable as you appear to be, I'm sure you'll be one of our soldiers by sunset."

Michael had to laugh. He didn't realize he looked so obvious to the locals.

"Is it difficult to have an audience with the Emperor?" he asked.

"No. Anyone can see him. All you have to do is walk up to the door of the palace and ask to see him. If he's home, someone will take you to him," the man replied.

"Remarkable," Michael said.

"That's just the way things are here," the man said. "If you don't mind my asking—just what kind of warrior *are* you?"

"I'm the last of my kind. I'm an Archangel," Michael answered.

"In that case, you'll fit right in," the man assured him.

"What do you mean?" asked Michael.

The man smiled.

"You'll understand when you meet him," he said as he walked off to tend to other business.

Michael left the Hall and continued on his way. Ten minutes later, he found himself in front of the royal palace, which was also painted white and trimmed with the same colors as the outer walls of the city. As soon as he dismounted, a stable boy rushed over and took the reins of his horse.

"I'll take care of him for you, sir," the boy said.

Michael thanked him and ascended the flight of wide marble steps to the front door. A guard stood on either side. One stepped out to greet him and asked him to state his business. The guard was polite.

"I have traveled many miles to speak with your Emperor," Michael said. "My name is Michael."

The guard opened the door and admitted him to the grand hall. Then he pulled a bell cord and left. A few seconds later, a short but pretty maid emerged from a side door. She stopped when she saw Michael and whistled.

"Just how tall *are* you?" she inquired.

"Seven feet," he replied, somewhat surprised at her directness.

"I'll take you to Arka-Dal. He's in the parlor," she said as she led him across the hall and through a double door.

In a corner of the large, open, comfortably furnished room he saw two men playing chess. The maid led him to them. They looked up when they approached.

"We have a visitor—and he's a *big one*!" the maid announced.

"Thank you, Lamani," Arka-Dal said.

She bowed slightly and scurried off. Arka-Dal rose and extended his hand. Michael hesitated at the informality of the gesture then clasped it. He noticed that the Emperor's grip was firm and strong.

Sincere.

"I'm Arka-Dal. This pudgy fellow here is Leo. What can we do for you?" the Emperor asked.

Again Michael hesitated. There was no ritual or obvious class structure. He was greeted as an equal. Arka-Dal sensed his confusion.

"Do you speak our language?" he asked.

"I speak *all* known languages," Michael replied as he tried to relax. "My name is Michael. I have been traveling for many years. Everywhere I've been, I have heard people say many wonderful things about Thule and its ruler. I have come here to meet you and to find out for myself if you are all they say."

"Well, I have no idea what people are saying about me, so I have no way to answer. As for Thule, the Empire speaks for itself," Arka-Dal said.

"I see by your weapons that you are a warrior," Leo observed.

"I have fought many battles. Perhaps too many," Michael said.

"I know exactly how you feel," Arka-Dal said as he offered him a seat.

Michael unstrapped the shield from his back and placed it against a nearby wall. He placed his bow and quiver beside it. He was about to unbuckle his sword belt when he heard a sound behind him.

At that point, Galya entered the room. The moment she and Michael laid eyes on each other, they froze in their tracks.

"You!" they both exclaimed at once.

That's when Michael reached for his weapon. So did Arka-Dal.

Before he drew his sword halfway out of the scabbard, Michael felt the tip of Excalibur at his windpipe. Although he was impervious to all Earthly weapons, he quickly realized that this particular sword had the power to slay him with ease.

Leo smiled at the expression on Michael's face. Apparently, Arka-Dal's actions had surprised him.

"Release your sword," Arka-Dal ordered.

Michael let go of the hilt and allowed the sword to slide back into the sheath. Arka-Dal lowered Excalibur and turned to Galya.

"You know each other?" he asked.

"Yes. We've met several times before and not under the best of circumstances," she said as she eyed Michael carefully. "Father knows him, too."

"From where?" Arka-Dal asked.

"The War," Michael said. "The war *we* should have won."

"But you didn't win. In fact, you were beaten rather badly," Galya reminded him. "By *my* legions."

"Are you speaking of the Forever War between Heaven and Hell? The war that destroyed the power of god?" asked Leo.

"Yes," Galya said. "*That* war. This is Michael, the last surviving Archangel. The last soldier of a false god."

"And *your* sworn enemy," Michael said.

"Not *here* you're not," Arka-Dal said. "If you attempt to harm Galya in any way, I'll bring an end to your race myself."

Michael stared at him.

"You *protect* her? She is the Devil's daughter, the Crown Princess of the Lower Planes…" he protested.

"And *my* wife," Arka-Dal said.

Michael's jaw dropped. It was several seconds before he could speak again.

"Are you not Arka-Dal, the Emperor of Thule and the champion of truth, justice and all that is good on this Earth? Are you not the wielder of the famous Excalibur?" he asked.

"I am indeed Arka-Dal, Emperor of Thule. As for the rest, well, that's a product of a lot of people's fertile imaginations," Arka-Dal replied modestly.

"Yet you are wed to *her*?" Michael asked. "Why?"

"Because we *love* each other," Galya said as she put her arms around Arka-Dal's waist. "We even have two beautiful children. Thanks to him, I no longer dwell in shadow and darkness. I no longer seek out souls. I am proud and content to be the wife of Arka-Dal and the mother of our children. Of course, I still maintain command of my 30 legions in Hell."

Michael shook his head in wonder.

"Even if god still lived, he could not have foreseen this. I stand humbled before you and I beg your forgiveness for threatening you and the disturbance I have caused in this house," he said with a polite bow of his head.

"Apology accepted," Arka-Dal said as he offered his hand.

Michael clasped it and bowed respectfully.

"Why have you come here?" asked Arka-Dal.

"I have come to offer my sword in the service of Thule and my loyalty for as long as your House endures," Michael stated.

"Why me?" the Emperor asked.

"God is dead. I was created to be a soldier. My life has no meaning without someone to serve. Someone who shares my ideals of justice. A man of honor and courage. Someone who is noble, compassionate and wise. *You* are that person," Michael replied.

"*Me?*" Arka-Dal asked.

"Yes. You have all of the qualities that my false god was devoid of. He deceived us on all counts but you are the embodiment of all he failed to be," Michael said.

"Wow! That's quite a compliment. You make *me* sound like some sort of god. I assure you that I'm *not* a god. I'm human and I have human weaknesses. I'm not perfect. I make mistakes but I try to learn from them. If I grant your request, bear in mind that it is not *me* you'll serve but the people and the Empire of Thule," Arka-Dal said.

"I understand," Michael said.

He drew his sword, offered it to Arka-Dal hilt-first and dropped to one knee.

"I am yours to command—*if* you'll accept me," he said humbly.

"I'd take him on," Galya urged. "He is a good tactician, an excellent and courageous fighter and extremely loyal to whomever he swears to serve. Father had great respect for him."

"With such a glowing recommendation, how could I even think of turning you away?" Arka-Dal said as he pulled Michael to his feet. "Get up, Captain. There's no need for you to kneel before me or anyone else in Thule. We have no such formalities here."

"Captain? You mean I'm in?" Michael asked as he took back his sword.

"I'll have Leo enlist you as soon as he draws up the papers. With your experience, I've decided to give you the rank of captain and place you in command of a troop of cavalry in the Central Army. After you've learned how we do things here, I'll award you a rank more befitting your vast experience," Arka-Dal said as they shook hands.

"I am grateful for the chance to serve," Michael said.

"Do you still have your magic?" asked Galya.

"Alas, no. We Archangels derived our magic directly from god. When he died, my powers died with him. All that remains is my immortality and telepathic abilities. What of your powers?" he asked.

Galya shrugged.

"I'm not quite sure. They became greatly diminished when I gave birth to the twins. Merlin said they might return in time," she said.

"Merlin still lives? That's amazing!" Michael exclaimed. "Do you see him often?"

"Yes. He visits us frequently. He's like one of the family now," Arka-Dal said. "By the way, are you hungry?"

"Yes. I have not eaten for the last four days," Michael replied.

"Then I insist you join us for dinner," Arka-Dal said.

As they walked to the dining room, Michael made small talk with Galya.

"I barely recognized you without your horns and wings. What became of them?" he asked.

She laughed.

"I lost them when I married Arka-Dal. What became of your wings?" she asked.

"They never mended properly so I had them removed. I ride a horse now," he replied.

"So do I," she said with a smile. "The last time I saw you, my soldiers brought you to me in chains. What have you been doing all this time?"

"Much. I guess you could say that I've been trying to make sense of what happened," Michael answered.

"And have you?" she asked.

"I'm not sure. Perhaps I never will," he said. "Do you ever think about those years?"

"There's no need to. What's done cannot be undone. Besides, we *won*," she said.

"So you did," Michael agreed.

At dinner, Michael was introduced to everyone in Arka-Dal's "family", including the Minotaur, Jun, who was visiting on official military business.

"For the next four weeks, you'll be working directly under Jun. He's one of my finest commanders and responsible for the entire army's training. If anyone can show you the ropes, he can," Arka-Dal said as Jun and Michael shook hands.

Michael seemed surprised when he met Jun. He was equally surprised to meet another of Arka-Dal's wives, Medusa. When she asked why, he answered honestly.

"I thought both your races had long ago vanished from the Earth," he said.

"Almost," Medusa said. "Like you, we are the last of our kind. If we had not come to Thule seeking refuge, we surely would have been killed."

"In our ancient homeland, people thought of us as monsters. They hunted us down and slew us until only we remained. Here, we are not monsters. Here, we are appreciated for our talents and abilities. We have been given a new lease on life—and it's all thanks to Arka-Dal," Jun added as he raised his glass.

"I fled to Thule to avoid being murdered. Since I speak several languages and can read and write many long-dead ones, Leo hired me to be his assistant. Soon after, Arka-Dal and I were married. I now have far more than I ever dreamt about," Medusa said as she squeezed Arka-Dal's hand.

"When I arrived, I enlisted in the Army of Thule. Because of my experience, Arka-Dal appointed me to be his chief training officer. It was more than I expected. A few years ago, he promoted me to the rank of Field Marshall and gave me the command of the Northern Army. Nowhere else could one such as me have attained such rank and honor," Jun said.

"Thule is a meritocracy," Leo explained. "A person can rise as high and go as far as his talent and determination can take him. There are no titles here. No class structures or castes. Thulian citizens are protected by a constitution and the rule of law. Arka-Dal safeguards those rights."

Michael nodded.

"I've heard this during my travels throughout this land. I have spoken with many of its citizens and foreign travelers. All had only praise for the Empire and Arka-Dal. I have been all over this world many times. Never have I heard any nation or its ruler held in such high regard," he said.

"Thule is that 'shining city on the hill' that everyone is drawn to," Medusa said. "That's why I came here."

"You and Arka-Dal have children together?" Michael asked.

"Yes. We have two," Medusa replied.

"Are they more human or Gorgon?" he asked.

"To tell you the truth, we really don't know. My Gorgon traits only come out when I'm frightened or very angry. I have not seen such traits in either of our children," Medusa replied.

Michael glanced at Leo.

"What religion to you subscribe to?" he asked.

"None," Leo said with a grin.

"But you are *Pope* Leo. The popes once ruled the Catholic church," Michael said.

"I am Arka-Dal's *religious advisor.* I advise him on matters that concern various and diverse religions, both living and dead, their customs, rituals, holidays, laws and histories behind each of them. I personally know every religious leader in the Empire but I practice none of them," Leo answered.

"What god or gods do you worship?" Michael asked.

"None. I've no use for gods," Leo said.

"Leo is also the keeper of our archives, our chief historical and archaeological researcher and he advises me on all matters dealing with civil and criminal laws. In another place and time, I suppose he would have been called the chief justice or attorney general," Arka-Dal explained.

"Why the title pope?" asked Michael.

"We couldn't think of anything else to call me," Leo said with a chuckle. "Pope is simple and easy to remember."

"Have you been with Arka-Dal a long time?" Michael asked.

"I met him when I was his teacher. He was nine years old then. I guess, in many ways, I'm still his teacher. Arka-Dal is like the son I wished I'd had—as are Pandaar and Kashi. We've been together for more decades than I care to think about," Leo said.

"And I've always looked upon Leo as my father. He helped guide me through many rough times and his teachings helped make me the man I am today," Arka-Dal added with a sense of pride.

"We are all one big family here," Mayumi chimed in. "And it is a very good, strong family."

After dinner, Arka-Dal showed Michael to one of the guest rooms.

"Make yourself at home here tonight. Take a hot bath and relax. My maids will wash your clothes and provide you with a robe until they are ready. You'll leave for your assignment with Jun tomorrow after breakfast," he said.

"Thank you, Sir," Michael said. "Will I be issued a new uniform and weapons?"

"If one can be found that will fit you. I think we'll have to have yours tailor made. You're a lot taller than the average soldier. You'll wear the traditional tunic and insignia that befits your rank. In battle, you can wear the armor and carry the weapons you normally carry. As a commanding officer, you have that right," Arka-Dal said.

"Commanding officer?" Michael asked.

Arka-Dal smiled.

"I expect you'll be commanding your own regiment quite soon," he said.

"Perhaps this is the destiny I was created for," Michael said.

"I'm sure it is. That's why your path led you here," Arka-Dal said. "I know that you'll serve the Empire well and with honor."

"I will do my best, Sir," Michael assured him.

"And that's all I ask of you—of anyone," Arka-Dal replied.

Afterward, Michael found his way to the roof of the palace. He looked out at the vast public park that surrounded it. After a few seconds, he caught sight of Arka-Dal and Galya walking hand-in-hand along the narrow brick path. A few yards away, most of the Dal children were engaged in a lively game of baseball with several children from the surrounding neighborhood.

It was a surrealistically tranquil scene that he still had trouble wrapping his mind around. The union between the Emperor and the Devil's daughter still amazed him. In fact, the situation he now found himself in was quite bizarre.

He heard footsteps behind and turned.

He nodded as Merlin walked over and stood beside him. Merlin smiled when he saw the happy couple.

"Their love grows deeper and stronger with each passing day," he commented. "And it's a true love. A pure and unconditional love that binds them to each other."

"You approve?" Michael asked.

"I didn't at first," Merlin admitted. "Now, I give them my blessings. Even her father approves of their union and he completely adores their children. Only Arka-Dal could have hoped to capture the heart of Galya."

"Are they as perfectly matched as they appear to be?" asked Michael.

"Oh, yes," Merlin assured him. "You'll see this for yourself as you come to know them. What do you think of Galya now that you've spoken with her?"

"She surprised me. In fact, I even *like* her," Michael replied. "This is so ironic for me. The last time we saw each other, she brought me before her father in chains. At that time, I swore I'd make her regret that. Now, I have sworn to *protect* her."

Merlin laughed and slapped him on the back.

"And so have *I*," he said. "I once detested Galya. Now, I love her as if she were my own daughter. To make matters even more ironic, her father and I have become very fast friends."

He smiled.

"Times have changed, Michael. The false god you served so long ago is dead. His power has been broken forever. You are an officer in the finest, most professional army the world has ever known and you serve an empire that is mankind's greatest hope for a bright, new age. You could not have chosen a better place or a better man to serve. Arka-Dal is everything you have ever heard—and much, much more."

Michael nodded.

"I hope I will prove myself worthy of such honors," he said.

"I'm sure you will," Merlin said.

Mayumi stepped out onto the roof and greeted them both with a gentle bow of her head. She looked down at Arka-Dal and beamed happily.

"Sometimes, I feel that life is perfect. Other times, I am sure that it is," she remarked.

"Except when things go terribly wrong," Merlin added.

Mayumi looked at him and wrinkled her nose.

"What is it this time, Merlin-san?" she asked.

"I'm not yet sure. I can tell you that this will be very strange and quite dangerous," he answered. "It may test all of our limits. Some of us may not even survive."

Mayumi frowned.

"Whatever it is, I am sure that you and Aka-san can handle it---as always," she said. "When will you know for sure?"

"In a few hours," Merlin replied.

"I know not what you speak of, Merlin, but I am more than willing to join you if you need me," Michael volunteered.

Merlin nodded.

"The danger is not immediate. We have time yet," he said.

He turned and left the roof. Michael shook his head.

"The old wizard still speaks in riddles," he said.

"Merlin says nothing until he is certain. If he is this concerned, something very dark must be waiting in the shadows," Mayumi said as she turned and bade him good night.

Michael smiled.

He now realized this was just the situation he was created for.

"She called him Aka-san?" Michael asked when he caught up with Merlin.

"She always calls him that. When they first met, she had difficulty pronouncing his name correctly. Aka for her, at that time, was easier for her to say than Arka. So she called him Aka-san, the 'san' being the honorific form of her language. It is also a term of respect and endearment. He never corrected her and, although she can now pronounce his name perfectly, she still calls him Aka-san. It's sort of her pet name for him," Merlin explained.

"But in her language, aka means crimson. Does that hold any significance?" Michael asked.

"Not really," Merlin replied.

"Does he speak Nihon-go?" Michael asked.

"Almost fluently—thanks to Mayumi," Merlin said. "He's fluent in several other languages as well. Arka-Dal is quite the scholar."

"I'm impressed," Michael said.

Merlin laughed.

"I'm sure he'd be embarrassed to hear you say that," he said.

"You and he started out as bitter enemies, did you not?" Michael asked.

"We did indeed. I made the mistake of underestimating him on every level imaginable—and paid the price for my folly. During our first war, I mistook him for a barbarian and tried to crush him. Instead, he ran my armies off the field and nearly killed me in the process. When I launched the second war against him five years later, I was testing him to see how he'd handle multiple levels of adversity. The more I threw at him, the more he impressed me with his determination and resourcefulness. We've been friends ever since. He continues to impress me to this very day," Merlin explained with a grin.

"Is he the legendary one true king?" Michael asked.

"If he isn't, he's the closest we'll ever come to it," Merlin said. "That's why I gave him Excalibur. He is the only man fit to wield it. It's as if the sword was made only for him."

Michael allowed this to sink in as he pondered his position.

"What more can you tell me of Michael?" Arka-Dal asked Galya as they strolled through the gardens.

"He is fearless and loyal. When he takes a vow or gives his word, he always keeps it. You can trust him with your life and the lives of all of us, if that's what you're wondering, my love," she said.

"And his experience in combat is vast," Arka-Dal mused.

"He has great command skills and is very adaptable to changing conditions. I was only able to defeat him because my legions far outnumbered the Angels. But he fought well and bravely until the end," Galya said. "It took ten of my best soldiers to disarm and chain him, too."

"Is he as good as you in combat?" Arka-Dal asked.

She laughed.

"No one is *that* good," she said.

He pulled her close and laughed at her false immodesty.

"I have this strange feeling inside of me, Galya. It's like something's going to happen. Like I'm waiting for that second boot to drop," he said as he looked up at the sky. "I feel that Michael's arrival is a harbinger of that—whatever it is."

"I feel it, too," Galya said. "If something bad is about to happen, I'm sure Father will warn us."

Arka-Dal nodded.

Michael had a long, hot bath in scented water. When he stepped out, two large soft towels and an extra long robe were waiting on the foot of his bed. After he dried himself and dressed, he decided to take a walk around the palace.

The first one he met was Pandaar, who was stumbling his way toward his chambers. The warrior hailed him with a slap on the back. Michael returned it and almost knocked him against a nearby wall.

"Damn! You're *strong!*" Pandaar remarked.

"You are one of Arka-Dal's closest friends," Michael began.

"*The* closest. He and I grew up together. We're like brothers—only closer," Pandaar said with a grin.

"Yet, from what I was told at dinner, he took your wife from you," Michael said.

"I *let* her go to him," Pandaar corrected. "There's a difference. Nobody owns Zhijima. Unfortunately, I learned that after the fact. When it was too late. Anyway, she deserves a good man—and there's none better than Arka-Dal."

"You mean you're not angry about this?" Michael asked.

Pandaar shook his head.

"Let me explain it this way, Michael," he said. "Arka-Dal, Kashi and I have been through more battles and trials than any men who ever lived. Our bonds are unbreakable. As far as Arka-Dal is concerned, what's mine is his. That included Zhijima. Although, it was *she* who wanted him and the other wives had to convince him to marry her. It's a long, crazy tale but it worked out in everyone's favor. Zhijima is happy. Arka-Dal and his other wives are happy. Hell, even *I'm* happy because she couldn't have chosen a better man. Does any of that make sense to you?"

"Not completely," Michael admitted.

Pandaar laughed and slapped him on the back again.

"It doesn't make sense to anyone—but that's the way things are around here. You'll see. You'll get used to it," he said.

Pandaar bade him good night and headed into his chamber. Michael thought he caught a glimpse of very naked Lamani greeting him at the door.

"Humans are still confusing," he thought.

The next person he met was Gorinna. She smiled when she saw him.

"I'm on my way to get a drink. Would you care to join me?" she offered.

He nodded and followed her to the bar in the living room. Gorinna poured herself a large brandy and dropped in several cubes of ice. Michael simply poured some blue wine into a large flagon. They sat down on the larger sofa together.

"What do you think of our family so far?" Gorinna asked.

"It's a very large and very diverse family," Michael replied. "I've never seen nor expected anything like this."

"But it works very well on every level. The ties are strong here and they grow stronger as time passes. And it works only because of Arka-Dal. We all love and respect him and each other. I think you've just become another odd relative," she said with a smile.

Michael laughed.

"I would really like that," he said. "I've never truly felt I belonged anywhere. Yet, I feel quite comfortable here in this house."

"None of us would ever dream of living anywhere else," Gorinna said. "Arka-Dal, Leo and I designed this house. Mayumi designed the gardens and we all had a hand in furnishing it. Arka-Dal says that a house should feel like a true home. It should be comfortable and easy to care for with lots of room for children, pets and visitors."

"Is there actually a throne room?" Michael asked.

"No. There's a room where official appeals trials are held. The high-backed chair in it is where Arka-Dal, and in his absence, Mayumi, sits when hearing pleas. But there's no throne or throne room here. Official business is conducted in the meeting room or in Arka-Dal's office. There's no need for a throne because Arka-Dal isn't a king," Gorinna explained.

"He sounds exactly like a man I met many centuries ago. He was the founder of his nation, too," Michael said.

"George Washington," Gorinna said. "He is one Arka-Dal's favorite historical figures."

"Is that why there is a figure of him in the Hall of Heroes?" Michael asked.

"Yes," Gorinna replied. "Merlin says that Arka-Dal has many of Washington's finer qualities and none of his vices. Leo taught Arka-Dal about that long-ago nation and the people who built it when he was a child. He even showed him copies of two ancient documents they wrote. It is those very documents that Thule's government and laws are based on."

"So the dream lives on?" Michael asked.

"Definitely. And we're going to make sure it doesn't end this time," Gorinna said.

"Over dinner, Arka-Dal introduced you as Kashi's wife. Then you said that was only when you weren't making love with Arka-Dal. Were you jesting?" Michael asked.

"No. I was merely stating a fact," Gorinna replied with a smile. "I have been madly in love with Arka-Dal for decades. We became lovers recently after we both admitted that we love each other. In case you're wondering, Kashi is fine with this as long as I return to his bed afterward. In fact, it was he who urged us to let our passions soar so we'd stop wondering about what might have been."

"This is more than a little strange," Michael said. "Under normal circumstances, any other house or family would have been torn apart by petty jealousies and lust for revenge. Yet, I see nor feel no such things here."

"This is *not* a normal house. And we are *not* a normal family," Gorinna said as she finished her drink. "You'll see after you've been around here a while."

That's when Michael saw her shudder. It was so obvious, he couldn't miss it.

"You see what Merlin sees, don't you?" he asked.

"Sometimes. Mostly I sense things. I see them in my dreams or get these odd sensations while I'm awake," she replied with a weak smile.

"Can you tell me more about it?" he asked.

"I see a huge, swirling, writhing black mass with hundreds of huge red eyes lying at the bottom of a deep chasm. It has been asleep for thousands of years but it's stirring once again," she said almost as if in a trance.

"Is this what Merlin saw?" Michael asked.

"I'm afraid so," she said. "And this is why fate has led you to us." Michael nodded.

"Whatever it is, I am with you to the end," he vowed.

She put down her glass and left. Michael watched her walk up the stairs and smiled. The legendary Red Witch was all he'd expected and more.

So was Arka-Dal.

Because of his wide variety of interests in the arts, sciences, history, culture and other arcana, Arka-Dal could be described as a true Renaissance Man. Michael felt that the Emperor had all of the finer qualities of Alexander the Great, Washington, Jefferson and even

Napoleon but none of their character flaws. If he did have a weakness, Michael didn't detect it.

Not unless one can call the ability to attract beautiful, intelligent and loyal women a weakness. Most men would consider this a great strength. So did Michael.

Arka-Dal's reputation for hating slavery and those who sold other human beings was well-known. Any "slave" who set foot on Thulian soil was instantly a free person and his "owner" had no choice but to grant that freedom. Anyone caught dealing in slaves in the Empire was punished severely and sent packing. Slavers took great pains to avoid entering Thule whenever possible.

Arka-Dal also detested anyone who slaughtered innocent people during wartime, hence his legendary treatment of the Turks who invaded Byzantium. Only the Janissaries who opted to switch sides were spared. [2]

Arka-Dal had a very keen sense of justice. The Turks were also known for trading in slaves, especially young women and children. This made them even more despicable to him.

That's why he didn't lift a finger to help them when one of their former slaves named Joshua gathered an army and destroyed what remained of the Turkish Empire a couple of years ago. But he did allow terrified Turkish civilians seek asylum in Thule after the last of their sultans was sent packing. Afterward, Joshua and Arka-Dal met in battle. When Joshua surrendered, Arka-Dal named him governor of the conquered Turkish lands and Trollegia. When these peoples voted to become part of the Empire, Joshua enlisted in the army of Thule and was promoted to the rank of Field Marshall by Arka-Dal.

This effectively increased the size of the Empire by one-third and a new army had to be created and trained to protect it.

Michael smiled.

"Arka-Dal's Empire is nearly as great as Alexander's was, but he didn't have to conquer it.," he said.

The next morning, Michael and Jun left for the training center of the Northern Army. Arka-Dal and Galya watched them leave.

"Just who *was* God?" asked Arka-Dal.

"He was my father's twin brother," Galya said. "His name was Jahweh. You might say I come from a very dysfunctional family."

---

[2] See Thirteen Skulls and Other Tales

He laughed.

"Who were their parents?" he asked.

She shrugged.

"No one really seems to know. Father never spoke of having parents. To my knowledge, supernatural beings don't necessarily *need* parents," she said.

"So I've heard," Arka-Dal said.

He'd often wondered if gods created people so that they would have someone to worship them or did people create gods in order to have something higher to believe in? Which came first? The chicken or the egg?

He'd asked the Devil, but even *he* didn't know. Somehow, men and gods became mutually dependent upon each other. In the past, that connection had been very strong. Now, it barely existed at all.

God was supposed to represent all that is good, noble and kind in the universe. Michael discovered, albeit too late, that this was simply not the case. His god simply put on a good front to hide the nasty, vindictive and vengeful personality that was truly his. It must have crushed Michael's spirit when he found out what a monster he was.

The Devil was supposed to be the embodiment of darkness, treachery and evil. Instead, it was he who brought mankind the gift of enlightenment, his thirst for knowledge and his desire to question everyone and everything. It was he who actually dispelled ignorance and superstition. Without him, human civilization never would have flourished. There would be no human history. No great empires. No science. No medicine. Nothing but a bunch of near-mindless worshippers of a false god.

Gods didn't exist anymore.

Perhaps they never did.

But demons and devils existed. He'd met far too many of them first-hand to deny their existence. His own father-in-law was the Devil himself!

Galya touched his arm and smiled.

"Don't trouble yourself with questions there are no answers for," she advised. "There are much more important things to think about."

"Such as?" he asked.

"How long you and I can make love without being interrupted," she said with a come-hither smile.

Gorinna saw Merlin seated on a sofa in the parlor. She walked over and sat beside him.

"Are you going to do this tonight?" she asked.

The wizard nodded.

"It's as good as any other night. The sooner he knows, the sooner we can devise a plan to put an end to it," he said. "Or it to us."

"Can it actually *do* that?" Gorinna asked.

"Indeed it can," he replied. "It has done this more times than I can care to think about. It has laid waste to more than a dozen worlds in a dozen different dimensions. That's why Arka-Dal must be told tonight."

"Can we stop it with magic?" Gorinna queried.

"I seriously doubt that," Merlin said.

"When will you do it?" she asked.

"Later—after he's asleep," Merlin replied.

"Once you show him what it can do, I'm sure he'll be convinced to act. But what can even *he* do? He's not a god," Gorinna said.

"I'm not sure that even the gods would be able to deal with *this*," Merlin said. "But we have to try or all will be lost."

Arka-Dal's sleep was a fitful one at best. In his subconscious mind, he saw images of crumbling cities, flames that engulfed an entire world and hellish figures taunting him from the outer edges of deep shadows. He saw a huge, dark mass of writhing energy undulating across the world, killing everything it touched.

He rolled over to put his arm around Galya. Instead of snug, warm body, his arm rested up something hard and cold. He opened his eyes and started as he stared into the dead, eyeless sockets of a dust and web encrusted mummified corpse. He jumped out of bed pulled the moldy covers away and nearly vomited at the sight of thousands of maggots and bloated worms that swarmed amid the fleshless ribs of the corpse that lay next to him.

It took several seconds for him to regain his composure. When he did, he turned to examine his surroundings. His comfortable bedroom had somehow become a surreal, decaying ruin.

There was a dull orange light streaming into the room through the dusty, tattered remains of the silk drapes that hung ghost-like from the rusted brass rods above each of the two paneless windows. One window had rotted out completely and leaned against the equally rotted sash as if waiting for the final push that would send it crashing to the ground below. The designs on the drapes were obscured by the ravages of time but he could still make out strange, almost terrifying designs in the fabric.

He looked down and saw he was dressed in his usual cotton tunic and boots.

"That's odd. I don't recall dressing last night," he though as he looked around.

The room was a complete wreck. Parts of the ceiling had fallen and everywhere he stepped, pieces of broken plaster crunched beneath his feet. There were long cracks in the walls and most of the decorative trim had fallen off.

The furniture was covered with layers of heavy dust and thick cobwebs obscured decorative objects and the right angles of the corners. The chandelier was covered with webs and hung precariously at an angle from its one remaining bolt. Both balcony doors had fallen from their hinges and lay shattered on the floor. Glass and bits of wood framing mingled with the fallen plaster from the ceiling and the carpet beneath the rubble was threadbare and riddled with worm holes.

Instinctively, he called out for Mayumi.

Nothing.

He turned to look back at the corpse lying on the bed and shuddered.

"Who were you?" he asked.

But no answer came forth from her open mouth.

He left the room and walked down the hallway to the stairs. The ornate brass light fixture had fallen from the ceiling and lay bent and rusted amid a pile of plaster and wooden laths. The wallpaper was stained with dark brown streaks and had even peeled away in several places. Along the way, he stopped to examine several large dust covered paintings that were mounted on the walls. The paintings were at least four feet high and three wide.

"There was nothing like this when I went to sleep last night," he thought as he stopped to brush the dust from one of them.

He expected to see a portrait of one of his wives or lost friends. Instead, a stern-looking bearded man with sharp eyes and a goatee stared back at him. He wrinkled his nose as he studied the man's face. His glare was cruel and malevolent.

"Who *are* you?" he asked. "And what are you doing on my wall?"

He did the same with the next portrait.

And the next.

None of the faces were familiar to him. He stepped back to study the features of the woman in the painting before him. Whoever she was, her malevolent glare gave him the creeps.

"You're obviously part of this family—but who *are* you?" he asked.

He stopped at the top of the staircase and called out again.

His voice echoing through the halls told him the palace was deserted.

When he descended into the foyer his was surprised to see that a huge weed tree had made its way up through the tiled floor and now commanded most of the area. At the roots, ugly green, yellow and purple briars and weeds had also sprung up and vines had spread across the floor like hideous green and brown ropes. Bits of plaster, splintered beams and marble shards were strewn about the entire floor.

The tree had made its way up through the second floor and broken through the roof of the palace and in effect had created a bizarre atrium of sorts. He heard and saw movement in the branches. He watched as several large birds fluttered from limb-to-limb. Their movements disturbed the loose plaster around the edges of the holes and sent it cascading to the floor where it kicked up a cloud of white dust.

"At least there are birds," he said. "Not everything is dead."

He shook his head in wonder as he walked into the living room. Instead of seeing comfortable, overstuffed sofas and chairs and side tables and his bar, he saw sharp-edged, sterile furnishings that were decidedly unwelcoming. The frames were made of steel and there was very little cushioning. It looked very official—like a place where men who were awaiting punishment sat.

He looked at the fireplace. The mantle had fallen to the floor years ago and now lay in several pieces on the hearth. Instead of his tear-drop shaped shield and Excalibur mounted on the wall above it, he saw a strange, twisted emblem of cold, black iron with crossed bolts of lightning running through it. It was symbol of unyielding power and it felt dark and cold.

And as heartless as the people in the portraits he's seen earlier.

Above the symbol was a portrait of a stern-lipped man with dark brown hair and cruel eyes. He had his hands folded across his chest and was dressed in a dark, steel-blue uniform. The man's gaze seemed to follow his every move. He looked even more heartless than the symbol beneath him.

"Who *are* you?" Arka-Dal asked. "You must have been a real monster in life. What kind of punishment befell you? What brought your line to an end?"

He walked back out into the foyer and called out again.

His cries disturbed several small birds that were nesting in the weed tree. They returned his cry as they flapped their wings and darted past him and left the palace through the wide open doors.

He looked around.

The entire palace was in a state of advanced disrepair and decay. The walls and floors were badly cracked in several places and large chunks of decorative plaster had fallen from the tops of ornate columns and medallions and now lay in hundreds of pieces across the floor. The plush draperies and tapestries were tattered and moldy and the banister was missing a half-dozen newel posts.

And dust covered everything.

Layers of it.

And cobwebs were everywhere. They clung to corners. They spanned open spaces and arches and they hung like eerie wisps of smoke from the chandeliers.

It looked as if no one had lived there for centuries.

He walked out into the rose garden and saw that it had reverted to wilderness. He shook his head and blinked. But the images remained the same.

Tall trees and weeds choked the cobblestone paths and sprouted from fountains. The lily ponds were now pools of thick, bubbling muck and the marble statues and benches were broken and discolored with green moss and mold. And the stagnant ponds now reeked of decaying plant life and fish.

There were no statues. No athletic fields. No well-kept plots of flowers. Everything was gone.

He looked up at the sky.

The clouds were wispy and sickly-looking. They rolled by in shades of purple, pink, orange and gold. The sky itself was a strange, unfamiliar hue.

It was reddish.

Almost like rust in places.

Amid this surrealistic nightmare, he saw a dull red sun instead of the warm, cheerful bright yellow sun he expected.

"Even the sun seems to be dying," he thought. "Just what happened here? How long have I slept?"

He followed the overgrown path past the Grand Basin. This deep, man-made lake was usually crowded with geese, ducks and other waterfowl. It was now weed-choked, muddy and deserted. Most of the water had drained out through the long, deep cracks in the bottom. This was barely visible beneath the layer of mud.

He shook his head sadly and kept walking.

He soon came upon the Hall of Heroes. To his dismay, the ornate dome had fallen down and the cascading rubble had destroyed most of the statues within. One large chunk had struck and crushed the fountain in the center. Weeds and vines were everywhere as well. Some had made their way across the floor and entwined themselves around a few of the statues.

The Hall had been the architectural gem of Thule. It was a masterpiece of art and engineering. Now, it was little more than a forgotten ruin.

He climbed the steps and walked through the arch. The floor was littered with debris from the collapsed dome and broken statues. Most were lying is pieces on the floor. Those that remained in their niches shocked him.

Gone were the images of Jefferson, Washington, Alexander and Caesar. Gone were Hercemes and other heroes of Thule. In their places stood a series of arrogant-looking, overbearing men in uniforms he had never seen before. All stood at attention with their right arms raised as if in salute.

"Just who the Hell were you?" he wondered.

The bas reliefs on the walls also shocked him.

Instead of depicting great inventions and historic documents and other peaceful scenes, there were scenes of marching soldiers, piles of burning corpses and forlorn people peering out from behind barbed wire fences.

"What has become of Thule?" he asked as he left the Hall.

He left the garden and traveled along the main avenue of the city. The beautifully paved streets were cracked and pitted. Large craters appeared where sewers had collapsed and weeds, wild flowers and grasses had sprouted through the cracks.

The government buildings, such as the Hall of Justice, Legislature, hospitals, Customs House, history and art museums and several smaller buildings were in the same state of neglect and decay as the Hall of Heroes. Roofs had collapsed. Walls had buckled inward. Doors and windows were either broken or missing and weeds, vines and other vegetation had covered almost everything.

The same went for the rest of the city.

He also noticed that the architectural styles of these buildings had been altered. Gone were the comforting, graceful and almost poetic lines and elements. The public buildings had been purposely designed to please the eye and make the average citizen feel comfortable while conducting official business.

Now, they seemed imposing.

Harsh and cold.

Almost sterile.

They looked more like places that people were summoned to receive punishment. Or worse.

Even private shops and homes looked more dull and uninviting.

The city looked dismal now. There was no joy in it.

"What happened here?" he wondered as he continued to explore the city.

No matter where he went, what street he turned down, the strange scene repeated itself time and again. The city was deserted save for an occasional flock of birds that flew overhead or the occasional rat that rummaged through the piles of debris in search of sustenance.

The people had obviously fled centuries before. They had abandoned the "Shining City on the Hill" and left it to the packs of wild dogs, rats and other vermin that now called it home.

"Just how did this come to pass?" he asked himself.

He heard birds chattering overhead and looked up to examine them. There was something strange about the birds.

Something off and different.

After a few moments, he realized that some of them actually had double sets of wings and even teeth. He watched as they flew out of sight and wondered just where those strange birds had come from.

That's when he decided to study the trees.

He saw bananas and oranges nearby and plucked two of each and sat down on a pile of rubble to consume them. When he peeled a banana, he was surprised to see that the fruit inside resembled that of a grapefruit or lime. It was citriusy in aroma and contained several dark, round seeds.

When he bit into it, he smiled.

It tasted like a fine, sweet wine and was quite juicy.

"Not bad. Not bad at all," he said as he finished it.

The oranges were even stranger.

Instead of the expected citrus sections, the inside consisted of a bright, white meat wrapped around a seedy core. And it tasted more like an apple or a pear.

"This is all wrong," he thought. "There's no fruit like this anywhere on Earth that I'm aware of. Where did this come from?"

He tossed the core over his shoulder and walked down toward the docks. When he arrived, he stared in disbelief. The once-colorful rows of shops, inns and warehouses and elegant homes now stood abandoned and dilapidated. The smoothly paved streets were cracked and choked with weeds and briars and parts of the magnificent piers had tumbled into the sea. The planks of the boardwalk were warped and split in places and long holes scarred the pier. The boards were rotted and weatherbeaten beyond repair. It was obvious that no one had attended to them for centuries.

He walked down to Pier 33 where his personal yacht was usually moored. Something resembling it was still tethered to the pier but the back end was now beneath the brackish water and its bow pointed skyward at a 45 degree angle. He studied the hull. It was—and wasn't the same yacht.

His yacht was gleaming white with blue, gold, red and green trim. It was a cheerful vessel that tourists could freely explore. This one was stark and foreboding.

The river, which was always clean and bright, was now brackish and cluttered with debris and dead fish.

He shook his head sadly.

"Everything's changed," he said. "The entire city is in ruins. But how did this happen?"

He walked over to the Great Bridge that connected both halves of the city. Along the way, a lone jackal crossed his path. The animal froze in its tracks when he saw him and bared its fangs menacingly. Arka-Dal picked up a nearby brick and hurled it. The missile struck the animal in the face. It yelped in pain and ran off down a side street.

He laughed.

Then a thought occurred to him.

Perhaps he was the first human being that jackal had ever seen? Maybe he was now the last human on the planet.

He pushed the thoughts from his mind and kept walking. The scenery remained the same all the way to the bridge, which was still intact. This didn't surprise him. The bridge had been designed and built by the Romans during the First Age. It was constructed from a specialized concrete which continued to harden over the centuries. His own engineers had attempted without success to duplicate that concrete. Although they did produce a concrete that was hard and durable, it never came close to the fabled cementum.

Despite their engineering genius, Rome had vanished. Only their ruins remained for people to marvel at. He wondered if the same fate had befallen his beloved Thule. Was it like this everywhere?

As he approached the bridge, he spotted a lone figure seated on the bank. He wore a wide-brimmed hat that shielded him from the sun. In his hands, he clutched a bamboo fishing pole that extended out into the water.

Arka-Dal called out to him.

No answer.

He walked over and tapped the man's shoulder and started as he crumbled to dust and fell into the river. He realized he'd been dead for years. As dead as the city that surrounded him.

He sighed and walked across the bridge to the eastern half of the city. He found it to be in the same state of disrepair as the western side. He moved on to the large plaza that also served as the commercial center of the city. Instead of the expected stalls, food carts, shops, he found himself standing in a deserted, rubble-strewn, weed-choked square. In place of the ornate bronze fountain that had been the masterwork of a Thulian artist and a gathering place for people looking to escape the mid-afternoon heat, the center was now dominated by a 20 foot tall granite statue of a man with his right arm stretched out in salute.

Vines and weeds had reclaimed most of it but he could still make out the stern—almost cruel—expression on its weatherworn face.

"Whoever you were, you must have been a real nasty bastard," Arka-Dal said as he looked up at him. "A real brute. This statue stands in testament of your ego. It tells me that you were a monster."

He could also tell from the features that the statue depicted a man who was accustomed to being obeyed without question. There wasn't even the slightest spark of benevolence in his expression.

He was garbed in a long-sleeved shirt and high collar, riding pants that flared at the thighs, high boots and a garrison belt. It was definitely a military uniform of some sort.

"A foreign conqueror?" he wondered.

But what was this statue doing in the market square?

He noticed a bronze plaque on the front of the pedestal. Although it was badly eroded, he could still make out a few of the letters. It was enough to tell him that the alphabet was *not* Thulian.

"Did Thule fall to outside invaders? Did it become *that* weak?" he asked.

And just who *were* they?

He'd never seen such a uniform. Did this occur in the distant future? But how distant?

If the empire was destroyed by the invaders, then the invaders also suffered a similar fate. Were they driven off by other invaders? Or did something else destroy the city—something much more terrifying?

He pondered several possibilities as he continued to explore the ruins. Several things could and did destroy empires through the ages. Things such as constant warfare. Invasions. Total economic collapses. Plagues and famines.

He headed back to the palace. When he reached the garden, the sun was already setting. He stopped to pick more of the strange fruit and walked inside. He went upstairs to the bedroom and sat down at the rusted table on the balcony to eat and think some more. He looked out over the bleak ruins and watched as the dull red sun faded in the west as the twilight pushed aside the light of day.

When night fell, he realized it seemed unusually bright for some reason. Much to bright even if the moon was full. He looked up at the sky and gaped in wonder. There, shining large and bright, was not one but *three* distinct moons.

"This isn't Thule. Hell, this isn't even Earth," he said with a sense of relief. "If this is an alternate Earth that means Thule is safe. But where am I and just how did I get here?"

"I brought you here, of course," said a familiar voice from behind him.

He turned and smirked as Merlin, Ned the Knower and the Devil stepped out onto the balcony.

"I should have known this was your doing, Merlin. But why did you bring me here?" Arka-Dal asked.

"I have my reasons," Merlin replied. "Good reasons, too."

"Care to enlighten me?" Arka-Dal asked.

"As you have already surmised, this is an alternate Earth in a parallel universe. This city is all that remains of a vast empire that once controlled this entire world. It was a very cruel, heartless empire that enslaved and brutalized its people," Merlin said. "The family that founded it reigned for more than 2,000 years without interruption. By anyone's standards, that was a remarkable feat in itself."

"It is very dead now—as you can see," Ned added. "In fact, no human life exists anywhere at all on this planet. The entire population was erased in the space of a single night many millennia ago. When I realized the cause of this, I informed Merlin and the Devil. They, in turn, decided to bring you here so you could see for yourself."

"This must be some kind of nightmare," Arka-Dal remarked.

"This is not a dream," the Devil assured him.

"What is it then?" Arka-Dal asked.

"The future," Ned replied.

"Whose future?" Arka-Dal queried.

"Earth's—if we don't prevent it," Merlin responded.

"Prevent what?" Arka-Dal asked.

"We must prevent the Beast and its Minions from entering our universe," Merlin replied.

"I'm listening," Arka-Dal said.

"I have been traveling between dimensions and parallel universes for millennia. In my travels, I have come upon more than 20 such worlds. All are cold and dead—just like this one. Each world is a mirror image of your own world. Each had vast human populations that were wiped out in less than a single day. All are in a direct line to Earth. This is the last such world. Earth will be its next logical target," Ned explained.

"Just how many parallel universes are there?" Arka-Dal asked.

"Far too many to be counted," Ned replied. "They all occupy the same space but in slightly different times."

"Like Chatha's world," Arka-Dal said.

"Exactly," Merlin nodded.

"All are interconnected by gates or vortexes. All may be reached through any number of lower, darker planes, such as the Abyss or Hell," the Devil added.

"And you think Earth is next?" Arka-Dal asked.

"After a slight detour taken by its Minions," the Devil said. "The Beast dwells in the very lowest reaches of the astral planes. You are already familiar with Hell and the region known as the Abyss. Beyond the Abyss, lies a dim, virtually unknown area populated by creatures we simply refer to as the Others. You ran into an advance force of them on

Chatha's home world. There are other, even darker realms beyond theirs. The Beast and its Minions dwell there."

"What, exactly is this Beast?" asked Arka-Dal.

The Devil shrugged.

"No one knows for certain. No one knows where it came from or what spawned it. It's ancient. Maybe far more ancient than Ned here," he said.

"It may be a bit older anyway," Ned said. "I can tell you that it is a life form and it is immortal. Other than that, I know very little about it."

"What are the Minions?" asked Arka-Dal.

"I don't exactly know. As the Beast awakens, it produces countless numbers of the creatures. They come in all shapes, sizes and temperaments. They are nasty, hateful and quite dangerous and they seem to be nearly mindless," Ned explained. "I guess you could say they are the Beast's shock troops."

"What else do you know about the Beast?" asked Arka-Dal.

The Devil shook his head.

"We do know that it mostly sleeps. It wakes every 10,000 years or so to feed. As it does, it produces hordes of Minions which out in all directions in search of another world they can enter. Once they do, they produce a reign of nightmarish terror you can't begin to imagine. Once the world is drowning in chaos, they awaken the Beast so that it may feed," he explained. "It devours every living thing within a fortnight and leaves the world barren and lifeless. Sometimes, through chance, some forms of animal life survive—like birds, fish and that jackal you encountered. But this is rare."

"You can see the results around us," Merlin added. "This will be Thule's fate if the Beast wakes."

"And it is about to be awakened. Even now, its Minions are knocking at the doors of the lower planes. They drive the Others before them. They, in turn, are trying to escape by forcing their way into the Abyss," the Devil said.

"If they overrun the Abyss, the Minions will be hot on their heels. Hell will be next and this war will continue until the Beast is destroyed or Hell falls. If Hell should fall, nothing will stand between the Beast and Earth and no army that man can field will be able to defeat its ravenous hordes. Thule—and every nation around it—will end up like this," Merlin warned.

"So this is why Mephistos and his people tried to enter our world," Arka-Dal mused. "They were trying to escape from the Others. When you shut the gate, you forced them to stand and fight against the very beings they were trying to escape from. In effect, you condemned them to eternal warfare against a foe they can't defeat nor dare lose to."

Merlin nodded.

"At the time, I did not know what drove them. Had I known, I might have been a bit more sympathetic," he said. "They have become our first line of defense against total obliteration more by chance than choice."

"Although the Others are more powerful than the creatures of the Abyss, they are not numerous enough to turn back the invaders. In fact, I fear they've been steadily losing ground to the Minions. It may only be a matter of months before their domain is overrun. That's why they seek a safer placer to retreat to. That's why they've invaded the Abyss," the Devil said.

"The Abyss shares borders with the lower planes of Hell. If Mephistos and his people start losing, they'll seek a safer place to retreat to as well," Ned explained.

"That means they'll invade the lower planes of Hell and this insane war will spread. What's more, the Others will be right behind them and the Minions behind them. If Hell should fall, Earth will suffer the same fate as this world," the Devil said.

"That's why we must make certain that the Beast never wakes," Ned warned.

Arka-Dal allowed this to sink in then looked up at them.

"How much time do we have?" he asked.

"That is unknown. It could be centuries. It could be minutes. On the lower planes, time has no meaning. It really depends on how long Mephistos and his people can hold the line," Merlin answered.

"How can we prevent this?" Arka-Dal asked.

"We must slay the Beast before it can be fully awakened," Merlin replied.

"That means we'll have to enter its realm, find its lair, fight our way past all of its Minions, as well as two other warring races, and kill it," Arka-Dal reasoned. "That's a suicide mission. It's pure madness!"

"Yet, it is our only hope," the Devil said.

"And the sooner we act, the better our chances of success," Merlin added.

"Or the better our chances of getting killed," Arka-Dal said with a smile. "This will take some careful planning."

"Indeed," Merlin said.

Arka-Dal stood and looked them in the eyes.

"We'll need help—and lots of it. Since Mephistos and the Others are already battling the Minions and they have the most to lose right now, maybe we can convince them to join forces with us?" he suggested.

"After the fate we condemned Mephistos and he people to, that would be a most difficult sell indeed," Merlin pointed out. "He has about as much love for us as he does for the creatures he's now warring with. I imagine that he's still more than a little miffed with me."

"If we approach him at the right moment, I'm sure we can convince him that an alliance is in everyone's best interest. Mephistos is no fool. He can be reasoned with, especially if he sees some benefits in it," the Devil said.

"How ironic. In order to save our world, we must forge an alliance with the creatures of the Abyss," Arka-Dal said. "And perhaps those who dwell beyond it."

"That's correct," Ned agreed.

Arka-Dal looked at Merlin.

"You used the Necronomicon to seal the portal between our world and the Abyss forever. How do we reopen it to go to their aid?" he asked.

"We can't," Merlin said.

"But *I* can take us there," the Devil offered. "Sealed portals mean nothing to me. In fact, I can take us straight to Mephistos' lair."

Arka-Dal laughed at the thought of them just popping up in the middle of the room next to the lord of the Abyss.

"Once we get there, we'll have to convince Mephistos that we have come to help. It won't be easy after our last encounter. He is the type to bear a grudge over such things," Merlin said.

"I'd hold a grudge, too, if you had done that to *me*," Arka-Dal said. "I wouldn't blame him if he refused to join us."

"Neither would I," the Devil agreed. "Still, I'm sure we can convince him that such an alliance, no matter how improbable, is in everyone's best interest. Even he knows the Beast must be stopped."

Arka-Dal nodded.

"I've seen enough of this cold, dead place. Take us home," he said.

The Devil raised his hand and snapped his fingers.

A moment later, Arka-Dal found himself standing in the parlor of the palace surrounded by the happy sounds of his children at play.

He looked around and saw Galya standing not ten feet to his left.

"It wasn't a dream, was it?" he asked.

"No. It was not," she assured him.

Mephistos, Lord of the Abyss, nervously paced his chamber. The battles at the edges of his realm had been raging without end for the last 1,000 years. The Others were tough and determined foes. They were bent on swarming into the Abyss. Mephistos' demons were just as determined to bar their way.

Beyond the realm of the Others and pressing them from behind were the twisted, nightmarish Minions of the Beast. The Others were also fighting to keep them out of their realm but were steadily losing the awful war of attrition.

For every Minion the Others slew, at least ten more were spawned to take its place. The Beast, it seemed, could produce limitless numbers of those creatures and constantly replenish their losses.

But the beleaguered Others and his own soldiers could not. Both strained mightily to keep from being overrun. The Others strove to keep the Minions at bay while his troops strove to keep the Others in check.

It had become an ugly, bloody stalemate.

At least for now.

And he was cut off from the world of men. Cut off from any hope of recruiting enough black hearted souls to replenish his dwindling army. Without such reinforcements, he had little hope of winning this awful war.

His people had been driven from their homes along the border by the sudden, unexpected assault from the Others. After centuries of brutal and horrific warfare, they had regained some of their lost territory. Ever since, each battle became a nasty holding effort to stem the rising tide of the invaders.

Mephistos didn't fear the Others.

But he *did* fear what drove them.

His scouts had reported that the Others were engaged in an even nastier war against the invading hordes of the Beast and it seemed like they had no way out. Sooner or later, Mephistos feared that the Others would be forced to abandon their defensive lines. When they happened, they'd come streaming toward the Abyss en masse and the Minions would be snapping at their heels like rabid dogs.

There was no way his soldiers could defeat both armies. The Abyss would certainly be overrun and his people would be slaughtered before they could reach the lowers planes of Hell. Even if they could reach Hell, would his cousin allow them to enter? Would even Lucifer be able to summon enough soldiers to hold back the invaders?

His people had nowhere to go. They were forced to stay and fight it out to the last.

This was all Merlin's fault, too.

And Ned's.

Because it was they who sealed the portal between the Abyss and the world of men. It was they who cut them off from their pool of souls so they could not replenish their armies.

When they did this, Mephistos and his people were condemned to fight this endless war. They were trapped forever. After countless millennia, Mephistos and his people faced possible extinction.

Mephistos snarled.

He realized it was a fate they probably *deserved*. Had he sent an emissary to the world of Men to try and explain their dire situation, things might have ended differently. Instead, he *invaded* their world, thinking his troops could easily defeat any army they encountered. He didn't know about the Demon Slayer then or his alliances with other nations and his friendship with the Knower and Merlin. Even when he found out, he shrugged it off.

It was a mistake he has regretted ever since.

A mistake that may have sealed the doom of his own people.

His thoughts were interrupted by the arrival of three, tattered-looking demonic officers. Mephistos raised an eyebrow at them as they saluted him.

"The enemy is about to break through our defenses in the Vale of Ashes. Our line is weakening there," one of the demons said.

"The line *must* be held at all costs. If it breaks, all will be lost," Mephistos said calmly.

"Shall I strengthen it with troops from the Dragon's Mouth?" the demon asked.

Mephitos shook his head.

"No. The enemy may be expecting such a move and redirect their efforts to exploit our weakness there. Send in the reserves instead," he decided.

"If we do that, we will not have enough soldiers to fight future battles," the second demon pointed out.

"If the line breaks, there will be no future battles. Send in the reserves. The line must be held. There can be no retreat. No falling back. You must fight to the last soldier. Do you understand?" Mephistos said.

All three of them nodded, then they saluted and left the chamber.

"A thousand years of this and still there's no end in sight!" Mephistos said as he looked into the mirrors. "I am doubly cursed!"

At the training center near Northern Army Headquarters, Michael set to work learning the entire military and command structure of the Empire as well as Thulian fighting techniques, battlefield tactics, logistics, engineering and military intelligence gathering. He learned rank and insignia identification, military customs, law and how a Thulian soldier was supposed to conduct himself at all times.

He learned that Thule had six standing armies of 200,000 men each and that each was assigned to a particular region. Thulian soldiers were well-paid, well-trained professionals who instantly obeyed orders. Like most soldiers, they liked to gamble, drink, womanize and travel. They sometimes got into brawls. They trained hard five days a week. They patrolled frontiers and borders. They guarded bridges and roads and manned small outposts.

And they believed in what they did.

Each army was commanded by a battle-tested, trusted field marshal. Each army consisted of scouts, light and heavy infantry, shock troops, light and heavy cavalry, archers, peltists, engineers, artillery, medical brigades, quartermasters, and other support troops. Each army was designed to operate on its own with minimal or no support from other armies and each commander was expected to make snap decisions that could affect the outcomes of battles. They were also trained to help in civil emergencies, such as flash floods and quakes.

There were no class structures or military academies. Thulian officers began as lowly recruits and could work their way up through the ranks through skill and courage. Good soldiers were rewarded and promoted. The few bad ones were either punished, busted or discharged.

Jun explained that Arka-Dal based the military structure on one that was created by Napoleon Bonaparte during the First Age. Of course he also blended in elements of Alexander's army and the armies of Imperial Rome. As time went on, he added ideas from the Atlanteans, Turks and even the Mongoblins.

"An army stays prepared by changing with the times. New tactics and deployment methods should be added every so often. It keeps the troops fresh and interested. Bored troops are unhappy troops," Jun explained.

He also learned about the Thulian Navy.

Thule had 1,000 ships of all sizes and functions. There were rammers, biremes, triremes, fireboats, galleons and even steamships. There were fast-moving shallow draft ships for patrolling Thule's rivers, lakes and inlets. There were supply and transport ships and even merchant ships.

These were divided into ten fleets which were strategically placed to protect harbors, coastal cities, shorelines and to hunt down pirates. Each fleet was commanded by a full admiral and two commodores.

Thule also had many independent merchant fleets, the most famous being the one owned by Sindbad. These fleets could be commandeered by Arka-Dal during emergencies and to perform special assignments. Sindbad was called upon the most and was Arka-Dal's most trusted and resourceful sailor and explorer. His ship, the sleek and swift Saracen Moon, was the most famous ship on Earth. Sindbad had designed it personally.

There was also a very large pool of reserves that could be activated to serve during wartime or other emergencies. These reservists numbered more than two million men and more than doubled the size of Thule's army.

Thule also had a women's auxiliary who acted as doctors and nurses in field hospitals and military hospitals. The women could also fight if they had to and underwent the same training as regular soldiers. At present, they were 40,000 strong and rising. It had become a very attractive career choice since Mayumi had formed it five years earlier. Arka-Dal immediately nominated her to command it. Leo quickly seconded it and Mayumi had no choice but to accept her new title.

Michael learned that he'd be serving in the Central Army as a cavalry officer. The Central Army was under Arka-Dal's direct command and had elements the other armies didn't. The bulk of it was like any other of Thule's armies and made up of soldiers from every part of the Empire. But it also included 24,000 crack Atlantean troops under Chatha's command and 12,000 Janissaries who had enlisted after the Byzantine incident. There was also Arka-Dal's best-trained, highly-skilled Special Technical Forces. These men were armed with rifles, pistols, explosives and other high-tech weapons and could fight and survive on any terrain and under any weather conditions. They were only used for special rescue and exploration operations, during which they usually accompanied Arka-Dal himself. There were only four squads of these men—48 in all. They were the best of the best in Thule.

To Jun's amazement, it took Michael less than two weeks to absorb all of this. Along the way, he even showed Jun a few tricks he'd devised while commanding troops during the Forever War. Jun was so impressed, he wrote a letter to Arka-Dal recommending that Michael teach these tactics to the rest of the training officers and that they be adapted for use by the entire army.

"You're training's over, Captain. Return to Thule and report to the Emperor. While you're at it, bring him this letter," Jun said.

Michael bade Jun farewell and left the training center that evening. He caught a passenger ship downriver and spent most of the journey on deck watching the scenery pass by. He arrived at the palace four days later. He was dressed in the uniform of a Thulian captain. As he approached the front of building, he happened to see Arka-Dal on the front lawn playing catch with three of his children. He walked over and saluted. Arka-Dal smiled.

"Back so soon?" he asked.

"Yes Sir. I have completed the training. Jun sent you this letter," Michael said as he handed the envelope to him.

Arka-Dal read it and smiled broader. Then he laughed.

"Jun wrote that you were the fastest study he ever trained. In fact, he said it was almost the other way around. I'm not surprised, given your background and experience. I just wanted you to become familiar with the way things are done here," he said as they walked up the steps and entered the palace.

They went into the parlor. Arka-Dal poured two tankards of ale and handed one to Michael.

"I've promoted you to the rank of colonel and placed you in command of the 9th Cavalry Regiment of the Central Army. I've already drawn up the necessary papers. But before you report to your new command, I want you to return to the training center and follow up on what you did with Jun. He's recommended that your tactics be taught to the other training officers and would like to see them added to our bag of tricks. If Jun thinks they're *that* good, then I'm all for it," Arka-Dal said.

"Than you, Sir. I appreciate your confidence in me. I will not let you down," Michael said as they shook hands.

"I know you won't," Arka-Dal said. "For now, I'm giving you one week's leave. You can stay here at the palace if you like. Relax and get to know the city. I'm sure you'll like it."

"What will my duties as a cavalry commander be?" Michael asked.

"The 9ᵗʰ is assigned to patrolling the major highways and back roads between here and Osumel. Mostly, you'll be assuring the safety of travelers against natural disasters and would-be bandits. In between, you'll train the men to ensure they stay in tip-top fighting condition, conduct inspections and make monthly reports to either Pandaar or Kashi. In time of trouble, you'll be directly under my command," Arka-Dal said as he poured them another drink.

"From what I've seen, Thule has the best trained, most professional army on Earth," Michael said. "It's reminiscent of Imperial Rome."

"And I want to keep them that way. That's why we need officers like you and Jun. You bring invaluable battlefield experience to the table and you're able to share that with your men. Oh, by the way, Thulian officers—even myself—eat and live like the rest of our soldiers when in the field. We lead from the *front* and never ask our soldiers to do anything we won't do. Understand?" Arka-Dal advised.

Michael nodded.

"Although saluting is a custom, I generally frown on it. I'll return a salute if it's offered but I never insist on it. And my men *rarely* call me 'sir', 'your highness', 'sire' or anything other than my name. Polite titles are used here only during very official functions where foreign dignitaries are present," he added.

"I'll try to remember that. After using them for thousands of years, it is difficult to forego them," Michael said.

"I understand," Arka-Dal nodded.

After dinner, Michael roamed the upper floors of the palace. He stopped before a long, many paneled window and looked up at the night sky. It was illuminated by a full moon and thousands of twinkling stars. As he peered up at the heavens, he thought about his situation.

When he enlisted in the Army of Thule, he swore an oath to defend and protect the Empire and all of its citizens against all enemies. By an incredibly ironic twist of fate, that also included the Devil's daughter, Galya.

And protect her he would, with all of his strength, courage and honor. His oath was his bond and he would never break it. He realized that times and circumstances had changed. His old life was gone forever. His old beliefs had been based upon lies. He had new friends now.

New allies.

Galya saw him gazing through the window. She walked over and tugged on his sleeve. Michael turned and bowed respectfully.

"Thinking of your new situation?" she asked.

"Yes. I must admit that my life has taken a most unexpected turn," he said.

"Does it bother you?" she asked.

"It did until I spoke with Arka-Dal about your father. He's not as bad as I was led to believe. In fact, I now see he is a man of honor. Someone I could actually admire and respect," he said.

Galya laughed.

The sound was almost like music to him.

And her eyes were deep, beautiful and magnetic.

"I never realized how incredibly beautiful you are. No wonder Arka-Dal fell in love with you," he said.

Galya smiled and thanked him.

"I think being married to Arka-Dal has brought out the beauty that was hidden deep inside me most of my life. Being truly loved and truly in love has transformed me in ways I never thought possible or expected," she said modestly. "Mayumi always said that true beauty lies within a person. I guess Arka-Dal saw something in me that no else ever did."

"I still find it remarkable that your father approved of your union," Michael said.

"Father and Arka-Dal have become quite close. Even Merlin likes Father now, despite all their past dealings. Father has sworn to protect Thule and its people for as long as a member of the Dal line exists. Merlin has sworn the same. This made them allies. And, given their past encounters, they both appreciate the irony in this. How do you feel about me now?" she asked.

"You're quite lovely without the wings and other accoutrements. You seem softer now. More relaxed and happy," he replied.

"That's because I am. My life is filled with joy now that I've found true love. Have you ever been in love, Michael? Do you know what it's like?" she asked.

He shook his head.

"I know nothing of love. God forbade his soldiers to have interactions with females or humans unless it was to punish or torment them. He didn't want us to become tainted by emotions," he said.

"And he always accused Father of being heartless," Galya recalled.

"I see now that it was all lies. I wasted my entire life fighting for the wrong side and championing the wrong causes. We *all* fell for his propaganda. In the end, it was for nought," he said sadly.

"Your god bullied and coerced people into obeying him. Father believed in allowing people to make their own choices. He's always believed in free will. Your god demanded unquestioned loyalty. He wanted a host of mindless zealots. That's why when the Christians and Jews began to question his supreme authority, he made a prophet of a madman called Mohammad and loosed Islam on the world. It was in that twisted version of Christianity he found his most fanatical followers.

Thank goodness both religions are almost gone from the world. What remains are but pale shadows. The power of the one god is broken forever," Galya said.

"Is not Hamid Kashi a follower of Islam?" Michael asked.

"Sort of. The Ayatollahs who raised him beat that religion into him. He prays—if one can call it that—to Allah out of convenience. He said he can never remember which god to call upon for what favor, so Allah is sort of a catch-all for him. Kashi is like Arka-Dal and Pandaar. They believe in no gods but they never mock those who do," Galya explained.

"I no longer believe. The god I followed proved to be a false one. He was only interested in extending his power. If I met him now, I'd spit on him," Michael said almost bitterly.

"An Archangel is nothing more than a demon who served the other side. We are all cut from the same cloth. At one time, we were all in Heaven. Now, Heaven exists no longer. The Afterlife is but an extension of life here on Earth without all the suffering and misery that goes with it. But I preach to the choir. You *know* this," she said.

He nodded.

"And Hell is for those who willingly go there," he said.

"True. For some, it's a just reward. For others, it's a fitting punishment. But it's not as bad as people think," Galya said.

He laughed.

"It can't be if the women all look like *you*," he said.

"Well, the Succubi are quite alluring. Perhaps I can introduce you to one of them?" she suggested.

"Perhaps," he hedged. "Let me get back to you on that."

"Maybe I'll just surprise you," she teased as she walked away.

Michael watched until she was out of view then smiled.

"I like her," he said to himself. "She's quite pleasant and exceptionally beautiful. To think I tried to slay her many times. What a pity *that* would have been!"

Then he laughed at himself.

"My life has been turned inside-out!"

The next morning, he went downstairs for breakfast. Arka-Dal was already seated at the table. He greeted Michael and bade him to sit across from him so they could talk. After a few seconds of uneasy silence, Michael took a deep breath and let it out slowly. Arka-Dal looked up at him.

"Something on your mind?" he asked.

"Sir, may I ask you a question?" Michael queried.

Arka-Dal nodded.

"When you first met Galya, did you know who she was?" Michael asked.

"Yes, I did," Arka-Dal said.

"Weren't you frightened?"

"No. I was intrigued by her and I felt attracted to her," Arka-Dal replied.

"When did you realize that you loved her?" asked Michael.

"A few days later when she allowed her real self to emerge. I loved what I saw in her then and I love her even more now. Do you find that strange?" Arka-Dal asked.

"I don't find it strange that you fell for her but I do find it amazing that she loves you so passionately and completely. It must have thrown her father for a loop," Michael said.

"It did. When he realized our feelings were genuine, he was most gracious about it. He seems to be very happy that it happened now," Arka-Dal said. "Have you seen or spoken with him since your last encounter?"

"No. I would like to though. There is much I need to ask him," Michael said.

"This is your chance. He's in the parlor now. Go on in," Arka-Dal suggested. "I think you'll like him."

Michael excused himself, got up and headed to the parlor. He was surprised to see his old enemy kneeling on the floor playing rough and tumble with Hawk and Melody. He stopped and looked up when Michael entered.

"Look Grandpa! We have an angel here today," Hawk squealed as he pointed to Michael.

"So we do. Michael, isn't it?" the Devil asked as he rose and offered his hand.

"Yes, it is," Michael replied as he hesitantly shook it.

"The last time I saw you, you were brought before me in chains," the Devil said as they both went to the couch and sat down.

"I remember that day vividly. I thought I was about to breathe my last but instead, you released me from those chains and returned my weapons to me. Then you told me to go in peace. I've thought about that day for many years. And for years, I thought that if we ever met again, there is one question I needed to ask you," Michael said.

"And what question is that?" asked the Devil.

"Why'd you do it? Why'd you free me?" Michael asked.

"You really don't know?" the Devil asked.

"No," Michael said.

"Then I shall keep you in the dark no longer," the Devil said. "I spared your life because I learned that you alone opposed and refused to take part in the truce-breaking attack that slew my beloved wife and nearly took Galya from me. I also learned that your master imprisoned you for opposing him and set you free only when the tide of war turned against him.

When I discovered you were commanding a wing of his army during that final battle, I ordered my soldiers to take you alive and bring you to me with as little damage as possible. Although you fought well, with honor and courage against my soldiers on many occasions, my war was not with you. In fact, I actually *admired* you. Galya herself told me that you were one of the most fearless and valiant fighters she'd ever seen, even when hopelessly trapped.

Besides, the war was over by then. Your master was dead and his power was broken forever. I saw no need for further bloodshed—especially not yours. So I set you free and bade you go in peace. I also threatened to kill any of my minions who might have decided to harass you on your trip through Hell," the Devil explained.

"I don't know if I should thank you or curse you for sparing me," Michael remarked.

The Devil grinned.

"There's no need for either. The past is past. There is only the future before us. It is time to move on with your life. You've made the right decision in coming here. Arka-Dal is a good and wise ruler and Thule is that 'shining city on the hill' come to fruition. It's no accident that Merlin bestowed Excalibur upon him," he said.

"Have you forsaken your evil ways?" Michael asked.

"Yes—and no. There are more than enough fools out there who desire my services and I am always ready to give them what they want. But I do none of my business in Thule. In fact, I have sworn an oath to protect this Empire for as long as a member of Arka-Dal's line still walks the Earth. And I *always* keep my promises," the Devil said.

"In effect, you and I are *allies*?" Michael asked.

The Devil nodded.

"You're a good soldier, Michael. Serving Thule will make you a better one—and a better person. You may be fortunate enough to become a member of Arka-Dal's trusted inner circle and close friends—if you prove yourself worthy," he said.

"I am proud to serve him in any capacity," Michael said.

"This is the Second Age. Things are different now, yet much remains the same. Humans still possess the same values and lust after the same things they always have. But Thulians, overall, seem to be above that. It's as if they purposely push themselves to follow Arka-Dal's example. They want to make Thule an even better place to live because that's what *he* wants. These people actually adore him. I have never seen anything like it," the Devil said.

Then he laughed.

"He *must* be something special. I sent Galya to seduce and corrupt him. Instead, she fell in love with and married him. Even *I* didn't foresee *that*!" he said.

Then he lowered his voice and smiled.

"There is something about Thule. Something quite extraordinary. You'll discover this for yourself after you've been here awhile," he assured Michael.

They spent the next hour talking like old friends. The more they spoke, the more Michael grew to like the Devil. He decided that if Arka-Dal liked him and considered him a friend, then he would, too.

Afterwards, when the Devil returned to the Lower Planes to conduct some business, Michael decided to take a stroll in the rose garden. To his delight, he encountered Galya who was out picking flowers to put in some of the vases in the palace. She smiled when she saw him.

"I see you and Father had a nice long talk," she said.

"We did indeed. He's quite interesting. I hope to speak with him again soon," Michael replied as they walked together.

"I'm sure you will. He visits here quite often. He said it's the only place he feels truly welcome and there are no strings attached," Galya said.

"There is something I'd like to say to you. I think it's been long overdue," he said.

"I'm listening," Galya assured him.

"Long ago, I attempted to prevent the attack that took your mother from you, but others of my kind imprisoned me before I could act. Now I have sworn an oath to protect and serve the people and the Empire of Thule. That oath includes you, My Lady," Michael said.

"That makes you and Father *allies*. Don't you find this to be even a little bit *ironic?*" Galya asked.

"My life is filled with such ironies. I see this as a way to redeem myself for failing to stop that attack on your family. Today, I have realized your father is a man of honor and worthy of my respect," Michael said. "That adds further to this ironic situation. When I came here to offer my sword to Arka-Dal, I had no inkling that you were his wife or that your father was now his friend and ally."

"You seem somewhat humbled now," Galya observed.

"I *am* humbled. But I am also proud to have finally gotten to know both you and your father," Michael replied with a smile.

Galya giggled.

"Your old master would be horrified to hear you talk like this," she said.

"I was deceived into fighting for the wrong side once. I will not be so deceived again. Arka-Dal is my commanding officer now. I will serve him and the Empire forevermore," Michael vowed.

"Arka-Dal is a very special man. There has never been anyone like him before," Galya said.

"He must indeed be special to have won *your* heart. I did not think that you were capable of loving anyone," Michael said.

"Neither did I until I met *him*," Galya admitted. "He told me about your promotion. You must feel quite pleased."

"I am. This is more than I expected. This country is more than I expected. So is everyone I've met," Michael said. "What's it like to be human?"

"I *like* it. I like the feelings of love and warmth that come with it. The joy, sadness and other emotions, too. I've never experienced them before I came here. I never knew love or understood why women go through so much pain to bear children. Now I understand these things and I appreciate them more than words can convey," she replied.

"Perhaps I, too, will find out what love is like one day," Michael said wistfully.

Galya smiled.

"I can *arrange* that, if you like," she offered.

He squinted at her.

His expression made her laugh.

"I know several women who would be good matches for you. But you may have to overlook a few, er, *unusual traits*," she continued.

"Like Arka-Dal did *yours* and Medusa's?" Michael asked.

Galya nodded.

"Think *you* can?" she asked.

He shrugged.

"That remains to be seen, My Lady," he replied.

"Don't be so formal. Call me Galya," she said. "Everyone here does. Titles are not used here in Thule."

"I'll try," Michael said. "But you are the Emperor's wife. As such, I must refer to you as *my Queen*."

"Mayumi is the Empress of Thule. I am just the wife of Arka-Dal—the same as the other women here. And if you called her my Queen, she would be astonished and ask you not to do that," Galya explained.

"I don't understand," Michael said.

"You'll learn. You've used titles for thousands of years and old habits are hard to break. The only time any formalities are used in Thule is on the battlefield. There, Arka-Dal and his commanders are called 'sir' by their soldiers. Sometimes, they are saluted but that isn't a custom here," Galya explained.

"What of you? Are you also one of his commanders?" Michael asked.

"Although I still command legions in Hell, here I merely serve as an advisor. The only one of his wives who holds a military rank is Chatha. She has retained command of her Atlantean Legion, which is part of the Central Army," Galya said.

"I see that still have much to learn," Michael mused.

"And so do *I*," Galya said. "And the more I learn, the more I love it here and the more I love Arka-Dal and the rest of our family."

"Any man who can win your heart and keep it must be quite remarkable," Michael said.

She smiled.

Arka-Dal emerged from a gap between two hedges just in time to hear part of their conversation. Michael bowed his head respectfully. Arka-Dal returned it and put his arm around Galya.

"He is. Father thinks so, too. In fact, they've become quite fond of each other," she said.

"Talking about me?" Arka-Dal asked.

"As always. When are you planning to hold council?" Galya asked.

Arka-Dal shrugged.

"When Ned arrives. He had some business to tend to elsewhere. I expect him any day now. Then we'll sit down and go over the details of everything. When Merlin sealed those things in the Abyss forever, I never once imagined that we'd return to help them. I guess this is one of life's many ironies," he mused.

Galya smiled and touched his cheek.

"The universe is filled with such ironies. Michael is still trying to figure out how he came to be my protector. Father sent me to seduce you and see what happened with *that*!" she said.

"Ours was a *mutual* seduction," Arka-Dal said.

"I became yours and you became mine, but that was for love and nothing else. I never did capture your soul," she said.

"Oh yes you did. You also captured my heart," Arka-Dal assured her as they kissed.

Michael smiled.

He could actually feel the love emanating from them.

"Does this council concern the menace you hinted at before I left?" he asked.

"Yes," Arka-Dal said. "Since you've already volunteered to be part of this mission, I want you at that meeting, too."

"You can count on that, sir," Michael replied.

Back in Hell, all 666 lords, one from each plane, gathered in the Grand Chamber and listened as the Devil told them of the perils that faced them and what they must do to overcome it. All but one of the lords nodded in agreement. That was Fraakxus, the lord of the 56th Plane and one of the largest and most powerful of all the Demons.

He stood and growled in anger.

"You want *us* to fight alongside those mangy curs of the Abyss? They are *inferior*! I will not stand with them!" he shouted.

The Devil squinted at him. The rest of the Demon Lords realized he had crossed the line and stepped back.

"You *will* fight alongside them. In fact, you may be under Mephistos' command until this crisis is ended. And that is my order," the devil said calmly.

"I refuse!" Fraakxux insisted.

The Devil stood and walked toward him. The rest of the mass of malformed, winged, multi-limbed, cloven hoofed, fanged, furry and scaled collection of Demons and their more sophisticated Devil counterparts silently waited for their Lord and Master to handle the upstart.

"I am the lord of the 56th Plane! I will not have my people allied with the mongrels of the Abyss—and that is my *final word*!" Fraakxus snarled as he stood his ground.

"I am the supreme Lord of all the Lower Planes. I *rule* here and *you* will obey me or suffer the consequences. You *know* what I can do to you," the Devil said.

"I refuse!" the Demon Lord growled.

"Very well then. Have it *your* way," the Devil said as he snapped his fingers.

The others watched with amusement as Fraakxus slowly changed into a pillar of salt. When the transformation was complete, they cheered.

The Devil pointed to another Demon.

"You are now the lord of the 56th Plane. Gather your regiments and prepare to enter the Abyss on my command," he ordered.

The Demon bowed respectfully and vanished to do as he was bidden. The Devil turned his attention back to the rest of the lords.

"Anyone else care to voice a complaint?" he asked.

The room remained silent. He smiled.

"I thought not. You have your orders. Prepare your regiments. We will cross over into the Abyss in a few days and fight the battle to end all battles. Do not fail me, my brothers! We must not allow the Abyss to fall!" he said.

The lords cheered wildly, then vanished. The Devil shook his head and smiled.

"That part is done. It's back to Thule for me now," he said.

His sudden appearance in the living room startled the half-drunk Pandaar and the other occupants.

The Devil laughed at their surprised reactions.

"My army is being assembled as we've discussed," he said. "When shall we meet?"

"How about tomorrow afternoon? We should all be sober by then," Arka-Dal said as he poured himself another ale.

"Good idea," the Devil agreed.

"Will we need to take any supplies, like food or water?" Arka-Dal asked.

"No. You will feel neither thirst nor hunger while in the Netherworld. You may not even grow tired," the Devil assured him.

"I always prefer to travel light," Pandaar said. "Just me and my weapons."

The following afternoon, the council gathered at the long oval table in the War Room. Arka-Dal sat in his usual chair at the head of the table with the Devil to his right, Leo to his left, and Jun, Michael, Pandaar, Galya, Gorinna, Kashi, Perseus and Ned to complete the group.

As everyone listened, Ned explained the situation in detail, with both the Devil and Merlin interjecting additional details to fill in the gaps. When they were finished, Leo shook his head.

"Incredible!" he said. "Truly incredible."

"And every word of this is true, Leo. I saw what that thing did to the last world. It wasn't a pleasant sight, either," Arka-Dal said.

"You say this thing killed everything on that world?" Kashi asked.

"Yes. Unless, of course, the people had the capability of interstellar flight—which they probably did not," Ned replied. "I'm certain that no one escaped."

"How soon before it can make its way to Earth?" asked Leo.

"That's impossible to say. It can be anywhere from 6,000 years to a single day. It all depends on how much longer Mephistos' people can hold out," Ned answered.

"So you're saying that we might all be long gone before it reaches here? That this may happen in the distant future?" asked Pandaar.

"That's a very real possibility. But bear in mind that the Beast has systematically wiped out dozens of inhabited worlds. Try to imagine this world completely devoid of all living things. Isn't that a future worth avoiding?" Merlin asked.

"It's not a pretty picture by any means," Kashi said.

"No. It isn't. That's why we must find a way to stop it before it can eat yet another world. It is by pure chance that its path has been diverted through the darker realms. It normally travels a straight path from one world to the next. Some interdimensional anomaly has changed its course and location. For this, we can be very thankful," Merlin explained.

"So it accidentally was sent through the wrong portal?" Arka-Dal asked.

Ned nodded.

"About 10,000 years ago, there was a great schism in the multiverse that opened several portals between the physical universes and the realms in between. After it devoured its last world and went back to sleep, a sudden shift in the cosmos sent it tumbling into a realm far beyond the Abyss. That realm is so distant from my own that I only became aware of the Beast's location after its minions began to move," the Devil said. "Even so, I'm still not 100% certain of where it exactly lies."

"Can we stop it with magic?" asked Leo.

"That is unknown at this point," Ned answered.

"What about weapons? Can it be killed?" asked Arka-Dal.

"No Earthly weapon that I'm aware of can harm the Beast. In fact, I doubt that any weapon made *anywhere* can harm it," Merlin said.

"There may be *one* weapon that can slay it," the Devil said as he looked at Arka-Dal.

"You mean Excalibur?" the Emperor asked.

"Exactly. Excalibur was forged neither on Earth nor any other plane that I know of and it certainly was not forged by Earthly hands. If there is one weapon in this universe that can slay the Beast, it would have to be Excalibur," the Devil said.

"And only one man can wield it," Merlin added. "The one true king."

"That's *you*, my love," Galya said.

"That means only *you* can use it to slay the Beast—if the Beast can be slain," Merlin said.

"And only Father can take us to where it is," Galya added.

The Devil smiled.

"Once again, I am called upon to be savior of humankind. Although I have fought against and defeated untold numbers of horrible monsters in my long life, this time, the outcome could be very different," he said.

"Can one such as you actually die?" asked Leo.

"Everything dies eventually. Even gods," the Devil replied.

"Do you fear death?" asked Michael.

"I do not fear death. But I do fear being *consumed,*" the Devil responded.

"If the Beast does eat you, it'll only shit you out later," Pandaar joked.

"*If* it shits," Gorinna said. "No one really knows what that thing does."

"Whatever it is, it's good there's only one of them," Michael said.

"In a manner of speaking," said the Devil. "In reality, I believe it's a rolling mass comprised of millions of nasty, ugly things milling around some sort of central core. The thing is *huge*. It eats everything in its path. The more it consumes, the larger it grows. The larger it grows, the more ravenous and nasty it becomes and the more it needs to eat. This thing is vile and evil beyond your imagining."

"And it must be stopped," Arka-Dal decided.

"I guess we'd better break out our silver edged weapons for this one—like we did the last time we fought the things in the Abyss," Kashi said.

The Devil stood and shook his head as he paced.

"The Minions of the Beast can't be killed by any earthly weapons—not even those edged with silver or blue silver," he said.

He stopped and smiled at Arka-Dal.

"Excalibur is the exception of course. No creature that dwells on any plane can stand up to it," he said. "But the rest of you will need something more. Something *special*," he said as he waved his hand over the table.

To everyone's astonishment, black armor, helmets, shields and weapons materialized before them. Each were exact duplicates of the weapons they normally wielded. Kashi picked up the black katana and smiled.

"It's perfectly balanced," he said. "But I don't recognize the material it's made from. What is it?"

"The blade is of onyx blended with several other rare minerals that can only be found on the lowest planes of Hell. It has no effect on any of those who dwell within my domain or in the Abyss. But it will work wonders against the Minions," the Devil replied.

Arka-Dal smirked.

The Devil laughed.

"You didn't think I would be foolish enough to provide you with weapons that can be used against my own people, did you?" he asked.

"Of course not. But how can you be certain these will slay the Minions?" Arka-Dal asked.

"This isn't the only time my people have had to battle those mindless bastards. We've had to deal with them on several occasions when the Beast woke. After much trial and error, my smiths came up with a combination of materials that actually works," the Devil replied.

"If these weapons can slay the Minions, why didn't you try to use them against the Beast itself?" asked Leo.

"We tried---and failed. Miserably I might add. The best we could do was to divert it to another parallel universe. That happened so very long ago that I had nearly forgotten the Beast exists. Now, after nearly 10,000 years, it has returned to plague us," the Devil said. "And I lacked the one thing that can, most likely, slay it."

"Excalibur," Arka-Dal said.

"Exactly. Even I'd had it then, I could not have wielded it. Only the one true king has the power to use it to its fullest potential. To everyone else, it's merely a sword, albeit a well-made sword," the Devil replied.

"And you say this thing lies in a region somewhere beyond the realm that belongs to the Others? Just how are we supposed to get there?" asked Arka-Dal.

"I can get us as into the Abyss. After that, we'll have to fight our way to the Beast's lair. Once we find it, only *you* can deliver the death blow. That means you will have to get close enough to be able to use Excalibur. You will have to enter the lair of the Beast," the Devil said.

"Since you are the only one who can wield Excalibur, you're the only one on Earth who can do this," Merlin added.

"This will be incredibly dangerous. Even with our protection, you might not come out of this alive," Ned said.

"So this is a *suicide mission?*" asked Arka-Dal.

"It is the closest thing to one," Merlin assured him.

Arka-Dal smiled.

"The difficult we do right away. The impossible takes a little longer," he said.

"I'm up for it!" Pandaar said. "I love a good fight."

"You can count me in—as always," Kashi chimed in.

"I'm in," said Perseus.

"So am I. I wouldn't miss this for the world," Michael said.

"We always said that we'd follow you anywhere, even to Hell itself. This is close enough," Jun said.

"Actually, the Abyss borders the last plane of Hell. You might say that it's a sort of backwater as it has none of Hell's refinements," the Devil said.

"Hell has *refinements?*" Leo asked.

"You'd be surprised," Galya said with a grin.

"But the Abyss is far more primitive. One might say that life there can be very brutish even on a good day," the Devil added. "This also applies to those who dwell there."

"Father is right. The demons of the Abyss are of a much more primitive variety. But you already *know* this, my love. After all, you have fought against them before," Galya said.

"How ironic! The dreaded Demon Slayer is about to return to the Abyss. But this time, he goes to *save* it!" Jun said.

"And I will be by your side every step of the way, my love," Galya said. "Where you go, I go."

"I'm in, too," Gorinna said. "You know you can't leave me behind."

"I wouldn't dream of it," Arka-Dal said.

"Looks like we have our expedition team. When do we leave?" asked Perseus.

"In three days. I have some affairs to take care of first. We can leave afterward," Arka-Dal replied. "A couple of more days won't make any difference."

"And just how are we supposed to fight our way past the Others and find that thing?" asked Pandaar. "There are countless numbers of demonic troops in our way."

"That's where *my* legions come into play," Galya said.

Arka-Dal squinted at her.

"We can use them to punch a hole in the Others' line and protect our backs as we search for the lair of the Beast," she continued.

"You're really going?" Arka-Dal asked.

She wrapped her arms around him and smiled up at him.

"Just *try* and keep me out of this one!" she said.

The Devil laughed.

"Galya is by far, my finest field commander and her legions are the best trained soldiers in all of the Lower Planes. They are also fiercely loyal to her and obey her commands without question. Galya has never lost a battle—that's something else you both have in common," he said.

"So you see, my love—you have no choice," Galya said.

"I see," Arka-Dal beamed. "Just how many soldiers do you command?"

"Each of my legions consists of 2,000 of Hell's finest warriors. I command 30 such legions," she replied proudly.

"That gives us merely 60,000 soldiers against perhaps *millions*," Arka-Dal observed.

"Don't let the numbers concern you, my love. If any of my soldiers fall in battle, others will immediately appear to take their places. That way, my legions are always at full strength," she explained.

"So the 60,000 may as well be 6,000,000 because you'll never run out of troops. I like that," Arka-Dal smiled.

"Exactly. I'll always have an unlimited pool of elite warriors to call upon. We are the vanguard and shock troops of Hell's armies. Most of my soldiers fought with me during the Forever War. They have served me for ages," Galya beamed.

"But we can't just show up in the Abyss with 30 legions of soldiers. Mephistos will think we're attacking him and respond in kind. We'll have to get his permission to bring our troops into his realm—after we forge an alliance with him," Arka-Dal pointed out.

"That's quite right, my lad," Leo agreed. "Diplomatic channels must first be opened or our efforts will be for nothing."

At that point, everyone's attention was drawn to Zhijima who emerged from a side door singing, skipping and twirling as she approached Arka-Dal. She threw her arms around his neck and gave him a long, deep kiss. Then she smiled up at him.

"I'm pregnant!" she announced cheerfully.

Galya laughed, then hugged her. So did the other women who came charging into the room after her. Arka-Dal smiled and shook his head. Pandaar slapped himself on the forehead and feigned despair.

"Oh no! Not *another* one!" he moaned.

"Congratulations—I guess," Kashi said as he shook Arka-Dal's hand. "How many does that make now?"

"You mean here in the palace? Or altogether?" asked Pandaar.

"Here," Kashi said.

"I don't know. I've lost count," Arka-Dal said.

"This will be your 10th child, Aka-san," Mayumi said as she hugged him. "At least here. I'm not sure how many you have elsewhere."

The others laughed.

The women took seats around the table to listen in on the conference. Leo filled them in on what had been said earlier.

"Now that we've decided to go to the aid of Mephistos and his people, just how are we going to get into the Abyss? I sealed them inside forever when I read the spell from the Necronomicon. That way is blocked forever. They cannot get into our world and I have no way of getting into theirs," Merlin pointed out.

"I can get us into the Abyss. No way is blocked to me. As I've said earlier, I can transport us right into Mephistos lair," the Devil said. "I can hardly wait to see the look on his face when we appear beside him. We'll probably scare the daylights out of him."

"Sounds good to me. Leave your legions behind for now, Galya. We'll bring them in after we've reached an agreement with Mephistos," Arka-Dal said. "Also, any information you can get me on the Others would be helpful. I need to know what they really are and who commands them."

Ned nodded.

"I'll do my best," he said. "They dwell in a part of the universe that I have never ventured into."

"Then this will be a learning experience for you?" Leo asked.

"In more ways than you can fathom, Leo," Ned replied. "I shall return in three days."

They watched as he slowly vanished in a cloud of green mist.

"Exactly what type of being is the Knower?" asked Michael.

"That's one thing I've never been exactly sure of," the Devil said. "Perhaps you should ask him when he returns."

"I think I shall," Michael replied. "The man peaks my curiosity to no end."

"I think we've gone over this enough for one day. Let's head over to the dining room and tie on the feedbag," Pandaar said. "I'm starved!"

Leo rubbed his belly and nodded.

"I feel somewhat famished myself," he said.

"You *always* feel famished, Leo," Arka-Dal said. "But I agree. Let's eat!"

They ate, drank, laughed and talked as always as several courses were served and plates were cleared and replaced. Leo and the Devil carried on a particularly interesting conversation while the other listened in.

"Just how many Hells are there?" Leo asked.

"Several," the Devil replied. "The major portion is my realm and its multiple levels or planes. There are 666 such planes, give or take. Beyond that lies the region we call the Abyss. That's where I used to send my demons who couldn't measure up to standards. The demons there are more primitive and unruly. Real low quality material, you might say. In the First Age, humans might have referred to them as 'trailer park trash' or 'hillbillies'."

"The Abyss is kind of like Hell's backwater," Galya added.

"Although Mephistos and I are distant cousins, I don't have much contact with him. I stay out of his affairs and he stays out of mine," the Devil said as he sipped his brandy. "In fact, we haven't seen each other since the last days of the Forever War. We were allies then, mostly due to necessity. God's armies were also trying to take him out at the time."

Leo sat back and entwined his fingers across his stomach, which Arka-Dal noticed, was getting bigger as time passed. Leo didn't miss many meals and there was almost no alcoholic beverage he didn't like.

"The more I learn from you, the more astonished I become," Leo said.

"There's really no need to be," the Devil said. "The Netherworlds consist of several realms. Each realm has a specific function or sphere of influence. It's not much different from this world or any other. Just think of Hell and the Abyss as two different nations."

"Actually, Father, Hell is more like an Empire. Each plane is like a separate state with its own governor. And each governor must answer to you—if he knows what's good for him," Galya observed.

"That's as good an analogy as I can think of," the Devil smiled.

"Where did Hell come from?" asked Leo.

"God created it then cast me and my followers into as a 'punishment' for having enough balls to challenge his authority. Later on, he tried to take that from us, too. And you know how that turned out," the Devil replied.

"Was he really a god?" Leo asked.

The Devil shrugged.

"He was my twin brother—and I'm certainly not a god," he said. "But his megalomania was certainly god-like. Looking back on it, I think he might have been more than a little insane, too."

"Absolute power..." Arka-Dal began.

"...corrupts absolutely." Michael finished.

The Devil laughed.

"I have found that to be true in all such instances. And most of those who wielded such power suffered miserable ends," he said.

"Like my father," Arka-Dal said. "He was real tyrant, even at the best of times. The people detested him, too. So did I. When Thule fell to invaders, I didn't go after them to avenge my father's death. I went after them to avenge the innocent people they slaughtered when the conquered the city. I wanted to rid my city of the invaders and establish a more benign government based on the rule of law instead of one man's ego."

"You certainly did that, my boy," Leo beamed.

"I couldn't have done it without everyone's help," Arka-Dal said modestly.

Michael looked at him and realized his modestly was sincere. Unlike most men in his position, Arka-Dal had never allowed power to go to his head. His only true concern was the welfare and safety of his people.

They ate, drank and talked some more. By midnight, the meal was ended and everyone shuffled off to bed for the night.

Michael trudged up to one of the guest rooms. After enjoying a nice hot bath, he put on a robe and walked over to the double door. He wasn't tired at all and decided to sit outside to relax.

As he stepped out onto the balcony, a tall, slender woman with jet-black hair, amber eyes and leathery wings suddenly appeared before him. Taken by surprise, Michael dumbly stared at her for several seconds.

She was beautiful beyond words.

Her smile was bright and bewitching.

Her figure was perfect.

Flawless.

Her skin was smooth and lilac tinted and she wore a very short white dress tied at the waist by a slim golden cord.

"Who are you?" he managed when he'd found his voice again.

"I am Viviana," she replied as she stepped closer.

"What do you want?" he asked.

"My master sent me. He thinks we should get to know each other. He thinks you and I might become friends. *Close* friends," she said with a sexy smile.

"You mean the Devil?" he asked.

She nodded.

"He thinks that you and I would be a good match," she said.

"But you're a *Succubus!*" he stated.

"And you are *not*," she countered. "Why should that matter? You are alone. I am alone, too. We are both in need of someone, so why should it not be each other?"

"An Archangel and a Succubus friends? Wouldn't that be a hoot!" Michael said with a smile.

She laughed.

He liked the way it sounded.

"The war is long over. There's no reason for us *not* to be friends. Besides, I was not yet born when that last battle was fought, so it does not concern me at all. In fact, it should no longer concern *you*," she said.

"That's true. I *like* you, Viviana. I would really like to get to know you better," Michael said.

She put her arms around his neck and looked into his eyes.

"What would you like to do first? Talk or make love?" she asked.

Before he could answer, she stuck her tongue into his mouth…

Down in the parlor, Arka-Dal noticed the broad grin on Galya's lips. He walked over and sat beside her.

"What's so funny?" he asked.

"Father sent Michael a Succubus to keep him company. She's very pretty, too. Her name is Viviana," Galya replied.

Arka-Dal laughed.

"I bet he liked *that*," he said.

"He did. They are in bed even as we speak. They seem to have really hit it off. I doubt that he's ever had such a companion," Galya said.

"Why'd your father do that?" asked Arka-Dal.

"I asked him to. Michael is lonely and miserable. Viviana was, too. She never quite got the hang of being a seductress. Father picked her because he felt they would make a good match. I think he's right," she said.

"What other reason is there?" Arka-Dal asked.

"Father *likes* Michael," she said as she put her arms around his neck and kissed him. "I hope you're not too tired, my love."

"I'm never too tired for you, darling," he assured her as he swept her up in his arms.

Mephistos paced the floor of his command center when two of his generals materialized before him. He stopped and squinted at them.

"What news do you bring?" he asked.

"The Others have forced a breech in our lines to the east," the first general reported. "I shifted several regiments from the northern frontier to help stem the tide, but the enemy increased their troop strength as well to try to exploit the breech."

"Interesting. They've been doing that a lot lately," Mephistos said.

"As soon we shifted the regiments from the north, the Others launched a heavy attack there," the second general added.

"Send in the last of the reserves to strengthen the line in both places. No matter what happens, the lines must be held. Let not a single one of them get past you if you value your lives," Mephistos ordered.

The generals vanished.

He scowled.

He'd always known that the Others were numerous and ferocious opponents. Until recently, he'd always considered them to be a mindless and leaderless mob driven by their fear of what was attacking them. He now realized his assumption was dead wrong. The way they've been probing for weaknesses in his lines before attacking in strength to force a breech, then sending more troops in to exploit it, meant that some higher intelligence guided them.

They had a field commander.

But who?

And while he didn't fear the Others, he *did* fear the beings that were driving them from their realm. If the rear lines of the Others should break, those monsters would flood into their realm like an unstoppable tide. The sudden influx of fleeing Others and their mortal enemies might be enough to break through his defenses and overrun the entire Abyss. He shuddered at the idea.

His people were fighting a terrible war of attrition. A war without end. They could expect not give quarter. They could never retreat. They were trapped forever inside the Abyss with nothing left to do but fight to the bitter end.

"Damn you, Merlin!" he shouted at the top of his lungs.

The next morning, Michael joined Arka-Dal, Pandaar, Kashi and Zhijima and Koto, on the field behind the palace for their usual training session. Instead of pairing off against Koto like he usually did, Arka-Dal smiled at Michael.

"Since you're our newest commander, I'd like to see how good you are in single combat," he said.

"Are you certain you want to do this, Sir?" Michael asked.

"I'm positive. Let's see what you've got—and don't hold back," Arka-Dal said as he drew the practice sword and went into a defensive stance.

Michael drew his blade and charged straight at him. He started with a flurry of thrusts, lunges and slashes that should have, or so he thought, thrown Arka-Dal off balance and enabled him to deliver the coup de grace. To his astonishment, Arka-Dal parried and dodged everything he threw at him with a speed and ease that was almost superhuman. Arka-Dal suddenly slashed at Michael's throat. The Archangel parried the blow as he leaned backward. At the same time, he attempted a leg sweep. Arka-Dal backflipped to avoid it, turned and lunged at Michael's stomach. Again, Michael parried it and replied with a strike at his chest. Arka-Dal knocked his blade aside, dropped to one knee and attempted to use the killing stroke. When Michael also blocked this, he stood and cheered.

"Bravo! Well done, Michael!" he shouted.

Both lowered their swords and bowed. Michael handed his practice weapon to Master Koto and thanked him in his own language. Arka-Dal slapped him on the back.

"You're as good as I expected. Better!" he said.

"I should be. I've had millennia to practice. You, too, are amazing. No other human being could have parried all those blows," Michael returned. "I realized how formidable an opponent you would be the moment you placed Excalibur to my throat. At the time, I thought you got such quickness from the sword itself. Now I know better."

"I've had a most excellent instructor. Koto-san keeps me at my best and he's always coming up with new techniques for me to learn," Arka-Dal said with a polite bow to his instructor.

"Can you teach me?" Michael asked.

Koto shook his head.

"After watching you, I believe there is very little I can teach you. The best I can offer is to help you sharpen your technique," he said politely.

"I would greatly appreciate that," Michael said.

"I'd like to see what you've got," Zhijima said as she walked toward him with her sword in hand.

"You? But you're just a little woman. What can *you* possibly do against me?" Michael asked almost arrogantly.

"You'd be surprised. Let's have a match. Fight me, if you dare," she challenged.

Michael glanced at Arka-Dal. The Emperor nodded approval.

"Don't let her size deter you. She's an excellent fighter," he said.

Michael smiled at Zhijima.

"Alright then. Let's have a match. Use all of your tricks. Everything you can think of. Hold nothing back," he said as he went into a modified fighting crouch.

"Alright. You've asked for it," Zhijima said as she stepped back and slashed at the air with her sword to get loose.

It made a comical match-up. Arka-Dal sipped his water and watched as the diminutive Zhijima warily circled to the left of Michael. Then she stopped, feinted with her sword and dodged away before Michael could react. He watched and let her play her little game for a while.

Then she shouted at the top of her lungs and charged. He sidestepped her attack and backhanded her. Although he tried to hold back, the blow sent her tumbling a few yards. She immediately jumped to her feet, circled to right, then lunged again. This time, Michael simply seized her by the scruff of her neck and threw her to the ground. She landed on her stomach and quickly rolled into a kneeling position.

Michael raised his sword and brought it straight down toward Zhijima's head. Before the blow landed, she scurried between his legs, spun and attempted to strike him from behind. He blocked it with his bracer. At the same time, he seized her wrist and lifted her several feet off the ground.

"You're helpless now," he said.

"Not quite," she said as she kicked him in the testicles as hard as she could.

Michael let her go and grabbed his groin as he slowly fell to his knees in pain. When he tried to stand, Zhijima made as if to kick him again. Michael held up his hand to cede the match.

"Enough! You've made your point—in spades!" he said.

Arka-Dal and the others laughed and applauded. Zhijima picked up Michaels' sword and handed it to him. She then curtsied. Michael bowed his head and smiled. Now he understood what Koto meant when he advised him to always be prepared for the unexpected.

"Do all Thulian women fight like you?" he asked.

"I don't know about *Thulian* women, but we *Dihhuri* women do," she said. "I'm sorry if I hurt you but you did tell me not to hold anything back."

"Now I'm sorry I did," he said.

"If you think *she* was tough, wait until you go up against Galya," Arka-Dal said as he handed him a cool drink.

"I've already had that pleasure. She kicked my ass good, too," Michael admitted. "I'm just glad she and I are now on the same side."

"I am, too. Although I did beat you, it was not easy victory for me," Galya said as she walked out onto the field. "A few times, I was afraid I would be forced to kill you."

"Why didn't you?" Michael asked as he sipped his drink.

"Father ordered me not to," she replied. "And you already know why."

Michael smiled and nodded as he saluted her with his cup. She returned it.

Everyone cleaned up and headed to the dining room for the usual long meal and longer chat. The jokes and insults flew one after another, with Pandaar bearing the brunt of the verbal assaults. He, of course, dished out his own insults and everyone roared at the exchanges.

Around midnight, the dinner came to an end. A tired Arka-Dal, flanked by Mayumi, Chatha, Medusa, Galya and Zhijima, excused himself and bade everyone a good night as he headed upstairs. Leo and Michael retreated to the Archives for more talk while Pandaar and Kashi decided to head out on the town for a few hours.

Unable to sleep, Merlin walked the halls of the palace to think about their upcoming mission. It was, by far, the most insane thing he'd ever imagined. As he strode along the longest corridor, he happened to see Galya. She was standing before the wedding portrait of Arka-Dal and Mayumi and smiling.

He walked up and greeted her.

"They make the perfect couple," Galya said of the portrait. "I doubt that two people have ever been matched better."

Merlin chuckled.

"What's so amusing?" she asked.

"You. From what I recall of our many past encounters and what I thought I knew of your personality, I would have believed that you'd be insanely jealous of Mayumi. Instead, you seem to adore her," he replied.

"I do. Mayumi was the first to befriend me and welcome me to the family. She is the kindest, gentlest and wisest woman I have ever known. That is why she will always be first in Arka-Dal's heart. The rest of us, however, are content to share second place. I would die for her, Merlin. In fact, I would forfeit my life to defend everyone in this house," Galya said.

"And I, my dear, would die to defend you," Merlin vowed.

Now it was Galya's turn to laugh.

"Now *that's* something I never expected to hear from *you!*" she said. "You said that as if you like me now."

"I do like you. I also like your father. I *trust* him, too," Merlin said.

"Did you ever get the feeling that the entire universe has been turned upside down?" Galya asked.

"All the time," he said.

"Isn't it *grand*?" Galya asked with a big smile.

Two days later.

Mephistos cursed as he peered into the mirror and saw several new regiments of the Others launch a major assault on the weaker part of his right flank. Before the line buckled, he ordered his generals to move one quarter of his reserves into that section to strengthen the line. The ensuing clash was chaotic and brutally nasty.

But the line held.

He took a deep breath and sat down.

Since the Others had probed for and located a weak spot in his lines, they were more intelligent than he'd imagined. Or someone was actually directing them. He'd always suspected they had a leader, but he was never able to confirm it. He just assumed that the Others just threw troops at his borders randomly in order to break through. But this was deliberately probed. They knew exactly where his line was weakest and concentrated a major attack there. This was *planned.*

He slammed his fist on the table and cursed aloud.

"What cruel twist of fate forces us to fight this endless war alone!" he lamented.

"You are not alone, Cousin!" the Devil announced as he and the others suddenly materialized behind him.

As predicted, Mephistos was so startled by their sudden arrival that he nearly jumped out of his long robes.

"Lucifer!" Mephistos said after he'd regained his equilibrium.

"Long time, no see," the Devil said as he stepped toward him.

Mephistos looked past him and scowled at the rest of the party.

"Merlin, Ned and the Demon Slayer! Have you come to gloat over the fate you've condemned us to?" he asked bitterly.

"Actually, we have come here to *help* you," Merlin assured him.

"Why would *you* help me? After all, this was *your* doing, Wizard. It was *you* who read the spell that sealed the portal forever and forced us to use all of our energies to fight this miserable war without end. Why should I believe anything you have to say now?" Mephistos asked.

"Because you have no choice," Arka-Dal said. "*None* of us do. We've come here with a proposal that will mutually benefit us all. You can either listen or we'll leave and you can keep fighting your nasty little war forever. The choice is yours."

"I'm listening," Mephistos said as he sat down.

"A most unusual and dire set of circumstances has come into play. Whether you realize it or not, we all now share a common enemy. One so deadly and so numerous that they threaten to overrun the entire cosmos," Ned said.

"And you know *exactly* who we mean, Cousin. You, too, have seen them. You know what drives the Others," the Devil said.

"I do indeed, Lucifer," Mephistos nodded. "I've seen them. I've watched them multiply with each passing moment, doubling and redoubling their filthy numbers as their slumbering master slowly begins to stir. It's like a living nightmare."

"The peril is quite real. If the Others break through your defenses, they will flood into the Abyss like wild animals with the Minions hot on their heels. Your forces will be overrun. Scattered. You will soon lose all hope of stemming the tide and your people—along with the Others—will be devoured," Ned explained.

"Once the Abyss is conquered, the Minions will infest my entire realm and the Beast will eventually find its way to Earth and lay waste to it as it has dozens of other worlds," the Devil added.

"To make matters even worse, without the Netherworld realms to acts as a buffer zone, the *Elder Gods* will return to the universe and chaos will reign. This, above all, must not be allowed to happen. The Beast *must* be located and slain," Ned warned.

Mephistos gaped at him.

The possible return of the Elder Gods had not crossed his mind. He thought about it and visible shuddered.

"The end seems inevitable," Mephistos said. "Even now, my soldiers are losing ground to the Others. We can't turn the tide. All we can do is die in place."

"That is only *if* you decide to fight alone," Arka-Dal said.

"What else *can* we do?" asked Mephistos.

"We've come to offer you assistance, Cousin," the Devil said.

"What kind of assistance? More soldiers to help hold the lines?" Mephistos asked.

"I can have 666 legions here within ten Earth days. My best soldiers from every plane of Hell will be at your disposal to use as you wish," the Devil offered.

"You mean you're willing to place them under *my* command? Will they agree to this?" asked Mephistos.

"They already *have*. I gave them no choice and they know what is at stake here. We are just as eager to stop the Beast in its tracks as anyone else," the Devil said.

"Every little bit helps, Lucifer. But even *they* might not be enough," Mephistos said. "At best, it may enable us to temporarily retake some lost ground. The war will still continue until all of our combined resources are drained."

"That's why we must find and slay the Beast," Merlin said.

"Once the Beast is dead, its Minions will also weaken and die and the threat will be ended," Ned added. "There is no other way."

Mephistos shook his head.

"Even if you *could* find the Beast, just how do you propose to *slay* it?" he asked.

"With *this*!" Arka-Dal said as he drew his sword.

"*Excalibur!* That *might* do the deed, but you'll have to get close enough to deliver the fatal blow. That in itself may prove to be impossible," Mephistos said.

He stood and paced.

"As far as I can tell, the lair of the Beast lies far to the other side of the realm of the Others. To reach it, you'd have to cross over some highly treacherous and toxic ground. You'll also have to fight your way through the land of the Others. If you manage to survive *that*, you'll have countless hordes of Minions to contend with en route to the Beast's lair— *if* you can find it. It's a *suicide* mission at best. Only a madman would even attempt such a thing," he said.

"Yet, this *must* be done," the Devil said flatly.

"How?" asked Mephistos.

"Arka-Dal has a plan. It's daring and brilliant enough to actually work," the Devil replied. "And more than a little insane."

"Care to tell me about it?" Mephistos asked.

"I will—when we have all the necessary pieces in place. This has to be timed perfectly and the enemy has to react in a predictable manner," Arka-Dal said. "In the meantime, we'll need you to keep fighting until we can return with more troops."

Mephistos paced the room and shook his head.

"Although we may be able to stem the tide of the Others with our combined forces, the Minions of the Beast double in number with each passing day. Even if we defeat the Others, we'll have to stand and face a far more numerous and dangerous foe," he said.

"Why continue to fight the Others?" Arka-Dal asked.

Merlin raised an eyebrow. He had an idea where Arka-Dal was going with this.

"What do you mean?" he asked.

"Can the Others be reasoned with?" Arka-Dal asked. "Are they intelligent?"

"I'm not sure. As far as I know, no one has ever *tried* to make contact with them," Mephistos replied. "Why?"

"Since we all share a common enemy, perhaps we can try to forge an alliance with the Others against the Beast and its Minions? The Minions are far too numerous to be defeated by any single race. If we can *combine* our forces, we may be able to stop them in their tracks and have a shot at locating and killing the Beast itself," Arka-Dal said.

"I'm not sure this would be possible," Mephistos said. "We've been battling the Others for millennia without end. As far as I know, they don't have any kind of command structure. In fact, they seem to be almost mindless."

"The key word is *almost*," Arka-Dal said. "Someone or something *must* control them. After all, even herds of wild beasts have their leaders. If we can discover who that is, perhaps we can bring him here under a flag of truce and try to work things out. Slaughtering each other with no end in sight is fruitless, especially when faced with a far more fearsome enemy. If we can turn our combined energies against the Minions, we may be able to win this thing."

"I say that it's worth a try," Galya said.

"I'm for it," the Devil agreed.

"So am I. Anything is better than the situation as it now stands. But how do we find out who leads the Others?" Merlin asked.

"Don't you know?" the Devil asked Ned.

"I have a very vague idea, but even *I* can't be certain of everything," Ned replied.

"But you're the Knower!" Merlin said.

Ned smiled.

"While it is true that I have spent my entire existence seeking the answers to all questions and trying to learn all there is to learn, the universe is vast beyond your imagination. For anyone, even myself, to know everything is impossible," he replied.

"You said you have a vague idea?" the Devil asked.

"I have paid very little attention to the realms beyond the Abyss thus far. But even I have become aware of certain legends and rumors. One name comes to mind. I'm sure that if you concentrate, that name will also come to you. It is, perhaps, a name you haven't heard or thought of in ages," Ned answered.

"Azathoth?" the Devil asked.

"That is the very one," Ned assured him. "I heard his name repeated as I probed the borders of their realm. At least I believe it was a name. Their language is difficult to comprehend at times."

"What makes you think it is *he* who rules the Others?" asked Galya.

"Who better?" Ned responded. "Given his legendary reputation for cruelty and mayhem, who else would be able to control the Others?"

"Isn't Azathoth one of the Elder Gods?" asked Michael.

Ned shrugged.

"According to the legends, Cthulhu created him and placed him in charge of the darkest part of the Dark Realms. Those who fell from favor with the Elder Gods were sent there as punishment," he explained. "Supposedly, they were the ancestors of those we call the Others. But the lore is very murky and uncertain."

"But Azathoth is merely a legend. He never existed—did he?" Merlin asked.

"Some people believe that *I* am only a legend. Yet, I have existed for countless ages," Ned replied.

Mephistos laughed.

"Point well taken," he said. "But how do we make contact?"

"Leave that detail to me," Ned answered. "In the meantime, I suggest you maintain the status quo. Combine your forces to halt the advance of the Others and keep them at bay until you hear from me."

With that, Ned vanished in a puff of glowing green smoke.

Mephistos laughed.

"If anyone can find Azathoth, it'll be Ned," he said.

That's when he made eye contact with Arka-Dal and smiled. As he did, Galya walked over and put her arms around Arka-Dal's waist.

"And what role do you play in this, Galya?" Mephistos asked.

"I go where my husband goes—and my legions follow," she said with a grin.

Mephistos raised an eyebrow.

"*You* are wed to the Demon Slayer?" he asked almost in shock.

She beamed and nodded.

"And they have made me a very proud grandfather of two wonderful children," the Devil boasted.

Mephistos laughed.

"The times are indeed changing," he said.

"How potent will your magic be outside of your realms?" Arka-Dal asked.

"Our powers are somewhat diminished in this region," the Devil replied. "There is something about the very air and soil that takes away from our ability to cast certain spells and weakens others. Once we pass beyond the Abyss, there's no way of knowing if our spells will work at all."

"We'll still be able to wield spells effectively enough but we won't be able to bend matter to do our bidding as we can in our own realms," Mephistos added.

"Each plane, dimension or parallel universe consists of slightly different types of energy and matter. One must be attuned perfectly to that energy and matter in order to bend it into doing one's will," the Devil explained.

"So this energy and matter manipulation is what we call magic?" Arka-Dal asked.

"Exactly," Merlin replied.

Mephistos smiled at them and shook their hands.

"You may go and tell your armies that they have safe passage through the Abyss. We will welcome you as brothers from now on," he said.

"We shall return in three days with the rest of our team. We will not fail you, Mephistos," Arka-Dal promised.

Mephistos watched as they vanished in a ball of light.

"I am now allied with the Demon Slayer! These times are indeed strange," he said as he shook his head.

Six days later, Mephistos received yet another visitor in his chambers. This one was Hyrrak, the Field Marshall of Hell's main army. He bowed respectfully and then saluted. Mephistos nodded and welcomed him and his soldiers.

"Our Lord has sent us to fight alongside your legions. I am to place my soldiers at your disposal and obey any and all orders," Hyrrak said in his gravely voice.

"You are most welcome, Field Marshall. How many legions did you bring?" Mephistos asked.

"All 666," Hyrrak replied. "That's 1, 332,000 of our best warriors. We are armed to the teeth and anxious to show what we can do. Command us!"

Mephistos led him over to a large mirrored table and showed him the layout of his lines and where they were weakest. Hyrrak studied the map carefully and nodded. Then he pointed to places he thought his troops would do the most good. Mephistos nodded in agreement.

Hyrrak saluted and vanished.

Moments later, the sound of trumpets blaring and loud cheers echoed through the valleys of the Abyss as the legions of Hell marched to fight alongside their newfound allies.

Mephistos smiled.

The last time the two armies fought together was during the Forever War. He never thought he'd ever see the day they would fight alongside each other again.

"And it's all due to the Demon Slayer!" he thought. "Without him, this would not be possible. Our worst enemy has become our would-be savior. Such a thing is enough to shake the very foundations of my entire belief system!"

The sudden surge of troops caused the Others to fall back and regroup. Mephistos watched as they divided into several regiments and moved up to square off against his strengthened army. Once this was completed, the Others attacked in earnest. They stormed the lines in several places with renewed ferocity only to be repelled time and again by the stubborn defenders.

Mephistos watched the battle unfold in his mirror.

"There's no doubting it anymore. Someone commands them. Someone who knows what he's doing. The Others are not mindless brutes after all. Lucifer's troops enable us to hold the lines for now. We'll need twice as many soldiers to launch a counterattack to retake our lost ground," he thought.

As he watched the waves of invaders break against he lines like waves crashing against rocks, he hoped that Arka-Dal's idea would make this part of the war unnecessary.

"Maybe he's right. Maybe we can forge an alliance with the Other," he said. "Anything is better than this!"

While the battle continued to rage on the front lines, Ned the Knower penetrated deep into the realm of the Others. What he saw surprised him. The realm was dismal, to be sure. And as bleak as any place he'd ever seen. But instead of endless barren plains and deserts, he saw several small cities and towns with somewhat chaotic street grids and interconnecting roads. The land of the Others had obviously been scarred by countless centuries of brutal warfare against the Minions, so many of the smaller towns stood in ruins.

Yet several more towns and cities remained and they appeared to be thriving.

Then he also saw the people.

Instead of the mindless brutes who assailed the Abyss, the actual denizens of the realm looked quite human. Most had lilac colored skin, either white or red hair and were tall and lean. They had catlike eyes to compensate for the eternal twilight conditions and were neatly dressed. Most watched as he wandered past but did not stop nor question him.

"Arka-Dal would be amazed if he saw this," Ned thought.

Since the people of the realm looked human, he surmised that the soldiers had been especially bred for combat. After a while, he stopped a young woman and asked what the name of their realm was.

"It has not a name that I am aware of. We simply call it *home*," she replied. "How do you know our language?"

"I know *all* languages," Ned assured her. "Do you have a ruler?"

"Of course," the woman replied. "Does not everyone?"

Ned laughed.

"Where can I find him?" he asked.

"One does not find Azathoth. He finds *you*," she replied enigmatically.

"How?" he asked.

"Since you are not of our kind, he will soon notice you are here and seek you out," the woman said as she walked away. "Be patient."

Ned watched her go and shook his head. The woman was quite lovely by anyone's standards—as were most of the woman he'd seen. They certainly weren't the mindless brutes Mephistos thought they were. Nor did they seem openly hostile to strangers. He *did* learn something important from his conversation. The woman referred to their ruler as Azathoth.

This meant that he *did* exist after all.

Since she did say that Azathoth would find him, Ned decided to keep wandering through the realm until that happened. As he wandered, he stopped to speak with more and more people. Most were quite friendly and as curious about him as he was of them. Their land had never been visited by an outsider and Ned found himself becoming a sort of tourist attraction.

The cities he explored were well-maintained, clean and orderly. Some showed the scars of several battles. Each city had cafes, markets and even stadiums. He learned that the Others ate, drank, laughed, loved and did just about everything humans did—except grow old and die. He also discovered that some had even heard of him. They asked him about other places and people and why he was there and what he thought of their country. He answered each question honestly and asked several of his own. They, in turn, replied with the same honesty. They had no name for their race or their country, but each town and city did have a name.

Until the war started, they said they thought very little about things that lay beyond their borders and they were terrified of losing to the Minions.

To Ned, this had become a real eye-opening excursion.

And, just as the woman had predicted, Azathoth *found him.* Intrigued by the arrival of this stranger, he suddenly materialized not ten feet in front of him. Instead of starting as most others would, Ned simply bowed his head respectfully.

Azathoth smiled and stepped toward him. Ned stood his ground.

"I take it that I am in the presence of Lord Azathoth?" Ned asked.

"I am he. Who are you and what is your business here? Our lands are not exactly a tourist attraction, so you must be here on important business," Azathoth said as he studied Ned warily. "I *know* you. You're Ned the Knower."

"I am," Ned replied.

"Then I've guess right. This is not a social call, is it?" Azathoth asked.

"Not in the least—unless you *wish* it to be," Ned answered.

"State your business, Knower. I have little time to waste these days. Our borders are beset by innumerable invaders and we are fighting a war on two fronts," Azathoth said.

"That is *precisely* why I've come," Ned said.

"Oh?" Azathoth queried as Ned's response caught his attention.

"I have come bearing an offer that may resolve all our problems," Ned replied. "You might say, it's an offer you can't refuse."

Azathoth smirked.

"I'm listening…." He said.

Three days later, Arka-Dal arrived at Mephistos' lair with his entire team. Besides Arka-Dal, the Devil, Merlin and Galya, there were Gorinna, Kashi, Pandaar, Perseus, Jun and Michael. Mephistos studied them carefully and smiled.

"I bid you welcome to my realm. Please feel free to make yourselves at home while you're here," he greeted them. "I must say that you are the most unique band of brothers-in-arms I have ever beheld."

"You're not the first who has said that," Kashi said.

"And you won't be the last," Pandaar added. "We took a little tour of the Abyss on the way here. I must say this is the most dismal place I've ever visited."

Mephistos nodded.

The Abyss was indeed a nightmare realm. It had to be from design. The ground was hard, barren and covered with a loose layer of fine brown dust which, in turn, was littered with rocks and boulders of various shapes and sizes. Twisted, grotesque and leafless trunks of would-be trees and shrubs jutted out of the soil in some places. A slow moving, sulfurous "river" meandered hideously through the center of the widest plain, spewing noxious fumes into the air as it crept along. The sky above was pale, orange and sickly- looking and scarred by wisps of purple/gray/ greenish clouds. A blood red "sun" dimly flickered in the distance and cast a sad orange light upon everything below.

"This is one miserable piece of real estate," Kashi added.

"I know what you mean," Mephistos said. "I'm not all that thrilled with the place myself. But *someone* has to rule over this tragedy and I'm elected."

"Did you win or lose that election?" asked Arka-Dal.

Mephistos laughed.

"What do *you* think?" he asked.

At that instant, Ned popped into view.

"It's about time you got here," Merlin said. "Did you locate him?"

"Yes," Ned replied as he stepped aside and pointed to the entrance.

They were surprised to see a tall, ruggedly handsome man with shoulder length snow-white hair, deep amber eyes and broad shoulders, stride confidently into the chamber. He was dressed in a dark green tunic, black trousers and knee-high black boots. A dark green robe with gold trim and cryptic symbols embroidered into it completed the outfit. At his side was a slightly shorter, lean and sexily built young woman with white hair. She was dressed in a filmy tunic made of a fabric that resembled almost see-through chain mail with a thick leather belt around her waist. Arka-Dal noticed that she wore nothing beneath her tunic and the place between her thighs seemed to be devoid of any pubic hair.

She saw where his eyes were and smiled at his obvious interest.

The man bowed his head slightly.

"I am Azathoth, Lord and Master of the Darkest Planes and ruler of those you know as the Others," he announced. "And this is my daughter, Alyana, and commander of my forces in the field."

Alyana was about five feet seven inches tall with cat-like emerald eyes that seemed to glow with an eerie light. She had full lips and an almost disarming smile that gave her a look of innocence blended with evil and magnetic mystery. She reeked of sex appeal, too.

Arka-Dal smiled at her and nodded his head.

Alyana also nodded and smiled at Arka-Dal.

Galya frowned.

"We have come in answer to your request for a parlay. Ned guaranteed us safe passage to and from here and indicated this might be in everyone's best interest," Azathoth said.

"You look nothing at all like your people," Mephistos observed.

"This is our *usual* form. Those you now battle against are my shock troops—and they can be quite formidable as you have discovered," Azathoth said as he sat down at the table.

Alyana stood behind him and kept her eyes on Arka-Dal.

Galya kept her eyes on Alyana.

The Devil made the introductions. Azathoth nodded to each of them respectfully Alyana again smiled at Arka-Dal.

"We've always referred to your people as the Others. What do *you* call yourselves?" asked Mephistos.

"We've never given that much thought, actually. We have no name for ourselves or the lands we dwell in. Such things aren't important to us. If the truth be known, we have always referred to *you* as the Others," Azathoth replied with a slight grin.

Arka-Dal laughed.

"Names aren't important anyway," he said. "Deeds are."

"Not intentions?" asked Mephistos.

"The road into *my* realm is said to be paved with good intentions," the Devil remarked glibly. "Sometimes, I believe that old adage is right."

"So is this about *intentions* or *deeds*?" asked Azathoth.

"Deeds, I hope," Arka-Dal replied.

Alyana smiled at him. Her smile, he felt, was a mixture of warmth and danger. It intrigued him.

"So you are the famous Emperor of Thule, the infamous Demon Slayer. I have heard so much about. Even in our remote realm, you have become somewhat of a legend. I had expected you to be some sort of a monster. Instead, I find that you are far more handsome than I ever imagined," she said.

"And he is *my* husband—so don't get any ideas," Galya warned defensively.

Alyana giggled.

"Do not worry, Galya. I am not your rival—*yet*," she teased.

"And you'll keep it that way if you want to continue living," Galya warned.

"Go ahead and try something if you dare. I fear no one. Not even *you*," Alyana said almost casually.

Azathoth raised his hand to silence his daughter.

"Be still, Alyana. This is neither the time nor place for such nonsense. When I received your request, it intrigued me. In response, I have called a temporary halt to our endless hostilities. No one has ever attempted to contact me before or invite me to a conference," he said. "I thought that the least I could do was come and hear you out."

"I thought it was worth a gamble," Arka-Dal said.

Azathoth smiled.

"Ah. This was *your* idea then? As I understand your message, you would like to forge an alliance with my people against the Minions of the Beast. Is this correct?" he asked now very much intrigued.

"That's right," Arka-Dal assured him.

"Fascinating. And just why would you think I'd be interested in such a thing?" Azathoth asked. "What's in it for us?"

"Survival. Yours and ours," Arka-Dal said. "We share a common foe. The Minions are far too numerous for us to individually defeat them. But if we pool our might and resources, we may be able to turn them back long enough for us to locate and destroy the Beast before it awakens."

"Individually, we have no chance against those monsters. You should know better than any of us what they are like because they have nearly driven you from your realm. Our combined forces may prevail. At least we'd have a fighting chance. If we can find and destroy the Beast, you and your people can return to your realm in peace and both the Abyss and Hell will be safe," the Devil added.

"And Earth as well," Merlin said.

Azathoth looked into Arka-Dal's eyes.

"Right now, my people are fighting a war on two fronts. Half of my warriors are trying to punch their way into the Abyss. The other half are fighting—and losing—a very nasty rear-guard war against the Minions," he said. "It's a lose-lose situation at best."

"Then join with us," Arka-Dal urged. "Let's set aside our differences and fight against the monsters that would destroy us all. Individually, we haven't got a chance. Together, we can defeat those things."

"What you propose makes sense. I see no deceit in your eyes, Arka-Dal. I know that your offer of an alliance is sincere. I see the wisdom in it as well. Rather than keep wasting the lives of my soldiers in a never ending war with Mephistos' people, I would rather use them against the monsters that now attack our rear. I agree to this alliance," he added as he extended his hand to Arka-Dal. "My people are tired of war. We want nothing more than to put aside our weapons and return to our normal lives."

Arka-Dal clasped it and smiled.

Azathoth smiled at him as he used his powers to sense what type of man he was dealing with. What he senses impressed him.

"There is a *greatness* about you that other humans have never possessed. You were born to lead," he said. "It is your destiny. Who is going to seek out and destroy the Beast while our armies hold his Minions at bay?"

The Devil nodded toward Arka-Dal.

"A perfect choice," Azathoth agreed.

"I would have expected nothing less from the legendary Demon Slayer," Alyana cooed. "Your courage is well known, even among my people. Who else goes with you?"

"All of us," Merlin said.

"In that case, I, too, shall go with you," she said.

"Not if I have anything to say about it," Galya said.

"Actually, Alyana would be a *perfect* addition to your group. She and her forces have been battling the Minions for a millennium now and she knows the lay of the areas beyond our realm," Azathoth said.

"I can lead you to the Beast," she assured them. "But it's a suicide mission. Most of us will likely die along the way as the path is well guarded and those who don't die may wish they had."

Arka-Dal nodded.

"I always *did* like going against the odds," he said.

"The realm of the Beast is filled with unspeakable horrors. It's fraught with danger and a thousand deaths await you around every twist and turn. Of all of our people, only Alyana and one of her legions have dared to venture into their realm—and she barely survived," Azathoth explained.

"I went there with 3,000 of our best warriors to locate and slay the Beast. Most of us died on the way. Most of the survivors died trying to return," Alyana said.

"Did you locate the Beast?" Arka-Dal asked.

"Not exactly, but we did learn that it sleeps in a deep pit at the end of a narrow canyon in the Mountains of Madness. We tried to go in but we didn't get very far. The very air was thick with Minions. When I got wounded, my warriors decided to get me out of there and the mission was abandoned," Alyana said. "Only seven of us survived."

"Alyana barely survived the return trip. It took her weeks of your time to mend. There were many nights I was afraid that I'd lose her, but her will is very strong," Azathoth said. "She possesses great determination and courage. She refuses to give up."

Arka-Dal nodded.

"Those are admirable qualities to possess in times like these," he said.

She smiled.

Galya snarled.

"I can lead us to the canyon. I'm not sure how long it is, but I do know we'll have to fight every inch of the way. We won't be able to stop and rest and we'll have to guard our backs to make sure we're not taken by surprise," Alyana said. "Those Minions are everywhere and their numbers are endless."

"Are you sure that you want to go back?" Arka-Dal asked.

"I have no choice. It is our best and perhaps only chance to end this madness. I'll either end it or die trying," Alyana said flatly.

"I like your fighting spirit," Arka-Dal said.

"Then I can go with you?" she asked.

"Yes. You can lead the way," he said. "How long would it take to assemble both your armies in one place and where would the best place be?"

"There is a wide, open plain just on the other side of the ridges to the east," Mephistos suggested. "It's large enough for both armies. I can have all of my soldiers there within one day."

"I can have all but my rear guard assembled there in two days," Azathoth agreed.

"Good. That will be our jumping off point," Arka-Dal said. "We'll go over the details of my plan once everyone's there. Galya—I'll need your legions there, too."

"They are already on their way, my love," she said.

"We will meet you on the plains in two days," Azathoth vowed as he and Alyana melted away.

"I've always liked the way your people travel," Arka-Dal said. "Let's head over to the gathering place. Along the way, we can familiarize ourselves with the terrain—just in case we'll need a backup plan."

"As you wish," Mephistos agreed.

They left the command center and stepped out onto a wide, flat plain that looked much the same as the other areas of the Abyss. As they walked across the tortured-looking wasteland, they heard no sounds of any sort. Nor did they see any signs of life save for a few small groups of armed demons who stopped to salute Mephistos. He simply nodded at them and told them to carry on.

"Those are my scouts. They patrol this area regularly," he explained.

"This region appears to be rather quiet," the Devil observed.

"It is," Mephistos said as he pointed to a mountain range. "The battle lines are beyond the cliffs in the distance. So far, my soldiers have managed to keep the invaders at bay but we're steadily losing ground. Now that we've forged an alliance with them, we no longer have to worry about that."

"How long have you and the Others been at war?" asked Gorinna.

"One, perhaps two thousand of your years. It's difficult to say exactly. For a while, the Others seemed to be winning this war. That's why we originally sought a way into your world—but Merlin put an end to that idea," Mephistos said. "I have cursed him ever since and even vowed to kill him if we ever met again."

Then he laughed.

"And now, we are allies! Don't you find this ironic?" he asked.

"More than a little," Arka-Dal said.

"Does that bother you?" Mephistos asked.

"More than a little—but I'll get over it," Arka-Dal joked.

Mephistos laughed.

"What is your first impression of Azathoth?" asked the Devil.

"I must admit his appearance surprised me. I got the impression that he was confident in his own abilities and used to having his wishes obeyed without question. I also felt that when he gives his word, it's a bond that he will never break," Merlin said.

"He's strong-willed, confident and I feel we can trust him to do as he says—just as *you* both are," Arka-Dal said.

"I am glad that you feel that way about me, my son," the Devil said. "You are a most excellent judge of character."

Mephistos laughed.

"I feel somewhat humbled by your assessment of me, but I assure you that it's correct. When the Lord of the Abyss gives his word, it's cast in iron," he said.

They continued past a circle of jagged rock pillars that protruded from the dark earth at off angles. Some were connected at the by stone cross beams. They walked through the tallest set and into a large, flat circular space. In the exact center was a circular hole. They stopped at the edge and looked down.

"This seems bottomless," Merlin commented. "Where does it lead?"

"No one knows," Mephistos said.

"Huh?" asked Arka-Dal.

"This structure precedes my people by eons. It is so old, no one knows who built it. I personally feel it dates to the time of the Elder Gods. A few daring souls have attempted to reach the bottom. None were seen again," Mephistos explained. "Perhaps Ned could shed some light on it?"

"I must admit that I knew nothing of its existence until this very moment. It does resemble Stonehenge somewhat, but it's much *darker*. I would guess that it was created as some sort of conduit between the Abyss and whatever lies at the bottom," Ned said as he peered into it.

"I sense something but I cannot tell what it is. It also senses our presence but seems indifferent," the Devil added. "Something tells me that its indifference is a *good* thing. What is down there is best left in peace."

"I, too, have sensed those same things. And I agree with you about leaving it be. If it doesn't bother us, we should not bother it," Mephistos said as they left the structure.

"Are there more such structures in your realm, Mephistos?" Arka-Dal asked.

"No. This is the only one like it. Why? Are you curious about what lies at the bottom?" Mephistos asked.

"Only if it decides to cause trouble," Arka-Dal replied.

They walked on for what seemed like an eternity and the bleak scenery hardly changed at all.

They soon called a rest.

Arka-Dal sat down with his back against a boulder. The boulder moved. So did Arka-Dal. The boulder stood on two legs, stretched, yawned and plodded away. Arka-Dal and the others laughed. Then he found another rock to lean against. Before he sat down, he tapped it with his fist to make sure it was really a rock.

Mephistos watched as Galya walked over and sat beside him. She leaned her head on his shoulder as he pulled her close.

"I'm truly amazed," Mephistos said.

"At what?" the Devil asked.

"Your daughter genuine loves him. That in itself speaks volumes for his character," Mephistos said.

"Arka-Dal is a most unusual and remarkable man and he and Galya make a perfect match," the Devil said proudly. "When I see them together and I spend time with them in their home, I realize that there is much good in this universe and hope for mankind. I also realize that those things are worth fighting for."

"You sound as if Arka-Dal has rubbed off on you," Mephistos said.

"I think he has. I do know that since we've come to know each other, I've softened my attitude toward humans, especially those who live in Thule. Unlike people of other realms, they've embraced Galya from the start. To them, she's not some demonic monster. She's the beloved wife of their beloved Emperor and they adore her," the Devil explained. "In fact, they seem to feel the same way about *me, too.*"

"Aren't you afraid you'll lose your edge one day?" Mephistos asked.

"Not really. There are still more than enough greedy, black hearted fools running amok on Earth and other worlds to keep me sharp and busy for millennia to come. Human nature is still what it always has been and I still write contracts on a daily basis. I just don't do any business in Thule," the Devil replied.

"It seems as if your life has taken a most interesting turn, Cousin," Mephistos observed. "Perhaps mine is about to as well."

"I would not be surprised if it did," the Devil said.

Michael noticed that Ned was seated atop the trunk of a fallen tree. He walked over and sat beside him.

"I have much to ask you," he said.

"And I have much to tell," Ned replied in his usual manner.

"I have heard of you ever since I was created by God. It seems like you have always existed," Michael began.

"That is because I *have* always existed," Ned replied.

"Just how old *are* you?" asked Michael.

Ned smiled.

"That is difficult to put into terms you would easily comprehend. You might say that I am ageless. Time has no meaning whatsoever to me. I have always been," he said. "To give you some perspective, I was already ancient when Jahweh and his twin brother, Lucifer, came into being."

"The Devil is God's twin brother?" Michael asked.

"Yes," Ned assured him. "Lucifer translates into 'Bringer of Light' or the Enlightened One. That in itself should tell you all that you really to know about him. Jahweh is a name without any real meaning, but the symbol stands for the exact opposite of Lucifer. The two always shared different points of view. So different, it eventually led to their long, bitter and bloody war.

Jahweh was more than a little egotistical and power mad. He demanded total adoration, total obedience and brutally punished anyone who dared to disagree with him. He wanted to keep mankind totally subservient and ignorant so he could force them to worship him forever.

Lucifer not only questioned him, he openly opposed him. Against Jahweh's orders, he infused mankind with the gifts of curiosity, courage, free will, ambition and all of their emotions. He also gave them the drive and passion to use those gifts to create a new life and world that would make them totally independent from Jahweh's will. Without Lucifer's gifts, human beings would be nothing more than brain-dead monkeys. They would have accomplished nothing to set them apart from other primates. Thanks to Lucifer, men learned to reach for the stars—and they nearly succeeded—and would have save for Jahweh's vindictiveness."

"So the wars really started because the Devil freed mankind from God's control?" Michael asked.

"That's one reason. The biggest one was jealousy. When Jahweh attempted to force Lucifer to knuckle under, Lucifer revolted. He split from his brother and formed his own realm with his followers.

In a fit of rage, Jahweh created an army and sent them out to slay Lucifer's followers and bring him back to Heaven in chains. As you already know, that didn't work out quite like Jahweh planned," Ned explained.

"The god I followed so passionately and blindly was little more than a vindictive and treacherous monster. As humans say, I hitched my chariot to the wrong horse," Michael said.

"But things have ways of working themselves out in the scheme of things. In this case, they did so with heavy doses of irony," Ned said.

"Indeed they have," Michael admitted. "Especially when one considers the incredible chain of events that have led me here. Through my service to Arka-Dal, I now find myself allied to the Devil and I've sworn an oath to protect his daughter and grand children. No one in his right mind could have foreseen this!"

Ned laughed.

"And what do you think of Lucifer now?" he asked.

"I like him. I find him to be a man of honesty and honor. He is the exact opposite of what I was told," Michael replied.

"Lucifer was always thus. His image was a result of propaganda put out by his enemies. If a lie is repeated often enough, it eventually feels like the truth. That is the intent of what the humans call a smear campaign," Ned explained. "I suppose your entire belief system has been turned inside-out since you came to Thule."

Michael nodded.

"I'm not sure what to believe in anymore," he said.

Ned pointed at Arka-Dal and Galya.

"You can start by believing in *them*," he said.

Arka-Dal stood and helped Galya to her feet.

"Let's get going," he said.

After another hour or so of walking, Galya turned to Arka-Dal.

"It's time for me to assemble my legions," she said. "I'll return in a few hours."

With that, she vanished from sight.

"Are her legions going to be in the initial assault?" asked the Devil.

"In a way," Arka-Dal replied. "I have something special in mind for them."

When they reached the line of rocky ridges, they were surprised to find both Azathoth and Alyana already waiting for them.

"I thought you said it would take you two days to assemble your armies," Arka-Dal said.

"Two of your days have already come and gone," Azathoth replied.

"Come and gone???" asked Pandaar. "But we've only been walking for a few hours!"

"I told you that time and distance have little meaning here in the Netherworld. While here, you can neither feel the time pass or age and a trek of miles is the same as walking across a small room," Mephistos explained. "But by human time measuring methods, 54 hours have passed."

"I'm not going to bother asking how far we've traveled," Pandaar said.

"That's just as well. You would not believe me anyway," Mephistos smiled.

Alyana was clad in her sheer chain mail tunic. This time, she wore a double horned golden helmet, grieves and bracers to protect her lower arms and legs and a wide heavy belt with twin swords. She smiled at Arka-Dal.

"I'm ready," she assured him.

"So I see," he said with an approving smile.

"Do you like what you see?" she asked.

"What man wouldn't?" he replied.

She beamed.

"In that case, I am yours whenever you desire," she said with a wink. "I have never had sex but I will gladly give myself to you."

"Let's discuss this later—after we've killed the Beast," Arka-Dal suggested.

"As you wish," Alyana replied with a smile.

Azathoth laughed at her boldness—and Arka-Dal's very diplomatic responses. He didn't rebuff her. In fact, he left the door open for her. He found this to be amusing and intriguing.

"Now what, Demon Slayer?" asked Mephistos.

"We wait for Galya's arrival," Arka-Dal said. "When she arrives, I'll outline my plan."

Azathoth walked over to Arka-Dal and nodded. Arka-Dal smiled and nodded in return.

"Please forgive my daughter for being so forward," Azathoth said.

"She did nothing to offend me, I assure you," Arka-Dal replied. "She does things in a very open and direct manner. There's no deceit in her. I like that."

"Alyana has been at war ever since she was tall enough to wield a weapon. You might say that she grew up fighting. There was neither time nor need to teach her tact or manners. Alyana is, first and foremost, a battlefield commander. She is a brilliant tactician and almost fearless. Her greatest traits are honesty and dedication. That's why our soldiers love her so much. She *is* nearly clueless when it comes to dealing with people and more than a little, er, crude at times. But she is what she is," Azathoth said.

"She did catch me by surprise and she sure as Hell seemed to irritate Galya," Arka-Dal said with a smile. "Once I got to understand her a little bit, I found myself liking her."

"I appreciate your patience and understanding," Azathoth said. "I hope Galya comes to know and like her as well."

"I'm sure she will before this is over," Arka-Dal said. "They have a lot in common."

"Indeed," Azathoth nodded.

When Galya arrived a few moments (or was it hours?) later at the head of her legions, she was seated astride a jet black, somewhat terrifying horse with bright yellow eyes. Each time it exhaled, flames shot out of its nostrils and its hoofs kicked up sparks when they touched the ground. The horse was covered with armored plates to protect its flanks. It also wore an armored face mask adorned with twin horns.

Galya herself was attired in her battle armor of onyx with gold trim. She wore a black helmet with twin horns and flaps that flared downward to protect her neck. Arka-Dal noted that her armor greatly resembled the armor worn by the samurai of faraway Nihon. He also knew that no Earthly weapon could penetrate it.

Even dressed for war, Glaya looked sexy. Irresistibly so.

"I'm ready," she said.

"Yes, you are," Arka-Dal smiled as she slid from the saddle and walked up to him. "And a more beautiful warrior I have never seen."

She laughed.

"Our armies are assembled as you've asked. What is your plan?" asked Mephistos.

Arka-Dal looked out at the sea of demons and other creatures arrayed on the vast plane. It was the largest army he'd ever seen. If they wanted to, they could easily overrun every nation on Earth. There were *that* many of them.

He also knew that just beyond the range of cliffs in the distance was an even *greater* force. One so vast its numbers couldn't be counted. And those numbers were increasing by the second.

"Where is the enemy's line the weakest?" he asked.

Azathoth thought for a moment, then pointed at twin pinnacles of black rock far to the east. They stood over 1000 feet high. Two miles separated the pinnacles.

"Those are the Gates of Sorrow. We named them thus because of the countless battles that were fought there," he said. "Our scouts have reported that their numbers are thinnest there."

"Do you plan to attack them there?" asked Azathoth.

"Sort of," Arka-Dal said. "Where is this canyon you discovered?"

"It was to the south of the Gates," Alyana said as she pointed. "It lies in between that distant range. The range marks the edge of our realm."

"The bulk of the Minions stand between us and that canyon. We cannot hope to fight our way through them," Mephistos said.

"We don't have to," Arka-Dal said with a smile.

"I've seen that look before—many times," Merlin said.

"I know what you're thinking, too," Pandaar added.

"Of course you do. We've been together so long we can almost read each other's minds," Arka-Dal grinned. "It's a gamble—but if we time it right, we can make it work."

"What do you have in mind?" asked the Devil.

"I want to throw every soldier we have—except for Galya's legions—right at their weakest point. Make it look like an all-out attack and have your people make as much noise as possible. I want them to get the enemy's full attention. I want them to draw most of the Minions to the Gates and hold them there as long as possible," Arka-Dal said.

"A diversion!" Azathoth beamed.

"Exactly. Once the Minions engage your troops, Galya and the rest of us will punch a hole through their lines to the south and make for the canyon," Arka-Dal said.

"My legions are the finest soldiers in all of Hell. We'll go through their lines like a hot knife goes through butter," Galya said confidently. "We have never lost a battle."

"Tell me about it!" Michael said.

Galya smiled and nodded at him.

"This may be the strangest band ever assembled for a common cause," Azathoth said. "When do we begin?"

"In one hour," Arka-Dal said. "This gives us time to make last minute preparations. I would like *you* to remain behind with the bulk of the armies. They'll need someone to command them and make decisions if battlefield conditions change."

"As you wish," Azathoth agreed. "Will your people obey my commands in your absence, Mephistos?"

"They *will* if they know what's *good* for them," Mephistos said.

"Keep those things engaged for as long as possible. We'll need plenty of time to find and kill the Beast—*if* it can be killed at all," the Devil said.

"If it lives, it can be killed," Arka-Dal said. "I'll find a way to rid the universe of this thing or die in the attempt."

"I won't let you die, my love. I promise!" Galya vowed.

"I won't, either," Michael swore.

Arka-Dal laughed.

"I have no intention of dying," he assured them. "Now, let's get ready."

Mephistos laughed.

"Your plan is insane enough to work. Let's get to it," he said.

"What will happen after we slay the Beast?" asked Michael.

"Once the Beast is dead, the numbers of Minions will cease to grow as they all spring from within the Beast itself. Those that remain will suddenly weaken and fall to dust because they derive their strength directly from the Beast," Ned replied. "At least, that is the way it is *supposed* to go."

"What if it *doesn't* go that way?" asked Kashi.

"Then I suggest that you bend over and kiss your ass good-bye," Jun said as he pounded his back.

"I never imagined that the likes of us would be united against a common foe. The gods themselves must be laughing at the sheer irony of this," the Devil mused.

"I think the gods are too stunned to laugh," Ned said with a grin.

For the next hour, Mephistos, Azathoth and the Devil walked among their troops and extolled them to fight harder than they've ever fought before. They made them all pledge to stand should-to-shoulder with their new brethren and not give an inch of ground to the hordes of the Beast.

"Your attack must be swift, fierce and relentless. You must take it to the enemy like never before and fix them at the Gates of Sorrow. You know what is at stake. Do not fail us," they said.

Merlin and Ned watched in fascination.

"Who would have ever imagined that creatures such as these would be mankind's best line of defense against evil?" Merlin mused. "Or that creatures from three alternate dark universes would stand together to fight a common foe?"

"Only one man could have imagined this and brought it about," Ned replied as he nodded at Arka-Dal. "Even your Arthur couldn't do *that!*"

Merlin laughed.

"Alas, but diplomacy and tact were not among Arthur's finer attributes. The fall of Camelot was my fault as I did not see the flaws in his personality until it was far too late. Arka-Dal's skills at bringing together diverse groups of people are unmatched by anyone living or dead. He never ceases to amaze me," he said.

"And that is why you very wisely extended his life," Ned added. "And the lives of those he cherishes most."

"The people who are close to him keep him grounded and he heeds their advice—especially Mayumi's. He needs them as much as the world needs him. It was an easy decision for me. I expected him to be angry when he found out, but he took it rather well. He didn't like it, but he said he understood my reasons," Merlin said. "I would have made him immortal if possible—but such things are far beyond my powers."

"Nearly four centuries is more than enough, thank you," Arka-Dal said as he walked up with Galya. "Any longer than that and I might develop some sort of god complex and go insane like some of the ancient emperors I've read about."

"*That* will never happen to you, my love," Galya smiled. "I won't *let* it. Neither will Father."

"So I have nothing to say about it?" Arka-Dal asked.

"Nothing at all, my love," Galya smiled.

Merlin and Ned laughed.

"I'm afraid your fate is sealed, my lad," Merlin said.

Alyana had been quietly listening to their exchanges the entire time. While she did, Galya noticed that she couldn't seem to keep her eyes off Arka-Dal. She also knew that Alyana would do something to get him to notice her. She also knew that this young princess from beyond the Abyss might be too sexy for him not to notice her.

Galya wanted to slap her silly to put her in her proper place. To let her know that Arka-Dal was hers and she didn't appreciate nor want any sort of rivalry for his affection. She wanted to do something. Instead, she remained quiet.

It was Alyana who made the first, and not unexpected, overture. She walked over and smiled. Arka-Dal returned her smile. Then Alyana upped the ante.

She batted her eyelashes at Arka-Dal and smiled seductively. Galya hissed and went for her sword. Arka-Dal stayed her hand and nodded at her.

"And what, exactly, is on *your* mind?" he asked.

"Even though I am inexperienced in sexual matters, I wish to become your mate," Alyana announced out of the blue. "I wish to bear your children."

"I am already married to Galya and several other lovely women. I have no desire to add yet another woman to the mix," he replied. "But I appreciate the offer nonetheless."

"Our household already has more than enough people," Galya added defensively.

Arka-Dal heard the bitter tone in her voice and winced. Galya's claws were coming out and she saw Alyana as a possible rival.

"If your household is too crowded, I can help you make room for me," Alyana said.

"Oh? And just how would you go about doing that?" he asked as he winked at Galya.

"I could start by killing Galya," Alyana replied matter of factly.

"Why you miserable little bitch! I'll rip your eyes out!" Galya growled as she lunged toward her.

Arka-Dal restrained her (and it wasn't easy!), then got between them. He looked into Alyana's eyes and realized she had only said what was on her mind without thinking. He decided to set things straight before they got out of hand.

"If you harm Galya or any of my other wives, I'll kill you. Then I'll cut you into small pieces and feed you to that thing in the pit," he warned. "Do you understand that? As alluring as you are, I would not hesitate to kill you if you threatened any of my wives."

Galya hooked her arm with Arka-Dal's and walked off with him. As she did, she smiled at Alyana. It was a smile that clearly stated that Arka-Dal was hers.

Alyana fumed and sat down on a nearby boulder just as her father, Ned and the Devil walked over.

"Well, at least he said I was alluring," she said. "What did I do wrong?"

"Much. If you wish to win the heart of Arka-Dal, you must do so without threatening those he loves," her father advised. "You must *charm* him. Be less forward. Tease him a little."

"I'm Alyana. I take what I want," she said arrogantly. "It's the only way I know how to be."

The Devil laughed.

She scowled at him.

"That's exactly what Galya once thought. You can see for yourself how *that* worked out," he said. "It was *she* who got taken."

"When you showed him your darkest side, you lost Arka-Dal. Perhaps completely. You cannot win a man's heart by threatening to kill his wife," Ned added. "This is especially true of Arka-Dal."

"Arka-Dal's love for Galya runs strong and deep. One might almost say it is an epic sort of love, one that never should have been possible in the first place. Theirs is the kind of love that inspires poets and musicians. I have never seen the likes of it in all of my years of existence," the Devil said. "It's quite miraculous."

"Just how many wives *does* Arka-Dal have?" asked Alyana.

"Seven—so far," Ned replied. "Five live with him at the palace and two elsewhere."

"If you would be number eight, I suggest that you start by displaying some of your most redeeming qualities—*if* you have any," the Devil advised.

"Of course I do! I am Alyana, princess of the darkest planes. I can terrorize, torment and destroy millions on a whim. I am dark power incarnate!" she boasted.

The Devil laughed.

"That's *not* what I meant by *redeeming* qualities. Such things would likely *repel* Arka-Dal," he said.

"Indeed. He might also consider you to be a monster," Ned added.

"I'm *supposed* to be a monster! I'm Alyana!" she said. "I don't know how to be anything else."

"If you would win the favor of Arka-Dal, now is a good time to start learning," the Devil advised. "Just as Galya did."

"Galya?" Alyana asked.

"Yes. Before she met Arka-Dal, most humans viewed her as evil incarnate. A real monster who corrupted men and delighted in destroying them. And she was exceptionally good at it. What you see before you now is a *different* Galya entirely. Arka-Dal—and to a large extent—Mayumi, have caused her better qualities to override her baser ones. Love does that," the Devil explained.

"Love *weakened* Galya?" Alyana asked.

"Quite the contrary. It has *strengthened* her in ways neither of us ever imagined possible," the Devil replied.

"I don't understand," Alyana said.

"You may—in time," the Devil suggested. "Just relax and be yourself. Let him see and know the real Alyana—just as he did with Galya."

When they walked away, Alyana pondered what was said. Outside of her father and the troops she'd commanded for the past 1,000 years, she rarely spoke or interacted with anyone. Diplomacy and tact were not in her nature and she had very little understanding of the way things were supposed to work between men and women. Until she met Arka-Dal, she never gave such matters a passing thought.

Now, thanks to her inexperience and arrogance, she wondered if she had permanently damaged any chance of forming a relationship with him. And she didn't fully understand why such a relationship was now important to her.

Azathoth read the turmoil in her eyes and sighed.

"This is my fault," he said. "When she was growing up, I neglected to teach her how to act around others. I only taught her how to fight and survive. Because of my negligence, she is sadly lacking in other, more important, areas."

"You raised her in accordance with the situation and time she grew up in—much as I did with Galya," the Devil said. "It was not until long after the war was ended that Galya developed other facets of her personality on her own. Her marriage to Arka-Dal enabled the true Galya to emerge in ways I never expected. Under the right circumstances, I'm certain that Alyana will do the same."

"I hope so—for her sake," Azathoth said as he saw a tear roll down her cheek.

She brushed it off and smiled at them as if to assure them she was alright. It was the first time he'd seen her weep since her mother was slain by the Minions centuries ago. It was then Alyana's heart also became filled with the desire for vengeance. When turned loose on the field of battle, Alyana was terror incarnate. Against the Minions, she neither gave nor expected quarter. She always fought to the death

And she always won.

"Alyana," he thought, "will now have to learn to fight a different kind of war."

Arka-Dal and Galya sat on a mound of dirt and talked. Mostly, they discussed what he expected her legions to accomplish once the real battle started. Galya assured him that her soldiers would protect the party from all sorts of attacks and from any direction.

"We'll reach the Beast intact. I promise," she said.

She looked over at Alyana and scowled.

"What do you think of her?" she asked.

"I think she's incredibly brave to return to the place she was nearly killed. Not many others would do that," he said.

"Not that. I mean what do you think of the way she looks? Is she beautiful?" Galya fished.

He laughed and put his arm around her.

"In a savage sort of way," he hedged. "She's like a tigress. Lean, sleek, sexy and dangerous. There's a sense of danger about her, too, that's kind of attractive."

"You think she's attractive?" Galya asked.

"I think every man on earth would say she's attractive. I'm no different," he replied honestly. "Even for all of her bravado and experience as a warrior, there's an almost childlike innocence to her because she's socially inept. Kind of like a bratty two year old."

Galya laughed.

"She is kind of clueless, isn't she?" she asked.

"What do *you* think of her?" Arka-Dal asked.

"I despise her," Galya answered.

"Why?" he asked.

"She's trying to become your mate. She even said so," Galya said. "You don't need another wife."

"No. I don't," Arka-Dal agreed. "I already have enough of those."

She laughed.

"I know who your favorite is and I'm fine with that because I love her dearly, too," she said.

Arka-Dal smiled and nodded.

"I love *you* dearly, too. More than I can even put into words," he said as he pulled her closer. "Don't ever forget that."

"I won't. So I don't need to feel jealous of Alyana?" she teased.

"Only if you *want* to be," he teased back.

Alyana heard every word of their conversation. She had to admit that Arka-Dal was right about her. She *was* socially awkward. Very much so. She had no idea how to correct that, either. But Arka-Dal said he thought she was attractive and sexy. No one had ever said that about her before.

"But *now* what do I do?" she wondered.

Mehistos, the Devil, Ned and Merlin chatted while they waited for, what they hoped, would be the battle that would end the war. Mephistos looked at Ned.

"There is something I would ask you," he said.

"Ask," Ned responded.

"You and Merlin both knew that the Others were driving us from the Abyss. Yet you chose to seal the portal and force us both to wage a relentless war of attrition. Why?" Mephistos asked.

"At the time, we failed to look beyond the immediate danger. We failed to see what drove the Others," Ned replied.

"Had you known, would you still have sealed the portal?" Mephistos asked.

"Yes," Ned replied.

"Why?" asked Mephistos.

"You and your people were a direct threat to all of the races who inhabit the Earth. We could not allow your demons to overrun the planet and throw it back into chaos," Ned answered.

"It was a choice between saving your people or the people of Earth. We chose to save the people of the Earth," Merlin added. "It seemed perfectly logical."

Mephistos nodded.

"I appreciate your candor. I am also grateful that you have returned to help us—and the Others—in our darkest hour. To be truthful, I had almost given up hope of surviving this war," he said.

"We now stand united against a common deadly enemy. Circumstances and the diplomacy of Arka-Dal has made brothers of us all," Ned said.

"But will this strange new fellowship last beyond this war we are fighting?" Merlin asked.

"I, for one, intend to make certain that it will," Mephistos said.

Zero hour.

Azathoth stood on the mesa and looked out upon the vast wasteland that had been the scene of countless battles between his rear guard and the hordes of Minions that sought to overrun his realm. He was flanked by six demonic generals. Two from his own armies. Two from Mephistos' host and two from Hell itself. Millions of battle hardened troops from their combined armies were arrayed in countless rows in the plain below. All were heavily armed and anxiously awaiting the signal to attack.

"It is time to take the war to the enemy," Azathoth decided.

"Where do we concentrate our attack?" asked one of the generals.

Azathoth pointed to the twin pillars of black rock in the center of the field.

"There at the Gates of Sorrow," he said.

"When?" the generals asked.

"In five human minutes," Azathoth replied. "On my signal, send every last soldier you have straight at the Gates and have them attack the enemy there with all of the fury and brutality they can summon. And keep attacking no matter what. There can be no retreat. Understand?"

The generals nodded and hurried off to join their units.

Azathoth smiled.

If Arka-Dal's plan worked, the sudden attack would buckle the enemy line and force them to send every available soldier nearby to plug the breech. As soon as both armies were fully engaged, Galya would spearhead an attack that would punch through the Minions' lines at their weakest point and provide cover for the group all the way to the pit. Then Arka-Dal could use Excalibur to slay the Beast before it could wake.

But what if the plan failed?

What if Arka-Dal fell in battle along the way? Only *he* could wield Excalibur. If he fell, all would be lost.

Azathoth shrugged these thoughts off.

"The others will see to it that he does not fall," he said. "Even at the expense of their own lives. Even Alyana would sacrifice herself to make sure he reaches the pit. She knows what is at stake here. There can be no failure. No turning back this time. It is all or nothing."

He smiled to himself as he thought of even more trite clichés, then he shrugged them off and said he was becoming too much like the humans. He stepped to the edge of the cliff and studied the vast army that was spread out below.

Azathoth had formed his armies into a gigantic wedge, with his more ferocious and heavier-armed shock troops at the point and the lighter, swifter soldiers from the Abyss making up the body. On either side, he had legions of winged archers, poised to attack and eager to rain death down upon their hated foes. The reserves were made up of the legions from Hell.

He had no idea just how many soldiers he had.

Millions perhaps.

He *did* know that the Minions numbered at least four times as many and those totals were steadily increasing as their hideous master spat out more of them with each tick of a clock. They were armed, fierce and they came in all shapes, sizes and forms. They were nearly mindless, too, although of late they had displayed some small organizational capabilities.

"Are they developing some sort of *collective* intelligence now? If so, is the Beast guiding them?" he wondered. "An eternity of battles and I still have no idea exactly what the Beast *is* or how it produces so many Minions. What sort of monster *are* you and where do you come from? Are there others like you lurking beyond the rim of the universe?"

At the precise moment, Azathoth launched his attack. It was a combined air-land assault that startled the enemy into inaction for few moments as thousands upon thousands of screaming, roaring demons descended on the Gates. At the same time, the airborne archers riddled the Minions with arrows, killing thousands on the first pass. By the time the archers turned to attack from the rear, the sky was filled with howling winged Minions that rose to counter it.

For a long time, both sides became embroiled in a strangely twisted dog fight as they fired arrows and other missiles at each other or collided in mid-air in brutal hand-to-hand combat. Azathoth's forces were faster and more aggressive than the Minions. They slew them by the thousands and their deteriorating bodies rained black dust down upon the troops below.

It was at that instant the point of the wedge slammed straight into the Minions' line. They struck with such brutal force that the line momentarily buckled and was in danger of breaking. As the Minions tried to strengthen it, the rest of the Demons also collided with them and the fight was on.

Azathoth smiled as his combined armies forced the Minions back through the Gates and slowly retook the lost ground. Although the initial assault was going well, he knew that once the rest of the Minions joined the battle, it would become a long, ugly and costly stalemate. But would they be able to hold the bulk of the Minions long enough for the others to find and slay the Beast?

Arka-Dal and the others watched as the struggle grew nastier and nastier as wave after wave of Demons assailed the Gates. After a few minutes, the Demons' shock troops broke through and started clearing the Minions from the gap between the twin pillars of rock. That's when the Minions did exactly what Arka-Dal hoped they would. They pulled as many of their troops as possible from surrounding areas and hurled them into the battle. Even so, the Demons managed to break through their lines and began to sweep the Minions from the field.

Arka-Dal and the others watched as the battle spread to the black plains and beyond. It was brutal, nasty and unbelievably noisy—just as Arka-Dal had hoped.

"Why do we wait?" asked Alyana.

"We wait because the other Minions have not yet abandoned their positions to stop our attack. We can't make our move until they do," Arka-Dal explained.

"What if they aren't intelligent enough to respond to the attack? What if they are as mindless as we think they are?" Merlin asked.

"Oh, they aren't *completely* mindless, Wizard," Alyana said. "But they *are* very slow- witted. Once they realize we are attacking their weakest spot, the rest will react."

After what felt like an eternity, Alyana proved correct. The Minions finally realized they were being flanked and rushed great numbers of their troops in to join the battle. The Devil watched from his vantage point and smiled.

"That's most of them! What remains behind can easily be handled by Galya's legions," he said.

"It's just as you planned, my love! The Minions have severely weakened their forces to the south to counter Azathoth's attack.," Galya reported. "They won't be able to keep us from going through."

"Let's move!" Arka-Dal said.

Galya began by launching two legions of aerial archers at the remaining Minions to the south. The attack was unexpected and horrifyingly lethal as arrow after arrow easily found its mark and caused the targets to fall to dust. The archers made a second, then a third pass with equally devastating results.

This attack was quickly followed by ten legions of heavy and light cavalry which punched a hole through the center of their pathetic line and sent the remaining Minions screaming in all directions. The infantry quickly followed, then came Arka-Dal and the rest of the party flanked by two more legions of infantry to protect them from any attacks.

Galya had told her soldiers that Arka-Dal had to reach the pit safely and ordered them to see to it that he did. She dismounted and ran beside him the entire way just as she promised.

"It's amazing. In less than an eye blink, we've managed to retake all of the territory we lost over several years of fighting," Mephistos observed as the wild running battle raged around them. "First, we lost it to the Others. Then the Minions drove them out. Now the land is ours again."

"I hope our soldiers can hold onto it—at least long enough to keep the Minions busy," Arka-Dal shouted above the clamor.

Mephistos smiled. Arka-Dal had *our* soldiers. He was now one with them.

As the battle grew more fierce, Arka-Dal, Galya and Alyana suddenly found themselves amid a veritable whirlwind of clanging weapons, shouts and curses as Demons and Minions swooped in from every direction. Galya's crack soldiers managed to hold the attackers at bay as they slowly advanced through enemy lines foot by bloody foot. As each of her soldiers fell, another materialized to replace him. As each Minion was slain, dozens more popped into being and joined the assault.

The two sides collided in the middle of the barren plain amid howls, screams, explosions, columns of flame and ash and metal-on-metal. Thousands upon thousands of evil-looking, malformed, winged, horned, taloned, and multi-limbed creatures fought fiercely for what seemed like several days.

Or was it years?

Time, after all, had no meaning in the Abyss.

Mephistos watched in fascination as Arka-Dal cut a swath through the demonic horde that sought to overwhelm them. One-by-one and two-by-two, the Minions fell before his determined and relentless onslaught like stalks of wheat fell to a sickle.

"Does Arka-Dal's courage and skill come from Excalibur or does *he* drive the power of the sword?" he asked Merlin who fought beside him with equal fury and determination.

"Arka-Dal's fighting skills and courage were already renown before he ever set a hand on Excalibur," Merlin replied. "The power of the sword has little to do with either."

No matter where they swung their weapons—up or down, sideways or in and out and around, their blades sliced through leathery demonic flesh and sent Minion after Minion to a dusty death.

But still they came.

By the hundreds.

With no end in sight to their ever-increasing numbers.

They swooped in from the sides, rained arrows on them from above. They shrieked. They cursed. They roared. They howled and they died by the hundreds with each attempt to overwhelm the invaders.

And the more Minions they killed, the more their numbers increased in this battle without end.

As Arka-Dal kept fighting, he thought that it was good the diversion drew off the bulk of the Minions, otherwise, they'd all be dead right now. The battle was heavy. It was incredibly fierce and bloody and the scenario was, at best, totally insane.

A true living nightmare as both sides slugged it out face-to-face and toe-to-toe. There was no chance to rest. No chance to breathe. No retreat and no quarter given nor asked for. It was combat in its deadliest, most brutal form that covered every foot of soil with layers of black dust, blood and ichor.

They soon passed beyond the black hills and crags and fought their through a sorry looking patch of trees and vegetation that could only be described as some sort of "forest". Here, two legions broke off to fight a rear guard action which held the bulk of the Minions at bay long enough for the rest of the party to race through the "forest" and along a foul, bubbling brook with little or no interference.

"We'll find rest and refuge on the other side of the forest," Alyana assured them as she ran beside Arka-Dal and Galya.

They soon found themselves in a quiet and barren area. Ned looked up at the sky. The Minions were circling overhead like vultures. But none made a threatening move toward them.

"How come the Minions don't attack us here?" he asked.

"They *can't*," Alyana replied. "This region is a place of refuge that only our people can come to. We are completely safe as long as we remain here. The Minions cannot enter this area. In fact, they can't even *see* it."

"We have a similar region in the Abyss. I like to refer to it as our *demilitarized zone*," Mephistos said.

"Each plane of Hell also has such DMZs," Galya added. "Even demons and devils need places of refuge on occasion."

"This region stretches almost to the mouth of the canyon. The moment we step outside of it, the Minions will fall upon us with all of their fury. We'll have to fight our way to the canyon," Alyana explained.

"How far is it to the canyon?" asked Arka-Dal.

Alyana shrugged.

"It's difficult to say as time and distances have no meaning here—at least not in the way you think of them," she said. "We'll get there when we get there."

As they strolled across the rocky landscape, the Devil related the tale of how Arka-Dal and Galya met and fell in love to a very curious Mephistos. Alyana walked one step behind them and listened intently.

"And their love is true?" she asked.

"As true as the very fabric of the universe," the Devil assured her. "Does that surprise you?"

"Yes it does. I never thought such a love was even possible. It's like one of the fairy tales humans are so fond of," she said.

The Devil smiled.

"I, too, never thought such a thing was possible. But there is no doubting it. Galya forsook everything she stood for to be with him and he willingly risked his life on more than one occasion to protect her without a thought for his own safety," he said.

"If that's not love, then there is no such thing," Mephistos said.

"He wed your daughter and asked nothing for himself in return?" Alyana asked.

"All he asked for was her hand in marriage," the Devil replied. "I sent Galya to tempt him with offers of more power and wealth and a greater empire and fame. He told her that he already had more of those things than he ever desired or deserved and wanted nothing more. All he wanted was for his people to live in peace and prosper. He is one of those rare people who are above such temptations. He cannot be corrupted."

"At all?" Alyana asked.

"At all," the Devil replied. "I sent Galya to abase him and drag him down. Instead, he elevated her in ways I never thought possible."

He smiled as Galya and Arka-Dal walked in front of them hand-in-hand.

"And Galya is truly happy. To me, that is the most important thing," he said.

"And what about *you*, Lucifer?" asked Mephistos. "Are you happy with this situation?"

"I'm *delighted*!" the Devil beamed.

"So who is more powerful now? The Devil or the Emperor of Thule?" Alyana asked.

The Devil laughed.

"I think I will allow *you to* decide that," he said.

"So did you win or lose this one?" asked Mephistos.

"Both," the Devil said.

"I think we *all* won, Father," Galya said over her shoulder. "I know that I did."

"I certainly have no complaints," Arka-Dal added.

"Nor do I—and I absolutely adore my grand children," the Devil said with a touch of obvious pride.

Michael was a few paces behind them listening.

"What," he wondered, "would God have thought of this? He sure as Hell wouldn't have approved of such a union."

Then he smiled.

"Who cares what he'd think? God is dead!"

Arka-Dal looked around and raised his hand to call a halt.

"Let's rest here awhile," he decided.

"But not too long, my love. The Beast is stirring even as we speak," Galya reminded him.

"I can use a rest right now. Every muscle in my back and shoulders is screaming with pain right now," Kashi said as he sat down against a large rock. "That was one hell of a gauntlet we just ran."

His tunic and trousers were ripped in several places and deep, red scratches could be seen on his bare flesh. Pandaar was in the same condition. Jun was breathing hard but didn't have a scratch thanks to his blue titanium armor.

"Great fun, eh, my friend?" Pandaar said as he slapped Jun's shoulder.

"I can think of other things to do that are much more amusing than this. But it'll do for now," Jun said stoically. "Every time I swing my ax or sword, I kill something. Yet they keep increasing in numbers and ferocity."

"That was just the beginning. We'll have to run an even worse gauntlet when leave this zone. It will get much worse than that once we enter the canyon," Alyana warned. "That's where the *heaviest* fighting will take place."

"That makes me feel so much better!" Pandaar quipped as he plopped down next to Kashi. "I was worried that the battle might taper off."

Michael walked to where Perseus rested and sat down next to him. The Greek was bathed in sweat and cut in several places. He grinned at the Archangel, then laughed.

Michael squinted at him.

"Why do you laugh?" he queried.

"I laugh because the sheer irony of this mission amuses me. You especially amuse me, given your history against these creatures," Perseus said.

"I know what you mean," Michael said. "Because of my service to Arka-Dal, I now find myself fighting side-by-side with the very demons I fought against so many centuries ago. I also find that I am allied to the very creatures of darkness I sought to destroy."

"Life is filled with such ironies. I suppose that's what makes it worth living," Perseus said. "I spent the first few decades of my life hunting down and killing Gorgons. I chased Medusa to Thule to slay her. Now, thanks to my service to the Empire, I am sworn to protect her. Since I've come to know and like Medusa, I feel great sorrow for having killed her sisters. This is my small way of making amends."

"You mean like a *penance*?" Michael asked.

"You could call it that," Perseus said with a grin. "To add to my personal irony, my brethren and I also hunted Minotaurs. Now, I serve directly under Jun in the Northern Army."

"Your life has also taken some very ironic turns," Michael said.

Perseus laughed.

"I'm Greek. Our lives are either tragic or ironic. But I think your bit of irony trumps mine," he said.

Galya saw Arka-Dal conferring with Merlin and her father and decided to give them some alone time. She found a large boulder and sat against it. She saw Alyana walk toward her and smiled.

"How did you do it?" Alyana asked as she sat down next to her.

"Do what?" asked Galya.

"Win the heart of Arka-Dal," she replied.

"Honestly, it was the other way around. I came to seduce him and change him. Instead of fleeing in fear or succumbing to my temptations, he greeted me with admiration and respect and declared me to be an emissary from my Father to his court. When Merlin and Gorinna tried to attack me, he intervened on my behalf and forbade them to harm me in any manner while I was guest in his house. No one had ever done that for me before," Galya said.

"Wow!" Alyana exclaimed. "He actually *protected* you? Even knowing who you are?"

Galya smiled and nodded.

"Arka-Dal is unlike any other man who has ever walked the Earth. He has an honor and nobility about him that is real and natural. He is the kindest, wisest, bravest, most just and loving man I've ever known. Father sent me to change him. Instead, he changed me—and Father to some extent," she said.

"What else is there about him?" Alyana asked.

"He is very modest about his achievements. Although he rules a vast empire, power does not go to his head. He is fiercely loyal to his family, his friends and the people of Thule. And all are just as loyal to him," Galya explained.

"You make him sound almost godlike!" Alyana said.

"Arka-Dal would blush deeply if he heard you say that. He doesn't feel he's anyone special. That's another reason he is well-loved," Galya said.

"Are you not jealous of his other wives?" Alyana asked.

"No. We are closer than most sisters and the best of friends. We love and support each other and we all have a hand in raising our children. And we all know where we stand in regards to Mayumi. She is Arka-Dal's first wife and the Empress of Thule. Mayumi is a very special person, too. In fact, we'd all gladly die to protect her—and she us," Galya said.

"And this is what the humans call true love?" Alyana asked.

"Yes," Galya replied.

"Then I really have no chance with him?" Alyana asked.

"None at all," Galya said smugly. "Not until you change your ways and show him that your changes are genuine. I think you have a very long way to go before you can do that."

Alyana nodded.

"I have never been attracted to anyone. Nor have I had any contact with humans. Until now, I stayed within our own realm. This war has brought changes to me. To us all. I am not sure how to behave anymore," she said.

Galya laughed.

"I know exactly how you feel," she said. "Until I met Arka-Dal, I treated all humans with utter contempt. Our love for each other has opened my eyes and enabled me to see things in humans that I had never bothered to notice."

"Did your love for him weaken you?" Alyana asked.

"Not at all. In fact, it made me even stronger," Galya replied. "But not in ways you think."

"I don't understand," Alyana said.

"You will after a while," Galya assured her. "There is something special about Arka-Dal and Mayumi. Something intangible that brings out the best in all of our natures. It's hard to explain in mere words. It's something you'd have to experience for yourself."

"Is that an invitation?" Alayan asked.

Galya laughed.

"Not really. But if Arka-Dal sees fit to invite you to visit Thule, I'll do my best to treat you as an honored guest. But if you get out of line or do something I don't like, I promise you that you'll regret it."

"I doubt that you'll need to concern yourself with that. I'm certain that Arka-Dal will never invite me to visit Thule after the impression I made on him," Alyana said.

"You're probably right. I hate to admit it, but I'm starting to like you—sort of," Galya said.

"I'm starting to like you, too. Maybe after this is over with, we can become friends?" Alyana suggested.

Galya smiled.

"Don't count on it," she said. "Did I hear you say that you've never had sex?"

"That's right. None at all," Alyana replied.

"Do you ever *desire* it?" asked Galya, somewhat intrigued by her new ally.

"Even if I do, it would not matter," Alyana said. "Just *whom* would I have sex with? Our soldiers are non-sexual and nearly mindless and, although there are many handsome and eligible men in our realm, they are also out of the question."

"Why is that?" asked Galya.

"None would have the courage to even approach me because I am Azathoth's daughter and they fear my father. To them, I am unapproachable. Hands off. Taboo," Alyana explained sadly.

"Are you *lonely*?" Galya asked.

Alyana smiled.

"What do *you* think?" she asked. "How did *you* feel before you met Arka-Dal?"

"Empty," Galya admitted.

"Now you know how I feel," Alyana said.

"Perhaps when this is over, you'll find someone," Galya said. "If I did, so can you."

Alyana laughed.

"I am no seductress. I don't even know how to talk to a man. I've already offended Arka-Dal. He probably will not speak to me again!" she said.

Galya smiled.

"I'm sure he's already put that aside," she said. "He is not one to dwell on a person's missteps," she said.

"I guess you don't either," Alyana observed.

"Why do you say that?" Galya asked.

"Well, you *are* speaking with me now. I meant no offense when I made my comments earlier. I've just no experience in social matters," Alyana said.

"So I've noticed," Galya said. "I speak with you because I consider you a potential rival and I want to understand just how much of a rival you might become. We've also entered into a rather tenuous alliance between our peoples and I don't want to sink this ship before it sails."

"I like you, too," Alyana laughed. "I'm surprised that you think I might be a rival."

"As beautiful as *you* are, I can't think otherwise. That's why I have to keep a close eye on you," Galya said with a grin.

"No one has ever said such nice things about me before," Alyana smiled. "Do you think Arka-Dal might find me attractive?"

"I'm sure he does. Any man would—unless he's the type who prefers other men or he's stone blind. I'm sure that many women would also find you attractive," Galya said.

"Do you?" Alyana teased.

Galya laughed.

"Let's not go there for now," she said.

A few yards away, Gorinna stood atop a boulder and looked out across what was, perhaps, the bleakest landscape she'd ever beheld. There were literally miles upon miles of blackened, ugly ground, its surface dotted with boulders, twisted leafless branches, and pools of bubbling slime and columns of rising purple smoke. The scene both depressed and intrigued her.

"So this is the realm of the Others," she said aloud.

"Only a tiny part of it," Alyana said as she climbed up and stood next to her. "There are larger parts. Some are just as barren. Some are less so. Yet this is the realm we call home. The realm that the Minions of the Beast want to drive us from."

"We won't let them," Gorinna vowed.

Alyana laughed.

Gorinna gave her quizzical look.

"I laugh because I know that when the Red Witch gives her word, she keeps it," Alyana explained. "So does the Demon Slayer."

"Arka-Dal never breaks a vow," Gorinna assured her.

"May I ask you something?" Alyana queried.

"Ask," Gorinna said.

"The one called Kashi is your mate, yet you have deep affection for Arka-Dal," Alyana said.

"Am I so transparent?" Gorinna asked.

"Yes. As the humans like to say, you wear your heart on your sleeve. By the way you look at Arka-Dal, I sense that you are lovers," Alyana said.

Gorinna smiled.

"Sometimes," she admitted. "We have known each other for a very long time. My feelings for him are—"

"---deep and strong," Alyana finished. "I also sense that Kashi knows this. Yet he remains fiercely loyal to Arka-Dal. I do not understand."

"The bond between Kashi and Arka-Dal was forged in the fires of countless battles and ordeals—as with all of us. That bond cannot be broken. Kashi not only understands, he *encourages* us to fulfill our desires. He said that my body is mine to give to whomever I please as long as I return to him afterward," Gorinna said.

"You humans are a strange lot," Alyana said. "I have much to learn."

"Yes, you do," Gorinna said with a smile. "So do it."

"I would like to be like you. I would like to be Arka-Dal's sometimes lover. But I fear that I have already repelled him," Alyana said. "How can I get him to look favorably upon me?"

Gorinna shrugged.

"Be yourself---but less, er, *demonic*. Do you know what I mean?" she suggested.

"I'm not sure. I will have to think about this," Alyana said as she jumped down from the boulder.

Gorinna smiled as she walked away.

"I hope you never do, Alyana. I don't need the competition!" she thought.

Alyana walked over to Merlin.

"What advice did Gorinna offer?" he asked.

"She told me to be myself," Alyana answered.

"And what is the real Alyana like?" asked Merlin.

Alyana thought it over and shook her head.

"I really don't know," she admitted. "I've always been what my father calls a 'holy terror'. A real, nasty bitch, especially in battle," she said.

"In that case, you need be *less* of a bitch. You need to reach down inside yourself, find the *real* Alyana, and release her. You must let the inner you shine through," Merlin explained.

"But what *is* the inner me?" she asked.

"That, my dear, is something only *you* can discover—just as Galya did," he said.

"Is such a thing even possible for one such as me?" she asked. "After all a tiger cannot change its stripes."

Merlin nodded toward Galya.

"*That* tiger did. So can you—if you really desire to," he said. "Granted, it will not be easy, but it can be done. Just don't expect it to happen overnight. And don't try to fake a change. Arka-Dal is very perceptive. He'll see through it immediately."

Alyana nodded as she let his advice sink in. Merlin had left out another, almost insurmountable obstacle: Galya was incredibly beautiful. In fact, she was by far, the most beautiful woman Alyana had ever seen. As long as Galya was at his side, Arka-Dal would have eyes for no one else.

After listening to all the advice from others, she decided to find Arka-Dal and ask him what traits he wanted most in a wife. She found him seated against what used to be a tree and walked over. He smiled as she sat down next to him.

"Can I ask you something?" she queried.

He nodded.

"What characteristics do you want most in a mate?" she asked.

"That's easy. It's the same traits all of my wives have. Trust, honesty, loyalty, intelligence, logic and passion," he replied. "I must be able to trust her above all others. She must be open and honest with me at all times and be at my side through good and bad times—especially the bad times. And she has to share the passions I have for her, our children, our nation and its people and be able to make good, well-thought out decisions when necessary."

"That's quite a list," Alyana said. "And you say that each of your wives posses these qualities?"

"Each and every one of them," he assured her.

"What about beauty and sex appeal?" she asked.

"If a woman has all of the qualities I've mentioned, then she is *already* beautiful and sexy," he said.

Alyana nodded.

"I have no chance of competing with them. I possess few of those qualities—maybe *none,*" she said.

Arka-Dal laughed.

"But you *do* have those qualities. You just don't realize it yet," he said with a smile.

"How do you know this?" she asked.

"I already see many of them in you," he replied.

"You do?" Alyana asked. "Really?"

"Yes," he assured her.

"I had no idea," she said in astonishment.

"You will, eventually, when this war is ended and you have time to relax and think," Arka-Dal said. "I imagine that Galya was a lot like you during the Forever Wars. She's very different now."

"I, er, apologize if I offended you earlier. I can't believe I actually said that. I'm so stupid!" she said.

"You're not stupid. You're socially naive. You blurt out exactly what's on your mind without considering the consequences. It's kind of childlike and innocent in a way. As charming as it seems, it can lead you into a lot of trouble. You need to stop and think before you speak. That's a skill you'll have to learn if you want to keep dealing with different people," he said.

"I'm truly sorry I said that. Please forgive me," she said softly.

He detected the sincerity in her voice and smiled.

"Apology accepted," he said.

She beamed at him.

The Devil saw Galya standing against what was nearly a tree. She was busy eyeing Alyana as she walked across the clearing. He walked over to his daughter. She smiled at him.

"How do you feel about Alyana?" he asked as he nodded toward her.

"I *detest* her," Galya said flatly.

"No—you don't," the Devil countered.

"Why do you say that?" Galya asked.

"Since you've been married to Arka-Dal, I feel that you no longer have the capacity to detest anyone. If you truly detested Alyana, the two of you would already have fought each other—perhaps even to the death. Instead, aside from a few barbs, you've been surprisingly civil toward her," the Devil said.

Galya laughed.

"I thought it best to restrain myself for the sake of this alliance," she said.

"Is that all?" the Devil pressed.

"Well, perhaps there's a little more to it," Galya half admitted.

"I thought so. Shall I tell you what that is?" the Devil asked.

Galya nodded.

"Alyana reminds you of *yourself* many years ago. You were much like her in many ways, especially during the wars. That makes you feel some sort of connection with her. And, despite what you've said, I sense that you *like* her," he said.

"Well—maybe a *little*," Galya replied. "But if she makes a play for Arka-Dal, I'll rip her eyeballs from their sockets and feed them to the Beast. And *that* you can wager on, Father!"

The Devil laughed.

"We shall see, my dear," he said.

"Let's get moving again," Arka-Dal said as he stood and looked around. "The more time we waste, the more time that Beast has to wake itself up."

They walked on for a great distance as they watched the ever-increasing numbers of the Minions that were circling overhead. As soon as they set foot outside the protected zone, hordes of the screaming, howling monsters attacked them from all sides. Galya's crack legions again provided them with excellent cover and managed to keep the major portion of the Minions at bay. The few that did manage to break through met their deaths on the blades of the weapons carried by Arka-Dal and his determined band.

But the numbers of the Minions kept increasing as more and more appeared to join the ever widening battle. And more and more of them managed to get past Galya's legions and attack Arka-Dal and his team with ever increasing ferocity. Before long, heads, limbs, weapons and battered pieces of armor and shields flew in all directions and the black dust of the dying Minions nearly obscured their vision. It filled their nostrils and mouths and caused some of them to cough and choke and sneeze.

As Alyana beheaded one of her attackers, she glanced over at Galya who was busily dispatching two others with her twin swords.

"That makes 29 I've killed so far," she boasted.

"I'm up to 44. You'd best step it up," Galya said as she disemboweled yet another. "That makes 45!"

"Bitch!" Alyana growled as she redoubled her efforts and counted out loud as she slew one after another with incredible ease.

"That's 30...31...32...33...34.."

Galya counted also.

"Fifty...51...52...53..."

After several hours of fighting over rugged, rocky ground, they found themselves standing before a large vertical crack in the face of the mountain. For the moment, the Minions had broken off their attack and were slowly regrouping high above them.

"There's the entrance to the canyon," Alyana said. Then she turned to Galya.

"How many have you killed thus far?" she asked.

"Seventy-seven," Galya said. "And you?"

"The same. I guess we are equally good at killing Minions," Alyana said. "There are far more waiting inside that canyon. Far too many to bother counting."

"I know," Galya said. "I can *smell* them. Truce?"

"Truce!" Alyana agreed.

They looked at Arka-Dal who was wiping black dust from the blade of Excalibur.

"I don't count them. I just kill them," he said flatly.

The ladies laughed, both at the intent of his comment and how silly he made them feel about their rivalry.

"I see what you mean about him now," Alyana said. "He admonished us without saying a single harsh word. It's what my father always does."

"Mine, too," Galya said.

Merlin, the Devil and Mephistos chuckled. Ned simply smiled and nodded at Arka-Dal for his subtle way of defusing and rebuking the rivalry between Galya and Alyana.

"You're right, Cousin," Mephistos remarked. "He *is* good."

Arka-Dal studied the entrance to the canyon. Alyana had described it in great detail. It sliced jaggedly through the black cliffs. In some places, it was wide enough for five people to walk abreast. In others, it narrowed to allow just two to pass at a time. The cliffs on either side were made of a hard black stone and almost featureless. They soared hundreds of feet upward on either side and came almost together at the top in some areas. The canyon trail was loosely packed, littered with small rocks, boulders and hideous-looking shrubs. It rose, sunk and leveled off intermittently and one had to climb over piles of debris in some places to get through.

Alyana had also warned them about the places where the shadows were very deep. It was there the Minions liked to wait in ambush.

"The canyon is heavily protected by those things. They'll come at us from everywhere. The ground, the walls of the cliffs, even from thin air. The closer we get to the lair, the heavier the fighting will become," she said.

"How far did you and your men get?" asked Arka-Dal.

"That's impossible to say. Halfway, maybe more," Alyana replied. "This canyon wasn't here 1,000 years ago. Then, one day, there was a horrific cracking sound that could be heard in every corner of our land. We only discovered the canyon after the Minions began to emerge from it. This is the gateway to the Beast."

Arka-Dal noticed her shudder and touched her shoulder.

"You don't have to go back in there," he said.

"Yes I do," she said.

"I understand," he said softly.

Galya smiled and nodded at her to show that she also understood and would be with her to the end.

"Let's get this show on the road," Arka-Dal said.

He raised his hand, then pointed. Both Kashi and Pandaar moved stealthily ahead to scout it. They returned a few moments later.

"It's very quiet. Too damned quiet," Kashi said.

"They know we're here. I can sense it. They're just waiting for us to go in so they can butcher us," Pandaar added.

"I'm not in the mood to be butchered," Arka-Dal said. "But I wouldn't mind doing some butchering myself."

The Devil stepped forward and stared into the crevice.

"I see a smoldering pit at the end of the canyon. Alyana is right. This will lead us directly to the lair of the Beast," he said. "We'll have to fight our way to it with every resource at our command. Galya's legions will guard our rear and prevent the Minions from overwhelming us."

"How far to the pit?" asked Arka-Dal.

"Space, time and distances have no meaning here. We'll just keep going until we reach it. This isn't the world you know, Arka-Dal. Here, physical laws do not apply," Mephistos said.

"But those things can still kill us?" Pandaar asked.

Merlin nodded.

"Oh, yes!" he assured him.

Pandaar laughed and drew his sword.

"It's a good day to die," he said.

"We go in together and come out together. *No one* dies. *No one* gets left behind," Arka-Dal said. "Watch the shadows and cover each other."

Alyana smiled and drew her sword.

"Those things nearly killed me before. This time, it is *they* who will die," she said.

"Let me remind you that although Excalibur does provide you with limitless energy when wielding it in combat, it cannot make you invulnerable.," Merlin advised. "You still risk being harmed or even killed by the Beast and its Minions, so try not to be your usual reckless self. You alone can wield Excalibur and only it can slay the Beast. You must reach its lair in one piece."

Arka-Dal grinned at him.

"Don't worry, Merlin. I have no intention of getting myself killed," he said.

"And I'll make sure you don't get killed," Galya vowed.

"We *all* will make sure," Alyana said. "Without you, we have little hope of slaying the Beast. We'll make certain that you reach that pit alive."

The path through the canyon was a gauntlet of nightmarish proportions. As they made their way along the narrow, twisting path, countless scores of the Minions attacked them from every direction imaginable.

They swooped at them from above. They sprang up from the ground. They emerged from the walls of the cliffs and the deep shadows and even materialized from thin air. All were ugly, twisted, well-armed and filled with fury and hate.

And they fell just as quickly as they appeared.

Alyana led the way. With each step she took, she found herself hacking off a limb, a head or cutting something to pieces. As the body parts and torsos hit the ground, they turned to dust and more Minions sprang forth from the dust. Alyana sliced off heads and arms that emerged from the ground and gutted each and every Minion who sought to bar her path and she never looked back.

Arka-Dal marveled at her incredible skill, nimbleness and courage as he followed close behind. He battered demons out of his way with his shield and ran them through with Excalibur then managed to slay others with his backswing as they tried to stop him. Each swing of his sword met and passed through demonic flesh and bone and elicited loud, painful howls from his opponents.

Behind him was Galya, with a sword in each hand, deftly carving a path of death and destruction through the hordes of Minions. Dressed as she was in her onyx armor and war helmet, she looked every bit like a goddess of war. Arka-Dal watched from the corner of his eye and smiled.

It was easy to see why her father had placed Galya in command of Hell's best legions.

It was even easier to see why god's army had no chance against her in battle. Her skill and ferocity almost awed him. She was veritable whirlwind of death and destruction and it made him glad that he never would have to face her in open combat.

Galya was indeed in her element now.

Behind her fought Michael and the Devil. Once bitter enemies, the two fought side-by-side like brothers-in-arms. Michael noticed that the Devil seemed to be remarkably skillful with a sword and told him so.

"Magic proved to be of little use during the Forever War. Because of this, Galya and I became experts in the use of all known weapons," he shouted above the din of battle.

To prove his point, he deftly side-stepped a lunging Minion and severed him in two on the fly as he kicked another in the face and finished it off with a downstroke that clove its head from crown to chin. On the return stroke, he disemboweled three more without missing a beat. It occurred to Michael that he'd never seen god actually participate in a battle. He always stayed in his lair and sent others out to do his fighting for him. He was too cowardly to lead his armies himself, while Galya and her father were always in the thick of things. They always led from the front.

"There's no end to these creatures!" Michael thought as he smashed in the face of a Minion with his shield and beheaded two others with a swing of his sword.

No matter where he turned, he came face-to-face with one of them. The more he killed, the more appeared to take their places. It was a lot like the battles he'd fought against the Devil's armies.

Mephistos and Ned followed close behind. Ned used what limited spells the strange makeup of the Others' realm allowed him to cast to slay bunches of Minions at a time while Mephistos took particular delight in swinging a sinister black battle ax with incredible and deadly ferocity.

"We're killing scores!" Ned observed.

"But more keep coming to take their places. There seems to be no end to these things!" Mephistos shouted as he hacked and chopped his way through demon after demon after demon until the black dust of their remains crunched beneath his boots.

Behind them came Gorinna and Merlin who used a combination of magic and swords to kill anything that dared to stand in their way. Both quickly realized that their spells now had limited range and power. This forced them to rely more and more on their weapons.

"Where'd you learn to use a sword like that?" Gorinna asked.

"Long ago, before I became a wizard, I was a warrior. I'm not as skillful as I once was, but I can still hold my own against mindless brutes like these," he shouted back above the din of battle.

Perseus was hot on their heels, battering his way through walls of demons with his shield and slashing at them as he moved past. After a while, his sword began to feel like lead weight and his shoulders ached from the strain. But he gritted his teeth and fought on because there was nothing else to do. To stop was to die.

Jun, Pandaar and Kashi were far to the rear and engaged in the fight of their lives as Minions assailed them from everywhere at once. The more they killed, the more appeared to replace them. The Minions spotted Jun at the rear of the party and descended on him in an effort to cut him off from the others. Jun saw them charging toward him and stopped. He pounded his chest with a fist and roared his challenge.

"Bring it, bastards! Let me see what you've got!" he growled.

Clad in his blue titanium armor, Jun resembled a living tank as he swung his huge sword with both hands and steadily carved a path through what appeared to be a veritable wall of the monsters. Each swing met—and passed through—demonic flesh and bone with ease and covered the ground around him with layers of black dust.

Up ahead, Alyana fought with a fury born of her loathing for the Minions and the Beast that spawned them and her determination to find and kill the creature. Her sword strokes were lightning-quick, accurate and deadly.

She slew them by the dozens.

But the Minions kept coming.

They swarmed around them, lashed out with swords, spears, axes, talons and teeth. They growled, hissed, cursed, threatened, spat venom, screamed in agony and died as they group steadily advanced through the canyon.

It would have been a bloodbath *if* the Minions could bleed. Instead, each one that died added its dust to those who had fallen before it. The only blood spilled was that of members of the group as demonic weapons found their marks time and again. Pandaar, Kashi, Perseus, Gorinna and even Arka-Dal were tattooed with minor cuts, scrapes, gashes and bruises, which they ignored as they continued to fight on and on...

The battle was, by far, the wildest any of them had ever fought. The canyon was wide enough to walk four abreast in most places, but narrowed in others so that only two people could walk through at a time. In some places, it suddenly widened. It was in the wider places that the battle became more ferocious.

More deadly.

The Minions were bound and determined to keep them from reaching the pit. They were just as determined to reach the pit and kill the Beast.

One waited until Galya was directly beneath him and launched himself off the face of the cliff. Before it could land a blow, Alyana intercepted it in mid-air, seized it by the throat and wrestled it to the ground.

Galya looked up just in time to see the two collide above her and dodged out of the way as they plummeted to the ground. When the dust cleared, she saw Alyana straddle the thing and drive the point of her sword through its face. The Minion fell to dust as it died.

Alyana grinned at Galya

"Thanks—but I could have handled him just as easily," Galya said.

"If you say so," Alyana smirked as more came at them.

The Minions swirled menacingly around them like hideous black tides and slashed at them with their weapons, talons and even teeth. Any of the things who came within reach were killed quickly. For each Minion that died, another—or two—appeared in its place. The battle raged on and on. And the distances between members of the party steadily increased.

Somehow, Perseus found himself to the rear of the group. He had been fighting alongside Jun for the past hour but had lost sight of the Minotaur when the latest wave of demons swarmed over them. He had no time to worry about Jun. He was up to his neck in demons and was struggling to keep up with the rest of the group.

Just as Perseus dispatched one foe, a second, much larger one appeared behind him. He turned and raised his shield. The ensuing blow resounded through the canyon and sent him hurtling into the side of the cliff. He struck hard enough to dislodge a few rocks along with his helmet and landed on his hands and knees. As he shook the cobwebs from his brain, the Minions moved in for the kill.

Again, Perseus raised his shield.

This time, the blow bent the shield and drove Perseus to the ground. As he lay akimbo, the creature straddled him and hissed.

"Now you die, human," it said as it bared its jagged teeth.

Unable to move, Perseus closed his eyes and awaited what would surely be the fatal blow.

It never landed.

From out of nowhere, Michael appeared and crashed into it shield first. The force of the collision sent the creature sprawling and, before it could regain its feet, Michael ran it through. The Minions hissed and melted into the earth.

Michael walked over and extended his hand to Perseus. The Greek took it and Michael helped him back to his feet. He then handed him his helmet and sword.

"Are you alright?" Michael asked.

"I think my left arm is broken. It hurts like Hell but I'm still alive thanks to you," Perseus replied as he gingerly placed his helmet back on.

"Since you apparently no longer have the use of your arm, maybe you should turn back?" Michael suggested.

Perseus grinned and shook his head.

"As long as I still have one good arm left, I will continue to fight. Let's catch up with the others before we miss most of the fun," he said bravely.

Michael smiled and the pair charged back into the thick of the battle.

A few yards away, Pandaar and Kashi were engaged in the fight of their lives as demons of all sizes, shapes and demeanors emerged from the canyon walls, floor and swooped down at them from above. Every swing of Kashi's sword either clanged against an enemy's weapon or slashed through flesh and bone. The air around them was thick with the sounds of swooshing blades, curses and cries of pain and anger as demon after demon met their ends and showered the combatants with fine black dust. Kashi's tunic was cut in several places and his arms ached from swinging his sword, but he grimly fought on.

Stopping, even for a moment, would mean death.

As Pandaar finished off a particularly nasty Minion by thrusting his shortsword through its face, another demon appeared behind him and reached for his shoulder. He saw it out of the corner of his eye and eluded its attempt to grab him. At the same time, he twisted around and lopped its arm off at the shoulder with his longsword. The Minion bellowed and struck him in the chest with the war club it carried in its other hand. The blow sent Pandaar tumbling head over heels for several years. He landed on his hands and knees and tried to shake the cobwebs from his brain as the Minion moved in to make the kill.

Kashi saw Pandaar's dilemma.

He quickly whirled around and decapitated his latest opponent. Then he leaped over its crumbling corpse and buried his sword in the skull of

Pandaar's would-be slayer. As the Minion died, it rained black dust all over Pandaar, who coughed and spat it out.

"Couldn't you have made it fall somewhere else besides on me?" he asked as Kashi helped him to his feet.

"Ingrate! Next time, I'll mind my own business and let these things finish you," Kashi countered.

Before they could say another word, several more of the Minions emerged from the walls and charged straight at them.

"I know I always say that I love a good fight, but this is ridiculous!" Pandaar shouted as the battle continued.

He quickly beheaded one and gutted another on the backstroke. At the same time, he ducked to avoid the blade of a third demon and delivered a killing stroke to its chest. But more rose up to replace them.

Kashi didn't reply. He was too busy fighting for every inch of ground he could gain. The Minions were everywhere now and there seemed to be no limit to their numbers. Just as they felt they were about to be overwhelmed, both Perseus and Michael hurtled into the fray and cleared a path through the startled Minions with their heavy swords.

Pandaar and Kashi followed in their wake and steadily fought their way toward Arka-Dal and the others. After what seemed like an eternity of endless and near hopeless combat, they caught up with Gorinna, the Devil, Jun, Merlin and Mephistos. They were seated against the canyon wall.

"This area seems unusually quiet," Michael said as he looked around. "Where is the Emperor?"

"Arka-Dal, Galya and Alyana are somewhere up ahead. I lost sight of them hours ago," Merlin replied.

Michael nodded and charged down the canyon after them.

"Why is it so quiet here?" asked Kashi as Gorinna hugged him.

"We combined our powers to create a safe zone so we can rest," she said.

"We sure can use a break. My entire body aches and I've been cut in several places," Kashi said as he showed her the ones on his upper arms.

"This should stop the bleeding," Gorinna said as she applied a gentle healing spell.

Kashi sighed as the pleasant sensations wafted through his battered body like a soft breeze.

"How long will this shield last?" asked Perseus as he plopped down next to Mephistos.

"Not much longer. I can sense it weakening already," the Devil replied. "Our powers are severely limited here. This place follows a different set of natural and supernatural laws. We can still cast some minor spells but they are less than half as potent as they are normally."

"The physics are skewed here," Mephistos added.

The immediate area around them was now eerily quiet. Arka-Dal, Galya, Alyana and Michael kept walking. As they did, they watched every shadow. Every nook and cranny of the canyon walls.

Seven of the monsters suddenly sprang at Alyana. She hissed menacingly and dispatched each of them with lightning-like ease. She turned and saw Arka-Dal smiling at her.

She smiled back.

"What do you think of me now, Demon Slayer?" she asked.

"I'm almost awed by your fighting skills and courage," he replied.

She laughed.

"My anger and hatred for the Minions and their foul father fuels my courage. My fighting skills are like Galya's. They have been honed by untold centuries of nearly constant battles. Is that all about me that you like?" she asked.

"Well, you're quite beautiful in a fierce, almost poetic sense. And when you relax your guard, I can see a softer side to you. You need to let that out more often," he answered honestly.

"You're not what I expected," she said. "You're different."

"Oh?" he queried.

"Not many of your race would come to the aid of the likes of us. Unlike other humans I've heard of, you seem to be quite comfortable among us," she said.

"His attitude amazed me as well," Galya said. "Arka-Dal doesn't view Devils and Demons as terrifying monsters like most humans do. To him, we are simply other races of people and he treats us as such."

"Do you feel that way about *my* people, too?" Alyana asked.

"Of course," Arka-Dal assured her.

"That is very generous and open minded of you. In fact, it's refreshing. Would the other people of Thule look upon us in the same light?" Alyana asked.

"Most of them would," Galya said.

"Thule sounds like a wonderful place. I'd love to see it," Alyana said.

"Perhaps you will one day," Arka-Dal said.

"Not if *I* can help it," Galya said.

"If you do visit Thule, you'd best work on letting that better side of you come out. The side you showed earlier," Arka-Dal said.

Galya glared at them but said nothing.

Alyana saw her expression and smiled. Her smile irritated Galya further, which pleased Alyana.

"If I have such a side, I am not aware of it," she said. "It comes out on its own and I cannot control it."

"Well, I *like* it," Arka-Dal said.

"No one has ever said such a thing to me. Of course, I've only spoken with my father and the soldiers we both command. I have no experience with humans or other races. I just lead our soldiers into battles," Alyana said almost modestly.

"That's another thing you do very well," Galya said.

Her comment surprised Alyana. She nodded her head respectfully to acknowledge it.

"I am not nearly as good as you are. Your victories are legendary, even in our bleak realm," she said. "Many of my people look upon you as a kind of goddess of war. I think they even pray to you before a battle."

Galya laughed.

"I owe my success to my legions. They made me," she said.

"I feel the same about our soldiers. A commander is only as good as the soldiers who follow her," Alyana agreed.

"I'm starting to like you—a little, anyway," Galya said.

"Well, that's a start, isn't it?" Alyana said.

"Here they come again!" shouted Michael as he moved to intercept another wave of Minions.

Azathoth stood atop the peak and watched as the waves of battling demons and Minions undulated across the field. The battle was a virtual draw as neither side gave an inch. The demons held their ground tenaciously against countless numbers of Minions who threw themselves at them with a fierce and wild abandon. As the casualties continued to mount, more and more Minions entered the fray in large, compact waves which broke against the shields of the stubborn demons.

As the battle grew even more heated, more violent and fierce, Azathoth decided to gamble. He ordered several of his legions in the rear to disengage from the front lines and attempt to encircle the Minions from the right and left. At the same time, the sky above was the scene of a most bizarre dogfight as thousands of bat and insect-winged demons fought each other to the death and showered the combatants below with battered shields, weapons and body parts.

The noise, mayhem and constantly shifting units of soldiers begat chaos and bloodshed on an epic scale. There were literally millions of demons battling on the plains with more and more Minions flooding into the fight with each passing minute. The battle now covered an area as far as the eye could see and was spreading further. Despite the overwhelming odds, Azathoth's combined armies stood their ground. Each of them knew what was at stake and each was determined not to retreat.

The battle seemed to be going in tides, like waves crashing against rocks. Azathoth's troops surged, retook some ground, then retreated as a more massive wave of Minions crashed into them. The demons would stop, regroup and counterattack, driving the Minions before them, only to have their advances halted by yet another, massive influx of enemy troops.

Azathoth was not only able to respond to the constant shifts. He was able to hold his own lines intact and launch occasional counter attacks whenever a gap appeared in enemy lines. These attacks forced more and more Minions to respond to plug the holes and kept their attention from Arka-Dal and the others.

He decided to try a new tactic. He turned to his generals who were watching the carnage with him.

"Gar, take five divisions and circle around to the left. And you, Xxrkk, take five more divisions and circle to the right. When you're in position, attack from the flanks with all of the fury your men can muster. Cut the enemy off and slaughter them where they stand and keep attacking until you're told otherwise," he instructed.

The generals bowed their heads slightly and hurried off to carry out their orders. One of the other generals, a big brute of a Demon named Harrakk, shook his head. Azathoth raised an eyebrow at him.

"You disapprove?" he asked.

"Yes. The maneuver will not carry the battle. The Minions are too many and their numbers increase with each passing second," the general said.

"True it will not give us a victory. But it will buy Arka-Dal and the others precious time to find and slay the Beast," Azathoth said.

Harrakk nodded.

"My soldiers stand ready whenever you need them, Lord Azathoth," he assured him.

"Thank you, General. They may be needed sooner than you expect," Azathoth replied as he turned his eyes back to the field.

Azathoth knew he couldn't hold the line forever. Sooner or later, his quickly diminishing forces would be forced to retreat from the field. Before that could happen, he hoped Arka-Dal would be able to slay the Beast.

At that point, he spotted a larger horde of Minions gathering far to the west and sent 10,000 of Harrakk's troops to intercept them. He watched as the two forces collided like twin tornadoes and cringed as the battle suddenly doubled in scope and fury.

A few minutes later, one of his scouts called his attention to yet another, even larger force of Minions approaching from the east only to be rudely intercepted by Gar's divisions as they completed their encirclement.

Worlds away, Arka-Dal's wives were seated around the long table in the Archives, anxiously awaiting news of him and Galya. While the others sat, Mayumi paced.

"Can you still see them, Leo-san?" she asked.

Leo shook his head and turned away from the clear crystal globe the Devil had given him so he'd know what was happening in the Abyss. The globe was about the size of a bowling ball but remarkably lightweight. In fact, it barely weighed a pound. Leo had placed it on a cushion in the center of the table the day they left. Ever since, he'd given Mayumi and the other women hourly reports of Arka-Dal's expedition.

"They have passed beyond the range of the crystal. That means they are in the realm of the Beast and its Minions. But I'm sure they're alright," he said with certainty.

Mayumi stopped and smiled at him.

"How can you be certain?" she asked.

"The Devil said that if they failed, this crystal would turn black. It's still quite clear. That tells me that everyone is alive and well," Leo replied.

"They've been gone for two weeks now. We're all growing anxious," Medusa said. "I didn't think it would take this long to fight one battle."

"Time as we know it has no meaning where they are. To them, only a day has passed," Leo reminded them. "Still, that is a long battle no matter how one measures time."

"I should have gone with them," Chatha stated. "I can fight as well as any warrior—better than most in fact."

"So can we *all*," Medusa said. "But Arka-Dal told us to remain here and run the Empire while they were away."

"As we do each time he leaves. It is our duty," Mayumi said. "Over the years, he has gone off to fight many times. I have never gotten used to it. I never will. I still miss him greatly. I still worry for his safety. It is what a wife does. To love is to wait."

"Every time he goes off like this, he ends up with another wife," Zhijima said. "I hope he doesn't bring back one *this* time."

"Me too. There's enough of us around here already. I'm not making room for another one no matter *who or what* she is!" Medusa said.

"I don't care who he returns with. I just want him to return," Mayumi said as she sat down at the table. "I want *everyone* to return safely."

Chatha nodded.

"But if he brings back another wife, I'll *kill* her!" she said.

Medusa and Zhijima laughed.

"You will *not*!" Medusa said.

"In fact, you will welcome and accept her as we did you," Mayumi said.

"I just hope he doesn't make her pregnant. We already have enough children running around here—especially after Zhijima gives birth," Medusa said.

They all laughed.

Leo smiled and looked into the crystal. It remained clear.

The canyon trail opened into a large circular valley surrounded by sheer black cliffs. Arka-Dal looked up at the hundreds of Minions flapping overhead. They were slowly circling the valley and waiting for the right moment to attack.

"Where's the pit?" he asked.

Alyana pointed to a crack in the wall of the cliff on the side of the valley.

"Through there. It's very narrow and well-guarded," she said.

Merlin looked up at the Minions then smiled at Arka-Dal.

"When I say run, head for that opening," he said.

Arka-Dal nodded.

"You said that you lost over 2,000 warriors in this canyon. If so, where are their bodies? I see no sign of them," he asked.

"The Minions *ate* them. They eat everything they kill. They devour flesh, bone, hair, organs and even clothing. They leave nothing behind," Alyana replied grimly. "There *are* no remains, Demon Slayer. None at all."

"What of their weapons and armor?" asked Michael. "The ground should be littered with it."

"The Minions are using them against us now. They manufacture nothing themselves. They simply arm themselves with the weapons of everyone they slay," Alyana answered. "They waste nothing."

"That makes perfect sense," Merlin said. "They left almost nothing on the last world they invaded."

"If those monsters overrun our realm, my people will cease to exist. We must stop them now, Demon Slayer," Alyana said with more than little touch of loathing in her voice.

"We *will*, Alyana," Arka-Dal assured her.

"We have no choice," Mephistos added.

"Get ready," Merlin said.

They watched as he walked out into the center of the valley and raised his hand above his head. He incanted a spell and sent a beam of explosive light from his fingertips right into the thick of the Minions. The creatures shrieked in anger, formed up and swooped down at them. Merlin looked at Arka-Dal.

"Run!" he shouted.

Arka-Dal, Galya, Alyana and Michael took off for the opening as fast as their legs could carry them. At the same instant, the Minions attacked the rest of the party and another huge fight was on.

"I think you pissed them off!" shouted Pandaar.

"This was exactly my intent! As long as their attention is on us, they won't go after Arka-Dal and the others," Merlin shouted as he swung his sword with two hands and killed for Minions at once.

"Not bad for an old man," Pandaar said as he threw himself into the fight with his usual reckless abandon.

"I may be old, but I can still outfight *you*," Merlin said as he slew three more.

Pandaar gutted one and beheaded another with one stroke and laughed.

"I'd hate to have to put that to a test," he shouted.

While the rest of the party fought for their lives, Arka-Dal and the others managed to reach the opening on the other side of the valley unscathed. As they approached, Alyana held up her hand. They stopped while she went ahead a few feet and looked around. She returned quickly.

"They're waiting for us in there. I can sense it," she said.

"So this is a trap?" asked Michael.

"In a manner of speaking," Alyana said. "The way to the pit is guarded by the largest and nastiest of the Minions. This is where I lost most of my soldiers—and almost myself."

"How far did you get?" asked Arka-Dal.

"Not far. I got wounded about 200 yards in. That's when my soldiers decided to get me out," she replied.

"Let's hope we have better luck this time," Arka-Dal said as he drew Excalibur. "We might as well go in. It's bad manners to keep our hosts waiting."

Almost as soon as they stepped inside, a particularly fierce looking Minion bounded from the top of the canyon and caromed off the walls on the way down. He landed directly in front of Arka-Dal and scowled at him. It was armed with a flaming sword and shield.

"None shall pass," it said as it brought the sword down toward Arka-Dal.

To its astonishment, Arka-Dal easily parried the blow. As their weapons collided, both were showered with flaming embers.

"Impossible! No weapon made can withstand my flaming sword," the Minion exclaimed.

"This one can!" Arka-Dal shouted as he parried a second blow.

And a third.

Before the Minion could strike again, Arka-Dal slashed through its sword arm right below the elbow. The Minion screamed in rage and pain as he watched his arm fall to the ground. Arka-Dal's second blow eviscerated the creature. The Minion clutched its ruptured stomach and fell to its knees cursing. Arka-Dal's next swing sent its hideous head rolling down the trail. The Minion's body struck the ground and turned to dust.

There was no time to celebrate as dozens more of the things emerged from various places and came snarling at them. Arka-Dal, Galya and Alyana charged straight at them with weapons swinging. The Minions fell back against their onslaught, rallied, and renewed their assault. But the three of them continued to carve out a path of death and destruction that littered the ground with heads, hands, arms, legs and battered bodies which all turned quickly to dust. As each one fell, ten more appeared to take its place.

"Is there no end to these things?" shouted Arka-Dal.

"None! The only way to bring about an end to the Minions is to slay the Beast itself. To do that, we have to reach the pit," Alyana replied as she sent another half dozen Minions reeling to the ground with her twin swords.

"How much further to the pit?" shouted Galya.

"Distance has no meaning here. We'll know we're there when we reach it," Alyana replied. "Do you ever grow weary of fighting so many battles?"

"All men grow weary of such things. I'm no different," Arka-Dal said. "How about you?"

"I have *been* tired. After so many years of fighting, I would like nothing more than to lay down my swords. I've been at this so long, I can't recall what peace was like," Alyana said bitterly.

"Once we kill that thing, you and your people will be at peace," Arka-Dal said.

"What about you, Demon Slayer? Will you also have peace?" she asked.

"Maybe for a little while. I'm sure something else will come up and bite me in the ass later. Something always does," Arka-Dal replied as he looked around.

Alyana laughed.

"Life is hard—," he began.

"—And then you die," Alyana finished. "Father says that all the time."

He laughed.

"Here they come again!" Galya shouted.

Michael didn't hear her. He was far too busy fighting a rear guard action against dozens of the creatures that tried to sneak up on them. When he glanced over his shoulder, he saw the others were several yards ahead of him. He beheaded two more of the Minions, and ran after them.

Out on the plains, Azathoth and his generals watched as a large group of winged Minions approached. They hovered above the battle for a few seconds, then began circling. They moved slowly at first and quickened their pace with each cycle until they moved like a black whirlwind. After a few more seconds, they shrieked and suddenly funneled downward toward the battlefield. Before they could join the fight, two large groups of winged demons closed in from two directions and stopped their attack in mid air.

Azathoth smiled as the bizarre and brutal aerial melee ignited as thousands of dark combatants covered the sky for miles in all directions. The no quarter combat rained body parts, black dust and battered armor and weapons down upon the armies battling on the ground.

And the din of the battle was becoming almost deafening.

"Those are the last of our aerial reserves, Lord Azathoth," one of generals pointed out. "Every last unit of our combined armies is now fully engaged."

"I know," Azathoth said as he watched the carnage. "Have our men hold the field as long as possible. Arka-Dal and the others must reach the lair of the Beast and we must keep the bulk of the Minions engaged so they can have time to complete their mission."

"This is becoming a very costly diversion," the second general said.

"And it will become far more costly if we fail," Azathoth said. "We must keep their army pinned here. There will be no retreat unless I order it."

"I understand, Lord Azathoth," the first general said. "Our soldiers know what must be done. They will not falter."

Azathoth nodded.

Back in Thule, Mayumi was sitting in her favorite chair on the balcony and reading a book when Zhijima stepped out of the bedroom and began pacing. She watched for a while, then closed the book.

"What is troubling you, Zhijima-san?" she asked.

Zhijima kept pacing.

"Anxiety," she said. "Our husband is on the other side of the universe, fighting a battle against unspeakable things and we have no way of knowing if he's safe. I got this way whenever Pandaar was away, too."

"I know. You were always on edge until he returned. I didn't expect you to act differently because you are married to Aka-san now," Mayumi said.

"How do you do it? How do you stay so calm?" asked Zhijima.

"I only appear calm on the outside. Inside, I am as anxious as you," Mayumi answered. "That's why I try to take my mind off of it by doing other things."

"How is the book?" Zhijima asked.

"I don't know. I've been sitting here with it open for hours and I have yet to read a single line," she said. "Where are Chatha and Medusa?"

"In the Archives with Leo. They haven't taken their eyes off the crystal for hours. I just left them. I couldn't take any more. I guess I'll try to relax in a good, warm bath. What about you?" Zhijima asked.

"That is a good idea. I think I will join you," Mayumi replied as she put down the book.

The fight at the entrance to the trail grew more intense by the second as hordes of howling, snarling Minions attacked in wave after wave. Caught in the forefront, Perseus was the first casualty. Despite his broken arm, he tried valiantly to stand his ground. But without his heavy shield, he was virtually defenseless as a Minion attacked from his left. The creature, armed with a war club, struck Perseus on the side of the head so hard that the blow split his helmet and sent it flying from his head. The Greek dropped his sword and fell on his back. Jun raced forward and straddled the unconscious Greek to protect him from further harm while Kashi and Pandaar fought the creatures off at the flanks. Mephistos and the Devil seized Perseus by the feet and dragged him out of harm's way while Gorinna blasted away at another horde of Minions with another weakened spell that killed less than a quarter of them.

Ned and Merlin were busy filling the air above them with a variety of spells that literally powderized dozens of Minions as they swooped in for the attack. Yet the more they killed, the more appeared from thin air to take their places and continued to assail the group from above and the front.

As another, larger group formed in the air above them, a regiment of Galya's winged troops who had fought their way past the first line of Minions, charged straight into them with incredible fury. The ones on the ground disengaged from their fight and rushed skyward to join the battle.

"Galya's soldiers have our backs! Let's hurry and catch up with the others," Ned shouted above the racket.

"I'll stay with Perseus until he regains his senses. He needs someone to watch over him," Jun volunteered.

"Catch up with us later—if you can," Gorinna said as she joined the rest of the group in a mad race along the rocky trail.

As Jun watched, the remainder of Galya's legions arrived to join the action. Their arrival sparked a counterattack from a huge wave of Minions that seemed to pop straight out of the ground.

And so began one of the deadliest, wildest and most bizarre battles the Netherworld had ever hosted as wild charges were met by even wilder counter charges as both armies clashed again and again and again without any signs of tiring. Each time one of Galya's men fell, another immediately appeared to replace him—and the numbers of Minions were increasing by the second.

"It's a stalemate," Jun said to himself. "If Arka-Dal fails to kill the Beast, this battle will last for eternity."

As Arka-Dal hacked a bloody path through what seemed like a wall of Minions, he watched out of the corner of his eye as Alyana ran up the side of the sheer cliff then back flipped toward the ground. As she did, she slashed her way through a large horde of growling, snarling Minions with her twin swords. By the time her feet touched the ground, the air around her was choked with black dust which was all that remained of her adversaries.

A larger Minion emerged from the ground behind her. Alyana ducked under its sword, whirled around and slashed upward with her own blade. She split the Minion from crotch to the top of its head. As it fell to dust, several more appeared and attacked, only tgo meet their doom on the edges of Alyana's swords.

A few yards away, Galya was also carving a path of death and destruction through a veritable wave of the creatures. As she fought, she hissed like a cat and her eyes took on an ominous red glare. It had been several millennia since she'd fought like this and she was beginning to revel in the action and excitement.

As Michael fought behind her, he realized that her had seen the Princess of Hell fight just like this during their final battle of the Forever War. Now he knew why she was Hell's most feared commander. Galya reminded him of a beautiful, dangerous wild animal that killed not for food but because she actually *enjoyed* the heat of a battle.

Galya's combat prowess was not lost on Arka-Dal either. HE was almost awed by her skill and ferocity and her unbridled courage.

Her father had told him she was unmatched in battle and that no army ever fielded on Earth or in Hell itself could survive an assault from her and her legions.

"She's as good as field commander as *you* are. Perhaps better," the Devil had said. "Neither of you have ever been defeated. The two of you should make a most formidable and unbeatable team."

Arka-Dal put these thoughts out of his head and concentrated on the task at hand. The Minions were everywhere now and they numbers just kept increasing with each beat of his heart. No matter how many they slew, twice their number appeared to replace them.

He couldn't recall ever being in such a long, hard, running battle or having killed so many enemy soldiers. Unlike his previous battles, this one appeared to be endless and it felt as if they were no closer to reaching their goal as they were when they started.

After fighting their way along the trail for what seemed like months, Alyana raised her fist. Arka-Dal, Galya and Michael stopped.

"The pit lies around that bend," Alyana said as she pointed. "We must hurry. I can sense the Beast stirring."

Before she could take another step, a huge winged Minion emerged from the side of the cliff and lashed out at her with its mailed fist. Caught by surprise, the blow struck her in the middle of her chest and lifted her nearly 20 feet off the ground. She sailed into the rocky wall, bounced off and slammed her right knee into a jagged rock on the way down. As she landed, she gripped her knee and writhed in obvious pain. The Minion moved in to finish the job, but only managed to get cut in half by Arka-Dal's sword as he dashed to Alyana's rescue.

While the Minion fell to dust, Arka-Dal attempted to help Alyana to her feet. The moment she tried to stand, she yelped in pain and sat down on the ground. He stooped to examine her. When she hit the rock, it tore through her flesh and exposed the bone. She was also bleeding badly.

He tore off part of his tunic and wrapped it around her knee to try and stem the bleeding. She sat and winced as he knotted it.

"Never mind me! Finish the Beast before it wakes. Hurry or all will be lost," she shouted.

"Are you sure?" he asked.

"Yes! Now go!" she shouted as she tightened the bandage.

Galya stopped and smiled at her. Alyana smiled back. Then Galya touched her shoulder and took off down the trail.

Arka-Dal, Michael and Galya raced along the trail and around the bend. As they headed for the pit, they were forced to fight their way past dozens of fierce, yowling Minions armed with a wide variety of weapons, sharp talons and fangs. Halfway to the pit, they felt the earth tremble beneath their feet.

"The Beast is stirring!" Galya shouted as she slashed her way through one Minion after another after another with her twin swords. "We have only minutes before it wakes!"

They redoubled their efforts and forced their way past another wall of Minions and moved further inward. The trail soon widened and made its way around a huge, deep chasm. A plume of noxious, green-gray-orange smoke and gas billowed out of it and out of this flew dozens more of the Beasts' hideous guardians.

The first batch immediately assailed them and quickly met their deaths as the trio slashed and hacked their way to the pit.

The ground continued to tremble and pitch. They steadied themselves as best as they could and peered through the rising, rolling mist that rose from the pit. Every few seconds, another hideously twisted Minion appeared. Some shrieked at them and rose skyward. Others ignored them as if they weren't there.

As the ground shook more and more violently, the mist momentarily parted to reveal the edge of huge, deep pit. They made their way to it and stared down at the writhing, misshapen black mass that lay at the bottom. The mass was stirring and it was its movements that made the ground quake.

As they watched, one-by-one, huge red eyes began to open slowly.

"The Beast is waking!" Galya shouted. "If it wakes fully, we're done for!"

"I can't let that happen. This ends...*now!*" Arka-Dal said as he gripped the hilt of Excalibur with both hands and pointed it downward.

Before Galya could react, he shouted and launched himself into the pit. Galya didn't hesitate. She immediately jumped in after him without the slightest thought for her own safety.

Michael was momentarily taken aback by her selfless act. After he recovered his senses, he leaped in after her. He landed at the bottom of the pit not five feet from Galya.

She grinned at him.

"At least I won't die alone," she said.

"No one is dying this day," Michael said. "We're going to find Arka-Dal and the three of us are getting out of this hole together. Alive!"

She nodded and plunged through the curtain of steam, rocks, bits of torn flesh, smoke and heavy black dust that suddenly filled the pit. Michael followed close on her heels.

By now, the air in the canyon was becoming filled with fine black dust as one after another, the monsters that fought to keep the rest of the party at bay fell to the ground and disintegrated. Some tried to escape by soaring skyward only to turn to dust in mid-flight and the canyon echoed with their dying shrieks and moans. It looked like it was snowing ashes.

"He did it! Arka-Dal has slain the Beast! Victory is ours!" the Devil shouted.

"But where *is* Arka-Dal?" asked Mephistos.

"The last I saw of him, Galya and Michael, they were headed up that path with Alyana," Merlin said.

"Let's hurry and find them!" the Devil shouted as they raced along the path until they came to the pit.

They saw Alyana seated on a rock, nursing her badly wounded knee. She grimaced at them.

"Where is Arka-Dal?" asked Ned.

"When last I saw him, he plunged into the pit to slay the Beast. Seconds later, the ground shook even more and the Minions started turning to dust," she said.

"Galya! Where's Galya? Have you seen my daughter?" the Devil asked.

"She and Michael went in after Arka-Dal," she replied as she attempted to stand. She grimaced with each ginger step then sat back down.

"Galya's love for Arka-Dal knows no boundaries. That is exactly what I would expect from her. But with her diminished powers, she can't hope to escape that pit," the Devil said as he raced toward the edge of the chasm.

The others followed after him.

The Devil stepped to the edge of the pit and looked down. The smoke, ashes and steam still rolled upward and the ground beneath their feet trembled slightly.

"Galya!" he shouted.

"I'm here, Father. To your right," she said.

He turned and smiled. She was kneeling on the ground and cradling Arka-Dal in her lap. Both were covered with mud, dirt and black dust.

"How?" the Devil asked as he knelt beside her.

"Michael. He seized us one at a time and tossed us out of the pit as if we weighed nothing. He still has great strength," she said weakly. "If not for him, neither of us would be here."

"And where *is* Michael?" asked the Devil as he stood and looked around.

She nodded at the pit.

The Devil walked to the edge, looked down through the billowing waste and concentrated until he located the unconscious form of the Archangel lying next to the bubbling, roiling remains of the Beast. He stepped back and waved his hand.

The others watched as he levitated Michael out of the pit and gently deposited him on the ground next to Galya and Arka-Dal. To everyone's astonishment, he tightly clutched Excalibur in his right hand.

Merlin walked over and took it from him.

"He threw himself into the belly of the Beast to retrieve it. He said that it must never be lost," Galya explained. "After he retrieved the sword, he threw us out of the pit. He is incredibly brave, Father."

"He always was," the Devil said with a smile.

"He still lives," Merlin announced as he examined him.

The Devil smiled at Galya.

"And what of Arka-Dal?" he asked.

"He'll be fine. He's scraped and bruised all over but he'll recover quickly. I'll see to it," she said softly.

"I know," the Devil said. "Let's take him home."

Moments later, the crystal globe in the center of the long table in Leo's study took on a strange, pulsating glow. Startled, Leo retreated to the other side of the room and told the ladies to come with him. As soon as Mayumi, Medusa, Chatha and Zhijima reached Leo's side, the globe shattered with a loud crash and bathed the room in a glaring white light. When the glare subsided seconds later, they were astonished to see the entire group standing before them. The women saw the unconscious form of Arka-Dal cradled in Galya's arms and rushed to them. Jun had Michael slung over his shoulder while Kashi and Pandaar supported a very battered Perseus between them.

"Take him upstairs to the bedroom," Mayumi instructed.

Galya and her father carried Arka-Dal upstairs and gently placed him on the bed. As Mayumi caressed his cheeks, he briefly opened his eyes and smiled at her. Then he fell into a deep, dreamless sleep.

"Where's Ned?" asked Leo.

"The Knower stayed behind to wrap up any loose ends he might discover," the Devil replied. "You should have been there, Leo. Arka-Dal committed the greatest act of bravery and self-sacrifice I have ever witnessed. No wonder Galya loves him so!"

"What of his wounds?" Leo asked.

"I already mended them. He'll sleep for a few days and be as good as new," the Devil assured him. "Perseus and Kashi are more in need of your healing skills right now."

"I'll tend to them immediately and meet you in the living room afterward," Leo said as he hurried off.

The Devil looked back at Arka-Dal lying on the bed surrounded by his adoring wives and smiled.

With his lines broken in two places, Azathoth was about to order his army to fall back so they could regroup and carry on the fight. Before he could give the order, several of his battered-looking officers raced over to him.

"Look!" they shouted as they pointed toward the advancing hordes of Minions.

Azathoth stared in disbelief as the hordes of Minions stopped in their tracks and began to wail and moan as if they were being torn limb from limb by some unseen force. Their cries reverberated through the land and grew so loud they actually caused the earth beneath their feet to tremble.

Then, just as suddenly, the wailing stopped and the Minions fell to dust.

"They did it! The Beast is slain!" Azathoth shouted as he pumped his fists in celebration. "The day is ours! The war is ended!"

He looked out at his stunned soldiers and raised both hands over his head.

"All hail Arka-Dal—slayer of the Beast!" he shouted.

The combined hosts of Demons and Devils raised their weapons and pounded their shields as they shouted with glee. Then they started chanting Arka-Dal's name over and over again. Each time, the chant grew louder and louder until their voices reached every corner of their realms.

Then a wild celebration ensued as the soldiers congratulated each other with slaps on the back, fist pumps, hand shakes, high fives and even hugs. After more than a thousand years, peace would reign in the nether regions.

"The fabric of the universe has truly been turned inside-out now. The Demon *Slayer* is now the Demon *Savior*!" Azathoth said.

"But where is the Demon Slayer?" he wondered.

When Arka-Dal opened his eyes, he found himself lying in his bed surrounded by his wives and children. Mayumi smiled as he forced himself to sit upright and she placed a pillow behind his back to make him more comfortable. Then she threw her arms around his neck and kissed him. He held her close. One-by-one, the rest of his wives and children did the same. Then most of the smaller children jumped onto the bed with him.

"It is good to have you back, Aka-san," Mayumi said happily.

"How did I get back?" he asked.

"Father and I brought you back right after the battle. You've been fading in and out of consciousness for several days now. It's good to see you sitting up and alert again. You had us all worried," Galya said as she hugged him again.

"Did we win?" he asked.

"Yes. You killed the Beast with Excalibur. Then Michael rescued you—and me," Galya said.

"The last thing I remember is jumping into the pit and plunging Excalibur into the middle of that black mass of eyeballs. Then there was this odd purple light. The next thing I know, I'm here in bed. Where is Michael?" Arka-Dal asked.

"I'm here, My Lord," Michael said as he stepped into the room.

Arka-Dal smiled at him.

"I'm no one's 'lord'—especially not yours," he said as they shook hands. "Thank you. You really saved our asses down there."

"I did what I pledged to do. I did what anyone else would have done at that moment. I am no hero. I just did my duty," Michael said modestly.

"Have it your way, Michael," Arka-Dal said. "Galya said that you were a man of great courage and honor. You've more than proven that. What of the rest of our party?"

"Kashi and Perseus were badly mauled but Gorinna helped to heal them with her magic. Pandaar and Jun only got a few scratches," Michael replied.

"So everyone made it out alive?" Arka-dal asked.

"Just as you vowed, my love," Galya said.

"Now that you're awake, I think you need to dress and come down to the parlor. You have a most unusual guest who wishes to speak with you," Mayumi said. "He has been waiting for three days now."

After Arka-Dal bathed, dressed, and went down to the parlor, he was surprised to find Mephistos sitting on the sofa and chatting with the Devil and Merlin. He rose and bowed respectfully when he saw Arka-Dal.

"You're looking well," he said.

"I am," Arka-Dal said as he walked over to them.

Merlin and the Devil also stood. At that point, Galya and the rest of the Dal wives entered. Mephistos greeted each of them in turn as introductions were made. He even went so far as to kiss the back of each of their hands.

He then beamed at Arka-Dal.

"What you did in that pit was nothing short of spectacular," he said.

"It wasn't all *that* spectacular," Arka-Dal said modestly.

"Ah, but it *was*! Thanks to you, my people and those of Azathoth's are safe. There are no words in any known tongue that are fit enough to describe how grateful we all are—to *all* of you," Mephistos said as they shook hands. "No one but *you* would have risked his life so selflessly to save us. You even had the foresight to bring us all together to unite against our common enemy. You did something neither Azathoth nor I ever considered. You brought peace to our realms. Thank you."

"I did only what needed to be done. If my act also ended the bloodshed between your peoples, then I am doubly grateful," Arka-Dal said.

"Yes, the war is over. The Beast and its Minions are destroyed forever. Things are very quiet on the edges of the Abyss right now as both my people and the Others are busy cleaning up the wreckage of centuries of endless battles. The cleanup will take many of your years," Mephistos said.

"The dimensions beyond the Dark Realm of the Others must be continually monitored. Right now, it is a vast dead zone but sooner or later, another, possibly more dangerous race may seek to make it theirs," the Devil warned. "No one, not even Ned, really knows what lies beyond the rim."

"That will be *our* task. Mine and Azathoth's. We'll see to it that all of our realms remain safe from unwanted invaders," Mephistos vowed. "Yours included."

He smiled at Arka-Dal.

"You know, Demon Slayer, I've become rather fond of you and your friends. While it's true you imprisoned us in the Abyss, you also came to our aid when we needed it most. No one that I have ever heard of in all of my eons of existence would have done that. You're a noble adversary and you have earned the respect of myself and my people," he said as they shook hands again.

He looked at the Devil.

"I now understand why you are proud to have him for your son-in-law, Lucifer. Galya has chosen very wisely indeed," he said.

He looked at Arka-Dal.

"I must return to the Abyss now and put things in order. There is much work to be done to rebuild after our long war. If ever you should need our help with anything, Demon Slayer, do not hesitate to call upon me," he said as he melted into thin air.

"Now that's something I didn't expect," Arka-Dal remarked as he walked to the bar and poured himself a drink.

"I must say that you have the most uncanny knack for making friends and allies of the strangest people," Merlin said. "And you have a most interesting collection of wives."

"It's good that Mephistos doesn't have any daughters to marry off to you," the Devil joked.

"But Azathoth *does*. And Alyana has quite a crush on you," Merlin said with a wink.

"That is one union I will never allow!" Galya insisted. "There is room for only one Devil in this family—and that's *me*!"

"That's fine with me, my love. I already have enough wives," Arka-Dal said with a smile. "And I can barely keep up with all of your demands!"

"Now that you are home, we are about to place even more demands on you, Aka-san," Mayumi said with smile and a wink.

"I hope you're healed enough to handle them," Chatha said. "I don't want anything vital to fall off or something."

They all laughed.

Azathoth walked through the wreckage-strewn field and watched as his war-weary soldiers helped their wounded comrades limp back into their realm. On the line of black, craggy ridges on the eastern edge of the field stood the equally weary soldiers of the Abyss. As Azathoth came into view, the demons raised their arms and weapons and flapped their leathery wings as they chanted their salute. He smiled and returned their salute.

The chanting grew louder.

Soon, Azathoth's own soldiers stopped what they were doing and joined in.

Their long war was over—thanks to help from a most unexpected source.

Azathoth chuckled.

Who could have possibly imagined that the feared Demon Slayer of Thule would become the savior of countless numbers of demons?

"The universe has indeed been turned on its ear," he thought as he continued his walk.

After a while, he came upon Alyana. She was seated atop a large rock looking up at the sickly purple sky. At the base of the rock were her helmet and twin swords. The swatch of Arka-Dal's tunic was still wrapped around her knee.

"You're wounded," Azathoth observed.

"I'll be alright in a bit," she said.

"You seem pensive, my daughter," he said.

"I saw it, Father. I saw it *all*," she said softly. Her voice was nearly a whisper.

"Oh? What *did* you see?" he asked.

She smiled.

"I saw Arka-Dal seize Excalibur with both hands and hurl himself into the pit to slay the Beast. It was the bravest, most reckless act I have ever witnessed. When the ground beneath us quaked and rolled, Galya leaped in after him without a single thought for her own safety. She just jumped in to save Arka-Dal," she said.

"I saw that, too," Azathoth said.

"Is that what the humans call love?" she asked.

"I'm certain of it," Azathoth replied. "The Beast was powerful enough to slay even Galya, yet all she thought about was going to the rescue of the man she loves more than life itself. She was more than willing to risk her own life to save his. If that isn't love, then I don't know what love is."

"It *is* a very powerful emotion, isn't it?" Alyana asked.

"I have heard that love is the single most powerful force in the entire universe," Azathoth said.

"I also watched Michael leap in after them both. He tossed them both to safety then risked his life further to save Excalibur," Alyana said. "Was that also love?"

"More like loyalty," Azathoth replied. "That, too, is quite strong."

Alyana sighed deeply.

"Will I ever find true love, Father?" she asked wistfully.

"Perhaps you will one day—*if* you heed the advice of Lucifer and Merlin. You might also consider following Galya's example," Azathoth suggested.

"How will I know it if it comes to me?" she asked.

He smiled.

"When you find someone who is far more important to you than your own ambitions, your own life and you are willing to sacrifice all you have for him, that will be true love," he answered.

She smiled.

Azathoth detected a touch of sadness in it.

"I think I already have," she said almost to herself.

The War Machine

The Yboe was a grassy plain that stretched for miles and miles in the western part of Thule. Although the day was warm and sunny, a low mist slowly rolled across the land. The mist wasn't a fluke of weather but the dust of battle. It was the remnant of a long, bloody afternoon.

Arka-Dal sat astride his warhorse and watched as his weary soldiers walked or rode past him on their way back to the encampment. Most were covered with dirt, mud sweat and blood. Their bodies were decorated with bruises, cuts and scrapes and their shields were scratched and dented in many places. Some stumbled wearily by without acknowledging the Emperor. Many looked at the ground as they were too tired to even lift their heads. Some had that faraway look of men who had been through Hell on Earth or of men who had fought too many battles. Most of them shuffled along in a daze. Some laughed and joked with their comrades. A few stopped to chat with Arka-Dal and to congratulate him for the victory.

Even the cavalry men looked battered and worn, as did their horses.

The battle had been long and hard-fought against an invading horde that neither asked or gave quarter. It had been a day-long battle to the death.

Arka-Dal sighed as he looked around.

The fields and streams were cluttered with dead and dying men and horses and broken equipment and tattered banners as far as he could see. Off in the distance, he saw the ambulance drivers loading wounded men into their carts while others scoured the field for missing and wounded friends.

Tomorrow, his commanders would be able to take a head count of the living. By the time they broke camp and returned to the nearest fort, he'd have a list of the dead and missing.

He smiled wearily at his soldiers as they cheered him.

Once again, Thule had come under attack.

And once again, his well-trained and disciplined soldiers had crushed the enemy on the field of battle.

And what a battle it had been!

It began in the early pre-dawn hours during a light rainfall. By the time the sun had dully lit up the sky, they found themselves fighting in a heavy downpour which lasted for the next seven hours. The rain had all-but ceased now and a low-lying mist was creeping slowly across the field.

This had been the third such battle against these nameless invaders in the last month.

All had been long and bitterly fought. Each time, the enemy had fought to the last man. They had refused to surrender.

Refused to retreat.

They stayed in place.

And they died in place.

"But why?" he wondered. "And just who were these invaders? Where did they come from? Who sent them?"

After a month of fighting, he was no closer to answering those questions than he had been at the onset.

The invaders carried no standards nor did the bear any symbols or markings on their shields. Their armor was uniform. Steel helmets and shields and long chain mail shirts covered by simple white tunics. They wore black trousers and boots and were armed with swords and spears.

Their forces were made up only of infantry and there seemed to be no noticeable field commanders. They had suddenly appeared as if from thin air and attacked the nearest military outpost or fort. During the battle their never spoke. Never shouted or cried out in pain. In fact, they had fought in complete silence each and every time.

And none seemed to be particularly skilled at hand-to-hand combat. They simply attacked and once engaged, they dug in their heels and fought to the bitter end.

He looked down at several invaders lying dead in a cluster exactly where they'd fallen minutes earlier. He studied each of them carefully, then dismounted.

"Something doesn't look right," he said as he walked over to the nearest one.

He knelt beside him and pulled off his helmet. The soldier had dark brown hair, straight lips and dark green eyes that stared up at the sky without actually seeing. Arka-Dal stood and walked to the next man and repeated what he'd done. This man, too, had dark brown hair and dark green eyes.

"Twin brothers?" he wondered.

He walked to the next and removed his helmet.

And the next.

And the next.

Each man looked exactly the same as the others around him. Arka-Dal stood and cursed.

"They can't *all* be brothers!" he said.

"Who can't?" asked Kashi as he and Pandaar walked over.

"All of our new foes," Arka-Dal said. "Look at their faces and tell me what strikes you most."

They did as he asked.

It took several seconds before they realized what Arka-Dal was getting at.

"They all look exactly alike!" Kashi exclaimed.

"That's impossible! I've heard of identical twins and even triplets, but this is ridiculous," Pandaar added.

"Let's check a few more of them and see what we find," Arka-Dal said.

They walked across the field and stopped to examine several more of the fallen invaders. After 20 minutes, they met in the center of the field. Pandaar shook his head.

"I've checked 15. All of them look alike," he said.

"Same here. That's impossible," Kashi said.

"I agree—yet we see it before us with out own eyes. There are nearly 25,000 of these men lying dead on the field. I'm willing to bet they all look exactly alike, too," Arka-Dal said as they walked back to where they'd left their horses.

"And each wears the exact same armor and helmet and carries the same shield. There's no markings to identify any of them and I see no flags or standards but ours anywhere. What's going on here?" Pandaar wondered.

"I don't know but something tells me that we'd better find out—and fast," Arka-Dal said. "As soon as we return to Thule, I want to have a meeting in the War Room. Maybe Leo can shed some light on this."

"Or Merlin—*if* he's around," Pandaar added.

To their relief, Merlin was in the living room when they arrived. He got up to greet them as they walked in, still covered with the dirt, dust and bruises from their recent battle. Arka-Dal walked to the bar and poured himself a tall glass of blue wine.

"Did you fight the same invaders again?" Merlin asked as Arka-Dal sat down on the sofa.

The Emperor nodded as he drank.

"With the same results. They fought and died to the last man. I'm glad you're here, Merlin. I need to discuss something with you and Leo. There's something very strange about our invaders," he said.

"Oh?" Merlin asked as he raised an eyebrow.

"We'll talk over dinner later. Right now, I need a good hot bath," Arka-Dal said as he finished his drink.

As they dined two hours later, Arka-Dal explained what he'd discovered about their strange foes.

Leo sat back and folded his hands across his belly.

"I've heard of identical twins or triplets, but not dozens of look-alikes. I swear to you that each man looked the same as another. And we checked dozens of them. They had the same facial features, same eye color, same hair—everything was exactly the same," Arka-Dal said.

"There's only one logical explanation, though I hope I'm wrong," Leo said.

"I think I know where you're going with this, Leo. I have similar suspicions," Merlin added.

"Care to let the rest of us in on it?" Arka-Dal asked.

"Sometime during the First Age, scientists perfected a method of duplicating living things in nature in laboratories. They duplicated plants, animals, internal organs and eventually entire human beings. This process was called cloning and the duplicates were called clones," Leo began.

"I remember reading about this in one of your books," Medusa said.

"At first, they had some noble ideals of cloning organs in order to cure several diseases. They took single cells from the damaged organs and fed them through a machine that would eventually create an entire new organ from it. This new organ could be transplanted into a human body to replace a damaged one. But this took weeks," Leo explained. "It was a long, slow process at first."

"Then the military got hold of the science and things changed. Dramatically, I might add," Merlin said.

"How so?" asked Arka-Dal.

"Wounded soldiers needed replacement parts. Arms, legs, lungs, etc. were needed in a hurry to repair and return those men to the battlefields. One country stumbled upon a way to clone needed parts on a grand scale and quickly. Had this technology been used for the good of the general population, it would have been the greatest boon in medical history. Instead, this nation decided that if arms and other parts could be cloned, why not entire soldiers?" Merlin said.

Arka-Dal stared at him.

"Did they ever achieve this?" he asked.

"They were on the verge of succeeding when the Great Disaster occurred and brought all such research to a halt—along with the rest of civilization," Merlin said.

"If that's the case, then why do all these invaders look alike?" Arka-Dal asked.

"Perhaps whoever is behind this invasion has somehow uncovered this ancient technology?" Medusa suggested.

"But Leo said cloning took a long time. How could anyone turn out an entire army?" Arka-Dala sked.

"Yes, it's true. **C**loning used to take several months," Leo explained. "And, only one or two clones could be produced each time. Whoever is behind this invasion is able to take this ancient technology to a degree of refinement that boggles the imagination. He can turn out vast numbers of clones in a very short time and transport them over great distances to launch surprise attacks against any point on the globe he chooses. This means he has an almost unlimited number of troops at his disposal."

"How many is limitless, Leo?" asked Arka-Dal.

"Theoretically, he could produce *millions*. Enough to overrun nearly every empire on Earth," Leo replied.

Arka-Dal whistled.

"In other words, he can produce them far faster than we can kill them," Medusa added. "We'd eventually run out of soldiers while he never would. This war could last for *decades*."

"And we'd be forced to fight one bloody battle after another," Arka-Dal said. "I can't allow that. We'll have to locate his device and destroy it—and him along with it."

"Whoever he may be," Leo agreed.

"Any ideas?" Arka-Dal asked.

"None," Merlin said flatly.

"If he was able to rediscover and improve upon some bit of ancient technology, what's to stop him from doing the same with even more dangerous relics of the First Age?" Leo asked.

"You mean like the bugs?"[3] Arka-Dal queried.

Leo nodded.

"Or worse," he said. "Remember what you used to destroy that island many years ago? Then imagine that power magnified several times over."

"It would be enough to wipe all mankind off the globe once again," Merlin added.

Arka-Dal envisioned entire cities going up in columns of fire and black clouds. The vision caused him to shake his head.

"We can't allow that to happen again," he said.

"Indeed not," Merlin said.

"Can we locate him?" Arka-Dal asked.

"We can try. I'll need your help, Gorinna," Merlin said.

Gorinna nodded.

"Any ancient device usually emits vast amounts of energy. Any device capable of producing entire armies would have to emit enormous amounts of energy. Such an unnatural spike should be easily detectable.

We'll have to wait until the device is activated again and then use its energy spike to pinpoint its location," Merlin explained.

"We'll have to work around the clock in four or six hour shifts in order to monitor for the spike. It's very draining. We'll have to sleep between shifts to conserve our energy," Gorinna said.

"Once we locate the source, we'll transport over there and destroy it," Merlin said. "With any luck, our adversary won't be able to reconstruct it."

"Especially if we kill him in the process. The machine isn't the real threat. The *operator* is," Arka-Dal added.

"Indeed," Merlin agreed.

---

[3] Read: Bad Lands

"But what if the device doesn't emit enough power to enable us to trace it?" asked Medusa.

"In that case, we'll have to resort to Plan B," Merlin replied.

"Which is?" asked Leo.

"We'll have to capture one of those clones so I can try to delve into his mind and track his memories to his place of origin—if he has any. We're not sure if these soldiers have actual memories, given they are merely copies of an original. But I may be able to track his genetic makeup to that original," Merlin said.

"Have you ever tried that before?" Leo asked.

"Never," Merlin replied.

"Will it work?" Medusa asked.

"I really haven't a clue," Merlin said honestly.

"And therein lies our problem," Leo said. "What if these clones have no actual brains you can tap into?"

"They might not have brains, but the living human being they're being cloned from does. All I need to do is find even the slightest trace of a brain in one of those clones. Once I do, I can try to use it to trace its cellular structure back to its original source," Merlin explained.

Then he smiled.

"Of course, this is only a *theory*. I've never attempted it," he said.

"In either case, we can't do a damned thing until another attack is launched," Leo added.

"I'll keep our entire army on full alert until then," Pandaar said. "No matter where they strike next, we'll be ready for them."

"Only this time, tell every field commander to try to take one of them alive," Arka-Dal said. "Just in case."

"Are clones considered living beings?" Kashi asked.

"Yes," Merlin replied. "They breathe, they eat, they feel, they have hearts and brains. They are most certainly alive."

"But these don't seem to have human free will. They've been cloned for a single purpose by someone who seems to have it in for Thule," Arka-Dal said. "When we get through with him, he'll understand that he picked a fight with the wrong people."

"If he already has his army in the field and we locate the device and destroy it, what happens to them?" Pandaar asked.

"They will continue to fight as they were programmed to do until every last one is killed," Leo said. "They won't just magically fall to dust simply because their creator is destroyed."

"Nuts!" Pandaar said.

"There's some in the bowl next to me," Kashi said.

"I wasn't asking for any. It was an expression," Pandaar said.

Arka-Dal paced back and forth a couple of times. He stopped and looked at Merlin.

"Each attack has come at a different location. The first was in the north, along the border with Garchem. Jun's scouts spotted them and alerted the Northern Army. That first fight lasted nearly ten hours and cost us over 850 dead and three times that number wounded. The second battle was to the south, near Larsa. That was bloody, too. This last one was the bloodiest of the lot. Each time, they hit us with at least 25,000 soldiers. Each time, they fought to the last man," he said.

"And they used the same tactics and the same battle formations each time, Kashi added. "They seemed completely unable to respond to any of our flanking maneuvers. In fact, they were almost sitting ducks."

"That tells me that they are following a pre-programmed order of battle," Arka-Dal said. "But is that order of battle set by the machinery that produces them? Or does it come from the mind of the operator?"

"The old chicken or the egg question," Medusa said.

"Exactly," Arka-Dal agreed. "If they *are* pre-programmed, is it even possible to capture one alive?"

"That, too, is unknown at this point," Merlin replied.

"That's a lot of unknowns, Merlin. Are there any *knowns?*" asked Pandaar.

"Just one: we'll be fighting them again and soon," Merlin answered.

Far away in the tortured realm of the Others, Lord Azathoth watched from the balcony of his mansion as his daughter, Alyana, her hands clasped behind her back, walked a wide circle around the structure. Every once in a while, she stopped and looked up at the tormented sky and sighed wistfully.

Azathoth had never seen her act like this. She ate little and barely slept and she seemed listless and forlorn.

"It's time to have a talk with her," he thought as he faded into thin air.

When he materialized next to her, Alyana barely noticed. Azathoth frowned.

"What ails you, my daughter?" he asked.

"I feel empty inside. Very empty," she said softly.

"And why is that?" he asked as they walked side-by-side.

"I miss him," she answered.

"Arka-Dal?" he asked.

Alyana nodded.

"I'd give anything to see him. Anything to be with him—even for a little while," she said.

"Alas, you cannot do that. You will probably never see him again," Azathoth said.

"Why, Father?" she asked.

"The terms of our treaty forbid it. We are prohibited from venturing beyond the limits of the Netherworld forever," Azathoth explained.

"Who came up with that idea?" she asked.

"Actually, it was the Knower's idea. He didn't think it would be wise for our people to suddenly flood into Earth. He said it would be in everyone's best interest," Azathoth explained. "At the time, it made perfect sense. Other than Arka-Dal and his friends, our people have never had any contact with outsiders. It's best to do such things gradually to minimize unwanted problems."

"Is it in writing?" Alyana asked.

"No. It's all verbal. The Knower conveyed the terms to Arka-Dal and he agreed to them. His word is as good as any written agreement. Better in fact," Azathoth replied.

"Is there no way around that?" she asked. "No way at all?"

"We *can* venture into the physical realm of Earth only upon being invited or when on official business," Azathoth said.

"Invitation?" she asked hopefully.

"Yes. If Arka-Dal should say your name three times and request you to visit, the gate will be opened and you will be able to enter his world at will. But such a thing is highly unlikely," Azathoth explained.

Alyana sighed deeply.

Azathoth frowned.

"My life no longer has any true meaning for me," Alyana said. "What's *wrong* with me, Father? What afflicts me so?"

"I believe your affliction is what the humans call *love*," Azathoth said.

"Love stinks!" she said.

As she walked away, she smiled. An idea formed in her mind. One she would have to find a way to convince her father to go along with. Azathoth had said that they could enter Earth on *official business*. But *what*, she wondered, might be considered such?

After giving it some thought, she smiled.

"I *have* it!" she said.

Arka-Dal, Leo and Medusa were in the Archives. They were going over a series of recently mapped areas of the Great Western Desert. The maps showed several new towns that had sprung up along rivers as well as a few ruined cities of the First Age that had recently been uncovered.

"This last one was partially uncovered by a wind storm three months ago," Medusa said as she pointed to a dot at the base of a series of foothills. "We haven't sent anyone out to actually explore or survey it yet, so there's no information on it."

"So we don't know if it was an actually population center or some sort of military base. There were many of both in those days. The entire world was an armed camp. A powder keg, if I dare say, just waiting for a spark to set it off," Leo added.

"How far from Thule is it?" asked Arka-Dal.

"Four hundred miles," Leo said. "There are no roads near it, either. It's in a very remote place."

"That makes me believe it was some sort of military base," Arka-Dal said. "If it was, there could be all sorts of ancient and very dangerous technologies hidden there. We'd best send our Special Technical Force to check it out to keep what may there from biting us in the ass later."

"I agree," Leo said. "We've had too many such incidents of that nature. It's better to be safe now than sorry later."

Arka-Dal paced.

"Do you suppose that ruin may be the source of our clone armies?" he asked.

Leo shrugged.

"Anything is possible," he said.

That's when Kashi raced into the room.

"I've just received a radio message from Jun. He said that some of his scouts spotted another army of those clones marching toward Dur," he said.

"How far from the city are they?" Arka-Dal asked.

"Jun said they were about 70 miles away and moving at a slow, deliberate pace," Kashi said. "He said there were at least 10,000 of them marching in formation."

"Tell him to have his men keep the enemy in sight at all times and to try and contain them if possible. Do not engage them in battle unless they attack first," Arka-Dal instructed. "Got it?"

"Got it!" Kashi assured him as he ran back to the radio room to relay the orders.

Arka-Dal looked at Merlin and Gorinna who had just entered the Archives.

"Did either of you detect anything?" he asked.

"I detected a huge energy spike about 250 miles directly north of where their army is. It's still throbbing steadily. It's near the ruins we call the Necropolis," she replied.

"Interesting," Leo remarked. "Those ruins were supposedly the location of a military laboratory during the First Age. This is starting to make sense now."

"It appears we have yet another ancient device running amok," Merlin added. "And we'd best find it and shut it down before it gets completely out of hand."

"Can you take us there fast?" Arka-Dal asked.

"Yes," Gorinna said. "I know exactly where it is."

"Let's saddle up, people! We've got work to do!" Arka-Dal said.

Everyone grabbed their weapons and walked out into the garden. They gathered around Gorinna as she raised her hands above her head and incanted a spell. A clear bubble suddenly surrounded them.

Seconds later, they rose several hundred feet into the air and zoomed northward. In less than an hour they were looking down upon a vast, ruined city in the middle of the desert. It was about two square miles in size and laid out in a neat grid pattern which was still visible from the air. Much of the grid was still buried under layers of shifting sand.

"So this is Necropolis," Arka-Dal said as they began to descend. "The Dead City."

"It has been thus since the latter part of the First Age," Merlin said. "Only recently has the radiation levels subsided enough to allow people to explore it."

"What secrets did it take to the grave with it, I wonder," asked Arka-Dal. "Who built it? What were the people like?"

"Alas, all of that was lost beneath the ever-shifting sands. It would take years of excavation to discover the answers to your questions. And we may not like what we find," Merlin said.

They touched down in the center of wide, sand-covered, rubble strewn plaza. Everywhere they looked, there were signs of terrible destruction. Only parts of ancient structures still protruded from the layers of sand: a flight of stone stairs here, a column there. A twisted metal light pole or street sign there. Only partial walls remained, some with openings that once held windows. Others were simply blank. All were deeply scarred by centuries of windblown sand and the ancient weapons that all but leveled the city.

And nothing moved.

Anywhere.

No rats skittered amid the rubble piles.

No jackals bayed in the distance.

No insects hummed in the still, dead air.

Nothing at all.

"This place gives me the creeps," Pandaar said. "It's too damned quiet."

"I must admit that I've seen more signs of life in graveyards. It's like Nature itself had shunned this place," Kashi added.

"No wonder it's called Necropolis. This city is truly dead," Gorinna observed.

"And yet, I have a feeling that something is watching our every move," Arka-Dal said as he looked around.

"And it's *not* friendly," Pandaar agreed as he drew his sword.

"What happened here, Merlin?" Arka-Dal asked.

"The people on the other side learned of its location and attempted to blow it off the map. They did quite a good job on it, if I dare say so," Merlin said. "Very little remained standing afterward."

"But they didn't destroy everything here. Something was missed. Now, we have to find it and destroy it," Arka-Dal said. "Keep your eyes open. If that machine can create entire armies, it can certainly create enough soldiers to protect itself. Be ready for anything. I smell an ambush!"

"Perhaps you should have bathed before we left Thule," Kashi joked.

"I'm glad you said something! I thought it was *you* I was smelling," Pandaar quipped.

Arka-Dal smiled at Gorinna.

"There's no need to be quiet. It already knows we're here. What direction is that energy spike coming from?" he asked.

She pointed to the right.

"About a half mile in that direction. It's still going strong, too. I can sense it," she replied.

"It will continue to run until its latest army is completely destroyed or we shut it down," Merlin said.

"What happens to the clones after we shut it down?" Arka-Dal asked. Merlin shrugged.

"At this point, that remains a mystery. It all depends what the machine has programmed them to do. They will either carry out their instructions to the last man or drop to the ground and die," he said.

"Let's hope they drop," Pandaar said. "We don't need to engage them in another long, bloody battle."

Jun and his unit commanders stood atop a large hill and watched as the cloned army slowly advanced on the city. Dur was still 55 miles to the south of them and Jun had positioned his troops between the clones and the city. He arrayed them in the classic Thulian formation, with his heavy infantry in a phalanx in the center, his archers directly behind them and his light infantry and cavalry on each wing. On a rise behind and above his troops, he arrayed his artillery pieces which would rain rocks and other heavy debris on the advancing enemy.

He estimated their strength at around 30,000. All were infantry, too. The clones never had cavalry. Perhaps, he thought, they were unable to clone horses. Each man was dressed and armed exactly alike.

He had brought 60,000 men in all.

More than enough, he thought, to stop the clones from reaching Dur. He just hoped that the battle they were now prepared to fight would never happen.

He snorted.

The enemy moved slowly. At their current rate of speed, it would take over two days for them to reach the city. That meant they'd have to fight in the dead of night. The darkness would probably nullify his artillery and his archers would have to fire blindly over the heads of their comrades.

Neither option was good.

He *could* force the issue and launch an attack. But that would go against Arka-Dal's orders not to engage unless attacked first. On the other hand, Thulian field commanders always were told to use their best judgment during a battle to adapt their strategies to fit any given situation.

He emitted a deep breath, then sipped water from his canteen.

"For now, we watch—and wait," he decided.

They left the plaza and followed a relatively flat path for a few blocks. When they turned a corner marked by to barely standing brick walls that were once part of a much larger building, Kashi spotted something lying on the ground. As they got closer, they realized that the 'something' were several large animals lying on the sides. Each had been partially buried by the shifting sands. They walked over to examine them.

"Horses. They look like they've been here a few weeks, but they still have flesh on their bones," Merlin said.

"They're also saddled," Arka-Dal observed.

Kashi squatted down and brushed the sand away from one of the saddlebags. He untied the flap and looked inside. He took out the contents one at a time and passed them to Arka-Dal.

"One compass," Arka-Dal said as he tossed it to the ground. "One map," which he passed to Merlin. "And one ham sandwich?" he said as he unwrapped it and tossed it away.

"That's all of it," Kashi said.

Merlin unfolded the map and nodded.

"This is a map of these very ruins with several areas circled in red. Apparently, these horses belonged to some sort of search party," he said.

Gorinna looked over his shoulder and pointed to one of the red circles.

"This is where the power surge is coming from," she said. "Maybe these people were looking for the same thing we are?"

"But why?" Merlin wondered.

"These horses have no marks on them. Nothing to indicate that they died from anything other than dehydration. They're almost emaciated. But they haven't ben touched otherwise, not even by vultures of jackals," Kashi said.

"Odd how no carrion birds of other creatures came to feast on their dead flesh," Merlin said. "It's as if all living things are too terrified to venture into this place>"

"I wonder why?" Gorinna asked. "What is it about this place that they fear?"

"I count seven saddled horses. That means there were seven riders. Who were they and what did they come here for?" Arka-Dal posed.

"Perhaps we'll learn the answers when we find that infernal machine?" Merlin suggested.

"Let's get moving," Arka-Dal said.

They walked on for another hundred yards and came upon the body of a man lying face-down in the hot sand. He was dressed in a khaki colored coat with many pockets and he had a canteen in his left hand.

Kashi picked up the canteen and turned it upside down. Nothing but sand poured out. He turned the man over and winced when he saw the fist-sized hole that was burned in his chest.

"I wonder what killed *him*?" he asked as he searched the man's pockets.

He found a billfold, a pocket knife, and a pair of spectacles in a leather case. He opened the billfold and counted out two thousand Dals in Thulian scrip. He slipped them back into the billfold, then went through the second compartment. He found a card with the man's name and address which he showed to Arka-Dal.

"His name was Karyl DJiorda. He was from someplace called Srbinka. I never heard of it," Arka-Dal said. "Since this has his address, we'll send it back to his family after we return to Thule. That way, they'll know what happened to him."

"Srbinka is in central Europe," Merlin said. "DJiorda is very far from home."

"He's not from anywhere anymore," Pandaar said.

"Let's get going," Arka-Dal said.

Ten minutes later, they found what they were looking for. It was a half-buried structure that leaned strangely to the left. It had an arched opening that was partially obscured by the sand and the door was opened inward.

"This is the place," Gorinna said.

"Check out the immediate area," Arka-Dal said.

Kashi and Pandaar nodded then took off in opposite directions.

"Just what type of men would be drawn to a place like this, Merlin?" Arka-Dal asked.

"Of hand, I'd say treasure hunters, scientists, scholars and even explorers. Ancient ruins are also magnets for tourists. Take your pick," Merlin said. "There was a time when you were drawn to such places. Remember?"

Arka-Dal laughed.

"I remember. I still am," he said. "Perhaps when this is over, I'll return to this place and do some digging of my own."

Merlin smiled.

"Even after all the trouble you stirred up exploring other ruins?" he asked.

"Even after that," Arka-Dal said.

"And I shall go with you—just to keep you out of trouble, of course," Merlin said.

"Of course," Arka-Dal smiled.

Just then, Pandaar and Kashi returned. They looked out of breath.

"Anything?" asked Arka-Dal.

"It's just as you said. We ran into about 20 or so guards on the other side of the street," Kashi said.

"But they won't be bothering us any more," Pandaar smiled.

"That's strange. We didn't hear a thing," Merlin remarked.

"Maybe it's because we caught them by surprise. It was over so quickly that we hardly made a sound. As usual, they didn't either," Kashi said. "They died without so much as a gasp."

"One thing's for sure—those guards didn't kill DJiorda. Whatever killed him was very high tech. I'm betting this entire place is booby trapped so we'd best be very careful where we step and what we lean against," Pandaar said.

Jun decided to force the issue. He ordered his archers to move forward and form a triple line. When the enemy moved within bow range, he gave the signal to fire. All three rows of archers aimed their bows skyward and fired. The missiles reached the height of their arc above the clones then rained down on them. The first volley found their marks with deadly accuracy. Jun watched as hundreds of clones dropped to the earth and lay still while their brethren simple marched relentlessly over them. The second volley struck the front of their column and dropped several more. This time, most of the clones raised their shields and took cover behind them. The third volley quickly followed but had little effect.

"Cease fire!" Jun told his signalman.

The soldier raised a red flag and waved it. The archers stopped firing, did an about-face, and returned to the main body.

Jun turned to an officer next to him.

"Move the artillery forward and set the sights low," he said.

The officer saluted and rode off.

"Are we going to engage them?" another officer asked.

"We will engage them only if we cannot stop them any other way," Jun replied. "I don't want to waste the life of a single one of our soldiers if we don't have to."

"They're shifting ranks," another officer pointed out.

Jun watched as the enemy slowly divided into four different groups, with two in the center and one on each flank. They did this slowly and with great precision, like the well-trained soldiers they were.

"Have the cavalry move to the right and left. Encircle them from the rear but don't attack until I give the signal," he said.

The officer saluted and galloped off.

He wondered if the clones would notice his maneuver. If they did, would they bother to react and adapt? Right now, he was testing them. He wanted to see if they could actually adapt to troop shifts like normal soldiers. If they did, it proved they were guided by some sort of intelligence. If not, they were just mindless copies of each other.

The cavalry moved as he'd ordered. They moved in plain view. The clones neither reacted nor seemed to notice. Jun nodded.

"Zombies," he said.

"Sir?" asked one of the officers.

Jun smiled.

"We are about to engage in battle against a horde of mindless zombies. They will just keep advancing toward Dur no matter what happens. Have the archers move to their flanks and bring down as many of them as possible until they run out of arrows," he said. "I'll have the artillery fire at the same time. That should greatly reduce their numbers."

Thule.

Mayumi and the other wives were seated in the living room after dinner when a soldier rushed in. He walked up to Mayumi and respectfully bowed his head. She returned it.

"My Queen," he said. "Our scouts have spotted a large body of soldiers moving south across the Yboe. They are headed toward the capital."

Mayumi looked at Chatha.

"I'm on it," Chatha said as she rushed from the room.

Mayumi and Galya smiled. The Atlantean princess loved a good fight and she was an excellent field tactician. In less than 20 minutes, she was clad in her battle armor and rushing out of the palace to assemble her regiments.

On her way out, she almost ran into Leo. He stepped aside and watched as she raced through the door and slammed it behind her.

"Where is Chatha going dressed like that?" he asked.

"Our scouts discovered another clone army marching toward the city. Since our men are elsewhere, she decided to handle it," Galya said with a smile.

Leo nodded.

"In that case, I feel sorry for the clones," he said.

When they entered the structure, they discovered that the walls and floors were made of a highly polished black marble. The front room contained a battered metal desk, some shelves and a couple rotted out padded chairs. On the wall behind the desk was a black, green and white flag with ancient Arabic writing.

"The banner was once the flag of something called the New Caliphate," Merlin said. "It rose near the tail end of the First Age. Their leaders tried to restore an old system of government by rallying every Muslim on Earth to its cause. Alas, all they triggered was the final stage of the war."

"So they were destroyed before they even got it off the ground?" Pandaar asked.

"Yes—and with good reason. They were bloodthirsty and power mad fanatics. Unfortunately, they managed to get their hands on some very nasty weapons and used them to attack the last two remaining powers. They Caliphate was destroyed within a week. After that, the two powers turned their weapons on each other again," Merlin said.

They walked past the desk and through the arched door behind it. They found themselves in a rubble littered corridor. The walls were cracked and had gaping holes in several places, along with a few scorch marks.

At the end of the corridor was a set of double doors. One had been slid partially open. Kashi raised his hand, then went inside. They saw a bright flash, followed by a shower of sparks that illuminated the corridor the room.

Then all went silent.

Kashi emerged with a sheepish grin.

"Damned trap almost got me," he said as she showed them his left shoulder.

His shirt had been seared open and the flesh beneath was slightly blistered.

"It was some sort of light weapon," he said. "I located the source and disarmed it, so it's safe now."

When they entered the room, long dormant lights suddenly flickered on. They saw four disheveled forms lying by the door. One was seated against the wall with a large hole burned through his forehead and scorch mark on the wall directly behind him. Two others lay on their backs staring up at the ceiling. The fourth was in a fetal position facing the door. Leather pouches, a few tools, hats and other gear was scattered among them.

"They're all dressed like the fellow we found outside," Merlin observed.

"Apparently, they weren't as lucky or as quick as I was," Kashi said. "You think that's all of them?"

"I don't know. But I think we'll soon find out," Arka-Dal said as they looked around.

The room was about 300 square feet large with a flat ceiling. There were several desks on either side and one large on in the center. The walls and floors were made of the black rock. Above them were a line of small barrels and lights, aimed at the door.

"That was the trap," Kashi said as he pointed. "Once I slashed through the cable that led into it, it became useless."

"Let's see what's behind the next door," Arka-Dal said.

"That's the place," Gorinna said. "I feel a huge amount of power coming from within."

"I feel it, too," Merlin said.

"Be careful," Arka-Dal said as he nodded for Kashi to take the lead.

He walked over to the doors, put his ear to it, then used his dagger to pry them open. To his surprise, they hissed open easily and the bright lights that came from the room behind them nearly blinded him.

"I hear a humming sound," Pandaar said.

"That's the machinery at work," Merlin said. "It's powering that army Jun's men spotted."

The room was large and rectangular with a vaulted ceiling. The walls and floor were made of the same black material and it was well lit by recessed lights. Banks of highly sophisticated machinery lined both the left and right hand walls. An illuminated, translucent blue cube stood against the far wall. There were cables and tubes running from it and into four of the machines on either side.

"There it is," Merlin said. "The source of the clones."

They spotted the shadowy form of a man inside. He was suspended in the middle with his arms and legs stretched out. On the wall he now faced was an illuminated map of the entire world. Two red lights blinked on different points of the map.

They walked over and studied the cube.

"The flashing light above his head is where Jun spotted that army. There's also a second light flashing to the south near the capital," Arka-Dal said. "That means a second army is now marching toward Thule itself."

Kashi looked behind them.

He saw two more charred corpses lying against the wall near the door. He shook his head.

"Looks like everyone in this party was killed but the guy in the cube," he said. "I wonder how he got in there?"

"Is he alive?" Arka-Dal asked.

"He's very much alive. The machine is feeding him. It's keeping him strong so it can use his energy to create the clones. After it creates a new army, it teleports it to anywhere it chooses," Merlin said.

"The technology is amazing!" Gorinna said. "It's almost like our magic."

"Amazing or not, we have to shut this thing down and destroy it o no one else can make use of it later," Arka-Dal said.

"If we kill the guy inside of it that might shut it down" Pandaar suggested.

"True—but then *you* might end up taking his place in the machine," Merlin warned.

Arka-Dal reached up and touched the cube. It jiggled and grew slightly brighter. He drew his dagger and plunged it into the mass. It went in easy but his hand tingled. He withdrew and stepped back.

"What's it made of?" he asked.

"That is not known to me at this time," Merlin replied. "It's some sort of gelatinous matter. It may even be alive. Some life form that was created for just this purpose."

"Interesting. Leo would love this," Arka-Dal smiled.

"How do we shut it off?" Kashi asked.

"There!" Gorinna said as she pointed to a large bank of lights and switched and dials. "That's its main power source."

"Trace the lines," Merlin said.

They traced the lines. Some led to the next bank of machines. Two went into the ceiling. A third went directly to the base of the cube.

"This has to be the one," Arka-Dal said as he squatted over it. "Merlin—what do you think the power source is?"

"Given the period this was created, I'd say it was nuclear," Merlin answered. "Destroying the machine may trigger an explosion."

Arka-Dal nodded.

He drew his sword, raised it over his head, and brought it down hard on the cable. The blade severed the cable with ease buy set off a shower of sparks. The room began to shake and a loud humming filled the air.

A few seconds later, all became quiet.

Arka-Dal looked at the cube. It was dark now.

"Get him out of there," he said.

Gorinna raised her hands and clapped. The cube solidified them shattered. As the pieces cascaded to the floor, the man imprisoned within it suddenly grew limp and hit the floor as well.

Arka-Dal dragged the battered man to a nearby wall and propped him up against it. He handed him his canteen and waited until the man was finished drinking. The man put the cap back on and handed it to him.

"Thanks. To all of you. I thought I'd never get out of that thing," he said.

"Who are you?" Arka-Dal asked.

"Thomas Boswitz. I make my living as a guide, explorer and treasure hunter. Or I did until I got myself trapped in that weird machine," he replied.

"How long were you in there?" asked Pandaar.

"What month is this?" Boswitz asked groggily.

"July," Arka-Dal said.

"Then I've only been trapped in there for five weeks," Boswitz said. "It felt like an eternity. But I guess I came out of this better than the people who hired me to bring them here."

"Oh? How many others were with you?" asked Merlin.

"Seven. None of them made it past that second door. They were all killed by hidden traps and other nasty devices," Boswitz said.

"That explains the bodies," Pandaar remarked.

Arka-Dal nodded.

"Just how *did* you get trapped in there?" he asked.

"As soon as I opened that door and stepped inside the room, something in the floor hurled me straight into it. I expected to hit it at full force. Instead, I became trapped. It absorbed me like a sponge and I couldn't get out of it," Boswitz replied.

"What happened while you were inside that machine?" Arka-Dal asked.

"I'm not really sure. I lost all track of time and even my sense of where I was. I think every few days I felt these intense waves of power surge through my body. The feelings lasted a long time. Maybe hours. In each instance, a map appeared on that screen in front of me. Each time, I saw a light blink on and off in a different location. This lasted until I blacked out. I have no idea what it meant, either," Boswitz said.

Merlin looked deep into his eyes.

"He's telling the truth," he pronounced.

"Good. Then we won't have to kill him," Pandaar said with a smirk. "Too bad. I was kind of looking forward to it."

Boswitz stared at him.

"Hey! What's going on? How did you guys even *find* me?" he asked.

"That's a long story," Arka-Dal said as he helped him to his feet. "We'll fill you in on the way back to Thule."

The Book

In the 57ᵗʰ year of the reign of Arka-Dal

It was a balmy summer afternoon. Just about everyone imaginable was lounging in the large living room after one the usual overlong breakfasts. Arka-Dal and Leo were playing chess and talking about things being nice and quiet for a change. That suddenly changed when the Devil materialized next to the gaming table with an oversized bundle in his hands.

"I've brought you a little gift, Leo. Since you are fond of collecting rare and unusual books from the First Age, I'm sure you'll appreciate it," he said as he placed the bundle on the table.

Everyone gathered around as he slowly unwrapped the bundle. When he was finished, an amazing large and heavy—and obviously ancient—book lay before them. The book was three feet long, 20 inches wide and 22 inches thick. It's was in a wooden folder that was covered with leather and the pages were made of vellum, or animal skin.

Merlin gaped in wonder at the heavy tome.

"The Codex Gigas! I thought it was lost," he said. "Where did you find it?"

"In the vaults deep beneath the Vatican," the Devil replied. "It was just sitting on a shelf gathering dust. I imagine it had been there for many centuries."

Leo untied the leather cord and slowly, gingerly, lifted the cover. Then, just as gingerly, he turned the pages. They had turned darker with age, but he could see that the book was richly illuminated and written in Latin.

"Codex Gigas is Latin for Big Book," the Devil explained. "But, thanks to a rather unflattering illustration of me on page 290, it became known as the Devil's Bible—but I take no direct credit for this work."

"This book is amazing," Leo said as he continued to examine it. "What does it contain, exactly?"

"It includes the entire Latin Vulgate version of the Christian Bible as well as Isidore of Seville's Entymologiae, Josephus' Antiquities of the Jews, Cosmas of Prague's Chronicle of Bohemia, various tracts of ancient history, etymology and physiology, a calendar with necrologium, a list of monks from a long vanished manaster, spells, potions and various records. It is quite an extensive work," the Devil said.

Leo turned to page 290 and smiled at the unflattering drawing. Other than the drawing, the page was blank and it had aged to a very gloomy color.

"Who wrote this?" Leo asked.

"Now *that's* open to debate," the Devil said with a grin. "As it's quite a long story, I think it best I tell it while we drink some of that delicious blue wine Thule is famous for."

Leo nodded.

He picked up the book and strained.

"This is heavy!" he said.

"It weighs 160 pounds," the Devil said as he took it from him and carried over to the large table in front of the sofas and set it down.

Galya smiled.

"I have never seen this book. Father told me about it when I was a child, but I didn't know it still existed," she said as Arka-Dal handed her a glass of wine and sat down beside her.

Mayumi sat to his other side. Chatha and Medusa also joined them on the sofa. Gorinna and Merlin took a seat on one of the smaller couches. Leo knelt at the table and kept gingerly leafing through the book.

"According to the legends, the book was written sometime in the 13th century of the First Age, probably in the bygone state of Bohemia. A note written on the inside states that it was pawned by its owners, the monks of Podlazice in the year 1295 A.D. Supposedly, it was the work of a single monk and he wrote the entire book in one night," the Devil began.

"Yes. I remember the legend and this may have something to do with its other name, The Devil's Bible," Merlin said with a smile. "The unidentified monk supposedly violated his monastic vows and was sentenced to be walled up alive inside the monastery. Desperate to avoid this severe fate, he promised to write in one single night a book that would both glorify the monastery forever and also contain all human knowledge. Of course, his superiors took him up on his offer but threatened to carry out his punishment if he failed to produce the manuscript."

"This is where I enter the picture," the Devil said. "As midnight approached, the hapless monk realized he would never be able to complete the manuscript on time so he called upon me for help. We supposedly struck the usual bargain. I got his soul and, in return, I completed the manuscript. The monk then added that horrid illustration of me out of gratitude for my aid. The legend further states that when the monk presented this masterpiece to his superiors, they realized that such a thing could only have been accomplished with the help of the Devil and walled him up anyway."

"Is there any truth to that?" Leo asked.

The Devil shrugged.

"True or not, the Benedictines did nothing at all to discourage the stories. They were good for business. People from all over the world came to the monastery to view this book and hear about the unfortunate soul who wrote it," he said. "If the abbot really believed this was done with my help, he would have had it burned rather than keep it on display."

"Did you make such a contract?" Leo asked.

"No," the Devil replied. "I had nothing at all to do with this book. What most likely happened is that a monk was ordered to write this by his superiors and he requested to produce it in solitude. It probably took him somewhere between 20-30 years to complete it. Some credit the work to someone named Herman Inclusus, or Herman the Recluse and say he did this to purge his soul of evil. If you examine the page directly opposite the one with illustration of me, you'll see it contains an illustration of Heaven. I believe it was meant to symbolize that good and evil exist side-by-side instead of anything sinister."

"The Codex Gigas has a long and colorful history," Merlin added. "From its origins in Bohemia, it remained under Benedictine control at the monastery in Broumov until the 16th century with several abbots and monarchs adding their names and dates to it. From there it went to Poland, then to Prague. It was taken to Stockholm after the Swedes overran the city in 1649. It remained in the Royal Library for centuries. Its history becomes quite murky after 2095."

"It certainly does. That was the start of the events that led up to the Great Disaster. I have no idea how or why it ended up at the Vatican, but it's yours now, Leo," the devil said.

"Just how did you procure it from the Vatican?" asked Gorinna.

"That's another strange story and it befits the Codex Gigas perfectly," the Devil said. "The Cardinal had no real use for it. To him, it was little more than an interesting and novel artifact from the First Age with a storied history.[4] In fact, he was shocked when I requested it in exchange for a small favor he needed from me."

Leo raised an eyebrow at this.

Galya giggled.

"Father and the Cardinal have known each other for decades," she explained. "Still, it's hard to imagine *him* asking you for help."

The Devil laughed.

"His summons surprised me, too," he said. "When I realized what he needed and why, I decided to forego the usual contract requirements. He expected me to ask for his soul. When I asked for the book, he was stunned."

"Out of curiosity, why didn't you take his soul? That *is* your usual custom," Merlin asked.

"That often depends upon the type and magnitude of the request. Since the Cardinal's request seemed quite minor to me and I happen to like him and support the work the Vatican does, I simply asked for the book instead. And I did that because I knew Leo would enjoy having it in his archives," the Devil replied as he sipped his wine.

"Destroying Opus Dei is hardly what I would call minor, Father," Galya said. "You did this because you despised them as much as the Cardinal did."

"That was only part of my reason," the Devil admitted. "The rest I'll keep to myself for now."

"You eliminated Opus Dei?" Leo asked.

"You mean those witch hunters are gone?" Gorinna asked.

"I merely lopped the heads off the hydra. I'm sure that another, perhaps more vile organization will sprout from its necks eventually.

---

4   Read: Hunter: Terror on the Bayou (Trafford)

There will always be madmen running amok on Earth and more than enough mindless sheep to follow them," the Devil said with a smile. "That's why my work is never done."

"There's a gap of nearly 2,000 years where the book is not accounted for. Do you have any idea where it was during that time?" asked Merlin.

"Near the very end of the Great Disaster, a rogue military commander named Axl Beritz led his marauders into Stockholm in search of the book. In the process, he leveled the city and his men raped and slaughtered most of the inhabitants. Around that time, a rumor circulated that whoever possessed the Devil's Bible had the power of Hell's legions behind him. Beritz believed the book would enable him to become the master of the world—such as it was at that time," the Devil said. "I'm not sure if he ever laid hands on the book, but it did vanish into the smoke of legends afterward. The Cardinal said the book was already in the archives when he became head of the Vatican and probably had been there for centuries. Either way, it belongs to Leo now."

"And I shall treasure it always. Thank you, my friend," Leo said as he turned another page. "I'm amazed at its condition. One would expect such a tome to be badly deteriorated after so many centuries."

"The book was badly damaged when I retrieved it from the vault. I restored it to the condition it was in when it was displayed at the Stockholm museum. I changed nothing. There are eight pages missing. They disappeared sometime during the 15th century. Most scholars believe they simply contained a list of the monks who lived at Broumov. But no one really knows for certain. One of the abbots removed them prior to selling it to the Swedish king," the Devil said.

"One of the legends associated with the book stated that it contained mention of the Necronomicon and *that*'s why those pages were removed. It makes sense when you think about it. After all, doesn't the Codex Gigas contain all of the knowledge that was available at the time it was written? If that was the case, then surely there was some mention of the Necronomicon in it," Merlin suggested.

"I did consider that more than I care to admit. Since the Necronomicon was the most detested and dreaded book ever written, the church went out of its way to erase all mention of it. I think they feared the Necronomicon more than they did me!" the Devil said.

"Is this the only copy of the Codex?" Leo asked.

"The one and only original. There were some attempts to translate it into Swedish during the 17th century but those were poorly made and never completed," the Devil replied. "What you see before you is the rarest of all rarities."

"Even rarer than the Necronomicon?" asked Leo.

"Much rarer. Several copies of that abominable manuscript were made and a handful of them still exist in one form or translation or another. But this is the one and only Codex Gigas," the Devil replied.

"You're right," Leo said as he turned the pages.

"About what?" asked the Devil.

"This *is* a most unflattering rendition of you," Leo said. "In fact, it's downright insulting."

The Devil laughed.

"I think so," he said. "And that unflattering image leant the legend wings. Because of that, I was given credit for something I had no part in whatsoever. But that's the price of fame, I suppose."

Leo ran his fingers over the heavy pages and wondered how many people had vied for possession of the book and their reasons for wanting it. The Devil smiled at him and nodded to show he could read his thoughts.

"Thousands have died over that book," he said. "But not until the end of the First Age was near. Up until that time, it had passed from one city to another where it was viewed as nothing more than a mysterious work of literature. The book itself is sort of an encyclopedia. It's the *myth* behind its creation that makes it fascinating. And what people choose to believe it contains."

Leo nodded.

"Anyway, it will make an excellent addition to the Archives," he said.

Just as he was about to close the cover, the book's pages began to leaf back and forth by themselves. They watched as the pages turned faster and faster, then slowly stopped. Leo looked at the Devil.

"What do you supposed caused *that*?" he asked.

"I don't know—but it *can't* be anything good," the Devil replied. "Whatever it was, made my skin crawl—and not many things have such an effect on me."

Before Leo could respond, the book began to take on an ominous, yellow-green glow. The glow lit up the entire room as it became brighter and brighter. Then, just as suddenly, it grew dark.

This was followed by a puff of bright red smoke. They gaped as a tall, dark figure emerged from the smoke and glowered at them with bright amber eyes. It turned its gaze toward Arka-Dal and emitted a strange, hollow, almost distant laugh. The sound made the Emperor's blood run cold and he was suddenly gripped by a deep sense of dread and terror so strong that it immobilized him.

Everyone else in the room just stood and stared as the demon flapped its leathery wings and beat its chest as if was mocking them. Before anyone could react, the creature began to swirl around.

Faster and faster and faster it swirled as it filled the room with a thick, purple smoke. Then it vanished in an eye blink—taking the book with it.

"The book! It's gone!" Galya shouted as she stood.

"That—whatever it is—took it!" Gorinna added.

"The entire room literally reeks of brimstone," the Devil remarked.

"I thought only *you* used that trick," Arka-Dal said as he looked around.

"Not hardly," the Devil said as he stepped to the table and placed his hands over it. "I'm feeling traces of energy. Dark energy. And nasty. That creature is a demon but it's not from any plane I know."

"Whatever it was, it scared the shit out of me," Pandaar said.

"Since you're so full of it, that might be an improvement," Kashi said. "But I know what you mean. I was too frightened to even move. I've never felt anything like *that* before. My entire body is riddled with chills."

"I admit that it terrified me, too," Arka-Dal said. "That thing broadcasts fear. A deep, bone chilling fear. I still feel cold inside. Did that thing dwell in the book?"

"No. It was sent to *steal* the book," the Devil replied as he lowered his hands.

"You mean someone *controls* it?" Leo asked.

"Yes. Someone summoned it for the express purpose of taking the book. Someone very vile and powerful," the Devil said. "Someone I think you and I know quite well, Merlin."

"But you did away with him," Merlin said. "Didn't you?"

"I was certain I did," the Devil said. "Yet I have the distinct impression that this was all *his* doing. I don't know how he managed to survive what I did to him, but I feel that he has returned to plague us once again."

"If it is him, why would he want the Codex? As you've already pointed out, it's nothing more than a curiosity of the First Age. It has no spells hidden within its pages. It would be useless to him," Merlin said.

"The man is quite mad, as you know. His lust for power twisted his mind centuries ago and destroyed whatever soul or humanity he possessed. He must believe that the Codex legends are true or he would not have gone through all this trouble to steal it," the Devil said.

"What if the legends are true? What if he knows something about that book we don't?" Arka-Dal asked. "If there's any chance, no matter how small, that the Codex will add to his powers, then we must get it back and kill him in the process—for good this time."

Merlin shook his head.

"I sensed nothing magical within the pages of the Codex," he said. "Nothing at all."

"But he stole it for a *reason*. And that gives us reason enough to take it back," Galya said with a smile. "If it really is him, then I owe him one."

"So do I," Gorinna said.

"We *all* owe him one," Arka-Dal agreed. "Him and his cat!"

"That's it!" the Devil said. "That's how he survived. He must have willed his essence into the body of his familiar a split second before my spell took effect. That's the only way he could have survived what I did to him."

"This time, we'll get rid of the cat first. That will keep him from making such a transfer again," Merlin said.

"What about that demon?" asked Galya.

"I'll handle him if he dares show his face again. I don't know where he got it from, but it's quite powerful. It must be one of those that dwell on the lowest planes of Hell. After all, I don't know *every* demon in my realm," the Devil replied. "But if he is one of mine, he'll regret his actions for all eternity."

Galya laughed.

Arka-Dal glanced at her. His expression made her laugh harder.

"I just pictured several nasty things that Father will do to that demon when we find it. Some are quite amusing," she explained.

Arka-Dal smiled.

"I've seen his work," he said. "Can you track that thing?"

"No. The last traces of its energy have gone. I did get an image of a tall, crumbling, stone keep in a mist shrouded valley. The image was familiar but I'm having difficulty placing it. I'm sure it will come to me later," the Devil answered as he folded his hands behind his back.

"I hope we can get the Codex back in one piece," Leo said wistfully.

"We will, my friend," the Devil assured him.

Far away, in the realm of the Others, Azathoth sat across the table from Alyana and listened as she questioned him about the treaty he'd agreed to with Arka-Dal.

"You said we could visit Earth on official business?" she asked.

He nodded.

"What would constitute such official business?" she pressed.

"What are you fishing for, Alyana?" he asked.

"Well, if you were to send an emissary or ambassador to Thule, would *that* be official business?" Alyana asked. "After all, many nations have ambassadors in Thule. Why shouldn't we?"

Azathoth smiled.

"I guess sending an ambassador to Thule to open diplomatic relations could be considered official business. After all, our realm does have all the trappings of an empire or nation. Before I could send an ambassador, I'd have to send an emissary to open diplomatic channels. If Arka-Dal agrees, then we could send an ambassador," he said.

"And it would be worthwhile for both nations, wouldn't it?" Alyana asked.

"I think there would be certain benefits in it," Azathoth agreed.

"And it would be fully within the conditions of the treaty," Alyana said.

"Indeed," he nodded. "So you think I should send an emissary to Thule?"

"Yes," Alyana replied with a grin.

"And I suppose you have someone in mind for the task?" he asked.

"I have the *perfect* candidate in mind, Father," she answered.

Azathoth laughed.

"I'm not too sure about that," he hesitated. "You might open a can of vipers instead of building good relations."

"I know I can do this, Father. Just give me the chance to prove it," Alyana said.

"If I do decide to send you, are you going there to fulfill your role as an ambassador or are you planning to try and land a mate?" Azathoth asked.

"Yes," she replied.

He laughed again. She giggled, too.

"Let me think about this awhile. Sending you to Thule as an ambassador could be like setting a flaming dog loose in a munitions factory—especially if you go after Arka-Dal and incur the wrath of Galya," Azathoth said. "While I like the idea of opening direct diplomatic channels with Arka-Dal, I'm not sure that you are the right person for that post. Subtlety isn't exactly one of your strong points."

"I can be subtle—when I *want* to be, Father," Alyana assured him.

She rose and walked out of the room. Azathoth watched her leave and smiled. He knew that Alyana was trying to take a page from Galya's book. He also knew that Galya was jealous of her and might react with all of her fury if Alyana made a play for Arka-Dal. He wondered if his daughter would be able to show some kind of restraint—at least publicly. Arka-Dal already had several very beautiful wives. But would he want to take on yet another?

Through an incredible twist of fate, he and Arka-Dal had become friends and allies. The last thing he wanted to do was jeopardize that alliance. On the other hand, in the unlikely event that Arka-Dal and Alyana married, their union would make the bonds between their worlds unbreakable, much as they are with Galya's father. The idea both intrigued and worried him.

The wizard sat at the crude table in his crumbling tower far away from Thule and gently opened the heavy cover of the Codex. He laughed at the crude depiction of the Devil on the first page, then gently turned it. As he perused the text, he frowned. His frown turned to outright anger then to disgust.

He slammed the cover shut and cursed through his cat as loud as he could.

The Codex was useless to him. All of the dark and powerful spells were purportedly written on the first eight pages of the ancient tome. And those pages were *missing*!

He grumbled as he paced the room.

It was plain to see that those pages had been torn out centuries ago. By whom and for what reasons he didn't know.

Were the secrets he needed on those missing pages?

Or were they still buried someone in the confusing text?

The cat sat on a nearby window sill and watched him pace, amused by his frustration. The cat stretched and yawned indifferently after a few minutes, then curled up and napped.

"All you ever do is nap!" the wizard groused/

"All *you* ever do is steal things that don't belong to you, then complain about them afterward," the cat replied disdainfully as it stretched up one of its hind legs and licked itself.

"If you're not napping, you're licking yourself!" the wizard snapped.

"You're just jealous because *you* can't do this. Perhaps if you could, you wouldn't be such an asshole," the cat said as it curled up and went back to sleep.

The wizard sneered at his familiar, then sat back down and began going through the Codex again…

"There's something troubling me about that crazed wizard," Merlin said.

"And what is that, my friend?" the Devil asked.

"I thought we destroyed him years ago. How does he manage to keep coming back?" Merlin asked. "Even if he does transfer into the body of his cat, how does he manage to return in human form time and again?"

"The same way *you* do, I imagine," the Devil replied. "You created clones of yourself and strategically placed them in deep caverns all over the Earth. The moment your physical body is destroyed, you teleport into one of them and keep going."

"You think he's hidden clones?" Merlin asked.

"I'd say that's highly probable. But where you can instantaneously make the transfer into a new body, he cannot. He needs to do it through a *conduit*. I believe the cat is that conduit. He transfers his conscious into the cat then the cat races to one of the clones and makes the transfer," the Devil said.

"So killing *him* accomplishes nothing?" Arka-Dal asked.

"All that does is give us a few months peace until he returns to plague us again," the Devil said.

"So to get rid of him permanently, we have to get rid of the cat?" Gorinna asked.

"It's not that simple. We have to strike at the cat the exact moment he makes the transfer. That way, we trap him inside the cat's body. It will take perfect timing and just the right trap to make it work," the Devil said.

"I suppose you have a plan?" Merlin asked.

"I *always* do," the Devil smiled. "And I need both you and Gorinna to make it work."

They saw three demons standing watch at the gate. There was the very demon who had taken the Codex and two slightly smaller ones. Each was armed with a flaming sword and were prepared to kill anything and anyone who approached the tower.

"I'll handle this," the Devil said.

He stepped into the open and walked up the path toward the tower. The demons watched him approach for a few moments, then moved to intercept him. The largest of them stood directly in front of the Devil with his arms folded across his chest and snarled. To the demon's shock, the Devil simply laughed at him.

"Turn back now or suffer the consequences," the demon growled.

"You'd best step aside and let me pass—*if* you know what's good for you and your friends," the Devil said calmly.

"Fool! I am Thraxx, Lord of 578th Plane. I stand aside for no one," the demon said as it brandished its sword.

"I know the lord of the 578th Plane and you are *not* him," the Devil replied. "You are nothing but a liar and a braggart and you shall suffer for your insolence."

"How could you know who the lord of 578th Plane is?" the demon said as it took several steps toward him.

Instead of backing off, the Devil stood his ground and smiled.

"That's simple enough. It was *I* who appointed him," he replied as he waved his hand.

In an instant, the flaming sword was transformed into a cloud of harmless moths which fluttered off in all directions. The astonished demon regained his composure and swung his fist at the Devil. The intended blow struck something invisible and the demons screamed in agony as its hand shattered like glass.

"Who are you?" the demon shouted as he dropped to his knees.

"I am your lord and master. I am the supreme ruler of all of Hell and your doom," the Devil said.

"*Lord Lucifer!*" the demon gasped. "Is it too late to offer an apology?"

The Devil clapped his hands twice. With each clap, parts of the demon's body fell to the ground and turned to dust.

"I—I guess it is," he groaned as he fell face-down.

The Devil kicked at the remains. The other demons watched as Thraxx faded into green mist. Almost immediately, they fell prostrate and begged for mercy. The Devil allowed them to grovel for a time then ordered them to stand. They leapt to their feet and snapped to attention.

"Since neither of you were involved in the theft of the Codex and did not try to attack me, I have decided to spare your worthless lives. From this moment forward, you are banished to the Outlands. If you ever set foot in another plane, I'll be far less merciful—if you get my meaning. Now go!" the Devil said sternly.

The demons bowed and vanished.

Arka-Dal and the others ran over. The Devil smiled.

"What are the Outlands?" asked Gorinna.

"It's a realm that lies far beyond the realm of the Others. It's where I send all of my troublemakers. There is no escaping from it, either," the Devil said. "Now, let's go and pay our respects to the madman in the tower."

Up in the wizard's chamber, the cat yawned.

"Your guards are no more. They have been made quick work of," it said. "Your visitors will be here soon. Then what will you do?"

"Greet them in my usual manner," the wizard said.

"Each time you do, you get your ass kicked. At least it's fun to watch," the cat taunted.

"It matters not. I'll just return and start over as always," the wizard sneered. "Just don't get yourself killed."

"Don't worry about that. I'm too quick for them," the cat said calmly as it licked its paw.

Halfway up the stairs, the Devil raised his hand. They stopped as he related the next step in his plan.

"I'll make myself invisible. You go on up and confront him. I want you to hit him with your most *destructive* spell. Once you destroy his body, he'll will himself into the body of his cat. As soon as he makes the transfer, I'll act," he said.

"That cat's awful quick," Gorinna said.

"I'm much quicker," the Devil smiled. "I have something in mind for him that will astound him. It's something not even he can escape from."

"What is it?" asked Arka-Dal.

The Devil smiled.

"Watch and see," he said as he slowly faded away.

"Just like an old soldier," Merlin remarked.

They continued their slow climb up the twisting, crumbling stairs until they reached the very top floor of the tower. To their surprise, the door was wide open and the wizard was seated in his high-backed chair waiting.

"I've been expecting you," he said through the cat which was still on the window sill.

"We've come for the Codex," Merlin said.

"It is there on the table. Useless," the wizard nodded. "It is not what I expected. You may take it if you like."

"That's not the only reason we've come," Arka-Dal said.

"We've also decided to rid the world of you once and forever," Merlin said. "You have caused far more trouble than you're worth. Before you can cause any more misery, you have to go."

The wizard laughed.

"Do as you see fit, Merlinus. But you can already guess what the outcome will be," he said defiantly.

Gorinna stepped forward and leveled a beam of light at him. He deflected it through the open window with a wave of his hand then pointed his finger and twirled it around. Gorinna was swept from her feet and spun like atop. He raised her several feet from the floor, then let her drop suddenly. She landed on her rear end with a dull THUD. The wizard laughed as she got up and massaged herself.

It was then that Merlin formed a fireball in the palm of his right hand and cast it straight at the wizard.

Just as Merlin's fireball struck the wizard, he turned to dust. At that moment, the cat leaped from the window ledge and darted across the floor as fast as his paws could carry him.

"I was *expecting* that!" the Devil said as he waved his hand.

In mid-stride, a clear, orange bubble engulfed the startled feline and brought his flight to sudden halt with a dull thud. The cat screamed and yowled as it clawed frantically at its prison while the Devil laughed. He walked to the bubble and squatted down. Then he smiled at the cat.

The animal scowled.

"You again! How many times are you going to ruin my plans with your interference?" it hissed angrily.

"I promise you this will the very last time," the Devil replied.

"Bah! This won't hold me forever!" the cat said smugly.

"It won't *have* to," the Devil said.

"What do you mean?" asked the cat as he realized the Devil was quite serious.

"I'm weary of having to deal with you time and time again. While the book you stole was worthless for what you wanted from it, I know you well enough to realize that you'll continue to be a thorn in my side and everyone else's. Therefore, I've decided to rid the world of you once and for all," the Devil said as he stood.

The globe levitated off the floor and hovered before him. The car hissed and clawed at it some more.

"You might as well stop struggling and accept your fate. That globe was designed to entrap your miserable energies. There's no escape.—except in death," the Devil said.

"Death?" the cat asked.

"Yes—if one such as you can suffer death," the Devil said as he raised his hands.

The globe spun wildly in place for several seconds. It was long enough to make the cat dizzy and sick. He laughed as it puked all over itself.

"It's time to be rid of you, Wizard," he said as he pointed toward the open window.

They watched as the globe sailed through the window and rocketed straight up into the sky. It was out of sight in seconds.

"Where'd you send him?" asked Arka-Dal.

"To the sun," the Devil replied. "The intense heat will disintegrate both the globe and the cat in less than a second. Not even *he* can escape that."

"What did the sun ever do to deserve him?" asked Merlin.

"Nothing at all that I'm aware of. It just seemed like the best place to send him," the Devil replied.

He walked over to the large wooden table and closed the heavy cover on the Codex.

"That fool gave up his life for a mere legend—a simple curiosity. I'm always amazed at what lengths some humans will go to in their lust for power, both real and imagined," he said as he tucked the book under his arm.

"At least he didn't damage it. Leo will be glad for that," Gorinna said.

"Indeed," Merlin agreed.

"I was wondering about those missing pages," Arka-Dal said.

"Oh?" the Devil asked.

"Yes. Does anyone have any idea what was written on them or why they were removed?" Arka-Dal asked.

"The only ones who knew what was on those pages are long dead. One can speculate based on the book's long and bizarre history, but the truth went to the grave with whoever tore those pages out," the Devil said. "Perhaps it's best we never find out."

When they left the tower, Gorinna stopped and looked up at the sun.

"How long until he reaches it?" she asked.

"An hour at most," the Devil answered. "Then we'll be rid of him forever."

"Are you sure about that?" asked Arka-Dal.

"As one of your philosophers once said, the only sure things in life are death and taxes. But not even *his* foul energies can survive a collision with the sun. No, my son. I'm sure that we've seen the last of that madman," the Devil said with a grin.

"I wonder," Gorinna said softly as she watched the sun.

The Ambassador

In the 57ʰ year of the reign of Arka-Dal

Arka-Dal had just finished his morning exercises. He walked into the back door of the palace and was about to head upstairs to bathe when Leo intercepted him.

"You have a visitor," he said. "A most unusual one, too."

"Oh? And just who is this visitor?" Arka-Dal asked as he dried the sweat from his face with a towel.

"He's a diplomatic emissary from Lord Azathoth," Leo replied. "He arrived just a moment ago and requested to meet with you."

"In that case, I'd better not keep him waiting. Where is he?" Arka-Dal asked.

"In your office. I've had refreshments sent in," Leo said with a smile. "It appears as if your expedition is about to bear some interesting fruit."

They hurried into the office where Arka-Dal usually conducted all official meetings. The emissary stood and bowed his respectfully. Arka-Dal extended his right hand. The emissary clasped it and smiled.

Arka-Dal studied the tall, lean gray skinned emissary as they shook hands. He smiled and bade him to have a seat at his desk. The emissary sat down and smiled. He seemed to be in his middle years—if anyone from their realm actually could age. His hair was long and almost silver, like most of his people. His eyes were almond shaped and cat-like.

"My name is Urmosa. I bring you greetings from my lord, Azathoth," he said as he handed him an envelope.

"Welcome to Thule," Arka-Dal said as he opened the envelope and read the letter.

"Lord Azathoth desires to open diplomatic and trade relations with your nation. He has sent me to clear the way for us to post an ambassador in Thule—if it meets your approval," Urmosa said. "The letter is his written request and requires a response in kind on your behalf."

Arka-Dal nodded as he read. He folded the letter and smiled.

"I see no reason not to agree to Lord Azathoth's proposal. I would be delighted to exchange ambassadors with your people," he said.

Urmosa watched as he took a blank sheet of paper from his desk drawer and carefully wrote that he accepted Azathoth's proposal. He then signed it and affixed the official seal to the bottom of the page. When the ink was dry, he passed it to Urmosa who read it and smiled.

"Lord Azathoth will be quite pleased," he said.

"Will you be the ambassador assigned here?" Arka-Dal asked.

"No. I am simply a messenger. Lord Azathoth will select the ambassador at a future date," Urmosa replied as he slipped the letter into his pouch.

They stood and shook hands again. Urmosa bowed respectfully and slowly faded from sight. Arka-Dal laughed.

Leo raised an eyebrow.

"That was fast. You didn't take much time to think it over," he pointed out.

"There was no need to, Leo. It was a simple, cut and dry request to exchange ambassadors and open embassies in each others' realms. Now that we are allied with the Others, I see no reason not to strengthen those ties," Arka-Dal said. "I wonder who he'll send as an ambassador?"

Leo laughed.

"Who, indeed?" he wondered aloud. "Will he be quartered at the palace?"

"At least until we can prepare a house that's suitable," Arka-Dal said. "When the ambassador arrives, we'll let him stay in the VIP suite in the east wing. There's room enough there for the ambassador and an aide."

"But what if Azathoth sends a woman?" Leo asked playfully.

"A woman?" Arka-Dal asked.

"Yes. I can imagine him sending one. So can *you*," Leo smirked.

"You mean Alyana?" Arka-Dal asked.

Leo nodded.

"If he does, then I'll accept her as an official ambassador—just as I did with Galya. To do otherwise would insult Azathoth and ruin our alliance," Arka-Dal said.

"I'm sure that Alyana is counting on just that, too," Leo needled. "She knows how you and Galya met and married. I'm sure she's hoping for lightning to strike twice."

Arka-Dal laughed.

"I don't want another wife," he said.

"*Wanting* one and *obtaining* one are two entirely different things, my boy," Leo said. "I can just picture Galya's expression if Alyana arrives!"

"So can *I*!" Arka-Dal said. "After I bathe, let's get back to our game. I'll worry about that if and when it happens."

As he stepped into the pool of warm water, Mayumi and the other wives entered the room. One by one, they stripped off their robes and entered the tub with him. He smiled as Mayumi scrubbed him down with soap and a brush.

"Galya told us that you had a visitor today," she said. "One of the Others."

"That's right," Arka-Dal replied as he soaped her down, too. "Lord Azathoth wishes to exchange ambassadors with us. He wants to open official diplomatic channels between our peoples. I think that would be good for everyone."

"And who will his ambassador be?" Galya asked.

"I have no idea," he said.

"I think I can guess," Galya smiled. "After all, she'd be a logical choice."

"You sound just like Leo," he said.

"I'm not sure how to take that!" Galya laughed.

"At least he didn't say that you *look* like Leo," Medusa joked. "Now that would be a *tragedy!*"

"Especially for Leo!" Zhijima said.

Galya splashed water on her and giggled. Zhijima returned fire and a free-for-all broke out that made everyone laugh.

When Azathoth received Arka-Dal's signed agreement, he smiled and handed it to his daughter. She looked it over and smiled back. It reminded him of the grin of a cat who was closing in for a kill.

"He agreed to exchange ambassadors—just as you expected," Azathoth said. "In fact, he said he welcomed this chance for our two people to engage in commerce and to get to know each other better. The Thulian Emperor is a most open-minded man."

"He is. But you knew this from the moment we met him, Father. He had a most unique way of viewing those of us who are not part of the human race. Now that he has agreed to your proposal, do you have anyone in mind?" she asked hopefully.

He laughed.

"If I send you, will you swear to me that you will be on your best behavior and not stir up any trouble with him or his household—especially Galya?" he asked.

"I swear that I will do my best to serve both our peoples to my best abilities as ambassador," she replied. "Galya did say that she likes me, so I'll build upon that. If I should slip in any way, I'm sure that Arka-Dal will understand that it is because of my lack of contact with other races."

Azathoth nodded.

"I'm sure he will. The two of you seemed to be getting along quite well toward the end of your mission. He said he admired your courage, fighting skills and determination—and your honesty and resourcefulness. He also said you were somewhat crude and naïve when it came to dealing with others," he said.

"Do you think he'll approve of me as an ambassador?" Alyana asked.

"He'll not only approve of you, I feel he's *expecting* you," Azathoth replied with a grin. "I'm sure that he's already guessed that this entire exchange was *your* idea. Somehow I feel that if I do not send you to Thule, he'd be disappointed—and maybe somewhat relieved."

"Have you chosen me?" she asked.

"Pack your belongings. You leave for Thule in five Earth days," Azathoth replied.

Alyana jumped up, threw her arms around his neck and hugged him. He beamed and patted her arm.

"Should I bring my battle armor?" she queried.

"Yes. But don't put it on. This is a diplomatic appointment. I think you should wear something more proper and feminine. Something that befits your new station," he replied. "And try to make it something that won't raise Galya's ire."

"I'll see what I can do," Alyana said as she virtually danced out of the room.

Azathoth laughed.

He'd never seen his daughter act so happy about anything. Until recently, she knew only war and death. Meeting and fighting side-by-side with Arka-Dal and his friends had turned her entire life inside out.

"I hope she can restrain herself," he thought.

Alyana walked down to the lower level of the castle and stopped by the shop of the royal seamstress, Hakar. Hakar was working on a new robe for Azathoth but stopped and looked up when Alyana entered. She smiled.

"Good evening, Princess. Is there something I can do for you?" Hakar asked.

"Father has just appointed me to the post of ambassador to Thule. He told me that I should act and dress the part. My usual attire won't do. I need something more appropriate. Something that befits an ambassador," Alyana said.

"Modest or revealing?" Hakar asked.

"Modest *and* revealing—but not *too* revealing. I want it to be attractive, too," Alyana said.

"See through?" Hakar asked.

"No. But I do think it should be of a light material, maybe in white with gold accents and accessories," Alyana said after some thought.

"Do you want undergarments as well?" Hakar asked.

"You know I never wear such things," Alyana smiled. "And I'm not going to start now."

Hakar laughed.

"Since you are entering the realm of the Humans, perhaps I'll design something based on their normal fashions," she suggested.

"That will be fine. Oh, I'll need at least five new outfits for official functions. My usual clothing will be fine for everyday wear. If I need anything else, I'll simply purchase it from the markets in Thule," Alyana said.

"I can have your dresses ready in one week," Hakar said.

"I leave five days from now—by Earth time," Alyana said. "Can you make them faster?"

"Three days fast enough?" Hakar offered.

"I knew I could count on you, Hakar!" Alyana said as she hugged her.

Two days later, Galya walked into Arka-Dal's office. He looked up from the pile of papers in front of him and smiled. She sat down on the edge of the desk as she usually did and touched his cheek.

"Have you heard any more from Azathoth about the exchange of ambassadors," she said.

"Yes. A letter materialized on my desk just ten minutes ago advising me that the ambassador will be here shortly," Arka-Dal replied.

"So when is Alyana arriving?" Galya asked.

Arka-Dal laughed.

"You and I think so much alike at times that is scares me," he said. "What makes you think he'll send Alyana?"

"Who *else* would he send? Besides, I'm almost positive it was *she* who came up with the idea," Galya said with a chuckle.

"Me, too. It's the most obvious way of getting around our agreement with Azathoth—and her only way of coming to Thule without my directly requesting it," Arka-Dal said.

"So when is she coming?" Galya queried.

"I'm not sure. Their way of keeping time is so much different from ours that I don't even want to guess. You know, once she's here, I can't send her back. Not without offending her father," Arka-Dal answered.

"Why would you send her back?" asked Galya.

"Oh? Then you don't mind if she comes here?" he asked.

"Not any more than *you* minded me when I arrived in Thule. I came to seduce you, but you declared me an ambassador and allowed me to stay. I think it was at that instant that I fell in love with you," Galya said as she hugged him. "As long as you don't fall in love with Alyana, I don't mind her coming here at all—in an *official* capacity. And I expect her to keep it official."

Arka-Dal laughed.

"You actually *like* Alyana, don't you?" he asked.

"I think so," Galya admitted. "She's like the little sister I never had. After fighting side-by-side with her against the Minions, I found it impossible *not* to like her. I'm sure the other women will like her, too."

Arka-Dal raised an eyebrow.

"Is that important?" he asked.

"I think so," she answered. "We'll have to take her under our wings—much like Mayumi, Chatha and Medusa did for me—and show her how things are done here. She's a little crude and inexperienced when it comes to dealing with people."

"You were far more experienced than Alyana is. After all, you'd had contact with humans for thousands of years and you knew how things worked."

"But they taught me how *Thule* worked," Galya said. "I'm still learning about it."

"So am I," he said. "I think Merlin is, too."

Galya laughed.

"Why else is it important for the other women to like Alyana?" he asked.

"You already *know* the answer to that, my love," Galya said.

Alyana was told by Gorinna that Thulian women wore short dresses made of light materials to compensate for the heat and humidity that was their everyday climate. Because of this, she chose to wear a sleeveless white dress with hints of gold thread throughout that caused it to glimmer in the afternoon sunlight. It was low-cut and very short—but not *too* much of each. She wore a narrow gold belt around her slender waist and matching sandals, gold bracelets which made for simple, yet eye-catching accessories. She kept her hair straight and well-combed.

Accompanying her was a slightly shorter, pretty young woman in a short, dark blue toga-like dress also with gold accessories. She had a dark brown, leather diplomatic pouch tucked under her left arm that contained copies of the trade agreements and introductory letters from Azathoth.

When her and her aide suddenly materialized in the conference room of the palace, they caused quite a stir. Arka-Dal smiled and walked over to greet them.

"Greetings, Alyana. I've been expecting you," he said.

"Father told me that you'd say that," she smiled. "This is my first time away from home, so I hope you'll understand and forgive any mistakes I may make."

"Consider that done," Arka-Dal assured her. "Please allow me to make the introductions."

He then introduced her and her aide to each of his wives and Leo. She nodded politely to each of them and smiled when she saw Galya. To her surprise, Galya gave her a warm hug.

"This is Ulla, my aide," Alyana said. "She will record all official contact between our governments and she and I will study your customs and civilization. We will gladly answer any and all questions you have about our homelands and people. Father wishes our relationship to become a strong and honorable one."

"I bid you both welcome to Thule. I hope your stay here will be a long and pleasant one," Arka-Dal said as he bowed his head to them.

Ulla handed him the pouch. Arka-Dal passed it to Leo who was standing next to him then everyone sat down at the table. Two servants brought out trays bearing iced drinks, fruit, nuts and cheeses and set them down on the table. Alyana and Ulla studied the trays and glanced at each other.

"I took the liberty of having refreshments set out," Arka-Dal explained. "Do your people actually eat or drink?"

"Yes, we do, but not the things you do. Our food is so different from yours," Alyana replied. "Yours is so, um, cheerful looking by comparison."

"Please help yourselves. Try a little bit of everything. I'd like to know what you think," Arka-Dal offered.

"I never ate before I came here, either. Arka-Dal encouraged me to try everything and I discovered that I liked it. The food here is delicious. I'm sure you'll enjoy it," Galya encouraged as she picked up an apple and bit into it. "I've even learned how to prepare a few dishes myself—thanks to the other ladies."

Alyana and Ulla tried several of the fruits and the cheeses while Galya explained what each was. Alyana remarked that she was right.

"Not only does your food look better than our usual fare, it tastes much better. Ulla and I could get used to this very quickly. I especially like this blue wine of yours," Alyana said as she sipped from her goblet.

Galya laughed as she looked Alyana over.

"Why do you look at me in that manner?" Alyan asked.

"I barely recognized you without your chainmail and helmet," Galya remarked. "You look so different in that outfit. So warm and pretty."

"Thank you for saying that. As you know, I've spent most of my life wearing armor and carrying weapons. Father said that such attire might not be considered appropriate for my new post, so I had our seamstress make this and several other dresses for me," Alyana said almost modestly.

"I like it. It's both simple and quite elegant. I imagine you'll start another fashion trend. Once the ladies of Thule see you, they'll all want to dress just like that," Mayumi said. "I might, too."

"What is it made from? I've never seen such material," Medusa asked.

"It is called zhril. It is made from the fibers in the bole of a tree that grows on the outer edges of our land. We can dye it any color and interweave various threads of other materials with it. It's very light, too," Ulla explained.

"That could become very popular here," Leo opined. "It may be the perfect commodity to open trade between our peoples."

"I'm sure almost every woman in Thule will want to have a dress made of it once they see it," Mayumi agreed. "It could become a very big fashion trend."

"Galya started a fashion trend after she arrived. So did her father," Arka-Dal added.

"I found that very flattering," Galya said. "I'd never had anyone emulate my dress style and Father was surprised that his attire had become a fashion statement among the men. Some even copied his horns."

Alyana giggled at the thought of hundreds of well-dressed men walking around Thule looking like the Devil.

"Your people seem to be very open-minded," she commented.

"That is because Aka-san is. I think our people try to be as much like him as possible," Mayumi said. "He is their role model."

"Father says the same thing," Galya added. "In fact, I think some of Arka-Dal is rubbing off on him, too."

"Enough of that," Arka-Dal said. "You're giving me too much credit where none is deserved. I just do the best I can for our people and the Empire."

"You're too modest, my love," Galya said as she stroked his cheek. "Everyone says that you are Thule and Thule is you. One can't exist without the other."

Arka-Dal blushed.

His reaction caused Alyana to smile. She never thought emperors or kings blushed or showed any signs of modesty. Yet she knew that Arka-Dal was genuinely reacting to what Galya and Mayumi said. He felt humbled by such praises. Alyana also knew Mayumi and Galya were right. There would be no Thule without Arka-Dal and he would have no reason to exist if it were not for Thule.

"We'll chat again later—after you and Ulla get settled into your quarters. They are in the west wing of the palace," Arka-Dal said.

"We'll show you the way," Mayumi said.

"Afterward, we'll give you a tour of the palace and Rose Gardens," Galya added. "Feel free to ask as many questions as you like along the way. I know what it's like to be among humans for the first time."

She watched them leave then turned to Arka-Dal.

"You know she engineered this, don't you?" she asked.

"Uh-huh. But now that's she's the official ambassador of her people, we'll treat her as such. Same as we did when you arrived," he said. "I'd say that worked out very well for both of us."

"Yes, it did. But I don't want it to work out the same way for Alyana," Galya said. "I see that you've decided to let them stay here at the palace."

"Only until we can construct an official residence. Then she'll move into that," Arka-Dal said.

"I'd rather that she stayed here—that will make it easier for me to keep an eye on her," Galya said.

Arka-Dal laughed and pulled her close.

"You're really beautiful when you're jealous," he said as he kissed her.

Mayumi showed Alyana and Ulla to their quarters. As Alyana unpacked, she began asking questions.

"How long have you and Arka-Dal been married?" she asked.

"Over 50 years," Mayumi replied.

"But you look so young!" Alyana said. "How long do Humans live?"

"On the average, about 125 to 135 years. Thanks to Merlin, I will live to be nearly 400 years as will Aka-san," Mayumi explained. "How long do your people live?"

"I really don't know. So many of us were killed during the war that our average life span decreased. I think we live about 50,000 of your years," Alyana replied. "I guess by your standards, that makes us nearly immortal."

"I think we humans have the shortest life spans of all the races. Aka-san always says that it's probably for the best considering all the wars we've started," Mayumi said. "How do you like your quarters?"

"I love them. They are so big and comfortable looking. We even have a private bath! I feel like I'm living in luxury!" Alyana said with a big smile. "Have you and Arka-Dal been married the longest?"

"No. Hetshepsut, the Queen of Egypt, wed him two years before I did. But that is a political marriage. She wed Aka-san so he and she would produce an heir to the Egyptian throne. They remain very close friends and she has not wed anyone else," Mayumi explained.[5]

"Did he produce the desired heir?" Alyana asked.

"Yes. His son, Arkaneton, is heir to the throne and the commander of Egypt's armies," Mayumi said. "And he looks exactly like his father."

"Then he must be very handsome," Alyana said.

---

[5] Read "The Gates of Delirium"

Mayumi smiled and nodded. She sensed that Alyana had talked her father into naming her an ambassador so she could be close to Arka-Dal. She also wondered how that would play itself out.

She excused herself and returned to the living room. Arka-Dal was seated on the sofa stroking one of the cats and sipping wine. She sat next to him.

"Your latest conquest is unpacking upstairs," she said.

"My latest what?" he asked.

"Conquest," she repeated with a smile.

"I didn't conquer anyone," he said.

"Yes you did. You just don't realize it yet," Mayumi said as she leaned her head on his shoulder. "Every time you go somewhere, you end up with another wife."

"You mean Alyana? She's not my wife and never will be," he insisted.

Mayumi smiled.

"We shall see, my love," she said.

The next day, Alyana asked if she could visit the Archives. Leo and Medusa happily agreed and showed her to the vast underground library beneath the palace. She listened carefully as Leo explained what they did there and what some of the books and artifacts were.

"If you have any questions for me, feel free to ask," Alyana offered.

"How did you learn to speak our language?" Leo asked.

"We can read your surface thoughts and pull images from your minds. Then we can find similar images in our language that relate to yours. All thoughts are normally in pictures and words, so that provides us with both language structure and definitions of various words. There are, however, many words in your language that have no correlation to anything in ours. I will need your help to understand them," Alyana explained.

"Fascinating," Leo remarked. "Communication must be incredibly easy for your people."

"Only when dealing with other sentient beings. Some creatures are impossible to communicate with—like the Minions," Alyana said. 'They did not think. They *reacted*. So we could not communicate with them at all."

She looked at the books on the shelves.

"Your books are in many different tongues. How many languages do the people of this week speak?" she asked.

"Far too many to even count," Medusa said. "There are thousands of languages and dialects and hundreds of dead languages that haven't been spoke for centuries. And more are being discovered as time passes."

"It must get confusing here," Alyana said.

"That it does—and sometimes, the confusion leads to tragic misunderstandings," Leo said.

"I can see how that would happen." She said.

"Do your people use magic spells?" Leo asked.

"Father can. Our high priests and priestesses can, too, but to a much lesser degree. It's mostly for healing, communicating with the dead and protection," Alyana answered. "But I think that most our people have the capabilities to learn how to use the most simple spells, which they often do. But when they get them wrong, strange and sometimes humorous things can happen."

They all chuckled at the idea of spells going awry at the worst times.

"But no one usually gets hurt. They just end up with extra appendages, or hair where it doesn't belong. Things like that. Then they have to seek out a priest to undo the spell," Alyana added.

"Have you ever tried to cast spells?" asked Medusa.

"I have done so many times. In the beginning, I made several mistakes and Father had to make things right again. I've become quite good at casting now—but I'm not in the same league as Merlin, Gorinna or Lucifer," Alyana replied.

"No one is," Leo said. "What is your culture like? Do you have arts and music? What are some of your customs?"

"It is difficult to answer that question," Alyana replied after some thought. "Ever since I can remember, our people had been at war with the Minions and later, the people of the Abyss. If we had any sort of culture like yours, it has been erased by the wars. We are a warrior culture. We are taught how to fight as soon as we are tall enough to hold a weapon. At one time, we had art and literature and music, but the war has devastated our land and made everything bleak and miserable for so long that we have forsaken those things in favor of necessities."

"That's similar to our ancient Spartan culture," Medusa said. "The Spartans were always at war with someone. The Spartans also had to be eternally vigilant against a possible slave revolt by the Helots."

"Our people enslave no one. Father detests slavery with a passion similar to Arka-Dal's. I think that's another reason he likes Arka-Dal so much," Alyana said.

"I thought Azathoth was an absolute ruler," Leo said.

"Only in the sense that Lucifer and Mephistos are. He must retain absolute control of our armies which were bred only to fight. Now, he is steering them towards more peaceful ways, like rebuilding our shattered cities and guarding our frontiers. He said it will take centuries to accomplish that," Alyana explained deftly.

"If you don't mind my asking—just how old are you?" Medusa asked.

"By your time keeping methods, I am about 2,000 years old," Alyana replied. "Since we are immortal, such things do not really matter. How old are you?"

"We Gorgons live about 5,000 years. I am more than halfway there," Medusa answered.

"At 88, I feel like the infant in this room," Leo joked.

"How long do humans live?" Alyana asked.

"Unsually, we last around 125 years. Merlin extended our lifetimes to triple that. It was his way of stabilizing Thule and the Second Age along with it," Leo said.

"Merlin believes that mankind would be plunged into another, even darker age if Thule collapses. Since Arka-Dal is the heart and soul of this empire, he wanted to keep that heart beating as long as possible. So he extended his life. Since he relies heavily on everyone in this house to help him manage the Empire, Merlin thought it best to extend our lives as well," he added.

"That is very wise of Merlin," Alyana said.

"Arka-Dal didn't think so at first. Now, you could say he has resigned himself to his fate," Leo said with a grin.

"In that case, he and father will have a very long relationship," Alyana said. "He instructed me to learn everything I can about your people and the way things work in Thule. Father also told me to be as honest and open as usual and to answer any questions you may have about us. And I have so many questions!"

"Why not take a grand tour of Thule? I'm sure many of your questions can be answered by traveling around our country," Medusa suggested. "That's the way I learned. One of us could accompany you."

"Who accompanied you?" Alyana asked.

"Arka-Dal," Medusa said.

"Maybe I can ask him to accompany me?" Alyana wondered.

Medusa laughed.

"Somehow I don't think that would sit very well with his wives—especially not Galya," Leo said.

"Oh, right. I don't want to cause a diplomatic incident during my first week on the job. I know—I'll ask Galya to show me around. It will give us time to know each other better, too," Alyana said.

"That might work," Leo nodded.

Galya stepped back and looked at her.

"You want *me* to travel with you? Any particular reason?" she asked.

"You know me and how I am. You could keep me from making a fool of myself. You know how naïve I am about interacting with others and I don't want to give your people the wrong impression," Alyana replied.

"Yes. You can be too honest and blunt at times. Very well. I'll accompany you just so I can keep you out of trouble. Besides, it might be fun," Galya agreed.

Alyana smiled and thanked her.

"When can we start?" she asked.

"How about next Monday? That will give us five days to prepare," Galya suggested.

"That's perfect! Where shall we go?" Alyana asked.

"Anywhere you like. It *is* your tour after all," Galya replied as she left the room.

She smiled to herself. Arka-Dal had suggested she take Alyana on a tour of the Empire so she could get to know Thule and its people better. Galya had expected Alyana to ask Arka-Dal to show her around. She was really surprised when Alyana asked her instead.

"That girl is smarter than I thought she was," she said.

Another relationship was about to bud.

Pandaar had been eying Ulla with more than just passing interest since she'd arrived in Thule. By any standard, Ulla would be considered more than simply beautiful and the filmy material of her dressed clung to her lithe body in ways that boldy highlighted her figure. He waited until she was in the garden alone before approaching her.

"Good morning, Ulla," he greeted her.

She smiled and greeted him the same way.

"This garden is so lovely. I've not seen flowers in many years. Our land is so devastated by the wars that almost nothing grows there anymore," she said as she stopped to smell a large, multi colored rose. "What are these called?"

"Roses. I don't know the variety. I never pay much attention to flowers" he replied as they walked together. "What do you think of our world so far?"

"I'm enchanted by it. Your world is so full of life and sound and color and smells. It fills me joy and wonder all at once. I would love to learn more about it," she said.

"If it would help, I'd be happy to escort you anywhere you'd like to go," Pandaar suggested.

"That would be wonderful—if it's no trouble," she said as she looked him over. She thought to herself that this seasoned warrior was quite handsome and he did seem to be interested in her.

"It would be no trouble at all. In fact, it would be a pleasure. Where would you like to go?" he said.

"Some of the maids told me about the nightlife here in Thule. They said there are many places they like to go to have fun. Do you know of any such places?" she asked.

"I know several night spots. It all depends on what you enjoy doing," Pandaar said.

"What do Thulians do for entertainment?" Ulla asked.

"We like to do many different things. There are many fine eating and drinking establishments. There are comedy, show and dance clubs. There are places to gamble. Places to watch sports. We could even take a cruise and dine and dance aboard the ship. Whatever you want," Pandaar said.

"Dancing! I haven't danced for a long, long time. Can we do that?" Ulla asked.

"No problem. I know a very nice dance club on the riverfront. What time would be good for you?" he agreed.

"Any time after sunset. I'm free all night," Ulla said.

"It's a date then. We'll go after dinner," Pandaar said with a smile.

"I'll be ready," Ulla said.

He stopped and bowed slightly. She held out her hand, expecting him to shake it politely. To her surprise, he leaned over and kissed the back of it then turned and walked away. She stood and watched until he was out of sight. She looked at her hand and smiled.

"He said it was a 'date'. I've never been asked on a date. This could be fun," she said as she continued her walk.

Pandaar saw Kashi and Gorinna sitting in the living room watching some of the Dal children playing board games while several cats lounged on the backs of the couches and atop the fireplace mantle. He walked to the bar, poured himself a drink then told them about his afternoon.

Kashi slapped his knee and laughed.

"I knew you'd ask her out. I saw the way you've been watching her ever since she got here," he said.

"Don't do anything stupid, Pandaar. We don't need a diplomatic incident," Gorinna warned.

"Oh ye of little faith! I promise that I'll be on my best behavior," Pandaar said with a smirk. "I won't do anything she doesn't want to do."

Kashi laughed again.

"She's been watching you, too. I think you may be in for a very interesting evening, my friend," he said.

"I certainly hope so," Pandaar smiled as they slapped hands.

Gorinna shook her head.

"Men!" she exclaimed.

When Galya told the other women that Alyana had asked her to show her around Thule, they looked at each other and laughed. Galya did, too. They joked about Alyana being clever enough to use Galya to get at Arka-Dal.

"She's not as naïve as we thought," Zhijima said. "The last thing I need is another woman to compete with around here. Alyana is very exotic and Arka-Dal has a taste for exotic women."

"We know!" the other wives said at once.

"Don't tell me you're already jealous of her," Galya teased.

"Of course I am! She's gorgeous! Aren't you jealous?" Zhijima asked.

"I must admit that I am. I wanted to cut her heart out when she made a play for Arka-Dal in the Abyss. I still might—if I could do so without causing a major diplomatic incident," Galya said with a smile.

"You won't," Mayumi said.

"What makes you think so?" asked Galya.

"Because you actually *like* Alyana," Mayumi replied. "You said so yourself many times since you returned from the Abyss. You said she was like the little sister you never had. Because of that, you won't harm her in any way."

Galya smiled.

"You know me too well, Mayumi," she said.

"The old Galya would have gutted her on the spot," Medusa said. "You won't. In fact, I can see you actually becoming sort of protective of her."

"Probably. But I'm still not too crazy about her having designs on our husband," Galya said.

"None of us are," Mayumi said. "But in the end, what happens will be up to them to decide."

"Damn! I guess we'll have to get a larger bed!" Zhijima said.

They all laughed.

When Arka-Dal sat down at his desk to finish some paperwork, Leo walked in and sat down in the chair next to the desk.

"I was in the observatory an hour ago and I saw a small impact on the surface of the sun," Leo said.

"The cat?" Arka-Dal asked.

"We can hope," Leo replied. "Whatever it was caused a very tiny solar flare to rise up. It lasted only a second or two then was gone. If it was the cat, he's been incinerated."

"I hate to see that happen to a cat, but in this case, it was necessary," Arka-Dal said. "Do you think we've seen the last of that wizard?"

Leo shrugged.

"Time will tell, my boy," he said. "By the way, Galya and Alyana left on their tour this morning. Galya said they were going to start on the docks.

"That's an excellent place to begin," Arka-Dal smiled.

Alyana was fascinated by the fact that humans traveled across the seas and along rivers in things they called boats or ships. She learned that the larger vessels were the ships and the much smaller ones were boats. She had never even imagined such vessels existed until she arrived in Thule. Water travel and the technologies that enabled it, were completely alien to her as were the vast oceans, lakes and rivers themselves.

"In our world, there are no such things as ships because we have no large bodies of water. What we call water is sluggish and dark and completely undrinkable. And there's not enough of it to bother to use for travel. While we have many such streams, there are no rivers, lakes or oceans that I am aware of back home," she said. "Until I came here, I never imagined that such large bodies of water existed or that humans traveled on them with such ease."

"Humans also get sustenance from the waters. They have done so for millions of years," Galya said.

"What kind of food do they gather from the waters?" Alyana asked.

"I think it would be easier to show you than explain it. Let's go to the market. It's just down the pier," Galya suggested.

"I'd like that," Alyana said.

They walked over to a long, open-sided wooden structure that took up almost a half-mile of space. There were hundreds of people milling around and hundreds of vendors selling all sorts of meats, produce and other items from stalls both inside and out. Galya led Alyana inside and past rows of stalls.

When they came to a large rectangular area they stopped. Alyana looked up at the hand-painted sign above the entrance.

SEAFOOD and SPICES

"This is the place," Galya said.

The first thing Alyana noticed was that the shop had a very distinct aroma. It was an odd mixture of sweet and pungent. She had never smelled anything like it before.

"Does it always smell like this?" she asked.

"Usually," Galya said. "You grow accustomed to it after awhile. Let's look around."

Alyana looked at the creatures arrayed on top of trays of crushed all around them. She'd never seen such creatures before and they held her attention like magnets.

"What are those creatures?" she asked.

"They are called fish," Galya said.

"Where do they come from?" Alyana asked.

"From the seas, lakes and rivers," Galya explained.

"They live in water? How do they breathe?" Alyana asked.

"Through organs called gills and various other methods. It's best you ask Leo about that. He's better at explaining such things than I am," Galya said.

"And people catch them?" Alyana asked.

"Yes," Galya stated.

"Why?" Alyana asked, now totally fascinated with the strange creatures.

"They're food. We eat them. We cook them in many different ways and we eat them," Galya said.

"You eat fish?" she asked.

"Yes. It's delicious. You have also eaten it. You ate a fish called trout at dinner last evening. It was the large white thing on your plate," Galya said.

"That was a fish? Did it come from the sea?" Alyana asked in surprise.

"No. The trout came from the lake up north. What did you think of it?" Galya asked.

"It was very enjoyable. Do all fish taste that way?" Alyana replied.

"No. Each fish has its own unique taste and it also depends on how it's prepared," Galya said.

"Is there a place I can go to see live fish? I'd like to watch how they move in the water," Alyana asked.

"We could go to the Thule Aquarium. It's just a few blocks from here. They have thousands of fish there you can observe and each tank has a sign explaining what types of fish they are and where they live. It is right next to our zoo," Galya suggested.

"Zoo?" Alyana asked.

"It's a park where you can observe live animals from around the world in their natural habitats," Galya explained.

"Can we go there, too?" Alyana asked.

Galya smiled. Alyana reminded her of a small child, which was understandable. Earth was totally new to her and she seemed eager to learn all she could about her new post.

"Sure. We can go anyplace you want," she said.

They left the market an hour later and walked down the pier to the large aquarium. It was opened to the public free of charge just four years earlier along with the famous Thule Zoo. Both were now major attractions for locals and tourists alike.

At the aquarium, they saw whales, dolphins, many varieties of sharks, octopi, several varieties of squid, eels. In fact, there were thousands of different species, including seaweeds, corals and sponges. Each habitat was designed to look as natural as possible. Alyana went from being an ambassador to a small child filled with awe and wonder. They didn't leave until the aquarium closed hours later.

Galya just stood back and smiled as Alyana read each and every sign on each and every tank.

"I am amazed at the many different species of fish and other creatures that inhabit your seas, rivers and lakes. Your world is filled with wondrous things that no one in my world can even imagine," she said as they headed back toward the city gates.

"I'm glad you enjoyed yourself today," Galya smiled. "I felt almost exactly the same way you do when this first opened. The architects did an amazing job."

"Can we visit the zoo tomorrow?" Alyana asked.

Galya laughed.

"Sure we can, she said as she realized how much like an excited child Alyana seemed to be at that moment.

The next day was more of the same.

They started at the zoo and ended at the vast open air market place just outside the city's walls. Galya explained what each item of produce was and how it tasted. She even purchased fruit for Alyana and got her to try it. She ate apples, pears, pomegranates, oranges and dates.

And she enjoyed them all.

She also tried various nuts and fruit drinks.

It was well after sunset when they returned to the palace.

Arka-Dal and Leo were seated in the parlor playing chess as usual while the other wives and several children busied themselves with various activities. Arka-Dal smiled when they approached.

"How was your day?" he asked.

"It was magnificent!" Alyana gushed. "Galya is a wonderful guide. She knows so much and we had so much fun."

Galya laughed.

"We did have a lot of fun," she said. "Where would you like to go next?"

"How about one of your museums? I'd like to learn more about your history," Alyana suggested.

"That will be fine," Galya said. "Right now, I need a good, long hot bath."

They watched as she headed up the steps. Alyana sat down at the table with Arka-Dal and Leo and asked them about the game. They both explained what each piece was and how one could use it and the strategies they employed while playing. She watched a few matches then asked if she could play.

Leo stood and offered her his chair. She sat down and arrayed her pieces like they'd shown her. She had the white pieces, so she had to start. Arka-Dal was surprised at some of her moves and how quickly she had absorbed the rules and strategies. It took him longer than he expected but he finally defeated her.

He won the next two matches as well.

Then Alyana managed to checkmate him in the fourth match. He praised her adapting so quickly. Leo mixed them all drinks and returned to the table. He handed Alyana a goblet of brandy which she had grown to like. They sat and played until midnight. By then, Alyana and Arka-Dal were the only ones left in the parlor.

"You've gotten good at this," he said.

"I had good teachers," she replied. "Father always said I was a very fast learner. But there's so much to learn here. Our world is quite simple compared to yours. We don't have so many different life forms and our lives have been very bleak for hundreds of years. Father said he'd like to see us bring it back to the way it was before the war. We had culture then. We had art and music and dance. We built things. We wrote books. We played sports and had schools. But that was all put aside because of the war. I hope that contact between our peoples will spark some sort of renaissance."

Arka-Dal smiled at her use of the old French word. She was indeed adapting quickly.

"I'm sure it will be mutually beneficial to everyone," he said.

Galya and Mayumi came downstairs. Mayumi mixed them drinks and they sat down near Arka-Dal and Alyana to join the conversation. Around two, Alyana yawned and announced she was going up to bed. They bade her good-night and watched as she ascended the steps.

"You two are getting along very well," Arka-Dal said.

"It's easy to get along with someone when you like them," Galya said. "She's smart and enthusiastic and eager to learn. And she's very naïve. Almost like a blank slate which is begging to be written on."

"I like her, too," Mayumi said. "I think she is a good ambassador. Just as Galya is."

"I guess I'm still sort of an ambassador," Galya chuckled. "I am the conduit between your people and my father."

"You're much more important than that," Arka-Dal said. "You're my wife and the mother of our children."

"Just please don't add any more children to the mix," Mayumi said with a smile. "I have enough trouble remembering the names of the ones we have around here now."

"Maybe you could have them wear numbers?" Arka-Dal joked.

"That might be of some help," Mayumi said. "Or you could try not to succumb to Alyana's charms."

She and Galya looked at each other and laughed. Arka-Dal smiled. His wives knew him all too well. But Alyana had been keeping herself very busy learning all she could about her new post.

"What do you think of her as an ambassador?" he asked.

"I think she is highly intelligent, a fast learner and she has a great curiosity and sense of humor. She's not as naïve as we first thought. In fact, she's exceptionally clever and can be very endearing. But she's still a little rough around the edges. Other than that, she's taking her post seriously and wants to be very good at it. She also wants to be sure everything she does works for the best interests of both our peoples," Galya said.

"I agree. On top of that, she is very nice," Mayumi added. "Her father made an excellent choice—even though it really wasn't his to make."

Arka-Dal laughed.

"She *did* maneuver him into making this decision," he said. "But he must have seen some real value in it or he would have sent someone else. He knew that she was familiar with us in many ways and that we liked her. So, the choice was obvious."

"I'm sure he sent her with his fingers crossed," Galya said. "Has she made any sort of attempt to seduce you yet?"

"Not a one," Arka-Dal said. "And I'd like to keep it that way."

"Dreamer!" they both said at once.

The next day, Alyana toured with Galya and Zhijima. The Dihhuri queen wanted to "keep an eye on the competition." Being well aware of Zhijima's jealous nature, Alyana engaged her in conversation as much as possible to sort of break the ice. As the day wore on, they began laughing and joking with each other.

They visited two large museums, strolled through the rose garden and watched young boys playing what was fast becoming Thule's favorite sport.

Baseball.

"Arka-Dal learned about from reading books. It intrigued him so he and his friends decided to learn how to play it. Other people saw them and joined in. That was about 15 years ago. Now, there are baseball fields in every park and each large city has its own stadium and professional team," Galya explained.

"What are the teams called?" Alyana asked.

"They have very strange names. They took the names of teams from the First Age so they don't make much sense. Right now, even the universities have amateur teams and there are several leagues for children and adults. It's surpassed wrestling and horse racing as Thule's favorite sport," Galya said.

"What is Thule's team?" Alyana asked.

"Arka-Dal named that team personally. They are called the Yankees after the most famous team of the First Age," Zhijima said. "Would you like to see a game? There's one tonight."

"I'd love to!" Alyana beamed.

They returned to the palace around midnight, looking flushed and acting giggly. Alyana saw Arka-Dal seated on the sofa reading a book and walked over. She smiled and sat down next to him. Then she told him all about her day.

"We had a great time," Zhijima said as she mixed herself a drink. "We need to do this more often."

"I'd really like that, Zhijima," Alyana said as Galya handed her a brandy.

"I'm glad that you ladies are enjoying each other's company," Arka-Dal said. "Have you contacted your father lately?"

"I spoke with him last night. He seemed very surprised and pleased that everything was going so well. He was worried that because of my lack of training that I would screw things up here—and rightfully so," Alyana replied.

She looked at the book in his hand.

"Is that the book you suggested I should read?" she asked.

"That's one of them. Once you've read it, we can discuss anything that you want to know more about. Leo gave this to me when I was just 10 years old. He was my tutor then. He still is, in fact," Arka-Dal said.

She looked at the cover.

"The Prince," she read aloud. "Who was Machiavelli?"

"He was a writer, advisor and statesman of a long-ago city state called Florence. He lived during the 16th century of the First Age and this book is considered to be his masterpiece. In fact, it laid down the foundations upon which many a ruler and business tycoon built his empire," Arka-Dal said.

"Did you use this for Thule's foundations?" she asked.

"In the beginning—but I made changes as time passed. The basic principles are still viable. Leo also gave me several other ancient books to read and study over the years and two ancient documents from the First Age that all of Thulian laws and rights are based on," Arka-Dal explained.

"Leo showed those to me. I was quite impressed," Alyana said. "He also suggested that I read your Constitution and Bill of Rights—which I will. Your people enjoy many freedoms and you have a very strong and efficient court system to protect those rights."

"The laws also apply to me and everyone in my household and circle. I am not above the laws of this land but I will fight to the death to maintain them," Arka-Dal said.

He looked up at the clock.

"I have to go to my office. I have a few dispatches to read and some papers to sign," he said as he got up and headed into the office.

The ladies stayed and chatted for a little while, then Galya and Zhijima headed upstairs to bathe. Alyana curled up on the sofa and began reading.

When Arka-Dal came down early the next morning, he saw Alyana seated on the sofa with her nose still buried in the book. He walked over.

"Good morning," he said. "Have you been here all night?"

She put the book down and smiled at him.

"This is a most interesting book," she said. "But you are nothing at all like the man he describes. You don't have any of his more ruthless traits, but I understand why you maintain a very large and powerful and well-trained military."

"To assure peace, be always prepared for war," he quoted.

"But your people love you," she said.

"It is better to be feared by one's *enemies*, not one's countrymen," he said. "I keep our forces modern, well-equipped and we train constantly. This causes anyone who thinks about invading Thule to pause to consider how stupid that idea might be."

"Leo told me that your soldiers employ a wide and ever changing variety of strategies and tactics and that each is provided with a manual that describes these things. Is that how your soldiers are taught?" she asked.

"That's just one of the methods. Most of the training is done in camps or while on extensive patrols and training missions. Many of our tactics and training methods have been adapted from the best armies of the First Age. I need my commanders and soldiers to be able to adapt quickly to shifting battlefield conditions and come up with new and better ways to use those shifts against our enemies.

Uninformed, poorly trained soldiers end up dead. Dead soldiers serve no purpose—unless you like martyrs," he explained.

She laughed.

"You and Father think along very similar lines," she said. "That's why he likes and trusts you. Leo compared you to several great generals of the First Age, like Alexander, Hannibal Barca, Julius Caesar, and a few others. I had never heard of these men, so I looked each of them up in the archives. I found the comparisons to be very accurate and impressive."

"Leo exaggerates," Arka-Dal said modestly.

"Not in this case. You are very much like those generals, but you have qualities they did not have and you have always managed to come up with very creative ways to defeat your enemies. I saw this during the Battle of the Abyss. And unlike those men, your empire endures and prospers," she said.

"The empire pretty much built itself," he said. "I'm just its caretaker."

"You are the glue that binds this nation together," Leo said as he entered the parlor. "Just ask anyone. They'll all tell you the same."

"This is true. Many of your people have told me this," Alyana agreed.

"Everyone gives me far too much credit," Arka-Dal protested.

"It is all very well earned and deserved," Leo said with a touch of pride. "Thule would not exist nor would it have prospered if it were not for your steady hand on the helm. You have turned enemies into friends and allies and have welcomed those who had been disenfranchised in their own lands. Thule is that 'shining city on the hill' that past leaders have spoken about but never achieved."

"I didn't build it," Arka-Dal said.

"Yes you did, my lad," Leo assured him. "There's no sense denying it. You are Thule and Thule is you. You are inseparable."

"I'm going to breakfast," Arka-Dal said as he walked toward the dining room.

Leo and Alyana followed.

As one who had led vast numbers of troops into battle for more than a thousand years, Alyana was particularly interested in learning all she could about Thule's military structure and tactics. Arka-Dal was only too happy to tell her all she wanted to know and they spent several long nights in his study going over each of Thule's six armies and its ten fleets.

Arka-Dal explained that since all of Thule's potential enemies have different weapons and tactics, it was necessary to learn and adapt new tactics in order to deal with those threats.

"We constantly change our ways of doing things. We adapt new tactics and encourage our field commanders to be innovative through war games and training and by observing other armies. We learn from our allies as well as our enemies and blend their tactics and weapons with our own. This enables us to stay ten steps ahead of anyone who thinks they can invade our nation. It's an old, proven idea. In order to assure peace, we must be prepared to wage war. Total, decisive war," Arka-Dal explained.

He explained that he had adopted the structure for his armies from First Age commanders like Napoleon Bonaparte and Julius Caesar. Many of Thule's tactics and battle formations came from his study of ancient generals like Alexander, Hannibal, Robert E. Lee, and Tsun Tsu. As he grew more accustomed to leading men into battles, he added touches of his own and encouraged input from all of his field generals.

"Jun is the commander of my Northern Army. He's also in charge of training and tactics. He's in charge of our officers' academy. Last month, I appointed Michael to assist him because of his vast experience. I'd like you to visit the academy when you have a chance so you can see how things are done here. I'd also like you to suggest things that have worked for you during your wars against the Minions," he said.

"I'll be happy to do that—if you think it would help," she said humbly. "I have never battled against humans, so our methods may be quite strange to you."

"If they're strange to us, they'll be even more incomprehensible to any potential enemy. We've adapted some of Galya's tactics and she has spent many hours teaching our generals how to work with them. In this army, nothing is off the table," Arka-Dal assured her.

Alyana was surprised. Arka-Dal had virtually asked her to become a military advisor. This was something she had not expected and she wondered how her father would react.

"And feel free to adopt any of our tactics that you think would be of use for your own soldiers. This alliance works both ways," he added. "Who knows? We may all have to fight side-by-side again one day and it would work better if we were on the same page, so to speak."

Another stunner!

Humans totally trusting and cooperating with her people!

"Father was right. Arka-Dal is not like any other human I've ever heard of. Who else would make such and open and generous offer?" she thought.

When she reported this to her father, Azathoth was surprised.

"The Emperor said *that*?" he asked.

"He certainly did, Father. And he was quite sincere. He considers our peoples to be close allies and has felt that way since we fought the Minions. If I were you, I would suggest an official military alliance between us and Thule and their allies. It would greatly benefit all concerned," she urged.

"Yes it would. Give Arka-Dal my regards and suggest that to him. Then let me know his reaction," Azathoth said. "You seem to be adjusting very well. I am proud of you, Alyana."

She grinned as she broke contact.

When she told Arka-Dal what her father had suggested, he nodded.

"I don't have a problem with that at all, Alyana. Although Thule has no 'official' military alliances with anyone, if it makes your father comfortable to set one down in writing, I'll be happy to have Leo draw up the documents," he said.

"You don't have any alliances in writing with anyone—not even Lucifer?" she asked in surprise.

"Not even with him," Arka-Dal said.

"Why?" she asked.

"A strong alliance is built on mutual trust and cooperation and the knowledge that those you count on will be there in time of need. Our nations are bound by trade, tourism, cultural exchanges and other things that are far too intangible to measure. When one needs help, the others respond. If one is attacked, the rest of us rise to defend it. You can't put that on paper," he explained.

She sat and allowed this to sink in.

"The only thing we have in official documents are trade and travel agreements—and that's to ensure that everyone involved gets a fair deal and that anyone who wishes to trade with Thule or our partners does not condone, own or trade in slaves. The rest is unwritten. It's simply understood," he continued.

"I think Father will like the way you do things," she said. "I'll tell him what you've said and let him decide how he wishes to proceed."

"That's fair enough," Arka-Dal said.

Azathoth laughed when she told him.

"Tell Arka-Dal that his word is worth more than every treaty that was ever written. I like the way he does things. He keeps them simple, honest and fair. You have chosen well, Alyana!" he said.

"Whatever do you mean?" she asked coyly.

He laughed again.

"You mean that you haven't attempted to seduce him yet?" he joked.

"Of course not. I'm far too busy learning my new post," she replied.

"Is that because Galya and his other wives are running interference?" he asked.

"Actually, they haven't. In fact, everyone here has been so nice to me and Ulla. They have taken us under their wings and made us welcome and comfortable," she said. "I'd love to seduce him but I have not had the time."

"It's just as well. I'd hate to have you ruin all that you've accomplished by being indiscreet," Azathoth said.

The next day proved to be a little more interesting. Alyana was talking about how she loved to watch the ships and boats sail into and out of Thule's busy harbor and how she would like to sail on one.

"Arka-Dal has a royal yacht that quite beautiful. Perhaps you can ask him to take you for a sail?" Leo suggested.

So as she dined with everyone that evening, she decided to follow up on Leo's suggestion.

"Leo told me that you have a royal yacht," Alyana began.

"Yes. I do. It's moored on Pier One," he said.

"May I see it?" she asked.

"No!" all of the other women shouted at once.

Alyana squinted at Galya.

"You can't set foot on that yacht—ever!" she said.

"Why not?" Alyana asked, puzzled by their behavior.

"If you do, you'll end up pregnant. Every woman who sails on that yacht with him comes back pregnant," Mayumi said with a smile.

"We sure did!" Zhijima added. "That's why you can't ever step aboard that yacht. Ever!"

"We already have too many children running around here. I have no idea where we'd put another one—or two," Medusa said.

"Wait! Zhijima—you said 'we'. Are you expecting?" Arka-Dal asked.

She beamed and nodded. Then she jumped into his lap and kissed him.

"See what I mean?" said Chatha. "That will make 11! And she did sail on the yacht with him only a few weeks ago. So you can't go on that yacht!"

Alyana looked at each of them and laughed at their expressions.

"You sound so serious!" she said.

"We *are*!" Medusa assured her. "Even Gorinna became pregnant while she sailed with him. So you can't board that yacht. We refuse to allow it."

Alyana looked at Mayumi.

The Empress smiled.

"I also forbid it," she said softly.

"What if we all went?" Alyana suggested. "That way, you can make sure that nothing happens."

"Sure! Take all the fun out of it for me!" Arka-Dal said in mock sarcasm.

"Oh, you can have fun, Aka-san. Just not with Alyana," she said.

"But what if we all end up pregnant again?" Chatha asked.

"In that case, we'd best have our architect draw up plans to add another wing to the palace," Galya said with a laugh.

"I'd better pack a large jar of vitamins," Arka-Dal said. "Maybe I'll pack two jars."

"Then we can go?" Alyana asked with a flush of excitement.

"I don't see any harm in it—under the circumstances," Arka-Dal said.

"Thank you! I can hardly wait! When can we sail?" she asked.

"I can have her ready in two days," Arka-Dal said. "We can sail downriver to the Gulf and spend some time at the beach house."

"Beach house?" Alyana asked.

"We have a vacation home on the beach. It has a large main house and two smaller ones. Our caretaker and his family stay in one. The other is for guests," Mayumi said.

"Will I be staying there?" Alyana asked.

"I'd prefer to have you in the main house with the rest of us," Chatha said.

"Right. That way, we can keep you out of trouble," Zhijima said.

"And Aka-san, too," Mayumi added.

Arka-Dal was in his office going over the latest military contracts, when Alyana entered. He put down the paperwork and smiled as she walked over and took the seat next his desk.

"How do you do it?" she asked.

"Do what?" he queried.

"Maintain such peace and harmony in your home? You have five beautiful wives, each with her own personality, traits and qualities, and yet they all live under your roof without any sort of apparent conflicts, jealousies or personality clashes. What I find even more fascinating is that they seem to take great delight in helping raise all of your children together. I think, based on what I have read of Human history, that such an arrangement would have been impossible in another palace," Alyana said.

Arka-Dal smiled.

"I actually have very little to do with that. If you observe them more carefully, you'll come to understand that it's Mayumi who is the glue that binds everything together. She was always the first to welcome and befriend each of them and treat them with kindness, respect, humor and even love. They just responded in kind. Mayumi has never shown any outward signs of jealousy or malice toward any of them. I'd go as far as to say that they are closer than sisters. They are the best of friends and their friendship just keeps getting stronger as time goes on," he said.

"Mayumi does make me feel at home here. She seems to have a real talent for that," Alyana agreed. "But I've read about other kings who had many wives and there always seemed to be political intrigues surrounding them. Why do I not see any such thing here?"

"That's simple. In those other kingdoms, the thrones were inherited. When the rulers died, the power then passed to the eldest son or the favorite if there were multiple wives. This led to plotting among the wives and concubines to eliminate potential competitors so they could place their own sons on the thrones," Arka-Dal explained.

"That can't happen here. As you know, the office of emperor can't be inherited here. When I decide to give up power, the people will hold elections to choose their next emperor. It can't automatically go to any of my children, so there's no need for any political intrigues."

Alyana thought about it and nodded.

"I understand now. That was very clever. It will also eliminate any possibility of a civil war over your throne. Is that also why you have no official titles here?" she asked.

"Exactly. Everyone in Thule is equal under our laws and everyone, including myself, is subject to those laws. As Emperor, I ensure that the rights of our citizens are protected at all times. I even hear and pass judgments on certain cases that come to me for appeal or in cases of national interest. When I'm away, that task falls to Mayumi. In each case, Leo sits in as advisor," Arka-Dal explained.

"What about in time of war?" Alyana asked.

"Even in times of war, the rights of our citizens are guaranteed. During war, I decide the fate of all prisoners taken in combat by my troops and of spies, saboteurs, terrorists and traitors," Arka-Dal said. "Since they are not Thulian citizens, they are not protected by our Constitution."

"Leo told me that you are usually quite merciful when dealing with prisoners of war. Is that true?" she asked.

"Yes. I give them the opportunity to join our army when the war is ended or to return to their homes in peace. If I treat them the way I hope my own soldiers will be treated under the same conditions, it turns them from enemies into friends," Arka-Dal said. "I've had thousands of opposing soldiers join our ranks over the years. Those that decide to return home tell their people how well they were treated and make others realize that we are not their enemies. The system works very well most of the time."

"Medusa told me about the Turks," Alyana said.

"I showed them the same 'mercy' they shoed to the people in Constantinople. They reaped what the sowed in that case. Those that butcher innocent civilians or sell them into slavery deserve no mercy."

"Back to your wives—do you have a favorite?" Alyana asked.

"Whichever one is with me at any given times is my favorite," he said diplomatically. "What do my wives say?"

"Galya said that Mayumi is your favorite. Hers, too," Alyana replied. "The others told me the same thing."

"Mayumi is the rock my ship is anchored to. She always has been and always will be. She makes everything work. What did Mayumi say when you asked her?" Arka-Dal said.

Alyana giggled.

"She said the exact same thing you did earlier," she replied.

He laughed.

"That's my Mayumi," he said softly.

"I always have the feeling that she is the one who is actually in control of everything here. I've watched the others come to her for advice many times on all sorts of matters," Alyana said.

"Mayumi does run the household, but she does it in a very subtle, unobtrusive manner. She suggests rather than orders. That leaves room for the others to express their own opinions as well," Arka-Dal said. "She's very clever."

"So I have observed," Alyana said.

"Mayumi likes you, Alyana. She likes you a lot, too," Arka-Dal said.

"I know but I'm not sure why," Alyana said.

"I'll tell you. She said that you remind her of herself when she first arrived in Thule. Like you, she knew nothing of the customs. The food and clothing were strange to her and she didn't even speak our language. But she was eager to learn everything she could and we spent many hours teaching each other our languages. Leo played a huge part in her acclimation, too. A few months after her arrival, I asked her to be my wife. That was over 50 years ago and our love is still going strong," Arka-Dal said.

"I see. Do I remind you of her?" she asked.

"A little bit. Mostly you remind me of a somewhat naïve version of Galya. The only reason I say naïve is because until we met, you had never set eyes on Humans while Galya has had millennia of contact with them," Arka-Dal answered.

"I'm doing my best to learn all I can," she said almost defensively.

He smiled.

"And you're doing extremely well. Take your time and ask as many questions as you can think of. You have a quick, sharp mind, but until now, all you've ever thought about are things related to war. Changing gears can be a long, tedious process," he said.

"I'm learning to adapt. This is by far, the longest period of time in which I have not worn my armor or carried a weapon. Peace is still fairly alien to me," she said.

"Chatha had the same adjustment problems," Arka-Dal said. "Her father raised her to be a warrior. It's in her blood. That's why I placed her in command of our Atlantean Regiment. Technically, she's their queen. The Atlantean troops are very loyal to her, too. And to the Empire."

"Can I ask a favor of you?" Alyana said.

"Anything," he assured her.

"I would like to stay sharp and battle ready. I've noticed that you train each day with Master Koto. Would it be possible for me to join you?" she asked.

"I have no problem with that. In fact, you can start tomorrow morning if you like," Arka-Dal agreed.

"I'll be there. Perhaps Koto can teach me a few new tricks, too," she said.

The next morning, she walked out onto the back lawn in a short, light tunic. Her sword was strapped to her back. She was surprised to see Chatha, Zhijima, Pandaar and Kashi there with Arka-Dal and Koto.

Koto bowed to her and welcomed her to the practice.

She returned the bow.

"Show me what you've got," Koto said as he drew his katana and lunged at her.

To his surprise, she blocked it with her sword, turned the blade aside and made a thrust of her own. He evaded it and batted her sword aside with the katana. They squared off and went at each other with incredible gusto.

The others watched as Alyana and Koto fenced for several minutes. After what seemed like a long time, Koto held up his left hand. Alyana stopped and sheathed her sword. Her movements were swift and fluid.

Koto bowed.

Alyana returned it.

"You are an amazing fighter," he complimented. "You are one of the best I have ever had the honor to fence with. Your experience shows."

"It should. I have been fighting almost every day of my life for the last 1,000 years," she said. "I appreciate your words of praise. I would also like you to teach me some of the moves you have taught the others."

"I'm not sure there are any moves I can teach you. I may ask you to teach me some of your methods," Koto smiled. "You fight like Galya and Michael but you have too much passion. Such passion could be used against you under certain circumstances. We can work on bringing them under control if you like."

"My father has told me the same thing. I would like to work with you. Please teach me how to manage my emotions during combat," she said.

Galya beamed.

The little firebrand was learning humility—just as she had.

"There's hope for you yet," she said.

"And you as well," Alyana smiled.

At the end of the month, Alyana contacted her father with the help of a small mirror she had brought with her. When Azathoth saw her image, he smiled.

"Your hair looks different," he noted.

"This is the latest style in Thule," she replied. "Do you like it?"

"It becomes you. How was your first month among the humans?" he asked.

"It was fascinating. There are so many wonderful and interesting things to see and do here. Compared to our realm, this is so alive. So vibrant. There are so many different customs and cultures. I think you should visit Thule," she almost gushed.

Azathoth detected the excitement in her voice and smiled.

"Maybe I will one day," he said. "How are they treating you?".

"Well, Father. Extremely well. I've made several friends here," she said with a grin.

"Is Galya among them?" he teased.

"Yes. In fact, she and I have just returned from a grand tour of Thule. I'm learning much from her, Father—and from Arka-Dal's other wives and inner circle. They all answer my questions and take the time to explain how things work—or don't at times. Nothing is hidden from me," Alyana said.

"I must admit this has worked out much better than I expected. You do our people credit, Alyana," Azathoth said proudly.

"Arka-Dal said the exact same thing to me a few days ago," she said. "He's looking forward to having open commerce between our peoples. He asked me to tell you that we are no longer bound by the treaty and that our people are welcome to travel freely in Thule if they have a desire to."

Azathoth laughed.

"Once word of that gets out, Thule will be inundated with tourists and merchants," he said. "Do the Thulians find you to be strange?"

"Not really. They are accustomed to seeing people from all races each and every day. There are Dwarfs, Trolls, Elves---all sorts of people here. Many of the Thulian women have copied the style of dresses I brought with me. Galya said that once they saw me wearing those dresses, I'd start a new fashion trend," Alyana replied.

"So we would be welcomed there?" Azathoth asked.

"Most definitely, Father," Alyana assured him. "Do you have a message for Arka-Dal?"

"Yes. Convey my sincerest thanks for lifting that travel ban. Tell him that I am looking forward to a long and prosperous relationship between our peoples."

"I will, Father," Alyana said as the mirror went dark.

Arka-Dal was seated at his desk reading the latest military reports from Jun. He heard someone approaching and smiled when he saw Zhijima. She sat down on the edge of the desk and kissed him.

"It appears that Pandaar has fallen for Ulla," he said.

"I know. They've been seeing a lot of each other. She told me she likes him, too. No one's ever paid any attention to her before so she's excited by it," she said.

"It doesn't seem to bother you," he observed.

"I don't care who he sees. I already have what I want and I'm very happy. I hope he doesn't tire of Ulla like he did me," she said. "Or you'll end up with yet another wife."

He laughed.

"I don't think I can handle another wife," he said. "You and the others keep me busy enough as it is."

"Is that a complaint?" she teased as she ran her fingers through his hair.

"Not at all. The gods have blessed me several times over. Sometimes, I feel almost too blessed," he joked as he stroked her thigh.

"From the way Alyana looks at you, I feel you're about to be blessed yet again," she joked back. "You know that she wants you?"

"For what?" he joked.

She laughed.

"The same things as the rest of us," she said.

"How do you feel about that?" he asked.

"I'd say that we already have more than enough little Dals running around here. There's no need to add more to the mix," she replied.

"I'll keep that in mind," he smiled.

"You'd best also keep it in your pants," she joked.

But yet another ripple was about to be added to the ever widening lake that is diplomacy. Once Mephistos received word of Alyana's appointment, he put into motion a plan of his own to open official diplomatic ties with Thule.

Down in the Abyss, Mephistos sat in his study perusing an ancient volume on human behaviors. He decided that it was time to learn all he could about his newfound allies. Although he'd always considered Humans to be beneath his contempt, his experiences with Arka-Dal had taught him that there was still hope for this bizarre species.

He heard someone enter the chamber and looked up as Fthrx, his major domo, entered.

"What have you to report?" he asked.

"It is as you feared. The war has cost us dearly. Half of our people are dead or missing and almost all of our lands have been laid to waste," Fthrx said.

Mephistos scowled.

As dismal as the Abyss normally was, the destruction caused by the long, bitter war, had made it even more dismal. He'd never imagined that such a thing was possible.

"That should play Hell with real estate values," he joked. "So we were on the verge of a total defeat?"

"Without question. We could not have survived much longer. Neither could the Others who suffered even greater losses. If we had not forged the alliance when we did, both of our peoples would have been annihilated," Fthrx said.

Mephistos smiled.

"A victory at any cost is nevertheless a victory. Our people have survived. We shall rebuild our miserable realm and we shall thrive once again. Just as the Humans have done time and again," he said.

"You seem to admire the Humans," Fthrx observed.

"I'm beginning to appreciate tenacity and incredible will to survive, even after major catastrophes. In order to for us to survive, we must learn how to be more like the Humans. We must never give up," Mephistos said.

"Any further orders?" Fthrx asked.

"Yes. Gather all of our remaining resources in a centralized area and have our people start the reconstruction process. I would also like to open official diplomatic channels with Thule. I want you to find our most suitable prospects for the post of ambassador and send them to me for screening," Mephistos said.

"As you wish," Fthrx said as he hurried out of the chamber.

Mephistos laughed.

"Not long ago, I *despised* Humans. Then Fate threw me a curveball and the Demon Slayer became the Demon Savior. I never saw it coming. Hell, I never even got a bat on it!" he said.

A few hours later, Fthrx returned with a group of six possible candidates for the ambassadorial position.

Mephistos carefully studied the six would-be candidates. Although they were all fine models of high level demons, he decided that they looked far too demonic to be considered for the post of ambassador.

He waved them away and looked at Fthrx.

"Are they the best you could find?" he asked.

"They are the finest of our first tier. The very cream of our society," Fthrx said.

"That they are, but their appearance is far too intimidating. I want to build a strong relation ship with the people of Thule. I don't want to frighten them out of their wits," Mephistos said.

"I might be able to find a suitable candidate from among our hybrids," Fthrx suggested.

The hybrids were the names they gave to souls that were transitioning from Human to demon. The transition took several centuries. When it was completed, all previous Human traits were gone forever and the souls became full fledged demons. What type of demon depended on where the souls came from and how foul a life they led when alive. Mephistos always had the final say in that.

"It's worth a try. Find me someone who still looks more Human than demon. Someone who has a pleasing personality and a sharp mind," Mephistos said. "In the meantime, I'll send an emissary to Thule with the proposal to exchange ambassadors."

"It shall be done. But the hybrid might become a full demon while serving as ambassador. Wouldn't that frighten the Humans?" Fthrx asked.

"If you find me a suitable candidate, I will permanently halt the transformation," Mephistos said.

Three days later, a tall, rather well-dressed demon appeared outside the palace. When the guards spotted him, they simply looked him over.

"My name is Vrfxx. I am an emissary from Lord Mephistos of the Abyss. I have been sent here on a diplomatic mission. Please escort me to your Emperor," the demon said.

The guards shrugged.

One went inside while the other stood his post. A few seconds later, the first guard returned with one of the palace maids.

"She will escort you to the Emperor," the guard said.

The emissary followed her to the office where Arka-Dal and Leo had been discussing a few legal matters. When they saw the emissary, Arka-Dal rose and shook his hand. The emissary sat down and smiled. He reached into his cloak, took out a letter, and passed it to Arka-Dal. Then he sat quietly while the Emperor read it.

"Lord Mephistos wishes to exchange ambassadors with your people and to make a trade arrangement between our peoples," the emissary said.

Arka-Dal passed the letter to Leo and squinted at the emissary.

"What sort of trade agreement? What does Thule have that Mephistos could possibly want?" he asked.

"Souls," the emissary replied.

"Come again?" Arka-Dal asked, unsure of what he'd heard.

"The souls of your executed criminals," the emissary explained. "As you well know, over a thousand brutal criminals are executed in the Empire each year. Sometimes, it is twice that number. My master simply wants the opportunity to *harvest* their souls before they leave their corpses so they can be used to replenish our population. They would already be dead and the dispositions of their souls should not matter to you."

"He's right. We've no use for souls. Neither do the executed criminals," Leo said. "We're discussing something that isn't even considered a commodity in any sense of the word."

"In return, Thule would have full access to any of our natural resources your people feel might be of use to them in any way. We would also like to exchange thoughts, ideas, information and artisans. Lord Mephistos believes that both our peoples could benefit from such exchanges," the emissary said.

Arka-Dal nodded.

"Condemned criminals deserve no respect and neither do their souls," he said as he signed the agreement and affixed his official seal to the bottom of the document.

"Then it's a deal?" the emissary asked.

"We have a deal," he assured him. "Now, as to the exchange of ambassadors, I'm more than open to that idea. It will establish strong lines of communication and promote good will between our peoples. I would also like to suggest that the barriers between our nations be struck down. That would enable our peoples to travel freely between your world and ours."

"Tourism? The emissary asked.

"Why not? That could prove to be even more beneficial than trade," Arka-Dal said. "We're working on a similar agreement with Lucifer and Lord Azathoth, although neither is exactly sure how people from our plane would be able to enter theirs."

"Yes. Working out such things might prove to be quite difficult to say the least," the emissary agreed. "But I'm sure Lord Mephistos will find the idea intriguing. But would your people actually travel to such a place? The Abyss is hardly a luxury resort."

Arka-Dal laughed.

"Thulians are a very curious people. Since Arka-Dal has been to the Abyss and back, I'm sure many of our citizens now want to travel in his footsteps, so to speak. Everywhere he's traveled has become a tourist magnet," Leo explained.

The thought of the Abyss becoming a tourist spot made the emissary laugh. He imagined hordes of tourists trudging over the burnt ground, eager to visit the site of Arka-Dal's battles.

"What do you think?" asked Arka-Dal.

The emissary beamed and signed the second copy of the document. Then he and Arka-Dal exchanged copies.

"I must say that you are, by far, the most open-minded individual I have ever spoken with. Are all Humans like you?" the emissary asked.

"Most people in Thule are. I can't speak for the rest of the people on Earth," Arka-Dal said. "When can we expect your ambassador?"

"As soon as Lord Mephistos finds a suitable candidate. He is seeking an ideal person even as we speak," the emissary replied as they shook hands.

"I'll put my trust in Lord Mephistos' good judgment," Arka-Dal said.

"Thank you again, Emperor. Lord Mephistos will be very pleased," the emissary said as he vanished into thin air.

"You really have to love the way those people travel!" Leo said.

"I wonder who he'll send?" Arka-Dal asked.

"If he sends a female, I hope it won't be someone else who wants to marry you! You already have far too many wives," Mayumi said as she entered the office. "Perhaps you could introduce her to Pandaar-san?"

Arka-Dal laughed and hugged her.

"Pandaar already has his hands full," he said.

Fleeth stood five feet two inches and had a nice, compact figure and a cute face. She had long, straight, jet black hair and a pleasant smile. Only her deep red eyes and slightly purple skin betrayed the fact that she was a demon in transition.

Mephistos smiled at her.

"You'll do nicely," he said. "I assume that Fthrx explained why you were brought before me?"

"He said you were seeking someone to be an ambassador. Someone who was still more Human than demon, with a good personality and demeanor and of good intellect," she replied.

Mephistos nodded.

"You seem to be exactly the type of person I need for this post, that is, if you desire it. This must be your decision alone. I will not force it upon you," he said.

"Where would I serve?" she asked.

"In the capital city of the Empire of Thule," Mephistos replied. "If you take the position, I will halt your transition process permanently. You will remain exactly as you are now forever."

"But what about--?" she began.

He smiled.

"That will still be blocked from your memory, as per the agreement you made with me when you joined us. Your past will remain forgotten," he assured her.

"Isn't Thule ruled by the man you call the Demon Slayer?" she asked.

"His name is Arka-Dal. We are allies now. I would like you to help us forge even stronger ties between our races. The position is new. We've never attempted anything like this before. It will be a real challenge and you'll have to make things up as you go along. The Others have already established an embassy there so you may be able to call upon their ambassador for advice," Mephistos said.

"It sounds like fun. I'll do it!" Fleeth said.

"Excellent. I'll draw up the necessary documents for you to take with you. Since you were once Human, being among them again won't be such a shock. Arka-Dal is a most interesting and unusual man. I'm sure the two of you will get along famously," Mephistos said with a broad grin.

"When do I leave?" Fleeth asked.

"In three Earth weeks. That should give you enough time to prepare yourself," he said as they shook hands.

Alyana saw Mayumi seated on a marble bench in the rose garden. She walked over and sat down beside her. Mayumi smiled and greeted her in her usual cheerful manner. Alyana greeted her back.

She liked Mayumi. She always felt at ease around her and the Empress always made her feel welcome.

"You look frustrated," Mayumi observed.

"I am," Alyana admitted.

"Is there something I can help you with?" Mayumi offered.

"I'd rather not say. You'd think I was being too forward or something worse," Alyana said as she stared at the bubbling fountain a few yards away.

Mayumi smiled.

"Does it have anything to do with Aka-san?" she asked.

Alyana smiled.

"Some of it does. Mostly it has to do with me," she replied. "I must be doing something wrong."

"Oh? Why do you say that?" Mayumi asked.

"Well, I've been trying to get his attention but nothing seems to work," Alyana said. "He just treats me as an ambassador."

"But you are an ambassador," Mayumi said.

"Yes. But I'd like to become much more than that," Alyana said.

"I know. In fact, all of us know," Mayumi smiled.

"Does that anger you?" Alyana asked.

"No. It sort of amuses us," Mayumi answered. "We see you trying to flirt with him and the way you sometimes dress to catch his eye. We can tell that you are new at this, too. There's a sort of clumsiness to everything you do. That is understandable considering your background."

"So everyone has noticed but him?" Alyana said.

"I would not say that. Aka-san notices you much more than you think. He has said that he thinks you are cute and sexy and he likes your enthusiasm. Oh, Aka-san has noticed you!" Mayumi said.

"Then why does he pretend not to?" Alyana asked.

"I think he wants to see just how far you will go," Mayumi replied. "Also, I don't think he really wants yet another wife that he has to keep happy. The rest of us put quite a strain on him."

"How do you feel about it?" Alyana asked.

"Whatever happens is up to you and Aka-san to decide," Mayumi replied diplomatically. "That is my feelings. I cannot speak for the others. Two are very jealous of you already. I think you know who they are."

Alyana laughed.

"Galya?" she asked.

"No," Mayumi replied. "She already feels as I do. And she likes you."

"Then who?" Alyana asked.

"Think about it and it will come to you," Mayumi said.

"Do you have any advice?" Alyana asked.

"Hai. Keep doing what you have been doing and be patient. Things like this cannot be hurried. They have to be nurtured over time," Mayumi said. "Also, I think you should be more playful. You are too serious about everything. Relax. Have fun."

The next day, Alyana walked into Arka-Dal's office. She was wearing a very short tunic, too. He smiled at her when she sat down at his desk.

"I've been told that Mephistos is sending an ambassador to Thule," she began.

"That's correct," Arka-Dal said. "Do you have any idea who he might send?"

"I confess that I know very little about the Abyss despite all of our battles with his people. I know that most of them are demons or souls in transition. If I were him, I'd send someone who is in the very earliest stages of transition to avoid scaring the Hell out of your people," she said as she crossed her legs.

He glanced at her smooth legs and smiled. She uncrossed them and leaned back. Her tunic slid up an inch or two.

"Will the ambassador stay at the palace?" she asked.

"Only until suitable quarters can be constructed. But that's months away. I haven't even seen the architectural drawings yet. We have several ambassadors in Thule at any given time. Most stay at official residences on the western edge of the Rose Garden. The new residences will be on the northern edge, which is a little closer to the palace," he explained as she parted her knees slightly.

"Will Ulla and I be moving to them when they're completed?" she asked.

"That's entirely up to you. My wives tell me they would prefer to keep you here in the palace so they can keep their eyes on you," he smiled. "And on me, too, I imagine."

She giggled.

"I've met some of the other ambassadors since I've been here. I must say they are a very diverse and interesting lot. I'm surprised at how many non-Human ambassadors are here. I didn't think your world had so many different races," she said. "And now I have added yet another to the mix. Does this make things difficult for you?"

"Not really," Arka-Dal replied. "Most of the ambassadors come and go frequently. They stay in Thule about six months of each year, then return home to tend to family matters. They drop by to chat once in a while, but mostly they're here to ensure the fairness of our trade agreements."

"Why did you allow me and Ulla to live in the palace?" she asked.

"For one, the other officials residences are occupied and we have a lot of extra room here in the palace. For another, you're kind of special," he said.

"Special? In what way?" she asked.

"In many ways. You and fought side-by-side against a brutal enemy and under extraordinary conditions. We got to know and like each other—as did Galya and Gorinna. So you are not a stranger to us. Galya thought it would be best for you to stay close to us so we could teach you about our society and government and I agreed. I knew you'd be a quick learner and would easily adapt to life here in Thule if given the proper guidance. You've exceeded all of my expectations, too," he said.

She beamed.

"I must admit that I was worried. I am still rough around the edges and perhaps too open and honest for my own good. I was afraid that I'd make some huge mistake and ruin everything," she said.

"I admire your honesty. Your people are incapable of lying—so Lucifer told me. I find that refreshing. You say what's on your mind and you hide nothing. If Human beings were like that, we'd avoid so much misery and war," he said. "And we understand your lack of diplomacy. You're a battlefield commander. You were raised to lead armies into battle and you're damned good at it. This post is quite different from anything you've ever done before—but again, you're handling it very well," he praised.

"Father would be delighted to hear you say that. He was worried sick about sending me, but since you already knew me and how I am, he agreed that I was the only logical choice," she said. "He also warned me not to do anything to upset your household—especially Galya."

Arka-Dal laughed.

"You haven't upset anyone and Galya really likes you. She took a liking to you in the Abyss because you reminded her of herself in many ways and she was impressed with your courage," he said.

"I do seem to upset Chatha," Alyana said. "Maybe Zhijima, too."

"That's because they see you as a competitor," he said. "Chatha was once highly jealous of Galya but now they're the best of friends. I'm sure it will be the same with you after a while."

"So she's jealous of me?" Alyana asked.

"I think she is," Arka-Dal replied.

"Do you think she should be?" she asked.

"That's entirely up to you," Arka-Dal replied.

Alyana stood and left the office. Arka-Dal watched her wiggle and shook his head.

"She's very attractive, isn't she?" Galya said as she entered the room.

"Yes. She is," he admitted. "I knew you were watching. I can always sense when you're nearby. You and I have a very special bond. I felt it the moment we made eye contact."

"So did I," she said as they kissed.

Alyana walked out into the Rose Garden to watch the Dal offspring go through their morning lessons with Medusa. She and Leo took turns teaching them about various things. The other three days of the week, they attended the local public schools like everyone else. Even though they were Arka-Dal's children, they didn't have any special privileges other than growing up in the palace. They played on local sports teams and were expected to serve in the military like everyone else who reached the age of 18. And they all had close friends outside the palace.

What Leo and Medusa taught them were subjects that generally weren't taught in schools. Arka-Dal was trying to take steps to correct that oversight but these courses would make for a highly unusual curriculum.

"Perhaps one day, your children will among them," Zhijima said.

Alyana turned and saw her smile.

"My children?" she asked.

"I imagine that you and Arka-Dal will have at least one or two. Don't you think so?" Zhijima said.

Alyana was at a loss for words.

"I thought you were jealous of me," she said.

"I am—but I think in your case, I'll have to bow to the inevitable," Zhijima said.

"Nothing is inevitable," Alyana almost sighed.

"It can be if you have some help," Zhijima smiled.

"What kind of help?" Alyana asked, unsure of where this conversation was going.

"Let me think about that," Zhijima smiled as she walked off.

Alyana watched and shook her head.

"Now I'm really confused!" she said.

"About what?" asked Gorinna as she walked around a hedge.

Alyana told her what Zhijima had said. When she was finished, Gorinna laughed and laughed.

"What's so funny? I don't understand," Alyana said.

"Maybe you don't understand right now, but I'm sure you will later," Gorinna replied. "The ladies are plotting something again."

"Again?" Alyana queried.

Gorinna nodded.

"They did it with Zhijima. Now, they're going to do it with you," she said.

"But what does it all mean?" Alyana asked.

"It means that Arka-Dal had better get ready to add another wife to the family," Gorinna smiled.

Alyana's mouth dropped.

Gorinna smiled.

"Now you're getting it," she said.

"But why would they even think of doing such a thing?" Alyana asked.

"They're doing it because they *like* you—a lot," Gorinna smiled. "So do I, but I'm really not too crazy about having you to compete against. You're just too damned pretty."

"I am?" Alyana asked.

"You sure are," Gorinna replied. "And cute on top of that. And bright."

"I appreciate the compliments, but I still don't understand why they would do this. I'm not even sure it's sane!" Alyana said.

"It's not," Gorinna agreed. "But sanity has nothing to do with it. Just be happy they like you enough to even think of it."

Alyana laughed.

Arka-Dal was in the conference room with Jun, Pandaar, Kashi, Michael and a few of the other top officers of his training command. Chatha, Galya and Alyana were also in attendance.

"After some consideration and first-hand practice, I've decided to add two more weapons to the arsenal of our infantry. Both were used with devastating effects by soldiers of the First Age," Arka-Dal said as he picked up what appeared to be a most unusual looking javelin.

"This first is called the *pilum*. Most of you are already familiar with it. It was carried by the Roman Legions, who were the most feared and successful foot soldiers of all time. It's a short, iron-tipped throwing spear with a wooden shaft. It can be thrown with great force and accuracy. It's designed to punch holes in enemy shields and armor. Once it penetrates a shield, it can't be pulled out. This renders the shield useless and the enemy soldiers have to throw them away," he explained.

He put the pilum down and picked up one of the strangest weapons anyone had ever seen.

"Once they discard their shields, they are sitting ducks for this," he said as he held it up. "This is called a *shangtu*. It's a short range throwing weapon. It has three razor sharp cutting edges and nine points. If used properly, it can have terrifying results. Even if an enemy soldiers attempts to hide behind his shield, the shangtu can go around it and strike him. There's no way you can protect yourself from this thing."

"Wasn't that used by a warrior tribe of central Africa during the First Age?" asked Kashi.

"Yes it was," Arka-Dal said. "It made them among the most feared warriors of their age."

"We will have to adapt some new tactics and training methods," Jun said. "When do you want these weapons introduced to the men?"

"The first 20,000 pilum will be ready at the end of the month. The shangtus take more time to produce, but you should have at least 5,000 by the end of next month," Arka-Dal replied.

He turned to Alyana.

"We change weapons and tactics often in order to be prepared to face any possible threat. Even if there are spies among us, when they see things like this, they don't know what to think. It keeps potential enemies guessing and afraid," he said.

"In order to assure peace…" she began.

"…be always prepared for war," Chatha smiled.

"Fifteen years ago, we adopted the horse archer tactics and composite bows of the ancient Mongols for use by our cavalry. Now, each cavalry regiment has one company of horse archers," Pandaar said.

"What about heavy cavalry?" Alyana asked.

"We eliminated them decades ago," Arka-Dal explained. "Our enemies never used heavy cavalry because they're too slow, so I eliminated them to keep up. Light cavalry is far more adaptable to changing battlefield conditions anyway."

"What about chariots? Do you employ them?" Alyana asked.

"No. But that's why I have horse archers. They can easily out maneuver and disrupt chariot forces. Our closest ally, Egypt, still employs chariots with great success, but even they have added regiments of light cavalry to their forces," Arka-Dal said.

When the meeting was adjourned, the commanders followed Arka-Dal into the dining room for some refreshments. Chatha spotted Zhijima and walked over to her.

"Are you sure you want to do this?" she asked.

"I'm pretty sure. Besides, we all agreed to it," Zhijima said.

"I really don't want to share him with yet another woman, but I understand. It's better this way. Isn't it?" Chatha said.

"Mayumi and Galya say it is. Medusa agrees with them. So I guess it is," Zhijima said with a hint of resignation. "They said it was inevitable and we should help it along."

"When are going to start?" Chatha asked.

"On the cruise," Zhijima said.

"You mean the cruise neither of us are going on?" Chatha smiled.

"Yes. That's the one," Zhijima laughed. "I sure as Hell hope that Mephistos doesn't send a woman to be his ambassador!"

"So do I! If he does, I hope she's unattractive," Chatha said as they walked down to the dining room.

But while Arka-Dal's wives were plotting to throw him and Alyana together, events were unfolding in faraway Egypt that were about to put their plans on hold.

The Head in the Jar

The edifice was ancient beyond words.

Beyond memory.

No record of the structure nor of those who constructed, existed anywhere.

It was carved out of the living rock on the side of granite cliff in the middle of desert wasteland. The façade featured eight ornate columns, each topped with the traditional lotus leaves, flanking an entry that was cut in three distinct phases. The outer phase was a massive rectangle topped by a reptilian figure. Only a few feet beyond was a smaller rectangle topped by a stone scorpion. Beyond that was an arched entry sealed by a smooth stone door.

Outside was a barely visible brick walkway flanked by 24 stone sphinxes that led up to a flight of 48 stone steps which ended at the structure's door.

At one time, the entire façade was covered with brightly painted hieroglyphs. All were so weatherworn as to be barely recognizable now.

The sorcerer studied the building. His thoughts took him back to the time of his youth. There was an entire city here then. There were thousands of people, parks, pools of fresh bubbling water, markets and travelers from all over. In those days, it sat at the crossroads of two major trade routes.

It was a busy, lively and exciting place.

"What has become of you?" he thought. "What has happened here?"

As he approached the structure, he noticed several odd looking piles on the sides of the steps. Upon further examination, he realized they were piles of bones and rusted shields and weapons.

"The remains of the temple's guardians?" he wondered.

As he climbed the steps, the bundles stirred. He stopped and watched as they came together. The bones began to reform into full skeletons. The skeletons began to take on new lives as they picked up their shields and weapons and stood. They stared at him with their empty sockets and took up defensive stances. They raised their swords and moved toward him.

He held up his right hand.

The skeletons stopped and bowed, then got down on one knee and allowed him safe passage into the temple.

He smiled.

"It is good to be home," he said as he walked up to the sealed door.

The limestone blocks looked weatherworn.

Ancient.

He studied their pitted surfaces as he ran his fingers over them. The last time he saw this place, it was painted a bright white with blue, red, green, black and even gold rings and trimmings along the top edges and around the columns and the hieroglyphs stood out. Almost of the colors were gone. Barely traces remained anywhere and the hieroglyphs were barely discernable.

"How long has it been?" he wondered. "Does Egypt still exist? What have I returned to?"

He stepped back and uttered a spell. The stones weakened and tumbled to the ground and a warm blast of stale, very ancient air greeted him. He waited for it to blow past him then stepped inside. As he did, web-covered ancient torches on the walls sparked to life and filled the room with their dull, orange light.

And dust was everywhere.

Layers and layers of it.

It covered everything.

From the shapes beneath it, he could tell that the ancient temple had been undisturbed. Everything seemed to be intact.

As he'd left it –how many years ago?

He smiled as he walked around. The temple's condition meant that everything should be exactly where he'd hidden it. He walked over to a space between two columns and knocked until he heard a hollow sound. He pulled out his dagger and jammed it into the edge of the stone block then pried it away from the wall to reveal a hidden compartment. He reached inside, took out a bell-shaped, covered container and carried it over to the altar. He pulled away the covering to reveal a twisted, dark and malformed head in an air tight glass container.

He tapped on the glass.

The eyelids flickered a few times then opened to reveal two, pale yellow orbs.

"I see that you're still here," the wizard said.

"I'm a head in a jar, Where *else* would I be?" the head replied sarcastically. "And just where in Hell have *you* been all this time? I've been waiting forever!"

"It's a long story and not a very happy one," the wizard said.

"I have time," the head said. "Hell, time is *all* I have."

The wizard laughed.

"The last time you came here, you were making plans to take over the kingdom," the head said.

"Things didn't go as well as I'd hoped they would," the wizard said. "How long have I been gone anyway?"

"How would I know? I've been in that damned closet all this time. It's not like I had a calendar with me," the head snapped.

The wizard sat back as he recalled recent—or not so recent--events.

The rejuvenation process had been painfully slow. It had taken months to gather the dust particles and turn them into bone. Longer still to fill the bones with marrow. Even longer to form the organs, muscles and tendons that provided movement. Then came the flesh, the hair, the nails.

For each step, he had to draw the necessary nutrients from the soil and absorb the life energy from the worms, bugs and other vermin that also inhabited his dark tomb.

"I live again," he said in his deep baritone. "Amenopur lives and woe be to anyone who crosses my path."

He looked around. His amber eyes penetrated the darkness. He saw the shattered remains of his coffin and the dried husks of the scarabs that had been interred with him. He recalled those final, terrifying moments.

He could still feel the strong ropes that bound him. Still feel the hot iron as it seared through his eyeballs and the horrid device that was used to rip his tongue from his throat. He remembered being placed into the coffin and how his flesh tingled insanely as thousands of hungry scarabs were tossed over him. He recalled how he felt as they scrambled over his naked body and gnawed at his flesh and the sounds of the coffin being nailed shut and the pitiable whimpering sounds of his mind as it slowly lapsed into madness before he died.

Bartada had caused that.

He was the head of the Pharaoh's household guard. It was he who had uncovered his plot to usurp the throne—or so he said. In the middle of night, Bartada and his soldiers had burst into his house, bound him in chains and dragged him before the Pharaoh. Then Bartada accused him of trying to seize power for himself.

Of course he vehemently denied those charges.

Of course the Pharaoh ordered him to be tortured until he confessed.

When days of interrogation failed to produce the desired results, the Pharaoh had his entire family arrested. Bartada and his men beat his wife, Kiriti, his mother and their children while he was forced to watch. His mother died from the beating and left his son, a boy of 10, crippled for life. He cursed Bartada and vowed to kill him. For his outburst, he was forced to watch Bartada and his men take turns raping his wife. To save her, Amenopur confessed to his "plot".

It didn't help.

Disgraced and defiled, Kiriti killed herself and their two children. The Pharaoh had their bodies hacked to pieces and tossed into the Nile to feed the crocodiles to keep them from entering the Afterlife.

That's when Amenopur swore he'd kill the Pharaoh and everyone involved in this tragedy. The Pharaoh laughed and ordered him to be buried alive in an unmarked grave and had his name expunged from all official monuments and documents. In short, it was the ultimate insult. It was as if he'd never existed at all.

He looked around.

"I'm in a cave," he said. "But where is the cave located?"

He saw a pile of dirty clothes on the floor. As he picked up the heavy cloak and examined it, he wondered who it had belonged to and how it had found its way into the tomb. He also found a heavy leather belt with a dagger in sheath, a pair of leather boots and a pouch filled with silver coins.

"I can make use of these he said as he donned the clothes. "At least now I won't have to travel the land naked."

He knew the book that was buried with him was gone. He had watched helplessly as the Devil destroyed it.[6] That was just as well. There were other copies of the book in the world. All he had to do was find one.

---

[6]   Read: In the Depths of Evil & Other Tales

The high priest of Amun had also buried two other artifacts with him. Both were far more dangerous than the book, especially in the wrong hands. He looked around and found two small wooden chests partially obscured by rubble. He quickly uncovered each then used a heavy rock to break the locks from each.

To his surprise, both chests were empty.

The artifacts were gone.

Stolen.

But by who?

Both chests had been locked and sealed. Only the high priests knew of them.

"No tomb robbers did this," he decided. "Tomb robbers would have broken the chest open to get at the contents. Whoever did this knew exactly where they were. He took the artifacts out of the chests and resealed them to make it look like they were still inside."

Only Bartada had the opportunity to do that.

But if he did take them, just what did he do with them?

The artifacts were dangerous.

Far too dangerous to be out in the world. When placed together, they could bring humankind to a most horrible end.

He had to find them before it was too late.

That meant he had to escape from his dismal tomb.

He searched the walls carefully for any sign of a doorway. When he found it, he saw that it had been blocked with tons of dirt and rubble.

"This will take time," he decided as he began raking up handfuls of dirt..

The head yawned.

"So you dug your way out?" it asked.

"No. I realized it was an exercise in futility and escaped by another means," Amenopur replied. "It took me days to summon up enough energy to do it, but eventually I turned myself into a vapor cloud and escaped through a crack."

"So you have regained your powers?" the head asked.

"Not fully," Amenopur said. "It may be years before they return to me—if at all. I used to draw my powers from the Earth and air. But something is different now. The energies are different and they don't nourish me as before."

"I can't help you with that. I have been imprisoned in this jar for as long as you were in your tomb. I don't know what has changed or why," the head said. "Many years ago, you and I were bitter rivals. I can still remember our final duel and how, after days of fending off spell after spell, I finally succumbed to your attack. It was bad enough that you had defeated me. But then you beheaded my and put my head in this jar. For what purpose?"

"Spite. Perhaps a twisted sense of justice based on years of anger against you. I truly can't remember what drove me to do this," Amenopur replied.

"What did you do with the rest of me?" the head asked.

"I burned it and threw your ashes in the Nile," Amenopur said. "Does it matter now?"

"I guess not," the head replied. "But did you preserve my head and hide it in the wall of this temple? Of what use am I to you?"

"I'm not sure why I did any of that. Perhaps I was caught up in a fit of madness. But you still live," Amenopur said.

"You call *this* living?" the head asked. "You truly must have been insane. So, why did you seek me out? What brings you here?"

"Something drew me back to this place. Some strange force I still can't comprehend. Perhaps it has to do with that peculiar wizard I met."

"Tell me about him. I have nothing but time—" the head said.

When Amenopur finally emerged from the tomb and reformed himself, he saw a curious-looking old man dressed in a dark gray, hooded cloak. He was seated on a rock just outside of the tomb. There was a black cat seated on his lap.

The cat looked up at him. That's when he heard it speak.

Or did the voice come from the strange old man?

"I've been waiting for you, Amenopur," the cat said.

"Who are you, old man? And how do you know my name?" he asked.

"I know many things. My name is of no importance and would be meaningless to you," the cat said.

He could sense a strange, almost black power emanating from both.

"Why did you come here, old man?" he asked.

"I need you to help me locate a few long-missing artifacts," the man said.

"And just why in the name of Amun Ra, should I help you?" Amenopur asked.

"Let us say that it would greatly benefit us both in ways that even you would appreciate," the man said.

Amenopur was about to walk away, but something about the old man and the cat intrigued him. He could sense that he was powerful.

Enormously powerful.

And that power was as black as coal.

He sat down next to him.

"I'm listening," he said...

Arka-Dal was seated at the dinner table chatting with everyone as usual when the Devil suddenly appeared.

"Father!" Galya said. "I wasn't expecting you today."

"Welcome, Lucifer. Please join us," Arka-Dal offered.

"This is not a social call," the Devil said.

"In that case, what troubles you?" Arka-Dal asked.

"He's back!" the Devil said with a touch of disgust.

"Who's back?" asked Galya.

"That foul wizard and his damned cat," the Devil said. "Somehow, he escaped the fate I'd assigned to him and has returned to plague us once again. I know he's back because I heard his nasty laughter inside my mind. He was mocking me—and I dislike being mocked."

"We'll have to find him and finish him off once and forever," Arka-Dal said. "where is he now?"

"That I don't know. He is one of the few beings I've always had trouble tracking. And I won't be able to track him until he uses his particularly unique magic," the Devil said. "I can tell you this---he's up to something very evil. I feel it in my bones."

Arka-Dal looked at the women.

"We'll have to postpone out cruise for a few days," he said.

"We understand," Aka-san Mayumi said. "There's time for that later."

Fifty miles from the mountain that had been Amenopur's tomb, Arka-Dal's grandson, Peace, sat before his campfire and slowly turned the rabbit he was roasting on a spit. As he took it off the flames to test it, Ned suddenly materialized next to him.

Peace started and nearly dropped his dinner. Ned smiled.

"I wish you'd announce yourself instead of just popping up like that. You scared the living daylights out of me," Peace said as his pulse returned to normal.

"Where are you bound?" Ned inquired.

"I'm heading into the mountains to check on Amenopur's tomb—like I do every year at this time," Peace replied.

"Save yourself a trip. I've just been there. Amenopur's gone," Ned said.

"Gone? You mean he's escaped?" Peace asked.

"I fear the sorcerer is once again at large," Ned replied.

"Can you find him?" Peace asked.

"Unless he uses his magic, I cannot locate him. But I'll keep trying. Egypt is vast. There is no telling where he's gone. I also have no idea what he looks like now. After all, he is one who can easily change his appearance if he desires. Amenopur is clever—and dangerous," Ned answered.

"As always, you are the harbinger of bad news," Peace said. "You keep searching for the sorcerer. I'll go to Memphis and warn Hetshepsut."

"I'll transport you to Memphis. We have little time to lose," Ned said as he waved his hand.

An eye blink later, Peace found himself standing in the reception room of the palace. As he looked around, he pinched himself to make certain it wasn't all a dream…

"That's all well and good. But what does any of it have to do with me?" the head asked.

"Perhaps nothing. Perhaps everything. The wizard asked me to help him locate two artifacts," Amenopur said.

"Which two?" asked the head.

"He didn't specify. He said that only I would be able to find them and that I would know them when I saw them. He also said I would need help in my quest from someone who knew the ancient world as well as I did," Amenopur replied.

"Me?" the head asked.

"Your name immediately came into my mind," Amenopur said.

"How the Hell am I suppose to help you? Look at me!" the head said. "It's not like I can go anywhere!"

Amenopur laughed.

"Go ahead—rub it in!" the head sneered. "Had things gone in my favor, this would be *your* head in this jar!"

"Perhaps you can help me remember," Amenopur suggested. "Those scarabs did a real nasty number on my body and internal organs. Part of my memory is still blank and it might never fully recover. But your mind has remained intact. You have been sealed within this jar, safe from the ravages of air, bacteria and time. Is your memory intact?"

"Yes. I have an eternity to strengthen it," the head replied. "But I've been in total darkness all this time and that has added touches of madness to me."

"I understand," Amenopur said.

Before he could say another word, Amenopur was knocked to the ground by a dark, unseen force. He rolled around in the sand before passing out. When he woke, the head was gone!

He stared at the empty space in disbelief.

Then he realized who took the head.

"When I find that bastard, I'll make him pay dearly for this!" he swore.

The first one Peace saw in the palace was Arkaneton, the Queen's son by Arka-Dal. Arkaneton smiled and extended his hand. As Peace shook it, he said:

"The evil one has risen from his grave."

"Dick Cheney?" Arkaneton asked.

"He means Amenopur," Ned said as he materialized next to them. "I've been out searching for him."

"Any luck?" Arkaneton asked.

Ned shook his head.

"It is as if he's dropped off the face of the Earth. I have tried every tracking spell I know of to no avail," Ned replied.

Arkaneton looked at them.

"What do you suppose he's planning?" he asked.

"If I were him, I'd travel the land for few days to get a feel for the way things are now. This is not the Egypt he knew anymore. There have been many changes since the six millennia he's been imprisoned," Peace said.

Hetshepsut entered the reception room and greeted everyone cheerfully. She smiled at Ned.

"If you're here, then something is amiss. Care to tell me about it?" she said as they sat down on nearby couches.

Ned explained the situation.

"The name is not familiar to me. What was he executed for?" she asked.

Ned went into a detailed history of Amenopur's rise and downfall. She listened as she considered the possible consequences of his return.

"His life reads like a Shakespearian tragedy," she said. "And you say he might have been falsely accused?"

"There is more than enough evidence to suggest that," Ned replied. "Amenopur was the most powerful and learned scholar, architect, physician, surgeon, scientist, astronomer and mathematician of his time. On top of that, he was an incredibly powerful wizard. But he had a rival.

There was another man almost as talented who coveted Amenopur's Grand Vizier position. At first, their rivalry was friendly enough. Then, one day, it boiled over in a long, vicious duel. Amenopur won but it nearly cost him life. In a fit of rage, he decapitated his enemy. Then he burned his body and scattered the ashes in the Nile."

"What became of the head?" Hetshepsut asked.

"No one knows," Ned replied. "His rival's son was the chief of the palace guards. It was he who accused Amenopur of high treason and talked the pharaoh into ordering his arrest and subsequent trial and execution."

Hetshepsut nodded.

"I kind of pity him now," she said.

"I could have our soldiers scour the city and drag him here," Arkaneton suggested.

"You will do nothing of the sort," Hetshepsut decided. "In fact, I order you to leave him in peace. He has already paid the ultimate price for something he most likely never did. The Egypt he supposed committed the crimes against is long gone. This is a new Egypt. A new age. He has committed no crimes against this land that anyone is aware of. Until he does, he has all of the rights and protections that are guaranteed to everyone under Egyptian laws."

"A cheetah never changes its spots," Peace said.

"Maybe this one has," Hetshepsut countered. "Let's give him the benefit of the doubt. For now."

"Alright, Mother," Arkaneton agreed. "We'll give him time to show his true colors. We'll allow him to make the first move. I just hope we'll be able to counter it when he does."

"That's settled. But there is one thing I would have you do, Ned," Hetshepsut said.

"Ask and it is yours," Ned replied with a bow of his head.

"If you find Amenopur, I'd like you to relay a message from me," she said with a smile.

Ned listened to her message, smiled and vanished.

Arkaneton looked at his mother.

"Is that wise?" he asked.

"Only time will tell," she replied.

The cat looked at the hideous head. The head snarled. The cat simply yawned and eyed the wizard questioningly.

"What's with the head?" it asked.

"That is the first object of Amenopur's quest. He will soon come to realize this and then he will also figure out what the second object is," the wizard said.

"I thought you were after some ancient artifact of great power," the cat said.

"I am. Two, in fact. One is already in my possession," the wizard said.

"*This* is an artifact?" the cast asked. "You must be joking—or you're totally nuts."

"I never do the first and the jury is still out about the latter," the wizard said. "But this head is indeed one of the artifacts I seek."

"How so?" asked the head.

"It's simple. You are quite ancient and you once possessed great magical powers. You know things. Things that I wish to know. Things that you will soon tell me," the wizard said.

"What makes you think I'll help the likes of you?" the head asked. "What's in it for me?"

"If you don't help me, then I shall toss your pitiful relic into the ocean. If you do help, then you will have the chance to avenge yourself against Amenopur," the wizard replied. "I learned of your existence centuries ago but I was never able to locate your hiding place. I thought that the best way to do that was to find the tomb of your arch enemy and wait for him to escape. Once he did, I'd convince him to help me search for two special objects—without telling him that *you* were one of them. Now you can help me find the *second*."

The head laughed.

"The cat's right. You're nuts!" he said. "I can't even get out of this jar. How on earth can I help you find anything in this state?"

"You won't have to leave the jar to search for the object. We will allow said object to come to *you* instead," the wizard replied.

"And when that "object" gets here, he will kick your ugly ass all over Egypt," the cat said.

"How can you say such a thing?" the wizard asked.

"That's easy. I've witnessed all of your big failures. Since you have an uncanny knack for picking fights with those you can never defeat, my money is on the "object", the cat answered smugly. "You should really consider getting out of the wizard business. You're not very good at it anymore."

"Bah! I'll make you eat those words!" the wizard said scornfully.

"I am sort of hungry right now. Got any tuna?" the cat asked.

Amenopur pondered his circumstances. He knew the wizard had taken the head. But at the moment, he had no way to track it down. His powers were still very weak. He knew he'd have to be patient and wait until he was fully restored before he could go after the madman.

For all intents and purposes, he was just an ordinary man. That meant he had to eat, drink and find places to live. It also meant that he needed money. He went back into the temple and pried a block of limestone away from the base of wall. He then reached inside and pulled out a small chest he had secreted there just before his arrest.

It was filled with emeralds, rubies, sapphires, and other semi-precious stones of all weighs and sizes. He selected six large emeralds and placed them into his pouch. Then he slid the chest back into the opening and replaced the block.

The following afternoon, he entered the city of Thebes. He made his way to the market place and asked a where he could exchange his jewels for money. The man pointed to a rather nondescript shop at the end of the street.

Amenopur walked into the shop. A middle aged man smiled at him from behind a counter.

"How may I be of service, sir?" he asked.

"I have just returned from many years abroad and I am in need of some spendable currency. I was told that you purchase gems here," Amenopur said.

"That I do, sir. Would you happen to have some you'd like to sell?" the man replied. "I give the best rates in all of Egypt."

"I have this," Amenopur said as he handed him the largest emerald.

The man held it up to the light, turned it over several times, then placed it on a scale. After it was weighed, he placed the emerald on the counter between himself and Amenopur.

"This is one very beautiful piece, sir. I'd say it's very old. Is it a family heirloom?" the man asked.

"You could say that. What will you give me for it?" Amenopur asked.

"I'll give you 5,000 dinar," the man said. "That's more than two years salary for most folks in Egypt."

"Done!" Amenopur agreed as they shook hands.

"Will that be silver, gold or scrip?" the man asked.

"What is scrip?" Amenopur queried.

"It's official currency made of papyrus. It's issued by the treasury and good as gold anywhere. It's much easier to carry," the man explained as he showed him a bill.

"How about 4,500 in scrip and the rest in gold and silver?" Amenopur asked.

"No problem," the man replied as he went to a strongbox, opened it and took out 45 100 dinar notes along with 25 gold and 50 silver coins. He handed this to Amenopur and explained their face values.

"Thank you, my friend. You have been most generous and helpful," Amenopur said as they again shook hands.

"It's a pleasure doing business with you, sir," the man said. "Please come again if you have any other pieces you'd like to sell."

"I will do that. Farewell," Amenopur said as he put the money in his pouch.

The Devil stopped pacing and smiled.

"He's shown himself," he announced. "He's used his filthy powers."

Arka-Dal sat up.

"Where is he?" he asked.

"Egypt. I don't know exactly where because I was only able to detect his magic for a split second. But at least we have a place to start," the Devil said. "If he's used it once, he will undoubtedly use it again."

"Why Egypt?" asked Galya.

The Devil shrugged.

"The man is mostly mad. He was driven over the edge centuries ago when he became corrupted by the very dark powers he so eagerly sought to make his own. It's kind of a pity in a way. He was once a very brilliant scholar and alchemist. Right now, he's so twisted, he doesn't care what is right or wrong," he said.

"Did you ever have dealing with him?" Arka-Dal asked.

"No. He never once sought me out. This is one foul creature that I refuse to take the blame for," the Devil smiled.

"He's *my* fault actually," Merlin said. "He and I once pursued the same things. Those pursuits nearly corrupted me. Had I stayed on the same path, I would have become just like him—or worse. I was able to leave the path and I warned him. We argued frequently and those arguments sometimes led to violence.

He was almost ma then.

He was also amoral. He didn't care who he hurt or the consequences of his pursuit of that dark power. The more he learned, the more he craved. I have no idea where the cat came in or how. I know that he seeks the Necronomicon and other forbidden books and scrolls. He may already possess some of them."

"It doesn't matter how he became who he is. We know he's insane, powerful and dangerous," Arka-Dal said. "But just how can we get rid of him? He's already survived everything we've thrown at him."

"That I don't know. I must admit that this one puzzles me. I don't fully understand the source of his powers or how he managed to survive my last spell. There must be a key—a clue—that I've missed," the Devil said.

Amenopur observed the people in the market place while he ate. This was not, he decided, the Memphis he remembered. Although much of it seemed familiar, it also felt different. The architecture was slightly different and of a smaller, neater scale. And some of the hieroglyphs that were carved into them looked slightly different as well. Some were symbols and words that he couldn't comprehend.

And the city felt cleaner.

Wider.

And busier than he remembered.

Even the people seemed different. They dressed differently and in an entirely new array of bright colors. There were bright reds, blues, greens. Whites with gold or silver trim. Dark reds and blues and orange and yellow and multi-colored patterns he'd never seen before.

Women's' hairstyles were quite different and their dresses were shorter.

Sexier.

More revealing.

There were also people of several different races. Some he had never seen before, like Dwarfs and Elves and Mongoblins.

He finished his meal and left two silver coins as payment. The waiter tried to give him change but he refused.

"You may keep the remainder," he said.

"Thank you very much, sir. Please come again," the waiter smiled.

He decided to stroll through the market. What he saw astounded him.

There were stall and shops filled with meats, vegetables and spices from all over the world. He saw shoemakers, dressmakers, barbers, dentists, doctors, toy stores, and stores that sold all sorts of household items.

And shoppers were everywhere.

There were also refreshments of every type available, including a heady blue wine and brandy from a place called Thule.

"Just where on Earth is Thule?" he thought.

He came upon a kiosk that sold something called newspaper. He asked the vendor about it and the man explained it to him. Curious, he purchased one. He then stopped at the next café and ordered an ale. To his surprise, it was brought to him ice cold and in a frosty mug.

"This isn't the Egypt I remember," he thought as he enjoyed the very first cold ale of his life. "Just how long was I entombed?"

The paper was called the Memphis Herald and was printed in an easy to read demotic script. It claimed to have all of the latest news of Egypt and the entire region. Then he read the date on the banner.

"Printed this 16th day of June, 272 S.A."

"S.A.? What's that mean?" he asked a passing waitress.

"It means Second Age," she said. "That's what we're in now."

"Second Age? When did the First Age end?" he queried.

"It ended about 2,500 years ago," she said. "I thought everyone knew that!"

"I—I've been away for a long time," he said. "Too long. So much has changed."

"I'll say they have. Things are a lot better since Queen Hetshepsut abolished slavery over 50 years ago. Everyone in Egypt is much happier now," the waitress said.

"There are no longer slaves in Egypt?" he asked.

"Not a single one and we're all better off for it," the waitress said.

The newspaper proved to be a revelation. Not only was it a good source of local information on recent events, it also contained satirical cartoons that lampooned the government and other local officials. And it appeared they were able to do this without fear of reprisals or arrest.

They also had a sports section that covered several pages. He learned that the most popular sport of the day was a game called "baseball" and that every major city in Egypt had a team.

"Perhaps I'll take in a game or two to see what it's like," he said.

He looked up at the strange globe atop a metal pole a few feet away. He had noticed such globes on every block throughout the city. He asked the waitress what they were.

"Those are street lights. They glow when the sun goes down," she said.

"You mean they're lanterns?" he asked.

"Sort of," she said.

"So someone lights them each night?" he asked.

"No. They're solar powered. They get their energy from the sun and come on automatically. No one lights them," she explained.

"Amazing!" he remarked.

"I guess you don't have them where you're from?" she asked.

"No. This is all new to me," he replied.

"There's lots of other stuff that we now take for granted that might surprise you. You'll see. Enjoy your stay in Egypt!" she smiled cheerfully.

"Thank you. I'm sure I shall," he said as he picked up his beer.

As he sipped, a familiar figure suddenly materialized in the seat in front of him. Amenopur finished sipping his ale. He smiled at his visitor.

"Ned the Knower. It's been a long time," he said.

"It's been 6,231 years to be exact," Ned said. "You look well."

"Thank you. I'm sure you didn't just drop in to say hello. Did you?" Amenopur said.

"You're right. I didn't," Ned frowned. "When I realized that you were out and about again, I thought I'd better find you to make sure you're not up to anything that would upset the Queen or the general balance of the universe."

"Even if I was, what business is it of yours?" Amenopur asked.

Ned scowled and leaned closer.

"You know me, Amenopur. I could destroy you in an eye blink if I so desired," he warned.

"Then why don't you do it and be done with it?" Amenopur asked.

"Hetshepsut, the queen, forbids it," Ned replied

His answer surprised the wizard.

"Why would she forbid it?" he asked.

"She said that any crimes you were accused of occurred in another age and time and you have already been punished. As far as she is concerned, your slate has been wiped clean. What you did long ago is of no concern to her. You have committed no crime nor have you shown any intentions of harming the Egypt of this age. As long as you conduct yourself honorably and within the laws of this land, she feels no need to worry about you," Ned explained.

"Fascinating," Amenopur said. "When we first met, you merely observed the doings of men. It appears that you have changed. You now seem to take a more active interest in human affairs."

"Circumstances have left me little choice," Ned said. "there are things—creatures—that dwell just beyond the rim of the universe. Nightmarish beings from the very dawn of time itself that now threaten our very existence. I have chosen to stand guard against them and their foul agents who walk the Earth. I now fight to hold back the darkness. On which side of the line do *you* walk, Amenopur?"

Amenopur shrugged.

"To be honest, I do not yet know," he said. "This is new Egypt. A new age. There is so much I have to learn. Right now, I have to figure out who this rather bizarre wizard is and exactly what he wants from me."

He told Ned of his encounter.

"So the bastard still lives!" Ned almost growled.

"You know him?" Amenopur asked.

"Oh, I know him alright. He's a twisted and dangerous sorcerer. He wields powers that only he understands. Powers he may have drawn from those same dark beings at the edge of the universe," Ned replied.

"The Elder Gods?" Amenopur asked.

"Yes. I believe he has somehow managed to tap into their dark matter and forced it into doing his bidding," Ned replied.

Ned stood and paced.

"The wizard is using you," he said.

"I am aware of that, Knower. I am using him as well. He promised to fully restore my powers if I helped him locate two ancient artifacts. I believe he already has one—which I've accidentally led him to. I have no idea what the second one is yet," Amenopur said.

"Do you plan to uphold your bargain?" asked Ned.

"In a manner of speaking. I'm biding my time until my powers return to me naturally. I have a feeling that those artifacts are very powerful and dangerous. I'd hate to see them fall into the hands of such a madman. I also know that he has no intentions at all of holding up his side of the bargain. I want to know what these artifacts are, what they can do, then find a way to destroy both them and the wizard," Amenopur said.

"Do not take him lightly. He has powers you cannot begin to imagine. This is no game," Ned warned.

Amenopur laughed.

"It is to me," he said. "Since you know him, is the man actually the sorcerer or is it the cat who wields the power?"

"I've never been able to figure that part out. I have never seen one without the other. I doubt they could exist independently of each other," Ned said.

"That makes this even more intriguing," Amenopur said.

"Be careful what you say. He could be anywhere. He could even be a fly on a wall," Ned cautioned.

"You mean like *that* one over there?" Amenopur said as he picked up the newspaper and swatted a fly before it could dart away.

Fifty miles away, the wizard suddenly toppled from his chair and hit the floor of his hideout hard. The cat, who was seated on a nearby table, yawned indifferently as the wizard painfully struggled back to his feet and massaged his lower back with both hands.

"That must have hurt," the cat said. "So much for the old fly on the wall trick, eh?"

"No matter. I was there long enough to learn what he's up to. Now, I can make plans to handle the situation when it arises," the wizard said as he leaned on the table and slowly lowered himself back into the chair.

The cat simply yawned again and began licking himself.

Ned looked Amenopur directly in the eyes.

"Until you decide which side of the line you will walk on, rest assured that I will be watching your every move," he warned as he vanished into thin air.

"Every move."

Amenopur shook it off and ordered another ale. Ned was powerful. Far too powerful to make an enemy of. He now found himself between a rock and a hard place. Queen Hetshepsut's benevolence had cast everything in an entirely new light.

Egypt had changed.

So much so that he barely recognized it.

Gone was the rigid, religion-oriented, conformist Egypt of his day. In its place was now a powerful nation of millions of people of all races and religions. The old symbolic style of art and writing had been subtly blended with more relaxed, natural styles. The colors were richer.

More vibrant.

Vividly lifelike.

He saw that the old monuments and temples had been restored by armies of skilled craftsmen. There were lush gardens, parks and athletic fields and hospitals and libraries and schools and markets galore. Happy children ran and played everywhere. Priests and nobles conversed easily with commoners and the clothing styles were varied and colorful.

The more he explored Memphis, the more it amazed and delighted him. He learned that titles of nobility had been abolished and everyone was considered equal under Egyptian laws. Even the once-powerful priests had been stripped of their status.

And the country was prosperous and at peace.

No longer surrounded by enemies, it had expanded its trade markets and had prospered like never before. And to ensure peace, it now boasted a standing, professional army of one million men and a 400 ship navy. That was ten times the size of the armed forces in Amenopur's day.

He also learned that the people loved the Queen and her son, Arkaneton and other members of the royal family. She had declared that she was not a living deity and she built no temples or monuments to herself. Instead, she used her wealth to construct bridges, roads, libraries and schools, dams and even a major irrigation project. She wanted her people to prosper.

And her son was also the first born son of the emperor of nearby Thule. Because of this, the two nations had formed an unbreakable bond and alliance.

Amenopur left the market place and walked to the Nile. He decided to take a leisurely cruise upriver to learn more about this strange, new world he'd awakened into. He boarded one of the traditional sailboats and sat down on a cushioned seat on the deck. A waitress asked if he'd like something to drink. He smiled and ordered another ale. To his delight, this also was nicely chilled.

He sipped and watched as the scenery slipped slowly by.

He also thought about the strange wizard.

Since he'd taken the head, that was obviously one of the two artifacts he sought. It was both ancient and, during the owner's lifetime, it was very powerful. Other than as an advisor, the head had no use now. Its powers had long ago faded and he had personally made sure they'd never return.

He smiled.

"I know who the second *artifact* is," he thought. "But he'll have a long wait until he gets me. I have more important things to do first—like find out who that madman is and where he gets his powers from. Then I can decide how to deal with him."

As the ship cruises toward Luxor, Amenopur heard a voice inside his head.

"It was good of you to lead me to the first artifact," the voice said.

He laughed.

"You'll find that to be quite useless at this stage in its existence. I took care of that 6,000 years ago," he thought. "I take it that I am the second?"

"Yes," the wizard said.

"Too bad for you," Amenopur replied. "You cannot have me."

"I can take you by force," the wizard threatened.

"You can *try*," Amenopur sneered.

"If I do, we may both be destroyed. That would be pointless, wouldn't it?" the wizard said.

"I'm betting that only one of us will be destroyed. Care to wager which?" Amenopur said.

"What would it take to assure your cooperation?" the wizard asked.

"I'll have to think about that for a few days. I will tell you this: the price will be very steep. You may not wish to pay it and I seriously doubt that you have the power to meet my demands," Amenopur said.

"Ask and it shall be yours," the wizard said. "I'll grant you anything you wish."

"Now you sound desperate. I think I'll have to up the ante quite a bit in that case," Amenopur said.

"Don't become too greedy—or you'll regret it!" the wizard warned.

"Bah! I doubt that even you can do anything worse to me than that which was already done. Make your idle and empty threats to someone who cares," Amenopur said sarcastically.

"Just what *is* your price?" the wizard asked in frustration.

"I'll get back to you in a few days," Amenopur replied as he blocked any further mental intrusions.

The wizard snarled and cursed at the top of his lungs. The cat watched him and smiled. He scowled at the cat.

"Aw, what's the matter? Your 'artifact' not acting the way you want him to? Poor baby!" the cat scoffed.

"Keep talking like that and I'll blow the fur off you!" the wizard threatened.

"And destroy your connection to your power source? I think not!" the cat replied scornfully. "You need me, wizard. Remember that. Also remember that it is only through me that you have nine lives. No more. No less. You have already used up four."

The wizard grumbled.

The Devil broke his concentration and sat back. He closed his eyes for a few moments to clear the buzzing from his brain. He had been trying to locate the wizard for several days now without success. He looked up at the others.

"He's good," the Devil said. "He can cloak his whereabouts in a way that makes it impossible for me to locate him until he uses his powers again."

Merlin paced nervously.

"This makes four times I thought we'd rid the world of him. Each time, he's found a way to return," he said. "I don't know what the source of his strange powers is, but I am almost certain it has to do with that cat."

"Did he always have the cat?" Galya asked.

"No. He acquired it—or vice versa—a few weeks before he parted ways. I attempted to dissuade him from following the darker path. I even threatened him. He ignored me and took off. The next time we met, it was over 100 years later. I met him and his cat in a tavern near London. He wasn't quite as mad then," Merlin replied.

"Was he speaking through the cat then?" asked Galya.

"No," Merlin said. "The cat simply sat on his shoulder while we spoke. He said he was on a quest to find every forbidden book ever written. I told him that some books were not meant to be found and were best left lost. He just laughed at me and called me an old fuddy-duddy."

"He's after books? Is that why you went after the lost books of Alzari?" Arka-Dal asked.

"That was the main reason. There were a few others that seem unimportant now. I just hope there are no copies floating around today," Merlin said.

"There is yet another sorcerer in the mix now," the Devil said. "Amenopur has returned from the grave and it seems our maniac wizard has contacted him."

"About what?" asked Arka-Dal.

"Helping him to locate two ancient and very powerful artifacts," the Devil replied. "According to Ned, he already has one of them. The second isn't being very cooperative right now."

"Should we worry about Amenopur?" asked Arka-Dal.

"No. In fact, I feel he hold the key in us being able to rid the world of the wizard once and forever," the Devil said.

"Amenopur is that powerful?" Arka-Dal asked.

"No. He'll need our help," the Devil said. "I'll have to bring him here and ask him to cooperate with us. If he does, I'm sure he'll want something in return—something only I might be able to provide."

Arka-Dal nodded.

"How soon can you get him here?" he asked.

"Right now, he's enjoying a scenic cruise up the Nile. I'd hate to interrupt that. Let's say we give him more time to get to know the "new" Egypt?" the Devil suggested.

"As soon as his feet touch solid ground, bring him here," Arka-Dal said.

Alyana had sat in on the entire meeting. She was amazed at the way everyone worked together for a common cause. The idea that Lucifer himself now protected Thule thanks to Arka-Dal's marriage to Galya was a concept that would have been impossible a few years ago.

The meeting adjourned.

Lucifer took his leave to tend to some business elsewhere while Merlin and Leo went to the living room to play chess and drink wine. Arka-Dal returned to his office to sign some official documents and Galya walked out into the garden. Alyana followed.

"Is it always like this around here?" she asked.

"Only when something pops up that might threaten Thule," Galya said. "Usually things range between chaotic and hectic. You've been here long enough to observe the way we live. How do you like it?"

"It's never dull and I enjoy interacting with all of you. I feel as if I've actually grown a bit since I've arrived. I still make mistakes, but hopefully they aren't bad enough to upset anyone," Alyana said.

"They aren't. No one is perfect here. Not even me," Galya smiled. "It took me a few months to grow accustomed to living here. Now, I wouldn't dream of living anywhere else. It's good to feel wanted, welcome, loved and trusted. No one's ever treated me like this before and I would die fighting to protect everyone in this house rather than see them harmed in any way. This is *home* and these people are my family. I've never had either until I came here."

"I wish I had such a home," Alyana said.

Galya put her hand on Alyana's shoulder and smiled.

"You do," she said.

The ship docked at Luxor two days later. Amenopur smiled and looked around at the fully restored temples and monuments. The city seemed larger and far more magnificent than he remembered.

But it also felt less formal.

Less "in your face".

Luxor, while impressive, was also built as a place to live.

He walked down the gangplank. As soon as his feet touched the warm sand, he found himself standing in the middle of large, well-decorated entrance hall. He stood and gawked at his surroundings.

Nothing seemed familiar.

"This isn't Egypt," he said aloud.

"No. This is Thule," came a voice from his right.

He turned and watched as Arka-Dal, Merlin, Gorinna, the Devil, Galya and several others entered.

A tall, lean and muscular man with brown hair strode toward him. Amenopur studied his. He seemed regal and noble. He sensed the man was in charge, but didn't flaunt it. Not knowing what else to do, he placed one hand on his chest and bowed respectfully. The man nodded.

"I am Arka-Dal. I bid you welcome to my home," he said.

"I have heard your name several times. You're the emperor of Thule," Amenopur said. "How is it you speak my language?"

"We speak one language here—thanks to a translation spell that Merlin cast on this house many years ago," Arka-Dal replied. "He did it to avoid misunderstandings."

"That was very wise of this Merlin," Amenopur said.

"Thank you," Merlin smiled.

Amenopur laughed.

"I seem to know your face," he said as they shook hands.

"We met when you first walked the Earth," Merlin replied. "You asked me about a certain spell. In fact, we learned it together. Our common adversary was also present."

"The wizard with the cat?" Amenopur asked. "I would have remembered him."

"He did not have the cat back then," the Devil said. "Do you know his whereabouts?"

"Unfortunately, I do not," Amenopur said as they walked into the living room. "We have only seen each other once but he has contacted me with his mind. What can you tell me about him? He seems quite mad."

"He is mad—and dangerously so," the Devil said as they sat down.

He went into a history of their recent encounters. Amenopur sipped wine as he listened. Then he smiled.

"I think I understand now," he said. "It's the cat."

"Would you care to explain?" Arka-Dal asked.

"You know the old story about cats having nine lives? Well, if he is indeed symbiotically and spiritually connected to the cat, then he would also have the same number of lives that cats are reputed to have," Amenopur theorized.

"So since we've killed him four times…" Galya began.

"You have to kill him five more times to be rid of him forever," Amenopur said. "But each time you do kill him, he will become more wary of you and thus become more difficult to kill."

"That makes sense," Arka-Dal said. "Now, what can you tell us about the artifacts he seeks?"

Amenopur told them about the head in the jar being the first of the two and then went on to tell him of his last contact. Arka-Dal stared at him.

"By the Gods! *You* are the second artifact!" he said. "He wants to steal your powers and add them to his own."

"That's exactly what I've come up with," Amenopur said. "Unfortunately for him, the powers that once belonged to my rival did not follow his head into that jar. He is merely a living relic with nothing more than comedic value."

"What about yourself? I sense strong power within you," Merlin asked.

"I am ever s slowly regaining my strength. I should be back to normal within another month or two. That's why I've been avoiding the wizard. When he comes to collect his 'artifact', I want to be at my highest level in order to be able to deal with him," Amenopur said. "Even so, I may need help. I know not how powerful he is nor do I understand the source of that power."

"What has the wizard promised you?" asked the Devil.

"I informed him that I'd get back to him about that later. Truly, there is only one thing I desire but I doubt he can provide it," Amenopur said.

"I sense a name and I see an image in your mind. Kiriti," the Devil said.

"Kiriti was my wife. I loved her more than life itself. She was my world. She was everything to me," Amenopur said sadly as a tear rolled down his cheek.

The Devil put his hand on Amenopur's shoulder.

"Grieve no more. Go and walk in the garden," he urged.

Curious, Amenopur left the palace and followed the path into the Rose Garden. After he'd gone about two hundred yards, he came to a large open area between several hedges. There was a man-made pond in the center and its dark green surface was covered with lily pads of all shapes and sizes. A fountain sprayed jets of water from the center. He stopped to look at it.

"It's beautiful, isn't it?" said a woman who had appeared behind him.

"I know that voice!" he said as he turned slowly around.

When he saw the woman's face, his jaw dropped and his heart skipped several beats. Tears ran down his cheeks as his vision clouded.

"Kiriti! Is it really you before me or my eyes playing tricks?" he said softly.

She walked up to him and touched his cheek.

"It's not a trick, my husband. I am truly here," she assured him. "I don't know how or even where this is, but we are together and this is all that matters."

He held her close.

He reveled in the feel of her warm body in his arms. Became intoxicated by the scent of her hair and the gentle perfume that scented her lithe body. As he held her, he wept for joy.

"Is this the Afterlife? Have I crossed over to be with you?" he asked.

"No. I have crossed into the world of the living to be reunited with you," she replied. "All is well now. All is right again. We are together."

He took her hand and they walked back to the palace. The Devil smiled.

"Is this *your* doing?" Amenopur asked.

"It is. This is what you desire most, so this is what I've given you," the Devil said.

"There is no greater gift in this or any other world. I am indebted to you forever, although I have no idea how I'll ever repay you," Amenopur said with a wide grin.

"I ask nothing in return but your promise to help us rid the world of that foul wizard and his cat," the Devil said.

"This is a promise I will gladly and freely give," Amenopur said as he extended his hand. "Amenopur's word is his bond. It shall not be broken."

They all shook his hand in turn.

Kiriti gaped in wonder at them and looked around the palace. She realized that she was not in Egypt—or any other place she had ever heard of.

"I will explain everything to you later, my love," Amenopur promised. "But first, I have work to do."

"I think I know how to find that wizard," Arka-Dal said. "We'll let Amenopur find him for us. Lucifer, you said that you are unable to track him. But most likely, he'll soon insist that Amenopur come to him. Since you are able to track Amenopur…"

"I was about to suggest the very same thing," the Devil smiled.

"You mean that I am to be the bait?" Amenopur asked.

"Exactly. We'll keep track of your movements at all times. Sooner or later, that madman will bring you to him. That will provide us with his exact location. Once we have that, we can go there and deal with him—again!" Arka-Dal said.

Amenopur nodded.

"That seems reasonable," he said. "What of my wife?"

"She'll be safe in the palace," Arka-Dal vowed. "No harm will come to her while I live."

"Then I agree to your plan. I suggest that you return me to Luxor so I can continue my travels. He'll be expecting that," Amenopur said.

Before he could utter another word, he found himself back at the dock of Luxor…

Arka-Dal smiled at the Devil.

"Is that really his wife?" he asked as he watched Kiriti walk into the garden with Galya.

"Most definitely," the Devil replied as he poured himself a brandy and sat down on the sofa. "It took me a long time to locate her wandering soul in the Afterlife. Once I did, it was a simple matter of restoring her flesh and other physical necessities. She is the one and only Kiriti and she and Amenopur have a long life ahead of them."

"Why did you do it—other than to assure his cooperation?" Merlin queried.

"In his day, Amenopur was a very powerful sorcerer and a man of many other amazing talents and qualities. When I realized he was on the verge of returning to his physical form, I decided to do whatever I could to bring him into our fold. Restoring his beloved Kiriti seemed the best way to do this," the Devil said.

"When did you know he was about to return?" Arka-Dal asked. "Was it in his tomb when we first met?"

The Devil nodded.

"I sensed his power growing. I could have easily destroyed him forever, but I knew of his tragic history. You might say that I felt pity for him in some small way. So I decided to allow him to return to see which direction he'd choose to travel once he began roaming this new Egypt," he said.

"Can we trust him?" Merlin asked.

"I trust him," Arka-Dal said.

Merlin smiled.

"That's good enough for me," he said.

Amenopur ate his dinner and smiled as he thought of recent events. The Devil's incredible gift all but cancelled out what he was about to extort from the strange wizard. He had already been given the very thing he was going to bargain for.

Not that the wizard would actually have lived up to any bargain they made. He knew the man wasn't the least bit trustworthy the moment he laid eyes on him. The man was worse than evil.

He was totally *amoral.*

That made him highly dangerous as well.

Amenopur decided to bide his time. He would force the wizard to contact him and to bring him to his lair. Then the others would be able to track him down and finish him—again.

"Just how many more times will they have to kill you to be totally rid of you?" he wondered.

The cat stretched and sat up. He watched as the wizard paced the floor of the crumbling tower.

"What vexes you now?" the cat queried.

"Amenopur. I am unable to locate him. He is shielding himself from me and it's driving me mad!" the wizard said.

"That's not much of a drive," the cat quipped. "You're already far madder than a hatter."

"Bah!" the wizard sneered.

"If that's your sheep impression, you'd better not quit your day job," the cat taunted. "If you can't locate him, just how do you plan on bringing him here so you can steal his powers?"

"Now you understand!" the wizard said.

The head looked at them and smiled. The wizard wrinkled his nose at it.

"Is that what this is all about? You want to steal our powers so you can become more powerful? Man, you're sicker than I had imagined!" it said.

"Well, maybe I am a little sick—but I know what I'm doing. You and Amenopur were once the most powerful wizards walking the Earth. Your abilities were legendary. I know that you fought a duel and it ended badly for you. But even though your head has been sealed inside that jar all this time, I believe that your powers are still intact," the wizard said.

The head laughed so hard it began coughing up dust. When he regained his composure, he smiled at the wizard.

"You believe wrong, old man," it said.

"Explain yourself," the wizard demanded.

"Even a total imbecile could see that if I still had even one iota of the power I used to wield, I would not still be inside this damned jar," the head pointed out. "I lost our duel badly. So badly, that Amenopur stripped me of my powers and sealed my head in this jar. So if you're planning to rob me of my powers, you're barking up the wrong tree."

The wizard sneered at the head.

"You can do nothing for me at this point. You are powerless," he said through the cat.

The head laughed.

"What's so damned funny?" the wizard demanded.

"I am not completely powerless, wizard. I still have power enough to perform one last act of magic," the head replied.

"Like what?" the wizard asked.

"This!" the head replied.

The wizard stared in silence as the head slowly turned to dust inside the jar. In less than a minute, it had totally disintegrated. The wizard cursed vehemently then he picked up the jar and hurled it across the room. It struck the stone wall and shattered into hundreds of small pieces, leaving nothing but bits of glass and dust scattered across the floor. The cat watched with amusement as he threw another tantrum. When he calmed back down, he looked at the cat.

"Since Amenopur stripped him of his powers, it must mean that *he* now has them," the wizard reasoned. "That makes it all the more important that I bring him here so I can absorb his energies."

"True. But you have no idea where he is, do you?" the cat asked.

"None!" the wizard admitted. "I cannot break through his shield. He is more powerful than I anticipated. But once I find him and bring him here, he won't stand a chance against me."

The cat yawned.

"I've heard similar rants from you before—and we both know how they worked out," he said smugly. "Maybe you should rethink your life ambitions? Perhaps you should join a monastery."

"Go fuck yourself!" the wizard snapped.

The cat laughed and hoisted his hind leg to do the next best thing…

The ancient temple sat atop a bluff overlooking the Nile. Although it had stood in this spot for over 7,000 years, it looked as if it had been constructed yesterday. The walls and huge columns were in excellent repair and the hieroglyphs had been fully restored to their original glorious colors.

In Hetshepsut's Egypt, no ancient monument or structure went unrepaired. She was almost fanatical when it came to preserving and restoring Egypt's legendary structures. She felt that as long as they stood, so would Egypt.

This temple was dedicated to Anubis, the jackal-headed god of the Underworld. It was here that Amenopur came.

He entered the inner sanctum and looked up at the huge statue of Anubis. It stared down at him with its burning, almost life-like eyes that seemed to follow his every move. He stopped and looked up at the idol.

"Why?" he asked.

"Because," the voice that filled the chamber responded.

"That's an ambiguous answer," Amenopur said.

"You asked an ambiguous question," the voice returned. "But if you were referring to your sudden rebirth, you need no answers other than those that are all around you and in plain sight. If you're asking about the meaning to your new life, that detail is entirely up to you to establish. It is what it is, Amenopur."

The eyes went dark, signifying that the god would entertain no further questions. Amenopur shook his head. He bowed respectfully, turned and left the temple. He saw Galya leaning against one of the massive columns. He bowed his head.

"To what do I owe the pleasure of your visit?" he asked.

"Father has sensed that your powers are almost completely restored. He sent me to tell you he feels it is time to put our plan into motion. Do you think you can handle the wizard?" she said.

He smiled.

"I'll make him regret that he ever came to Egypt," he said. "Before I deal with him, there is something else I must do first."

"I understand," Galya said as she vanished.

Just before he boarded the ship back to Memphis, Amenopur relaxed his shields. Just as he expected, a rather anxious wizard soon contacted him.

"I've been expecting you," he thought.

"You have some nerve blocking me out. Who do you think you are anyway?" the wizard snapped.

"I am Amenopur, High Priest and advisor to kings. I do as I please, wizard. I allow you to contact me at my discretion—not yours. I have a message for you," Amenopur thought.

"What is it?" the wizard asked.

"I will come to you in six days," Amenopur replied as he again raised his shield.

On the other end, the wizards slammed his fist on the desk so hard that he winced in pain and shook it. The cat grinned at his pain.

"He did it to again," the cat said smugly. "If I were you, I'd leave this one be. No good can come of trying to screw *him* over."

"He thinks too highly of himself. He doesn't know who he's fucking with!" the wizard growled.

"Neither do *you*, old man," the cat warned. "I think you should take up safer pursuits—like basket weaving."

"How about I start with you?" the wizard asked.

"You can *try*," the cat dared. "But first, I suggest that you gather together plenty of bandages in order to cover the wounds you'll receive."

What the wizard failed to realize is that Amenopur was able to extract a visual image of his hiding place from his mind during their brief contact. Now that he had that, he concentrated on opening a mental channel to the Devil. It took several minutes. He was about to give up when he heard the Devil's voice in his mind. He smiled and transmitted the image.

"Interesting," the Devil said as he received it. "It doesn't appear to resemble anything at all in Egypt."

"No it doesn't. Yet I got the impression that he was within 200 miles of Luxor—if that's any help," Amenopur said.

"At least we now know his general location. Thank you," the Devil said. "I shall relay this to Arka-Dal."

"And I'll continue my journey. I have something very important to do in Memphis," Amenopur said as he signed off.

Arka-Dal nodded when the Devil told him about his contact.

"Do you know this place?" he asked.

"Not offhand," the Devil replied. "Have a look at it yourself."

He raised his hand and projected the image onto a blank wall. The other studied it.

"I know that design. It's a Crusader watch tower," Merlin said. "They built several dozen of them throughout this area to protect roads that pilgrims traveled. From the looks of the designs around the entrance, I'd say this was built by the Templars."

"Any idea where this is, Merlin? Amenopur said he felt it was within 200 miles of Luxor," Arka-Dal asked.

"Sorry," Merlin said after some thought. "The Templars built several in Egypt. I'm sure more than one was near Luxor."

"I'm afraid this puts us back to square one. We'll just have to wait until Amenopur is brought to the wizard's lair," Arka-Dal said.

Alyana sat on the bench in front of the lily pond and watched the ripples made by the water spurting from the fountain. Water fascinated her. She was amazed that even in such a hot, almost arid climate, there seemed to be an abundance of it. She was also amazed at how many different forms of life called water home. Some of those forms were incredibly beautiful and bizarre.

Earth, she decided, was the most blessed place in existence. It had remained so even after countless wars that all but ended human civilization. Somehow or another, the planet had managed to renew itself each and every time.

Mayumi walked up and sat beside her. Alyana smiled.

"You are the most fortunate woman on this planet," she said.

"I know," Mayumi said. "But it wasn't always so. I thought my life was miserable until I met Aka-san. He saved my life in more ways than one."

"How come you are not jealous of me?" Alyana asked.

"Should I be?" Mayumi queried.

"I'm not sure. Right now, I'm too busy learning your ways and trying not to make a fool of myself. And he has been very busy with other things," Alyana replied.

"Be patient and all will work out for the best," Mayumi said as she patted her knee. "Whatever happens, remember that I am your friend and you can come to me if you need to," Mayumi assured her. "Are you alright?"

"I am now," Alyana smiled.

Three days later, Amenopur reached Memphis. He disembarked and headed straight for the royal palace, which was on a hill overlooking the city. To his surprise, he saw only one sleepy guard leaning on a spear outside the entrance. The guard looked at him warily.

"I wish to speak with your queen," Amenopur said.

"I'll go in and announce you. What's your name?" the guard asked.

He told him. The guard nodded and went inside. A moment later, he returned and opened the door.

"The Queen will see you now," he said. "Just follow the carpet to the throne room. You can't miss it."

Amenopur thanked him and did as he said. The entry room was large and had a vaulted ceiling with a large, oval window that admitted sunlight. The walls were decorated with tapestries and traditional hieroglyphs, life-sized paintings of Gods and past rulers and everything gleamed like glass.

It was indeed a palace.

He followed the carpet through a vaulted arch and stopped when he saw the tall, lithe and beautiful woman seated on the throne. She wore the traditional crown that signified she ruled both upper and lower Egypt and was clad in a long white, form hugging linen dress. She had a gold strap around her waist and a simple golden necklace. She smiled at him warmly.

With her was her son Arkaneton and Peace.

He bowed respectfully.

Hetshepsut studied Amenopur. He saw no fear nor malice in her deep, dark eyes. In fact, she seemed to be perfectly calm.

"I've been expecting you," she said. "Why have you come here today?"

"Something foul walks this land," Amenopur said.

"Don't look at me—I bathed this morning," Peace joked.

"And you have come to warn us?" Hetshepsut asked.

"Yes, Your Majesty," he replied. "Perhaps you know of him. He as a wizard of indeterminate age and power who speaks through a black cat."

"Oh, we know of him alright. You mean to say that he's here in Egypt? For what purposes?" Arkaneton asked.

"He is seeking to steal power from two ancient artifacts. I am one of those artifacts," Amenopur replied. "I have already visited your father and his friends in Thule. We have worked out a plan to locate and trap this madman. I am the bait."

"It appears that you've already decided how to handle this. So, again, why have you come here?" Hetshepsut asked.

"To thank you, My Queen," Amenopur said. "You know me and my history. You could have had me arrested and thrown into prison, yet you pardoned me. Ned told me this and I felt I should at least thank you in person."

"What you did so many centuries ago had nothing at all to do with Egypt today. Guilty or innocent, you have already been severely punished for your crimes and I see no need to punish you further. You are free to live as you please and do as you like. As long as you respect our laws, you will be treated as any other citizen of this nation," Hetshepsut said.

She stepped down from the throne and walked up to him.

"You have great skills as an architect, physician, scientist and in all things occult and magical. You were highly regarded and respected in your past life. Do you still possess such skills?" she asked.

"I do—but I shall have to bring them up to date. This is a new Egypt and I still have many things to learn," he replied.

"When that day comes, how do you intend to use those skills?" she asked.

"To be truthful, I haven't given that much thought. I have been too busy exploring this wonderful new country I've been reborn into," he said.

"Has Egypt changed *that* much since your time?" she asked.

He beamed. She saw the enthusiasm in his eyes.

"The differences amaze me more each day. This is a remarkable land and the people tell me that it is because of your inspired rule. They say you are their greatest and most beloved pharaoh ever," he replied.

She smiled and blushed a little.

"I am somewhat aware of the myths and legends concerning your past deeds. Too much of it makes no sense. Perhaps you can sit down with me one day and tell me what really happened?" she suggested.

"I would be honored. But I must remind you that you might only learn the story from my perspective. Since my name was expunged from history, there are probably no official records to back or counter anything I might say," he advised.

"You are uncommonly frank with your answers. I like that," she said.

"I have nothing to hide, Your Highness. There is no reason for me to speak anything other than the truth," he said.

"Why did you return?" she asked.

"Vengeance. I wanted to find and destroy the descendants of those who wronged me and my family. I wanted to make them suffer as me and my family were made to suffer. Instead, I found myself in a new Egypt. A new world and time. I have learned that all those blood lines have vanished from the Earth. There's no one left to seek retribution from," he said.

She laughed.

"I dare say that you are most likely the last of the true original Egyptians. You come from a time when no other races dwelled in this land. No one today, not even I, can trace his roots back to those times," she said.

She looked him in the eyes.

"You can be quite an asset to me here at court. You are part of our history. You know things that have long since been forgotten. You could help us to understand the way things were. I would like to offer you a position as my chief historian and archivist once you grow accustomed to your new life," she said.

He stared at her in disbelief.

"I—I humbly accept your most kind and generous offer, My Queen," he said with a bow. "But first, I must rid Egypt of that madman."

"I understand. The position will still be here when you are ready. May the gods be with you," she said.

"And with you as well, My Queen," he said as he bowed and vanished.

Peace looked at her.

"Are you sure that was a wise decision? He's still quite powerful and he will grow stronger with each passing day," he said.

She smiled.

"You sound as if you fear him," she said.

"I do. You should, too," he warned.

"We have no reason to fear or mistrust him. All that he hated, all who were responsible for his execution and the death of his family, are long gone. By offering him the position, I have hopefully gained his trust and assured his loyalty," she said.

Arkaneton laughed.

"That's something Father would do," he said.

"I've learned much from him over the years," she admitted. "Think of what Amenopur can bring to the table. There is much he can teach us about our past. There is much we can learn from him. He is indeed, a very valuable asset."

"I hope you're right," Peace said.

Amenopur reappeared on the banks of the Nile several miles from the palace. He looked up at the sky and dropped his mental shield. Almost instantly, he felt himself being gripped by a powerful, almost electrified force.

Then he was gone.

He materialized in the upper chamber of a crumbling Crusader tower nearly 450 miles from Memphis. He was surrounded by the force field and staring at the wizard who sat in a chair before him, stroking the cat as it sat on his lap.

"I thought a man of your self-importance would dwell in a far more opulent place than this," he said. "This place is barely fit for camels."

"It serves my purposes nicely," the cat said. "As do you."

Amenopur laughed and raised his right hand. The wizard started as the force field vanished.

"I am here of my own volition—not yours," Amenopur said.

"As are we, wizard!" the Devil said as he and Merlin materialized behind him.

The wizard jumped to his feet and snarled as the cat took off for parts unknown.

"How did you find this place?" he demanded.

"That's easy. I brought them here," Amenopur said. "But before I step aside and allow them to deal with you once again, there is something I must give you. Something you need more than anything else on Earth."

The wizard faced him.

"And what is that?" he asked.

"This!" Amenopur said as he punched him square in the nose and sent him tumbling to the floor.

The wizard struggled to a seated position as he rubbed his broken nose. Amenopur stepped aside and gestured.

"He's all yours, my friends. Do with him as you wish!" he said.

Before the wizard could reach, he found himself imprisoned in a bell shaped, see through container. He cursed at Merlin and attempted to use several spells to escape from it. But none worked.

"You might as well relax," the Devil said. "The container negates your magic and you have no way of escaping it."

"So you're just going to leave me here forever? I'll escape. I always escape and when I do, I'll come after you. All of you!" the wizard threatened.

"Perhaps—but that won't be for a long, long time," the Devil said as he raised his left hand and pointed to the floor.

The floor opened up beneath the container and the wizard found himself hurtling down into what appeared to be a true bottomless pit. As soon as the container dropped, the floor closed behind him.

"Impressive!" Amenopur remarked.

"Coming from you, that's quite a compliment," the Devil smiled.

"Where did you send him this time?" asked Merlin.

The Devil shrugged.

"I simply created a true vortex that has no ending or exit and dropped him into it. He will continue to fall for eternity or until he finds a way out of it. Either way, we won't be seeing him again for many years to come," the Devil said.

"You hope!" Merlin said.

"Indeed. With him, one never knows," the Devil said. "The container has very little air. He'll suffocate to death soon."

"That will leave him with only four lives," Amenopur said. "I have a very bad feeling about him."

"So do we," Merlin said.

"Now, let's return to Thule and reunite you with your beloved Kiriti," the Devil said as he snapped his fingers.

"What about our children?" Amenopur asked.

"You and your wife will have many years with which to create new ones," Merlin smiled as they materialized in the living room of Arka-Dal's palace.

Kiriti had been seated on the sofa and chatting with several of the wives. The moment she saw Amenopur appear, she rushed over and melted into his arms...

Getting to Thule

Travelers who desire to visit the Empire of Thule may reach it via several well known routes. The easiest is by water. One can sail across the Mediterranean through the Great Canal of Egypt and around the Arabian Peninsula to one of Thule's great southern port cities. From there, you can embark on a River Transport Ship up the Tigris-Euphrates River to any of the major Valley Cities, including the opulent capital city of Thule.

Overland, Thule can be reached from any of the Peninsula's other nations by taking one of the main caravan trails across the Great Western Desert or Southern Desert. One may find it wise to pay a caravan master the going rate in order to travel under his protection as the desert regions are fraught with roving bandits and unspeakable monsters. All caravan trails lead to the mountain range known as the Great Gray Wall, and to its only real pass into the lush Valley region. The pass is known as B'Aalikh ad-Dum (Door of the Damned) and several other names. In bygone eras, three great battles were fought here and uncountable thousands died.

To the northwest lies a nearly impenetrable swamp region bordered by another rocky chain of gray mountains. There is no known pass through this range.

To the northeast lies the puppet state of Darthool, with decadent Sundar to its immediate south. Darthool and Sundar both vied for mastery of the Valley against Thule and both lost so bad on the battlefields that they became militarily and economically crippled by the wars. Both states had to concede several smaller provinces to Thule. This left Sundar wide open to attack, and eventual conquest, by the powerful Persian Empire. Darthool is hotly contested by Persia and Scythian tribes.

All resent and fear Thule, which is the military and economic powerhouse of the Middle East.

It is wise not to travel through any of the above mentioned areas without a strongly armed escort.

About Thule

Thule covers approximately 11.7 million square kilometers and claims most of the desert regions to the south and west. It has 17.3 million inhabitants, at least 14.7 million of which are Human. There are nearly 1.8 million Alfar (Elves), 1.2 million Goblinoids of various types, and the rest are Dwarfs and their related races. All live relatively peacefully within the borders of the Empire.

The heart of the Empire is the Valley Region, highlighted by three massive lakes and the twin Tigris-Euphrates Rivers. This gives Thulians access not only to other major cities along the rivers but a quick outlet to the sea. Naturally, the Empire has become a powerful maritime nation and boasts a military fleet of 1,250 ships (mostly of the Viking Longship type, the ancestral ship of the Thulians), and Middle Eastern warships. It also has a merchant fleet of 2,200.

The Valley Region is lush rolling hills and rich farmland. It boasts several major crops, the most important of which is wheat, and has several large cattle farms. There are also many thick wooded areas off the beaten tracks and travelers are advised not to travel through them alone, especially at night.

Beyond the Valley to the west is a large open grassland called the Yboe. Beyond that is the Great Gray Wall.

Thule's common language is called Rithvuli (Thule Tongue). Originally, it was close to Norwegian. When the Thulians migrated to the Valley at the beginning of the Second Age, Rithvuli had mutated to include several Greek, German, Egyptian, English and Russian words. When the Thulians conquered Sumer and changed its name to Thule,

Rithvuli had merged with the local dialect. It bears little resemblance to Norwegian today.

The Thulian alphabet is Skandian Runic with Egyptian symbols thrown in for good measure. Although they still worship ancestral gods such as Odin, Thor, Baldar and Sif, many Egyptian Gods have also become part of the Thulian religious pantheon (See The Pantheon of Thule pamphlet). The local religion is called the Brotherhood of Mitre and is secular head is the aging Pope Leo Asugundis I, a childhood mentor of Emperor Arka Dal.

All other religions are practiced freely and openly within the Empire but human sacrifice is outlawed.

The government is known as an Enlightened Monarchy (see the copy of Thule's Constitution, drafted by Arka Dal and Leo when Arka Dal took the throne). No one is above the law, not even the Emperor. All citizens and visitors are treated equally and fairly by the law and there is a set code of punishments (see Laws of Thule). Of course, all criminal acts committed against the clergy are handled by the Papal Court (see Religious Laws). There is true separation of church and state in the Empire, but Arka Dal often asks Leo for advice on civil matters.

Most cities are policed by a well-armed Night Watch after sunset and by Army patrols during the daylight hours. The roads and pathways are patrolled by the cavalry, which also guards the major caravan routes. There are several military garrisons throughout the Empire as it boasts and army of nearly 650,000 men.

The major roads between cities and large towns are well paved and cared for. There are many public coaches one can take when traveling and horse-drawn taxicabs and omnibuses within the cities. The standard fare is 1 copper per mile, a real bargain in this day and age.

River boats cost 3 coppers per mile and are well worth the price.

Prices on standard item may vary within the Empire. They are reasonably lower in large cities near major trade routes, but can run between 5% to15% higher as you go off the beaten track. Prices include a 2% sales tax or service charge.

Tipping is allowed in the Empire. The standard tip is 5-10% of the bill, depending on the quality of the service, which is good in most places. Thulians take pride in their work and it shows.

Inns are clean and well kept for the most part and the food is usually good. Smaller inns cost less and country inns cost less still. The marketplaces are normally located in the center of each town or village and are open year round, except on major festival days. There one can get anything imaginable for a price and it is considered proper to haggle over the prices.

The money is standardized in the Empire. In fact, it is Arka Dal who came up with a standard measures and weights system which is now used by most of the known world. A money table is included in this guidebook. You'll find is quite similar to any you've used before.

Thulian cities are crowded but well-planned and clean. Thulians prize cleanliness and this is shown by their well-kept, scrubbed homes and shops. It is also the custom of Thulians to bathe at the end of each day and brush their teeth.

Thulian men are tall, mostly blond or brown haired and about half are bearded. Their hair is normally cut to shoulder length or braided in the Viking manner. Their skin is a deep tan mostly due to the merging of the Thulians and the ancient Valley Peoples. About 30% have ornate tattoos on their arms, chests or backs and half of these have golden rings dangling from their earlobes. They are gruff mannered, boisterous, love to gamble, drink, party and fight. They are true Viking stock.

The women are a subtle blend of dark Valley People and Thulian stock. They are about 5'3" to 6'2" tall, well- built and keep their hair in long braids. Many act much like the men and several are feared warriors. In Thule, both sexes are considered equal.

The Thulian climate is temperate to arid, depending on what part of the Empire you're visiting. Rain is rare outside of the Valley Region, and it doesn't rain much there, either. Thule has four distinct seasons and sometimes gets snowfall during winter months.

Thule is an adventurer's paradise. It is teeming with horrible monsters, nightmarish ruins, underground lairs, gambling, wanton women, fighting pits, gladiator rings and attracts people from every known nation and race on Earth. Whatever you want (or don't want) you can find in Thule.

Most Thulians pay about 5% of their annual income in taxes. Businesses pay the same and the rate can go up to 20% in time of war or national emergencies. About 40% goes into the military budget. Another 25% goes into public works, 10% goes into medical care, 10% goes into education and the balance is used for whatever is needed. If you stay in Thule for a year or more, you will be subject to the same tax. There is an "adventurer tax" which is 10% of the loot you garner while adventuring.

Firearms and particle beam weapons are strictly forbidden within city limits, although gunsmiths abound. These, along with spears, bows and crossbows and other pole arms, must be checked at the Gatehouse upon entering each city. Those refusing to comply with this law are either forbidden to enter or arrested, depending on the mood of the guards.

Prostitution is legal, as is gambling, pit fighting and other strange things, but only within each city's Red Zone (entertainment district). The capital's Red Zone is just outside of the city to the southeast. There are few police in the Red Zone, so don't get too drunk and watch your back--and purse--at all times.

Thulian Customs

When entering each city, it is proper to pay your respects to the local Meister (mayor) or the Captain of the Guard. Not to do so is considered an insult and may result in harsh treatment from local police and city officials.

Never invite yourself to a party, someone's home, or any private get together unless specifically asked. When asked, ALWAYS accept. To refuse is a great insult. Also, when offered food or drink, be sure to partake and thank the host. This can be done by a hearty handclasp, slap on the back or raising one's cup in salute. When eating, always use a knife to cut your meat and do NOT throw bones or scraps on the floor unless your host says it's all right to do so. They might not have a dog. ALWAYS return a toast or salute at the table and never leave the table until the host does so first. This could lead to several all night drinking binges, for which Thulians are famous.

Never vomit in anything other than the vomit urns provided by your host. Also do not urinate or defecate in other than the designated toilet. To do so would result in a trip to the local hospital for you or your host, depending on how well you can both fight.

Fighting and brawling is permitted if started by the host. If insulted, it is considered unmanly and rude not to return the insult. If struck, strike back.

Never talk to a married woman unless you are introduced. Single women are fair game and often make the first move. Virginity is not very important to Thulians, but a good time is. If asking a Thulian woman out, one must first have permission from her father or eldest brother. There are chaperones.

Thulian marriages are usually unplanned. About 95% are freely made. About 2% are political arrangements and the rest are matched at birth. Each bride must bring a dowry equal to 10% of her father's annual income. Grooms must give the bride's father a fine weapon, armor or a good horse when arranging the wedding. The bride's and groom's fathers each share the expenses of the grand wedding feast and the happy couple is wedded in a traditional Druid ceremony. This is followed by 2-4 days and nights of feasting, dancing, drinking and brawling until all are passed out or dead from exhaustion.

The birth of the first male child is celebrated in a like manner. Girl children may also be celebrated, but usually that feast money is set aside as part of her dowry. Interracial marriages are permitted in Thule.

When entering a Thulian house, always bow your head to the woman of the house and lightly kiss her on the left cheek. This is not, however, a proper greeting in public places.

When meeting a Thulian, clasp his right arm about halfway to the elbow. He will do the same and give a hearty, warm handshake. This shows that you are a friend and bear no weapons to do him harm. Similarly, be sure to hand all personal weapons on a peg near the front door of any home you enter. Not to do so may result in armed combat because this tells your host that you intend to do him harm.

Thulians are known for their honesty, warmth, humor and generosity to strangers and friends alike. They are practical jokers, so be prepared to have some fun. Sometimes, their jokes are embarrassing, but that's part of the charm of visiting Thule.

Most Thulians are literate and well-schooled, so don't try to treat them as inferiors. Many speak several different languages, so don't let their gruff exteriors fool you. They are also clever traders and bargainers.

Thulians do not keep slaves and slavery of any type is forbidden in the Empire. Any slave you take into the Empire is considered a free person as soon as his feet touch Thulian soil. So be prepared to lose your slaves when coming to Thule.

Thulian wines, ales and meads are very potent. Those who are unused to strong drinks had best take it slow. Anyone who can't hold his drink is considered a "sissy" and becomes fair game for all sorts of pranks and insults. So, if you can't drink, stay out of the taverns.

Thulian meals begin with a platter of thick stew and loaves of dark, dense and aromatic breads. One eats the stew by scooping it from the bowl with slices of bread, then licking it from your fingers. The next course is a platter of roast meat or boiled meats, potatoes, grains, mixed vegetables, more bread and a tureen of hearty gravy. large spoons and knives are provided for use. Forks are sometimes offered, but Thulians prefer spoons and fingers to them. Dessert is usually fruit or cakes. All during the meal, strong drink is served. Each meal lasts from 2-3 hours. This is usually followed by a game of chance (dice or cards) and more strong drinks. Bragging is mandatory at mealtimes and the bigger the boast, the better your host will appreciate you.

In battle, one must boast about one's prowess and declare how many enemies he will slay. Once such a boast is made, the typical Thulian will do his damnedest to live up to it. To do otherwise would dishonor him. Also, Thulians never leave a friend behind on the battlefield. They'd rather fight to the death to save their friend than to be marked forever as deserters and cowards. Thulians have a strict honor code among warriors.

THULIAN LEGAL SYSTEM

All foreigners have the same legal rights as Thulian citizens while within the borders of the Empire. If you should run afoul of the local law and find yourself under arrest, do NOT under any circumstances, attempt to resist arrest or escape from confinement. Such things are treated with deadly force and, if you're dead, you have no legal rights.

Once officially placed under arrest, you should be aware of the following rights and/or privileges while in custody.

Everyone is entitled to a lawyer. If you cannot afford one, the governor will appoint one to represent you. While in jail awaiting trial, you are entitled to daily visits from your family members, your attorney and your friends. They can, if you wish, bring you food, clothing, cards, dice, writing and reading materials. While in custody, the State will provide you with bathing facilities, toilets, a one-man cell (if possible), a clean bunk, desk and chair for you cell, medical, dental and tonsorial services.

If you are a family man and cannot practice your trade, the State will pay your family whatever your daily wages would be as specified by local Trade Guilds until such time as your trial and appeals are completed. So your family does not become destitute if you are convicted, the State will provide them a monthly stipend of 200 silver pieces for the entire time you are serving your sentence. Also your imprisonment automatically cancels all of your existing debts and mortgages. This is to ensure that your family will retain their property and places to live. If you are sentenced to death, the State will cancel all of you family's debts and pay them a lump sum of 25,000 silver pieces to keep them going for several years. After all, why should your family have to suffer for your crimes?

There is no bail in Thule. Once imprisoned, you must conduct all of your business from your cell. Everyone MUST be tried within 30 days of his arrest or the charges are automatically dropped. There is NO EXCEPTION to this law.

If you are found innocent, you will be released immediately. You will also be paid the sum of 20 silver pieces for each day you were confined, plus all of your legal fees. There are no court fees in Thule.

You will be tried before a Tribunal of experienced judges, appointed by the Emperor on their merits alone. If accused of a minor crime, a vote of 2-1 is enough to convict you. If you are accused of a major crime, short of murder or High Treason, you can only be convicted by a unanimous vote.

All crimes, other than murder or High Treason, are tried in the capital cities of the provinces they occur in. Murder and High Treason are FEDERAL OFFENSES and must be tried at the capital city of Thule. Usually, the Emperor himself presides over these trials and his vote can break a deadlock. He also has the authority to grant clemency, overturn verdicts, or dismiss charges.

If convicted, you may appeal your case first to the Provincial Governor. If the appeal is denied, you may request that it be brought to the attention of the Emperor. If this fails, just grit your teeth and take your lumps like a man.

If you are found innocent after you have served all or part of your sentence, the State will

(1) Issue you a full written apology, signed by the Emperor along with your full pardon.
(2) Return any lost properties.
(3) Arrest the one who's testimony convicted you and force them to serve out your sentence.
(4) Turn over all of your accusers' property, money and other assets to you permanently. The last two usually ensures that anyone who bears witness against someone stays honest. This system works incredibly well and few innocent people end up in prison this way.
(5) The State will pay you 2,000 silver pieces for each year you spent in prison.

Although everyone arrested for a crime in Thule is assumed innocent until proven guilty, do not take this justice system lightly. If convicted, you'll discover that Thulian punishments are quite nasty and hard prison time is just that. While in Thule, make every effort to learn the laws and customs and try your best to observe them.

SLAVERY

Slavery of any kind, even indentured service, is expressly forbidden within the Empire's domains. If you are traveling with a slave, it is advisable to send him home before you enter Thule.

EVERYONE is free in Thule. The moment a slave sets foot on Thulian soil, he is automatically and permanently free with all of the rights and protection afforded everyone in Thule. As a slave owner, you will be given 50 silver pieces for your slaves' freedom and it is advisable to take it and smile. If you refuse the offer, the slave will be freed anyway and you'll be forbidden to enter the Empire. If you refuse to leave, you will be arrested and put on trial for slave trading, which carries heavy penalties.

It is this feature that makes Thule a veritable magnet for people of all races, nations, religions and beliefs. Thule symbolizes freedom and equality. And rightly so.